i

The Sommelier

Published by Keldaviain Publishing

ISBN: 978-0-9928599-9-2

Chapter 1

Yusuf realised immediately that something was not right when the Toyota Land Cruiser suddenly braked. Thrown violently forward he turned his head sharply towards driver to see the man's arms ramrod straight against the steering wheel, his knuckles had turned white and there was fear in his eyes. It was enough for Yusuf to know that he was in mortal danger. The driver reacted and within an instant, his door swung open as he attempted to escape the vehicle and even before he had left his seat, Yusuf was scrambling out of his own open door. With a racing heart, he jumped out onto the desert floor, his adrenalin telling him it was time for flight. Behind him, his two bodyguards did likewise and as the Land Cruiser ground to a halt, the four men rolled across the desert the floor.

Yusuf scrambled to his feet, half-crouching as he looked anxiously for cover and seeing a line of boulders not far away, began to run towards them but the roar of powerful jet engines overhead transfixed him even before he had gone five meters. It happened so quickly, there was no escape; he could do nothing

save gape at the two black shapes skimming away
across the landscape. At least he was not the jets' target
and for a few fleeting seconds, he felt nothing but relief
until the explosions concentrated his mind.

Twelve hours earlier, as the desert sun slid slowly
behind the horizon, its orange glow giving way to the
night, a shape emerged from the shadows, a trail of
dust growing in its wake as it picked up speed.
Bumping over the uneven terrain the Land Rover was
in its element, ideally suited to these desert conditions
with specially designed air filters to keep the fine sand
at bay, double silencers and wide tyres facilitating
silent running, a machine with an ability to travel
almost unnoticed through the desert night. In its
confines, the four members of an elite Special Forces
patrol sat alone with their thoughts.

Not for the first time was the patrol crossing the
desert on a covert and dangerous mission, analysts had
identified an enemy base and their task was to seek it
out and to destroy it. In the driver's seat Corporal Barry
Thornton concentrated, gritting his teeth and staring
intently through his night vision goggles. The ever-
changing terrain was difficult to negotiate and he
struggled to keep the vehicle on a steady course. For
hours, his concentration was absolute until a tap on his
shoulder reminded him that he was not alone.

'One mile to target corporal,' said the sergeant
leading the patrol who leaned forward for a better view,
gazing through the windscreen, his night vision goggles
turning night into day. He scanned the barren

landscape searching for the landmark, feeling his pulse race as it came into view, a gap in the low hills, the entrance to the valley that would lead them to their target. With a gesture of his hand, he directed the driver and gradually the vehicle turned towards it.

'Pete, Malcolm, see anything?'

'Nothing,' retorted the two remaining members of the patrol sitting at the rear.

'Right Barry, slow down a touch more, we do not want any surprises.'

Sergeant Nicholson scanned the landscape, his owl-like eyes searching for any sign of danger as the broken ground forced a further reduction in speed. Any one of the large rocks could be hiding an enemy and each of the was aware of that possibility. For a tense half hour the soldiers remained vigilant until the driver finally guided them beyond the boulder line and across terrain where an ambush seemed less likely.

'Pull up here,' said the sergeant. 'Mally, get over behind that vegetation and watch our rear, Pete get up to the ridge, see what's beyond it.'

The Land rover was by now traveling at crawling speed and nearing the top of a shallow incline it ground to halt and the soldiers leaped out. Ducking low, with their weapons held close to their chests they disappeared into the night,

'We will give them five more Barry. If we get the all-clear then we'll find some level ground and you can set up the mortar,' said the sergeant slipping the safety catch off his modified Colt Carbine.

The Sommelier

The driver nodded, felt for his handgun, he was ready and as he waited for the sergeant's next command, he peered out at his surroundings. The desert was a different kind of desert to Afghanistan and as he recollected a previous mission he felt the hairs on the back of his neck begin to raise, the memory of it rather too vivid but before he could dwell, the sergeant's radio crackled into life. One of the patrol was calling in and then the second soldier called and the sergeant began to open the passenger door.

'Okay, let's get started. Pete and Malcolm have signalled the all-clear. Drive over there,' he said, pointing towards his choice of a temporary base. The driver pushed the gear lever forward and drove the Land Rover towards an area of flat ground. After switching off the engine he pulled his short-barrelled weapon from bulkhead clips above his head and checking the safety catch, climbed out to head for the rear of the vehicle. The sergeant was already there, a haversack slung across his back and after helping him lift the mortar from the vehicle the two Special Forces soldiers negotiated the last of the incline towards Corporal Blake's position. Lowering their burdens to the ground they lay flat, surveying the area and moments later Blake murmured, 'over there Nico, two o'clock, maybe a kilometre and a bit.'

Sergeant Nicholson switched his field of view and through the gloom could make out the shapes of several tents.

'Looks promising, Barry you can deploy the mortar while I take a closer look.'

Silently the driver slid back from the ridge, leaving the sergeant and Corporal Blake in position. After almost three years of working together in Afghanistan and Iraq, they had built up a trust that had little need for the spoken word. The driver knew his job and skilfully he prepared the mortar, insurance should they need to leave in a hurry.

'Okay, this is as good a place as any, let's dig in before anybody sees us,' said Sergeant Nicholson returning to clear the ground.

'Pete, go back to the Land Rover and help Mally with the camouflage netting. I want that Land Rover invisible before the sun comes up. Be ready for a quick getaway if we're spotted.'

'Right oh Nico.'

The driver slipped away from the ridge, Sergeant Nicholson pursed his lips and turned his to the valley below where the first grey light of dawn was beginning to appear. Taking out a pair of powerful binoculars from the pouch attached to his waist, he substituted them for his night vision goggles and lifted them to his eyes, careful to avoid the rising sun's reflection and for several minutes, he scanned the landscape.

'Got 'em now,' he said pointing towards the object of his interest.

The clusters of camouflaged, light brown tents over a kilometre away was the militant training camp all right and now that they had located it figures were moving about, the camp was coming to life. Through the early morning haze Sergeant Nicholson could see silhouetted men performing the ritual *Fajr*, each dressed in dark *salwar kameez*, the loose-fitting pants and shirt of the Arab. Wrapped tightly around their heads they wore the white *keffiyehs,* revealing no more that their eyes and he judged that they had come from Egypt, the Gulf, Libya to join the struggle. More than their dress though, it was their ideology that united them, a desire to destroy the West.

Obscured by the tents Sergeant Nicholson did not see the two men standing together and watching the trainees. One was stocky, well built, Hazem, the commandant of the camp and he was every bit the experienced fighter. The other man was tall, slender, and not a warrior in the normal sense. Yusuf's contribution to the struggle was different. As Osama bin Laden, he was the product of a wealthy Saudi family and during a brief meeting in Afghanistan the great leader had convinced Yusuf that his talent for mixing with Westerners and his grip on finance would be of far more use than that of a foot soldier.

'You are impressed Yusuf?'

'Yes I can see that you are doing a good job Hazem and yes, I am impressed. How long before you send these men out to repel the infidel? Will you send them south to Samarra or Baghdad perhaps? Al-Qaeda in Iraq is gaining in strength, Abu Musab al-Zarqawi is showing the way his strategy of sowing sectarian division among the Shi'ite is beginning to pay off. He will keep the Iraqi security forces busy, weaken them and afford us the opportunity to extend the reach of our organisation. Hazem, Al-Qaeda will spread across all of the Muslim lands wherever they are. We shall prevail.'

'It shall be so. Come Yusuf, come and see the recruits. I know your time is precious but I would like you to witness the brothers' training, see the kind of fighters we are producing before you leave us.'

'Allah be praised I would like to but first I must complete the task with which I am entrusted and give you the American dollars.'

'American dollars, why is it always American dollars?'

'Because those who supply us with weapons insist we pay in dollars. Never fear, once we crush our enemies we will have little need for their dollars, we will simply take what we want.'

'It is so. Come, the brothers are making ready for live fire. They become better marksmen each day, their instructors are the best, men who have seen action in many places, in Afghanistan against the Americans and in Georgia against the Russians, good men, dedicated and dangerous, qualities we are instilling in the recruits.'

Yusuf managed a smile, but that only served to cover a deep-seated disappointment. The setbacks in Afghanistan and Pakistan were still fresh in his mind. The training camps spread out across the northern desert were the key for with an endless supply of volunteers, they would prevail and he, Yusuf Ahmed Abdel Rahman Muhammed al-Hudaybi, was proud to be at the forefront of that fight. He turned away from the line of soldiers, strode across the open ground, past tents constructed in the Bedouin style and made his way towards the Toyota Land Cruiser. Opening the rear passenger door he reached inside and pulled out a canvas bag that he carried back to the camp commandant.

'Here is thirty thousand dollars, enough to keep your enterprise going for a few more months I think.'

'Allah be praised, thank those that help and protect us Yusuf. Tell them to be in no doubt that we will use the money wisely.'

'I know you will and when I can arrange it, I will have more weapons and ammunition sent here to your camp. Take this, spend it wisely.'

Yusuf handed the bag over to Hazem and together they approached the line of fighters.

'We are ready Hazem,' said one of the instructors, his dark eyes just visible through the narrow folds of his *keffiyeh*.

'Let them begin,' said the leader.

The instructor barked out a command and one by one the AK-47s spat fire at a row of wooden targets painted with crude facsimiles of human heads and one by one, the targets flinched, splintered, as the bullets struck home.

'You see my friend, we are expert at shooting, every brother has hit the target and, with God's help, the targets will soon be Iraqi police or better still American soldiers.'

'It shall be, praise Allah that he may guide them and be with them as they martyr themselves in his name.'

'Come, let us take coffee before you leave us, you have a long journey ahead of you.'

The Sommelier

'Thank you no, I wish to perform the midday prayers first and then we will leave you.'

'As you wish.'

It was uncomfortably hot, the temperature almost forty degrees as the sun reached its zenith and Sergeant Nicholson needed a drink. Not for a moment did he take his eyes away from the cluster of tents shimmering in the distance as he felt for his water bottle and after taking a drink, he again lifted his field glasses to his eyes to study the line of men.

'They have been doing some shooting and now are on their knees praying again. I don't know how they manage in this heat. Can you get some more pictures of their faces Pete?'

'Okay Nico though I will not get much, they rarely remove their scarves. I'll keep at it.'

The sergeant slowly traversed the binoculars from side to side, examining every detail until something attracted his curiosity.

'Looks like the four-wheeler is on the move, three men just climbed in. If I am not mistaken some of them are leaving. Get some shots.'

Beside him, the corporal adjusted his camera lens and for several minutes, the two of them watched the vehicle slowly make its way past the tents before stopping for a minute at the edge of the camp and then it proceeded into the desert.

'They are coming this way,' murmured the sergeant, reaching into a pocket in his fatigues and pulling out a small two-way radio.

'Mally, incoming, make yourselves scarce.'

'Roger that.'

It was brief but it was enough; the two soldiers guarding the Land Rover began to check their weapons, prepare themselves for possible action as Sergeant Nicholson watched the Toyota's progress, relieved to note that its path was far enough away from them not to have much chance of discovering the Land Rover.

'Get some pictures, get their faces if you can Blake, they are near enough, it's your best chance.'

The Nikon 300 mm lens slowly extended, focusing on the Toyota and more importantly on the men inside. For fifteen minutes, Sergeant Nicholson and Corporal Blake observed their subject's passage and as it disappeared over a ridge, the sergeant looked at his watch.

'Time to get ready, pass me the haversack, they will be here shortly.'

Reaching into it, he retrieved the laser designator, the piece of kit he would use to pinpoint the target for the jets. An hour earlier, he had transmitted the coordinates to the two McDonnell Douglas F-15 Eagles circling high in the sky fifty miles away. They were making ready to cover the distance to the terrorist's camp in less than five minutes and the time was running down.

He glanced towards the Toyota now a kilometre or more from the camp, a faint cloud of dust marking its path. He was not the only one to watch the vehicle's progress for from his vantage point on the crest of a small hill at the camp perimeter Hazem also watched. He was pleased the meeting with the paymaster was a success and he relished the chance to demonstrate to his superiors his undoubted ability. Soon they would learn of his achievement as the recruits dispersed throughout the war zone and with the American dollars given him by Yusuf, he would produce the next batch of martyrs. He gave a final wave, turned away from the road and watched with some pride as his trainees gathered for their meal, fifty hungry men, well-trained fighters, a sight that filled him with pride.

Those thoughts were amongst his last for he was unaware that the two F-15s were homing in on the camp, guided by the laser. It took only a second for the pilots to arm the GBU-10 Paveway bombs and with a roar, the fighter-bombers suddenly appeared. It was a total surprise, the camp's occupants had no time to retaliate and all Hazem could do was watch in a state of total fixation as the two dark shapes skimmed towards him.

It was over in seconds, the crump of exploding ordnance and the columns of black smoke rising above the desert, the fires and the charred bodies littering what had been a lively and vibrant camp. The roar of the jets receded, nothing remained but an eerie silence and some distance from the carnage Yusuf stood stock-still, sick to the pit of his stomach, the disaster leaving him with a feeling of intense hatred for the Americans. He searched the sky in case the jets should return but there was nothing and he turned his anguished face towards the columns of smoke.

'We should go back Yusuf?'

'No, we don't know if they will return. There is nothing we can do for them; as soon as it becomes dark we will leave,' he said.

The driver nodded, relishing a return to neither the camp nor pushing on through darkness and beside him, a thoughtful Yusuf regained some composure as he began to question how the Americans had discovered the whereabouts of the camp. Who had told them of its location, a spy? If so, he would root him out and kill him with his own hands. Perhaps it was one of those accursed satellites looking down on them. No, he did not believe that, the tents would appear as no more than shadows from above; and with clothing almost the same colour, he was sure they were invisible in the desert. Nevertheless, the Americans had found them.

Unknown to Yusuf satellite it was imagery that had indeed exposed the camp. Although it was invisible to the satellite's camera there were vehicle tracks imprinted into the desert floor, in part were detectable. An alert analyst had noticed them and from there it was a relatively simple exercise to examine the photographic series, to follow the tracks to a dead end – the campsite and now it was no more, obliterated. On the ground, the Special Forces soldiers still had one further task to perform. They would kill if they had too but their task was more one of intelligence gathering and that meant exploring the camp's grizzly remains.

As night returned, they once again donned their night vision goggles to visit the remains of the terrorist training camp, to pick their way past burned-out tents and charred bodies, all which remained of a once bustling encampment. There was not much to find, simply a laptop computer and thousands of dollar bills scattered everywhere like confetti.

Ten years later

The men smoking the traditional hookah looked up to see a tall Arab dressed in traditional garb crossing the courtyard with a self-assured air, though that was not completely genuine. Yusuf knew that to show fear in the company of such men was not something that would endear him to them. Dressed in black robes, each with an assault rifle by his side, these were dangerous individuals, yet they and men like them were necessary to the cause. Since the American-led invasion of Iraq many things had happened, Al-Zarqawi, their leader was dead and in late 2006 remnants of Al-Qaeda had killed a senior Anbar sheik, turning the local population against them. It was a grave state of affairs and to compound Al-Qaeda's difficulties in Iraq, Daesh had appeared on the scene. Although Yusuf admired their progress, he did not agree with their aims. Creating an Islamic state was one thing but the real objective should be to bring down Western civilisation and in particular America. Certainly, they were draining America's treasure but Daesh were never going to hurt them in their own lands, whereas Al-Qaeda could and would do so. Nevertheless, this new force was far more useful as an ally than as a foe and under the order of the ruling council, he had come to discuss an area of mutual benefit. As one of the organisation's bankers, Yusuf's job was to scour the Middle East for donors and sympathisers. He had contacts throughout the Arab world, had been involved in financing Al-Qaeda in the Middle East for many years and today he was hoping to conclude a deal from which Al-Qaeda in Syria would benefit.

'*Assalaam alaykum*,' said one of the men as he approached.

'*Wa 'alaykum assalaam*, and peace be upon you also.'

'How goes the fight in Yemen, we see you are doing great things?'

'Well, it goes well, and in Syria our fighters are holding their own against the regime of Assad.'

'It is to be hoped he is toppled soon. We control much of that country and soon we hope to control it all,' said one of the men with an air of superiority.

Yusuf nodded; aware that Daesh looked upon Al-Qaeda as the junior partner.

'You have come to discuss the oil we have for sale? Before we talk, we have an execution, an example, a spy in our midst, a Shi'ite from Iran who tells us he is of the faith but he is not. It is time, bring out the traitor.'

Two of the men jumped to their feet and hurried across the courtyard.

'Come my friend, the people are gathering. Executions are both entertainment and a warning. The man will lose his head and the crowd will comply with our law, sharia law. Praise be to Allah.'

Yusuf bowed his head in acknowledgement and followed his host through an archway into a square where a gathering of several hundred people waited in silence. Then the two black-clad terrorists returned, dragging a struggling and bound man through the same archway, pushing him through the crowd towards an open area where they forced the sobbing victim to his knees. It took no more than a minute, a few prayers and the curved sword swung down to a collective sigh as the crowd witnessed yet another beheading.

'Let this be a warning to you all, Islamic State rules this land and we will not tolerate anyone working against us, we will not tolerate anyone who defies the will of Allah,' said one of Yusuf's hosts.

Yusuf looked at the man, then at the subdued, obedient people and he knew that Daesh really was a force to be reckoned with, a force that could very well dominate the whole of the Middle East. It was an unnerving thought, and turning his eyes towards away he took a deep breath, unaware of the slender surveillance drone loitering high overhead.

Chapter 2

After the harsh Russian winter, once the snows melt Moscow becomes a relatively pleasant place to be as spring flowers add much-needed colour to the city. It is a time for the people to rediscover the great outdoors and for the two men, their fur ushanka-style winter hats discarded for more sober trilbies, a walk through Gorky Park was very welcome. The park had been transformed, the the drab Soviet style replaced with new and elegant gardens complete with fountains, the ramshackle and illegal buildings of the past replaced with modern structures and for the two men the park's open spaces offered a rare degree of privacy as they walked along secluded pathways, a rare chance to talk freely. They had much to discuss for both were well aware of the momentous change that was coming.

'Igor shall we sit by the river for a while, the sun is warm and I do so enjoy looking at the gardens? We have much to discuss and perhaps the riverside is a good place for a little privacy.'

'You do not really believe that Alexander, do you?

We have been in this game too long to expect our meeting to remain unnoticed. We can at least talk freely here in the park so long as we take the right precautions.'

'Why would we want to take precautions my friend? We have nothing to hide.'

'That is true, I invited you here to give you this,' said Igor, a slim bespectacled man with a serious face who reached into his jacket pocket to produce a small colourfully wrapped package. 'A birthday gift for you Alexander, a small token of my gratitude for the support you have given me during my career at the ministry. How was the birthday dinner last evening by the way?'

'I am touched by your thoughtfulness. My birthday was two days ago but we know it is unlucky to celebrate early.'

'Yes, it's pointless arranging something you might never see,' said Igor falling silent as he handed the small package to his friend, his silence an acceptance of the foolishness in believing that even the best-laid plans would work out as intended. After all, they were both professionals and as professionals in the world of espionage had seen much change in the order of things. Since completing their education at the FSB Academy twenty years earlier, they had worked for the Russian Secret Service and now in their mid-forties were accomplished spymasters. As heads of their respective departments they had a vast collective experience, Alexander in charge of operations in the Americas and Igor those nearer home, Poland, Germany and as far south as Italy.

'There will be big changes in the next few years Alexander, maybe we should not think about birthdays for a while. The Americans will be starting their presidential election cycle soon and we both know our own president will not be standing again. Twenty twenty four could be a very interesting year.'

'A power vacuum perhaps?'

'Perhaps and if there is then maybe now is the time to break the habit of a lifetime and to look our own future.'

'And if we do perhaps there may not be any more birthdays for us Igor. Nothing in this life is without risk.'

'Quite. We should walk a little.'

The two men began to walk slowly along the path running parallel to the river, Alexander turning over the small gift still in his hand before finally slipping it into his pocket and Igor looking towards the sun with half-closed eyes. How many more birthdays *would* they see he wondered before turning his head towards his fellow spymaster.

'We are Russians Alexander; we should not fear the future, instead let us cross the park to the fun fair. I like to hear the children enjoying themselves.'

Alexander nodded his head, understanding, for amongst babbling voices they could speak a little more freely. In the open air there was always the chance that someone was observing them; they were not immune to surveillance even by their own people. Experience had taught them that amongst a crowd even the most sophisticated listening equipment would find it difficult to completely overhear their conversation.

Millennials on roller skates sped past them as they walked, and the crowd enjoying the Moscow sunshine became ever denser. Pulsating fountains, shooting water high into the air were a draw and from not far away the sound of trumpets and drums reached their ears.

'Ah, the happy sound of a happy people Igor. Russia is a happy place I think.'

'On the surface yes, but we both know that Russia is at its happiest with a strong man in charge and in less than two years he will leave office. We must make sure someone equally as strong takes his place to lead this great nation.'

'You have someone in mind?'

'Come Alexander near to where the noise of those musicians will cloak our conversation.'

'You are paranoid my friend.'

Igor Andresov's eyes narrowed behind his glasses as he looked at his colleague, rendering his message clear, unmistakable, and Alexander pursed his lips in understanding. Igor was guiding him towards a new and dangerous world.

'Let us cross the path, there by the cafe, a seat near the band. Everyone is too busy enjoying themselves to notice two middle-aged men.'

Igor looked across the path, past the crowd, teenagers' zig zagging on their roller skates, some veterans in a family group bedecked in medals, looking proud and carrying flowers, posing for photographs.

These were men who had fought for their country, men who deserved the fruits of their labours and Igor silently saluted them.

'There, that is as good as anywhere, come Alexander we can chat a while longer, then let us take a coffee before we return to the office. I have some information about the Politburo, who are the most likely to succeed the president.'

Rosemary Pennington had enjoyed her job in the United States navy but her naval career was over; she had decided to take the retirement package on offer before moving to her new job in Washington. But before doing so she had headed back to Arizona for a well-earned break. She still had family in Scottsdale, the place where she had spent her teenage years, the desert city just to the east of the state capital Phoenix. She had fond memories of those days, particularly learning to play golf in the spa resorts where her father worked as a groundsman and the times she had riden the trails through the McDowell Sonoran Preserve with Taylor, her then boyfriend.

Taylor was the one who had introduced her to the military; he had wanted nothing more than to become a fighter pilot and when he won a scholarship to the military academy north of Colorado Springs it signalled the end of their relationship. She had felt sad though not exactly heartbroken at the time and they had remained friends and Taylor's move to the military had inspired her. She was growing up, the future beckoned and two years later she too joined the military. For her it was the navy, a seemingly strange choice for the girl from landlocked Arizona but it seemed that the sea held some attraction for her. To begin with she failed the selection process but at the second attempt she made it to the Officer Candidate School at Newport, Rhode Island, and she loved every minute of it. She had always been near the top of her class at school though never outstanding but at Newport, she discovered that she had a talent for mathematics, particularly mathematical psychology, a branch of growing importance to the military. There were distractions it was true but after Taylor men, unlike to some of her friends, were never of much importance,. Instead, Rosemary found a career path, worked hard and towards the end of her time began specialising as a military analyst.

At the end of the course, she passed out with honours, her first posting to the cryptographic department at the San Diego naval base where she became absorbed in the craft of naval intelligence. Two years later she received a second posting, to Naples, Italy, working with the Sixth Fleet and it was there that she met her future husband, Commander John Pennington, also in military intelligence responsible for deciphering the Russian fleet communications. Like Rosemary, he was a talented analyst and cryptographer and it was not long before they were working closely together. Work spilled over into their private lives and consumed as they were by its intricacies often they would leave work only to meet for dinner to discuss the latest analysis techniques. Eventually it became obvious that they were in love; they married and because they were a talented team doing crucial work, the navy kept them in Italy for much longer than a normal posting. That was all in the past, the couple were now living in Washington and working for the CIA. Recognised as outstanding intelligence officers nearing the end of their naval careers, the Firm had come looking for them.

'Have you seen the news this morning John?'

'Er . . no, what's happened?'

'There has been another terrorist incident in Paris, eleven-thirty European time.'

'ISIS?'

'We don't know yet but I would guess so. There have been predictions that they would strike European cities. With so many refugees streaming into Europe some of them were bound to be ISIS plants.'

'What are the details?'

'It was on CNN about ten minutes ago when you were in the bathroom, it seems a gunman managed to get into the main railway station.'

'Casualties?'

'Lots, reports seem to indicate maybe as many as ten dead. The security services were quick to react though, killing the terrorist and now France is back on a high state of alert.'

'Not surprising.'

John looked at the television; a weather report was just ending and the picture switched to Paris. A French reporter stood outside the Gare du Nord and as he spoke, subtitles appeared on the bottom of the screen.

'The police killed the gunman almost as soon as he opened fire but the reporter is saying that he did manage to fire into the crowd before he died. He had an automatic weapon and there is speculation that he must have acquired some sort of military training.'

Rosemary was standing near the doorway to the kitchen and read the lines of text at the bottom of the screen. She did not need her husband's running commentary.

'John?'

'What?'

'I don't think it is ISIS.'

'Who then, Al-Qaeda?'

'Yes, I think it's one of their operations, ISIS is not too interested in causing trouble in the West, not yet anyway, and they are a weakened force. It's the stated aim of Al-Qaeda to attack the far enemy, as they call us, ISIS are more concerned with what is left of their caliphate. They have enough trouble there.'

'I think you might be right. Is the coffee on? I need a strong coffee because I have a feeling it is going to be a long day.'

John's experience of working in Italy and the United Kingdom had elevated him to the CIA's European desk and this was a European issue for sure. The news was disturbing and with his mind starting to assimilate what they knew, he went into the kitchen, filled a cup from the percolator and reached into a wall cupboard for a granola energy bar. It would have to suffice; a hurried breakfast was all he could manage today.

'Are you ready?' he asked, lifting his cup for one last

drink.

'Sure,' said a thoughtful Rosemary slipping on a thick, warm jacket.

She was enjoying her work at Langley and was glad she had made the decision to join John rather than grow lazy in retirement. A comfortable life can appear desirable when the pressure becomes too much but after her sojourn in Arizona she was glad to be back in the saddle. With an exceptional ability to interpret intelligence she was an asset to the CIA and though they were comfortably off with a nice house and generous pensions from the navy the chance to be at the heart of things was just too good an opportunity to miss.

They had a son, Chuck aged twenty and studying at MIT majoring in mathematics. It seemed that he was taking after his mother. Chuck had left for Boston just a day earlier and would not be back until Easter, leaving his parents free to take a long-planned holiday to Hawaii though it now appeared as if they would have to forego their vacation.

'I will take my car today John, I do not expect our hours of work will synchronise too well for a day or two.'

'Good idea, will you lock up if I leave straight away?'

'Sure, who else is there?'

'Sorry, yes, I forgot Chuck is in Boston. Good job he is not here because I think this place is about to become very lonely.'

John joined Interstate 495 from Rockville, running

into a long line of vehicles and causing him to swear under his breath. He had left it just a little too late, the rush hour traffic was building up and he suffered a fraught twenty minutes before he finally crossed the Potomac. The George Washington Parkway was less congested and he hit the speed limit, passing through Langley's security gate just half an hour later.

'Morning Commander,' said the guard, saluting and leaning forward to scrutinise his pass.

John returned the salute and smiled to himself; after twenty years in the navy, he could not help but return a salute. Leaving the car in the parking lot, he grabbed his briefcase, made his way past the rows of cars towards the main building, and headed for his department. He was not the first to turn up for already congregated around the coffee machine were several colleagues and from the tone, he guessed that they were discussing the shooting.

'Morning John, I guess you've heard the news from Paris?'

'Some, only what I saw on television. The French reporter gave a few details. Are we any wiser?'

'Not much,' said the section head. 'My office in five minutes, okay?'

'Sure,' said John, pressing the black coffee, no sugar button, and minutes later he was pulling up a chair in his boss's office. Two other men were already there, Leo Patrice, a liaison officer dealing with the French security services, and Charlie Fuller, the visiting head of the Paris station.

'Gentlemen, as you are aware the Europeans have

had another terrorist incident. Information is still patchy, the operation in France is ongoing but so far, this is what we know. A gunman somehow smuggled an automatic weapon into the railway station and managed to kill or wound around twenty people before the local police shot him dead and right now they are conducting a manhunt for suspected accomplices.'

'Do we know who they are?'

'Not yet no, and it seems the French do not know either. The gunman was under the radar and they suspect a new and previously unknown terrorist cell perpetrated this attack. We've had some signals from your office, Charlie, but we are no wiser.'

'I got a call just after the incident became known to my people and told them to get a couple of spooks to the area, see what they could turn up.'

'Okay gentlemen, you know where this is leading, does it affect us here in the States, should Homeland Security be involved? My feeling is that this is a local matter for the Europeans and we can stay out of it but these damn terrorists are beginning to pop up more and more and I fear it will not be long before we see some of them over here. What do you think John?'

John finished his coffee, screwed the thin plastic cup into a ball and dropped it into the waste bin before turning his attention towards his boss.

'I have spent some time looking through reports on terrorist attacks that have taken place during the past couple of years. Clearly they are on the increase, and for the most part, we believe are driven by Islamic State rather than Al-Qaeda. These people are media savvy;

they exploit social media like no one else to spread their doctrine and recruit fighters. We see it on the news most days, sympathisers joining the fight from all over the Middle East, more come from the Caucuses, men who fought the Russians and others who have left safe countries in the West. They are mainly young men disillusioned by their lives, young men without work or a decent income who have time on their hands, radicalised by the real culprits, the imams and subversives in their societies. These are the people with the long-term aim of hurting us.'

'We're well aware of that John; question who is doing it and what we can do about it.'

'Sorry, got a little carried away. I think we are doing all we can, there is always room for improvement I know. Between us, the French and other security services we have managed so far to keep the attacks to a minimum but my fear is that amongst all the refugees who have been fleeing the conflicts in the Middle East for the past twenty years there must be quite a few radicals in amongst them. They are lying low until they receive the word, and that worries me.'

'Sleepers?'

'Like the Cold War? No, I do not think so, these guys are not lone wolves, more tight-knit cells. Their weakness is that they are not watertight, there are usually several members of each cell and eventually one will let something slip – trouble with the police for a misdemeanour usually or maybe they get caught buying banned chemicals, you know for home-made explosive devices. The security services need to be vigilant and we need to be at the top of our game analysing what comes in.'

'Who do you suspect on the limited information we have.'

'Rosemary thinks they are al Qaeda and I tend to agree with her. Whoever they are they are interested in hurting the West and that probably means al Qaeda.'

'Charlie, see what your people can turn up, I will call my opposite number across the water, see what he can tell me. In the meantime, John, I agree with your comment regarding our work here. I want you to gather the intelligence coming in, play with your statistics and see what they can tell us. Leo, get in touch with our bases in Europe, I expect they are already on high alert, see if anyone has information. They have not attacked any United States installations yet and it is our job to make sure that they don't. Get back to me as soon as you can. That is all for now people.

As the meeting broke up John Pennington headed towards his office and as he did so, a thought crossed his mind. Why would Rosemary believe that al Qaeda were the culprits? To be fair he had a gut feeling that was the case but he knew his wife, she would have had something more than a simple hunch.

Rosemary arrived at Langley shortly after her husband and made her way to her office. The place was waking up, the night shift was on its way home and the more numerous daytime staffers were heading for their workplaces. She passed through security and like most of her colleagues grabbed a coffee from the machine.

'Good morning Rosemary,' said a young black woman her hair tied in a bun and wearing thick-rimmed glasses.

To the untrained eye, Sarah Lovell was a typical geek, not particularly attractive nor with a great personality, a view that would greatly underestimate one of the brightest minds at Langley. She had received her doctorate from Stanford at just twenty-two, and with her glasses removed and her hair down, she certainly was not unattractive. However, Sarah was not in the least bit vain, she was a computer scientist and was completely absorbed in her work. Before coming to Langley, she had indulged herself for several years working in the computer gaming industry where she had helped develop more than one successful outcome and that had brought her to the attention of the CIA.

'Hi Sarah, how are you today?'

'I'm good. How's Chuck, I here he is back at MIT.'

'Yes, he left a couple of days ago. Say you have not been for dinner of late. Chuck always enjoyed your company. You're the one that inspired him to try for MIT.'

'He's a clever boy, takes after his mother I understand,' said Sarah with a cheeky smile.

Rosemary smiled back but the air of frivolity soon wore off and she got down to business.

'So, where are we with the graphics analysis program?'

'I've done a few trials on some intelligence shots from the library and the results are promising. I have my juniors checking out the code for errors because we are not quite there yet. It may be there are errors in the program code but it could be a deeper problem and we might need to completely rethink some of it.'

'How long will that take, I can't wait to see what you have? It sounds so exciting, a heck of a boon to the drone surveillance department if you can make it work.'

'Give me a few more days and I will see what I can do. Maybe I can rig up a demonstration using some recent footage.'

'That would be great, I look forward to it.'

'Bye for now Rosemary.'

Sarah began walking away and Rosemary turned towards the large open-plan office, beginning to wonder what the rest of the day might bring. That was part of the attraction of working for the CIA; there was never a dull moment and walking into the room, she became aware of a low murmur. The analysts and security specialists were preparing for their day's work but not before discussing anything from who was seeing whom to how the Washington Red Sox were getting on.

For the past few years, the department had focused its efforts on the Middle East and Afghanistan but now there was a sense of change. As security officials, they were the first to understand deeper consequences behind the events of the day. It was their job to extrapolate the present into the future for the protection of the United States and it was becoming apparent that home-grown terrorism was the new paradigm. The cancer of Middle Eastern terror was likely to spread across the Atlantic.

She walked to her desk, put down her briefcase, and finished her drink. From the office window, she had at least a partial view of the countryside and after casting her eyes over the greenery for a few moments, she slipped into work mode. The Russians were becoming a problem, talk of a re-set after the Cold War was a fantasy. Her prime task these days was to examine reports from the joint NSA-CIA Special Collection Service, teams stationed in United States embassies around the world, read the intercepts, analyse what she could and then, after collating that information, she would file it ready for interrogation by computer programs written by Sarah and her colleagues. The computers would compare the intelligence with that of other departments and, with luck, throw up leads to pass on to the spooks.

Rosemary was expert at statistics; she had used them to good effect in the navy, saved millions of dollars teasing out efficiencies in procedures and procurement and these same techniques, she had discovered, worked well in counter-espionage. She sat down, clasped her hands in front of her, and spent a few minutes connecting with the events of the previous day. She turned over in her mind the report she had read about a ship the navy had tracked from South America. The automatic identification system transponder it was supposed to use to inform other ships of its position and course had failed to transmit for long periods. The silence had aroused suspicion, were they running drugs or possibly even smuggling armaments? Both scenarios were possible but after examining the erratic transmissions she believed that it was more likely to be incompetence or poor maintenance and to be sure she had advised a boarding well out at sea.

The post trolley arrived breaking her train of thought and a young clerk handed her the morning's post, depositing it on her desk with the usual 'good morning ma'am'.

'Good morning, thanks.'

She picked up the first envelope, slit it open, read the contents and placed it on the desk ready to support an ever-growing pile. Most were routine traffic with details that she would enter into her database. Then she picked up a signal from the Cheltenham headquarters of GCHQ, the centre of British intelligence. It seemed innocuous enough, a report of a Russian billionaire's superyacht docked near Odessa on the Black Sea. In itself, it was not a particularly thought-provoking event unless of course taken in the context of the Russian annexation of Crimea, just a stone's throw away and the more serious events of just two years before.

The agent's report said that several men had visited the yacht but that he did not recognise any of them. Rosemary reread the report: why would a billionaire's yacht not have a stream of visitors? After all these men were powerful and could use their position to lever influence with lesser mortals. Perhaps the owner was Russian mafia; maybe he was an oilman or a financier;

it seemed to Rosemary that only someone in that bracket could afford a superyacht.

She entered the details into her computer and added a note to keep an eye on its movements. Then a thought occurred to her that if it were up to no good then the transmitter on this vessel could also be turned off?

She turned to her computer and initiated a search for the yacht, the Lady Galina, and an image filled her screen. The vessel was impressive, seventy metres long and weighing in at more than two thousand tons and she was capable of crossing the Atlantic without missing a beat.

Several thousand kilometres away in the Black Sea a stocky, balding man in his mid-fifties walked onto the flying bridge of the Lady Galina. Leonid Borisovich was a very rich man and had connections all the way up to the Politburo. However, those connections were not without ties, the favours bestowed upon him by those in power were not free. Leaning on the rail, he gazed out across the mouth of the Sukhyi River towards one of the few jetties big enough to accommodate a yacht of Lady Galina's size, a jetty that was well away from the city of Odessa and prying eyes.

'We have made good time Captain,' said Leonid, walking onto the bridge as the yacht began manoeuvring alongside.

'Just over thirty hours sir. We will be ready to lower the gangplank in ten minutes or so.'

'Good, I will go ashore for a few hours and when I return set a course for Istanbul.'

'Aye aye sir.'

Leonid turned back to the doorway and for a minute or two watched the deck crew secure the mooring lines, and then the gangplank appeared from out of the yachts hull, sliding gracefully towards the shore. It was time for him to leave and leaning over the rail, he called out to two men below who were watching the operation.

'Alexie, Viktor, swing the car out and fetch your weapons, we are going ashore.'

They were big, muscular and aggressive-looking and one turned towards the bridge, waved an acknowledgement before leading the way aft towards the deck crew who were mustering to begin swinging a black BMW car onto the quayside. Leonid watched for a time and as the car landed on the quayside he descended to the passerelle deck and casually walked down the gangplank.

'Alexie you know where to go I think. The area is familiar?'

'Yes boss, we were here a few years ago.'

'As Little Green Men, without insignias, I think?'

'Yes.'

The two men had been part of Russia's land grab, officers in Spetsnaz GRU, the Russian Special Forces, each of them a specialist in explosives and radio communication and experts at unarmed combat. As well as those skills, they were proficient in the use of the English language. Their job today though was no more than to drive Leonid to a dacha on a deserted stretch of coastline and as the oligarch reached his two bodyguards Alexie opened the rear passenger door for him.

For half an hour the car followed the estuary before turning inland to cross an area of flat, barren land eventually reaching a single-storey wooden construction in the classic style. It was a building of no particular note except for one feature, the eight-foot high razor wire security fence surrounding it. This was no ordinary dacha and as the BMW pulled up at the gate, a man in a pair of dark green overalls appeared.

'Can I help you?'

'I have come to see Alexandr Petrovitch,' said Leonid. 'My name is Vladimir Semyonov,' he lied.

The man's eyes narrowed and he produced a short-wave radio; it crackled into life and after a brief conversation with someone in the building, he spoke to the new arrival.

'Wait here, someone is coming.'

A minute later, a door opened at the side of the dacha and a man with an automatic weapon slung over his shoulder appeared. He was carrying a photograph taken on board the Lady Galina only hours before, a supposedly fail-safe security measure for verifying the authenticity of the visitor and after a brief comparison he said 'let him in.'

The guard reached for the bolt on the gate, swung it open and allowed the visitor to enter to be met at the doorway leading in to the building by a fat, balding man in his mid-sixties.

'Vladimir,' he said, 'come in come in, welcome. Would you like some coffee, we have the finest Arabica mountain coffee from Ethiopia, I can recommend it.'

"Vladimir" nodded and his host called out to a heavily built woman with muscular arms and sturdy legs to bring coffee. While she attended to the refreshment, the fat man ushered Leonid into a poorly lit room containing nothing more than a large table with several piles of papers and a telephone on it.

'Take a seat my friend and let's get down to business. The cash is in dollars, one million in fifty and one hundred dollar bills. It is surprisingly bulky, any less a denomination and you would not be able to transport so much by car. It is solely for use in financing the terror groups. Don't go spending it on yourself or you could finish up dead or in prison.'

'Prison?'

'You don't think the Americans printed them do you and you don't think our masters in the GRU will take kindly to you if you are seen to be squandering their funds?' the man said, an expressionless look on his face.

'Oh I see, no of course not.'

Leonid began to feel a little uncomfortable, the reality of the situation sinking in. He had agreed to help his country after a reception in the Kremlin where the state apparatus both feted and pressurised him, convincing him that his cooperation was tradeable for state favours. He was not a stupid man; he had not become wealthy by being naive and was well aware of the fate visited upon those who were less cooperative. For the state to accuse him of tax evasion or treasonable offences could leave him facing a hefty prison sentence so he was never going to refuse the Kremlin's request for help and after a short lecture from a high ranking intelligence officer he had begun a new chapter in his life as a facilitator for the FSB. Not only that, but Igor had confided in him, giving him just enough sensitive information to implicate him in any future investigation should he step out of line. It was a standard ploy of the FSB; insurance should the operation go wrong. Those that dreamt up these schemes were never around when the shit hit the fan and the realisation had made Leonid squirm as the true position dawned.

'I take it you had a good journey from the motherland,' said Petrovitch, signalling to the woman to pour the coffee.

Leonid nodded, the refreshment was a welcome distraction. After rubbing shoulders with some of the people he now had to deal with, he had been having second thoughts but it was too late to turn back, there was no escape, and taking a sip from the cup, he waited for the caffeine-rich liquid to help steady his nerves.

'Go and tell Ivan to let our visitors begin loading the boxes,' said Petrovitch to the woman after she had put the coffee pot on the table. 'This operation is important to us; I am told we have made contact with the people with whom you are to give the money. They will send a representative to meet you in Istanbul and you will give him the money, then you are to go to Naples in southern Italy and await further orders. Here is an envelope with your instructions, meeting places etc. You should cruise around and enjoy yourself, invite a few friends, look as if you are doing that which anyone might expect of a man in your position and we will be in touch. I am also to tell you that once the operation is completed the Order of Lenin awaits you. There is no greater honour for a true Russian.'

'I am humbled, grateful, and I will make the operation a success,' said Leonid, beginning to feel a little more in control.

The journey towards the Syrian border was slow, uncomfortable and fraught with danger. Until he was safely on board the overnight train to Ankara, Yusuf felt unable to relax. On edge, he was exhausted from a journey that had begun amongst the remnants of Al-Qaeda in the war-torn city of Idlib. Cornered and dodging bullets alongside fighters he had fought government forces witnessed many good men die and then with the survivors he had gone to ground finally escaping the city even as his comrades dispersed to the far reaches of the Islamic world. They had melted away to Yemen, Libya and North Waziristan to await better days.

'We are across the border, your escort is waiting,' said the driver, breaking into his thoughts.

Yusuf had escaped in a battered truck alongside tired and exhausted fighters, spent an anxious night avoiding government checkpoints before finally he was able to make his way to safety. It had been a hard lesson and he knew that if they were ever to rekindle the fight in Syria then they would need supplies, ammunition and explosives. Without more and better armaments, they could not continue the struggle for much longer.

Yusuf looked up to see a vehicle parked in the shade of a palm with two armed men leaning nonchalantly against it. Narrowing his eyes, he squinted into the sunlight, relived relieved to see not twenty metres away was a road sign in Turkish. Quickly he made his way to the waiting vehicle, introduced himself and as they headed away from the Syrian border he thanked Allah that least the roads were better here than in Syria and as he thanked his god for his safe deliverance he remembered his parting words.

'Soldiers of God do not be afraid; although I must leave you but I will return one day with American dollars for you to buy guns.'

'Where will you go?' asked one inquisitive soldier, his eyes ringed with fatigue, his face dirty with the dust from the wrecked city.

'That is for me only to know. Be assured the ruling council have sanctioned this journey and they have negotiated with people who are prepared to help finance our fight.'

Yusuf remembered the looks on their faces, brave, committed soldiers, all that was left of Al-Qaeda in Syria. God willing, they would one day establish a zone of influence across Anbar and the desert, a real Islamic territory, one where the people would welcome them.

Three hours later, after travelling at speed the vehicle reached Adana and it was with some relief that Yusuf boarded the train for Ankara. His goodbyes were necessarily brief and within minutes he slumped onto the bunk in his sleeper cabin, lulled into an exhausted sleep by the rocking of the train, a troubled sleep. His mind filled with the images of triumphant fighters shooting into the sky, raising the flag of the Al-Nusra Front, images of Afghanistan, American bombers and the training camp in the Iraqi desert. Vivid memories flashed through his mind, very real, the sight of the two American jets coming towards him causing his body to convulse. Unable to do no more than twist and turn in the confined space his eyes opened with a start.

He could not help but let out a cry, wondering where he was and sat up rubbing confused eyes before looking at his watch in the low light. It was four in the morning, it would be another hour before they reached Ankara and he would board the train for the last stage of his journey. Istanbul was where he would meet the man who would provide the finance the group needed. Although the deal he had brokered with Islamic State had proved fruitful, it had lasted for just eighteen months before American and Russian forces working together had displaced them. How could that have happened, they were enemies?

The world had changed so much during the past four years; Al-Qaeda had retreated on so many fronts. Yemen was the only real success where they had raided the central bank and netted almost one hundred million dollars From there they had created a mini state that provided much needed income but then the military intervention of the Saudis had put an end to that. The movement was becoming desperate for funds.

Since his days chasing round the desert paying local commanders and tribal chiefs Yusuf had become older and wiser, learning how to use bribery to convince them to remain loyal. It was during those days he had learned about international finance, working with some of the best bankers in the Middle East. Those men were in general sympathetic to the cause, and with this newfound knowledge, he had become a valuable asset in the fight against the West. As he expanded his reach, he made unexpected allies in the Russians. They had backed Assad and the regime, and now they were suddenly offering to help with the financing of Al-Qaeda. What was the catch?

He was still wondering hours later as the train pulled into the railway station on the Asian side of the Bosporus and lifting his bag from the overhead shelf, he disembarked to stand for a few minutes to check his phone. There it was, the message he was expecting. After replying, he left the station and stepped out into the sunshine to look for the Turkish bar as instructed to meet his contact. The man would be an Arab like himself and would be reading a copy of the Jordanian Ad-Dustour newspaper.

Looking left and then right along the street, he noticed the bar not far from the station entrance and sitting alone outside was a well-dressed man of Arab extraction. Approaching him Yusuf said, 'I expect the sun will rise again tomorrow.'

'Of course, it always does. Welcome to Istanbul, I

am your guide while you are here. My name is Mustafa. Please take a seat and you can breakfast, you can try some *börek* and you can tell me what you need from me.'

The man clicked his fingers, attracting the attention of the proprietor and, in the few minutes it took for their breakfast to arrive, Yusuf's contact told him of the arrangements he had made.

'I have a car waiting and a safe house in the city where you can rest should you need to.'

'I will not be here long. I have made travel arrangements already. I leave tonight when I have concluded my business.'

'Then I will stay close to you, at your command. Anything you need just tell me and it shall be done.'

'I require the services only of someone with local knowledge and transport. I do not anticipate trouble but if it occurs . . .'

'Have no fear, I have contacts and the ones to whom I owe my allegiance have told me to take good care of you as you are a special one. Here, the briefcase I am to provide,' said Mustafa, sliding a black leather case along the floor.

As Yusuf examined the case, a waiter appeared with a silver tray to deposit two cups and a pot of tea together with the pastries.

When he had gone Mustafa asked, 'you have travelled a long way my friend?'

Yusuf did not answer immediately, simply looked the man in the eye before picking up his cup.

'You do not need to know from where I come nor

where I go, simply convey me to my destination and you will have provided a great service to the cause.'

'Now which pastries do you prefer?' said Mustafa, taken aback by Yusuf's admonishment. 'I am sorry if I seem too inquisitive, please, help yourself to breakfast, I have already eaten, and then I will take you to your destination.'

Bowing slightly, Yusuf acknowledged his contact's curtesy and selected a pastry from the plate.

'The Turks make good tea,' he said, drinking from his cup. Perhaps another ten minutes and we will go.'

'My car is parked over there, where is it I should drive you?'

'The Marina Ataköy.'

'Ah, I know it well, just a short drive from here. Waiter,' he called, taking out some money from his pocket.

A short distance from the marina gate Yusuf got out of the car and finished his journey on foot. Pulling out his smartphone as he went and he selected a number and almost immediately heard a gruff voice answered in English.

'Who is calling Lady Galina?'

'I am Mohammed from the Egyptian Bank.'

There was a short pause.

'Wait at the gate and someone will come for you.'

The phone went dead and the newly created 'Mohammed from the Egyptian bank' looked round a little nervously. He was happier in the flowing Arab robes but today he was wearing European clothes and they were making him feel uncomfortable. Reaching the gate, he attempted to appear relaxed as he waited for his contact looking nonchalantly at the array of expensive motor yachts moored side by side, noting that they were probably worth a great deal of money. He wondered what he might achieve if he could lay his hands on so much wealth. His people were poor, most of them having no more than the clothes they stood up in, and yet here, not a hundred metres from him, was good reason to destroy the West. Their desire for wealth and power had drained the Arab lands, his lands, tainting even the emirs and the sheiks.

Chapter 3

At her desk in the MI6 building on London's Embankment Anita took the envelope from the office mail carrier. She was still recovering from a heavy cold and as it was her first day back at work she was not fully alert. She had been on sick leave for a week and picking up her coffee cup, she took a few sips. It was always like this on her first day back and it did not matter the reason. If it was because of illness, holidays or some covert mission, she always seemed to need a cup of coffee and a few minutes to gather her thoughts. The nature of the job and events surrounding it would normally sweep her along but she was not yet up to speed but wanted to read the intelligence relating to the recent terrorist incident in Paris. The French still seemed to be taking the brunt of the backlash started by the American invasion of Afghanistan so many years ago.

She took a mouthful of coffee and at the same time switched on her computer to catch up on her emails, mainly routine traffic, messages from colleagues and superiors and for half an hour, she read them to bring herself up to date. GCHQ had played a crucial role in tracking down the terrorists involved in the Gare du Nord incident. The gunman had made the fatal mistake of contacting someone in Belgium, the French security services had received information from the British and made several arrests and after interrogating the suspects, it had become clear that there was more trouble brewing and that was of interest to Anita. Of course but her expertise lay more towards the Russian end of the spectrum but recently she had been working on possible connections between the terrorists and the GRU, the Russian foreign intelligence agency, until her cold had laid her low. She had noticed a few spikes during her investigations but in general, the Russians seemed quieter than they had been for some time. In itself, that seemed encouraging, but Anita knew that radio silence often meant quite the opposite. She considered the accumulated intelligence before taking one last drink of coffee, screwing her face as the realisation dawned that it was stone cold. It seemed that her ability to concentrate had returned and picking up the envelope, she opened it and slid its contents onto her desk.

There was a single sheet of paper, several photographs. Reading the text she discovered that an agent from the Istanbul bureau had spent some time photographing a Russian oligarch's superyacht and its visitors' comings and goings. The page told her that the reason he was taking pictures was that the tracking signal it must transmit by international law was absent and when the automatic identification device had become live in the middle of the Black Sea GCHQ had taken notice and suspicions were aroused. Then she discovered that on the day before the Americans had asked the British to keep an eye on the yacht after one of their satellites had located it in Odessa. An operative was despatched immediately from the embassy in Kiev to have a look but by the time he arrived, the vessel had put to sea, switching on the automatic tracking system once it was clear of Ukrainian waters. From then on, MI6 decided to keep it under surveillance, following it to Istanbul and sending and intelligence officer to investigate.

Anita had the results of that surveillance in front of her and working slowly through the photographs she looked for any clues as to what the owners of the yacht might be doing. Were they smuggling drugs, arms maybe, or was it simply a false trail? There were several people in the pictures, none of them familiar, but three men stood out under her expert eye. Two appeared to be Russians, big, muscular-looking men. That at least gained her attention; they were very possibly GRU and that was enough for her to begin making a few notes. Then she looked at the third man, swarthy skinned, of Middle Eastern appearance. He was good-looking, tall and slender, not at all like the other two.

'What was the Arab doing on a Russian's yacht,' she mumbled to herself. Maybe she was reading too much into the situation but he was in the presence of possible GRU personnel and that made her uneasy.

She picked up her telephone and pressed a pre-programmed button. 'James, I think I might be on to something. Can I come and see you?' The answer was in the affirmative and Anita was soon leaving the office clutching the brown envelope.

Rosemary rubbed her eyes, after concentrating for hours on her computer screen she was feeling drained. Information from the French security services and her own people had poured in and she had noticed several trails leading across the border into Belgium and Germany, then information from GCHQ relating to telephone calls had arrived and reaffirmed her suspicions. Immediately she had spoken with her superiors and within hours, the French security services were making arrests. It had been a gratifying experience to know that she had helped.

'I need a coffee,' she said aloud as she stood up to make her way to the coffee machine.

'I think I might just join you,' said a familiar voice.

Rosemary turned to see the beaming black face of Sarah Lovell.

'Hi Sarah, you are looking pleased with yourself.'

'Maybe I am but then perhaps I have reason to be. I have the program up and working, still a few bugs but it looks promising. I have a meeting in the morning with the director of drone surveillance at DDI. The details are secret but I can tell you a little as you will be involved shortly.'

'Really, congratulations, when do I get a demonstration?'

'Tomorrow afternoon, at about three o'clock, come to the lab and bring a few overhead shots from one of the drones. I think you will like what you see.'

Rosemary pursed her lips in a puzzled smile. Some of the stuff this girl got up to truly amazed her and she, as much as anyone, was well aware of how significant computer analysis was when applied to intelligence gathering and it looked as if Sarah and her team at the Directorate of Digital Innovation were taking the science, or was it an art, to a new level.

'I look forward to that Sarah.'

The young woman smiled broadly and left Rosemary to return to her desk but for a few moments she did not move, instead she pondered Sarah's statement. It had intrigued her and she decided to dig out one or two overhead shots from drone surveillance as soon as she returned to her desk. With access to a large file of photographs taken in Iraq and Syria over the past few years, she had plenty of choice and, at random selected some overhead shots of several black-clad figures of Islamic State militants. Amongst them was a man in traditional Arab robes and looking through the folder, she selected two more of the same scene taken from different angles. Inserting a USB drive, she transferred the pictures and placed the drive in her drawer before turning back to her ongoing work.

James Hill was distracted and looked up to see Anita peering round the cubicle screen.

'Anita, what can I do for you?

'Have a look at these,' she said sitting on the chair opposite and placing her photographs onto his desk.

'That's a fine-looking yacht. Is that what you have

come to show me?'

'Partly, we've been tracking the yacht ever since we became suspicious of it.'

'What caused the suspicion?'

'We believe the vessel left Sochi on the Russian Black Sea coast some days ago without transmitting its identification signal. There have been one or two situations like this but never a superyacht leaving the Russian president's favourite place. The owner of this boat must be wealthy, very wealthy, probably an oligarch, probably with ties to the president.'

'Who is he?'

'That is why I'm here. I do not know, can you find out for me?'

'That's easy,' said the secret service officer turning to his computer. 'What's the yacht's name, any other registration letters?'

'She is called Lady Galina and she is registered in Panama.'

'Hmm . . I suppose she would be. Lady Galina, nice Russian name,' he said, entering the name into the computer. After a pause, he continued, 'She is owned by a Russian billionaire all right, one Leonid Borisovich. Have you heard of him?'

'The name rings a bell but I have not come across him. Anything else?'

'Just a minute,' he said his fingers almost a blur as he typed in several search parameters. 'It seems he's made his money from iron ore.'

'Not oil?'

'No, I admit we would expect these Russian

oligarchs to be oilmen but this one is not it seems. He has interests all over the world, South America, Australia, and he has a stake in the biggest iron ore deposit in Africa, in the Simandou mountains of south east Guinea.'

'Guinea, well I would think a Russian oligarch would feel at home in a place like that, with all the corruption that goes on there.'

'Yes, there have been rumours of scandals for years surrounding the Guinea raw materials deposits. I would not be surprised. So have I answered your questions?'

'Not quite, I need to know who these men are. I think these two are GRU but the other, the one is a complete mystery. Can you do anything, have we records on the Russian Special Ops people?'

'Some, but like us they play their cards pretty close to their chests. Leave the pictures with me; I will do what I can. Will sometime tomorrow do?'

'It will have to James, but in the meantime I have a few other lines of enquiry I can follow that will keep me busy. Just let me copy what you have already turned up.'

'Email?'

'Yes, that will be the easiest I guess.'

'Done, the information will be waiting for when you return to your desk.'

'Thanks James,' said Anita. 'Let me have the photos back when you have finished with them.'

The young man nodded and Anita left him to walk back to her desk, her mind already working on possibilities. A Russian metals oligarch, GRU, an Arab and a superyacht. It was a heady mix; if subterfuge of some sort was involved, she could not yet see what it might be.

Rosemary tapped on the half-open door and pushed it wide enough to look inside the laboratory.

'Can I come in?' she asked the technician.

'Sure, are you looking for Sarah?'

'Yes, she asked me to come here for three and it's about that by my watch.'

'She is over there look, with those two men standing near the white board. Just go over.'

'Thanks,' said Rosemary, walking past laboratory equipment piled high and towards the two standing men and in front of them she saw Sarah sitting in front of a large monitor screen.

One of the men sensed her presence and turned, alerting the others and Sarah looked up from her keyboard.

'Rosemary, glad you could come. We are just finishing off, take a seat and I will be with you.'

Rosemary nodded and pulled up a vacant chair as Sarah continued her discussion with her colleagues for a further few minutes before they moved back to their own workplaces.

'Have you brought some surveillance pictures?'

'Here,' said Rosemary, handing over the USB stick.

'Okay, pull your seat a little closer and I will show you what I have been doing. You may already know that they construct a lot of the three-dimensional buildings and features on Google Earth from drone footage. They fly the drone around a building, take pictures logged with GPS positions, then the computer stitches the images together and hey presto another building is mapped. It's a tried-and-tested technique and I have, I think, taken it a stage further.'

Rosemary did not reply, she felt a little out of her depth.

'Let me show you a short video demonstrating the principle.'

Sarah logged on to the internet and brought up a video for Rosemary to watch. A drone flew into view and proceeded to circle an isolated building; the images from its on-board camera appeared in a side panel and then graphics took over. A series of lines appeared and then two-dimensional faces filled the spaces between them building up a three-dimensional facsimile of the building.

Rosemary watched with interest. 'That was pretty impressive but what has it got to do with espionage? Am I being stupid, should I know?'

'No, I'm not actually doing anything with buildings or a street scene, my work is more to do with people. Let's load your images and see what we can do.'

The screen changed as Sarah loaded her program, and as the pointer flew across the monitor, the images Rosemary had provided appeared. There were three of them, one from overhead and two from steep angles. From those images, the subjects were impossible to identify, which was normally the case.

'Okay, I just need to adjust the sizes to make them

compatible. Now if I incorporate them into the software you can see what we have developed.'

Sarah pressed a key, sat back and together the two women watched the computer create a new image on its own.

'My God Sarah, that's pretty darn clever.'

Sarah hardly heard the compliment, busy as she was refining the image.

'The rendering isn't as good as I would like and the proportions are not real but look, I can stretch the image to give a more realistic impression of our target,' she said working the image with her mouse pointer.

She had taken the three images, combined them and worked out their perspectives allowing the computer to create what was almost a hologram of the subject. To anyone familiar with Yusuf, the three-dimensional image slowly rotating on the screen was a good likeness.

'I will copy several views of the man and you can take him away with you. Do you know who he is?'

'No, I don't, it was just a random set of images from an old shoot in Iraq. If memory serves me right they were taken several years ago.'

'Well maybe you can figure out who he is.'

'The images are from an old file, probably not much use now, but hey, a great exercise. I can see how useful this program will be for use with overhead aerials. We do have a problem identifying suspects sometimes without a full-on face image.'

Rosemary studied the man's face as he slowly rotated on the screen and marvelled at the detail Sarah had managed to capture. Apart from a few small imperfections, it was almost as if she were looking at him in the flesh.

Anita picked up her desk telephone after the second ring. 'Hello, oh James, what have you turned up? So you think they are GRU, I am not surprised, and the yacht owner, Leonid Borisovich, what have you on him? What about the other man, the Middle Eastern one?'

For several minutes James spoke, outlining his findings and before ringing off said that he would email everything he had. Anita put down the telephone and chewed on her lip for a moment or two. So, the two thugs most probably were GRU, which posed the question of why Russian Special Forces personnel were on the yacht belonging to an iron ore billionaire? Then there was the Arab, was there any real connection, was he somehow involved with Borisovich? She had no idea yet but her curiosity was aroused and she was not about to let go. Then, wondering if the email from James had arrived, she reached for the computer mouse and opened her mailbox. It was there, along with at least a dozen others she had not yet opened; ignoring the earlier messages, she clicked on the latest arrival. James had already briefed her on its contents, explained everything he had found out and cleared up a few of her questions but he did have something new. Tucked away at the end of the message was a breakdown of Borisovich's known assets and standing out from the rest was a property he owned in London, near Belgrave Square – also known as Red Square for good reason.

Interesting, she thought, he must visit Britain on occasion. What was his motivation; Britain was not as welcoming to Russians with Kremlin connections as it once was. She would like to know, wondered if bugging the place was an option, and made a note to ask Border Control to inform MI6 each time he planned to enter the country. The two GRU personnel were not so important, most likely bodyguards she guessed

It was getting late and she would soon be finishing for the day but before she left, she would do one more thing. The Americans had a huge database full of information on terrorists, insurgents and the like. After nine-eleven, the CIA had woken up to the fact that they needed more and better intelligence and had turned to MI6 and GCHQ for help. Anita had found herself involved during periods when she was not working in the field and during trips to the States; she had made a good friend in Rosemary Pennington. Though their dealings were brief and infrequent, they had hit it off from the start and on the rare occasion when Anita had paid Langley a visit, Rosemary had invited her for dinner. Both Rosemary and John were experts on the Russians and those dinner dates had proved fruitful, interesting, and now she needed their help.

Logging on to the secure email server, she looked up Rosemary's address, composed a short note and attached the best image she had of the Middle Eastern mystery man. She considered that she had provided as much information as she could and she hoped that it would bring results. She clicked on the send icon.

The Russian, Borisovich, intrigued her; a billionaire on a superyacht accompanied by GRU operatives appeared extremely suspicious to her questioning mind. What was he up to, was he under the direct orders of the Kremlin, or was he acting as a lone wolf and were the thugs his bodyguards or perhaps even involved in some operation of their own? She was not sure about any of it but a little more digging would not go amiss. Perhaps the Americans would turn something up, but in the meantime, she would talk to her section head to see if she could make a case for keeping an eye on the Russian. Biting her lip again, as she did in moments like these, she picked up the telephone and made the call and an hour later, she was sitting across the desk from the head of the Russian counter-espionage department.

'We know a bit about your man Anita but not a lot. Since your call, I asked for his file and to be honest there is not much in it. He was not one of Boris Yeltsin's confidants, did not reap the benefit of the sell-off in state assets like one or two other high-profile oligarchs. His beginnings are murky but he was in St Petersburg when Putin was mayor and it was not long after that he took possession of an iron ore mine in Siberia and from there he has grown an empire spanning the globe. Now, it may be he is a genius in business or it may be he has the ear of the Kremlin.'

'But you don't benefit from state patronage if you have nothing to give in return sir.'

'Quite. There is a note here that he provided funds

towards the football World Cup and we know whose pet project that was.'

'You think he might be connected to the Kremlin?

Most of the oligarchs and gangsters in Russia do seem to have connections to the centre of power. We have kept an eye on a few of them over the years and we know that a high percentage is involved in spying.'

'Yes, and this chap will be no different I am sure and he has taken Israeli nationality to get round our ban on Russian undesirables.'

'I would like to have a closer look at him sir; I have a strong feeling he is involved in something the Russians are planning but as yet I have no idea what that might be. He has a house in Belgravia and I would like permission to have the place wired.'

'I don't see why not, I respect your judgment Anita, you have been right before and I must say I am leaning towards your appraisal. I will write an order for the surveillance department to plant some of their toys in the house and we will see what that turns up. By the way, I have had the French on to me; they have been picking up signals from the Middle East indicating some sort of threat to mainland Europe. My opposite number tells me that they are finding links between Al-Qaeda and some unexpected associates. I have told him that I will set up a discussion group to go over the intelligence we have already and arrange for one of our spooks to meet with representatives of their Directorate for Internal Security. We know they have had their problems over the past year or two and I believe they have coped as well as they could. Home-grown terrorism is on the up over here too, but so far we have managed to keep the lid on and now maybe we have yet another problem, the Russians.'

'I don't know that for sure sir but I would like to pursue this Borisovich character and find out what he is up to.'

'Well he's Russian with an Israeli passport and we believe he has the ear of the president,' he said, looking at Anita. 'That tells us a lot I think.'

'Yes sir, I believe it does.'

'Right, there is no need to consult the lawyers on this one. You have my permission to carry out surveillance of his property in Belgravia. If you find anything then you are to let me know immediately, is that clear? I don't want an incident because we've trampled on someone's toes.'

The flight by private jet from Istanbul to London City was uneventful, taking only seven hours even with a fuel stop at Frankfurt. Leonid Borisovich had used the time to read his latest sets of company reports paying particular attention to his interests in Australia. The Chinese market was sluggish, gone were the days when anything you dug out of the ground would turn a profit. The retreat from globalisation was having a profound effect on his business and the rate he was losing money meant that it might not be too long before he would need to begin a major restructuring of his operations. Perhaps it was time to retire, perhaps the rough and tumble of the business world was becoming too much for him, he thought, as the aeroplane swept in low over the River Thames. He was feeling sorry for himself, it happened periodically and a sure way to shrug off his melancholia was to throw a party, reconnect with old friends. Yes, that was what he would do and just over an hour later, as he walked through the front door of his impressive six-bedroom town house he finished concocting his guest list.

Waiting for him was Lyudmyla, his trusted housekeeper, alerted to his arrival and ready for him.

'I am preparing you a light dinner mister Borisovich. It will only take a few minutes to cook. Would you like it serving immediately?'

'No, not straight away, I will settle in, change my clothes first. Give me half an hour and see if we have any of the Barolo I enjoyed last time I was here.'

Lyudmyla did as she he asked, checking through the unopened bottles in the cellar and checking the time began to cook dinner.

'That was very good, and you found the wine. I feel that I have come home but it has been a long day and I still have a little work to finish off so I will retire to my bedroom and have an early night. Don't bother to wake me in the morning, tomorrow is a day off.'

The sun was streaming through the lace curtains when Leonid Borisovich finally woke and looking at his very expensive watch was surprised, ten o'clock was late for him. Half the day had already gone on this his first day back in London but he was feeling so much better after a good night's sleep. After almost three months away, he was looking forward to a little self-indulgence. First, he would take a shower, then take a stroll before returning for a very late breakfast and give Lyudmyla her instructions.

He gazed down at the street below and noticing the line of parked cars he realised that something had changed. During his previous visits, every other vehicle was a tradesman's van or small truck but now there were gaps, large gaps. The work must have dried up, a sign of the times he thought. Then he noticed a few pedestrians, Chinese tourists by the look of them, and in a doorway, a man was speaking into a mobile phone, but other than that, the street was practically deserted. He had never noticed it so quiet.

Leonid liked London, especially Belgravia; he felt at home, could walk into any restaurant and feel welcome, and more often than not hear at least a snatch of his native language. Numerous Russians had settled in London, a welcoming place until only a few years ago but attitudes were changing, Europe was beginning to disintegrate, forces were emerging to disturb the status quo, the British economy had weakened and he had read that in the north, industrial unrest was beginning to manifest itself.

That was good news; he could report to the Kremlin that their predictions were accurate; the work of the keyboard warriors at the St Petersburg Internet Research Agency was bearing fruit.

There was a knock on the door and he turned away from the window.

'Come,' he called out and the wide white-painted door slowly swung open.

The Sommelier

'Your morning tea sir,' said Lyudmyla in Russian.

'Thank you Lyudmyla, put it over there on the side table,' he replied in their common language. 'Lyudmyla, I am considering a dinner party, a special dinner party for friends and business associates. I have just about completed a list of guests, there should be around twelve. For the event I want you to engage the services of a well-respected caterer who can put on a Russian evening, remind me of home.'

'I can arrange that; let me know the date you are proposing and I will make enquiries. Will there be anyone for dinner this evening?'

'Yes, there will be one guest. He is arriving at six-thirty. Please let me know as soon as he enters the house.'

The woman addressed him again in Russian before leaving him to reflect on his evening's guest, Mikhail Mikhailovich, the SVR London bureau chief. While crossing the channel in his Cessna jet, Mikhail had called him, saying they should meet for dinner. That could only mean one thing – state business. Leonid knew very well that he was treading on dangerous ground; he was in a foreign country with a sophisticated intelligence service and the Russian intelligence chief was coming to dinner. Not for the first time did the hairs on the back of his neck stand up, even before the yacht had left Sochi two men had arrived from Moscow to speak with him. They were agents of the Federal security services, the FSB, sent to brief him on his mission. Although he did not know the true focus of what he was to do, he did know that it was of importance to the state and, if successful, it would bring him favours, and as they left, they told him that two GRU Special Forces personnel would be joining the crew of the Lady Galina.

Anita was not one for vulgar expression but she came very close when she received the report of the surveillance team in Belgravia. They had not been able to plant any listening devices without risk of detection and then they reported seeing a visitor. At least they had managed to get a shot of him, and as she pulled the photograph from the envelope, she recognised Mikhail Mikhailovich.

'Damn, that was a missed opportunity,' she said to herself. What she would give to be a fly on the wall when those two met, to hear what they had to say to each other.

Then she had a second report to read, from the embassy spook in Istanbul tasked with keeping an eye on the Lady Galina. Two men of Middle Eastern appearance had turned up early in the morning in a Fiat Panda and one had gone aboard the yacht carrying a briefcase. The agent had not been able to follow them onto the dockside, though he did manage to take some hurried shots with his camera.

Rosemary was just starting work when Anita's email arrived, jogging her memory, causing recollection of the original request.

'Oh gosh, I'd forgotten about that,' she said to

herself.

Perhaps she should attend to the British request immediately, get it out of the way to allow her a free run at her current project analysing the movements of the remnants of Islamic State. There were reports of them springing up in diverse theatres such as Libya and Kenya, even far-flung states of the former Soviet Union. It was already clear that the Russians had stolen the limelight in the Middle East and Russian state involvement troubled her. They had finally completed their base on Syria's Mediterranean coast and the brutal strategy they were pursuing had established them in Libya where a second Mediterranean naval base was under construction. Perhaps more worrying was the subdued reaction from POTUS and there were rumours that the he was about to withdraw Sixth Fleet. That was a real problem but at least someone had persuaded him to order the revival of the Second Fleet to strengthen the North Atlantic command and that had settled more than a few nerves. She had also seen plenty of ELINT traffic from spooks on the ground informing her that the Russians had met with several known Al-Qaeda leaders. That was disturbing, what was going on?

She clicked on the icon to open her inbox and within seconds a flood of new emails appeared. They would have to wait. Scrolling down she found Anita's original message and opened it, reading the first few lines to refresh her memory, and then she opened the attached image for the first time, the sight of it a real shock. Only days before the face she was now looking at had come to life on Sarah's computer screen. It was the same man she was sure, older and less lean, but it was him alright. She picked up her telephone and rang Sarah; she needed to have no doubts and by the time she walked into Sarah's laboratory the computer whiz had the two images sitting side by side on the large monitor.

'It's him all right. Look, if I stretch the image a little to put some weight on him, and lighten his hair, match the features . . .'

'My goodness, it really is. Sarah you are a genius.'

'Thanks for that Rosemary but I think you are going a little overboard with your praise. I'm just doing my job.'

Rosemary smiled a smile that masked her racing mind.

'Perhaps he's somewhere else in our database; perhaps this is someone we have missed, under the radar as they say. I think I might have to change my workload today.'

Taking her leave, Rosemary walked back into the main building and along the corridor to her desk. She hardly remembered the short journey, the security checks, the odd greeting, deep in thought as she was. She had been tracking most known Al-Qaeda affiliates for some time and was almost as familiar with some of them as with her friends, but the man in the photographs was unknown to her. How could that have happened? It was time for a little more help from her researcher.

Chapter 4

Rosemary, aware that Edward was walking towards her looked up from her work. He was carrying a light brown folder and his jaw was set, a clue that his research had turned up something of importance. She knew better than to pre-empt his report, to pressurise him, for Edward was a researcher not a toughened field operative. Instead, she simply nodded a greeting and with an outstretched hand offered him a seat.

'Morning ma'am, I thought I should call you as soon as I had some information worthy of discussion.'

'Of course, it's what I would expect,' said Rosemary in anticipation. 'What have you got for me?'

'We think his name is Yusuf al-Bana, I could not find a birth certificate or school records so we believe that at some time he may have changed his name. All we have to go on are the images and I must say that, by the look of it, the geeks have come up with some weird software.'

'Yes they have, so what else?'

'Well, as I said, there were just dead ends, nothing in any of the databases I searched, and I searched I can tell you.'

'I believe you Edward.'

'Then I thought perhaps I was not looking in the right area.'

'What do you mean?'

'Well I had been searching names and places, connections, but I kept drawing blanks. Then I thought about that weird three-dimensional image so I wondered if I might be more successful doing an image search, facial recognition and all that stuff.'

'You sound like a computer whiz yourself,' said Rosemary, intrigued.

'Ha, I wish, no ma'am, but I went to Sarah's department and she seconded one of her people to help me and between us we came up with this.'

Edward opened his folder and spilled several photographs onto the desk, rearranging them in neat order. Rosemary leaned forward, recognising two of them but the others were new.

'Look, in the car, the passenger. We think it is the same man, this Yusuf.'

Rosemary picked up her glasses and scrutinised the three new images, all taken in quick succession by the look of it.

'Goddammit boy I do believe you are right. Where did these come from, they look old?'

'Second Gulf War, northern Iraq, they were taken by the British during an operation to knock out a terrorist training camp. British Special Forces located the camp and called in a couple of F15s to obliterate it but these characters were already on their way out when the jets struck.'

'And the Brits took a few holiday snaps. Well done Brits, so what was our friend doing there in the camp?'

'We don't know but the Special Ops boys picked up a laptop and reported seeing literally thousands of dollar bills floating around. They were all over the place, scattered by the bombing presumably.'

Rosemary pursed her lips, moved her spectacles to her nose end, and as her vision lost focus her brain moved into overdrive. Opposite her, the researcher remained silent, witnessing with some wonder the operation of one of Langley's best minds swinging into action.

'This guy has been around for quite some time, it seems, and no one has ever picked him up. Strange, intriguing, okay thanks Edward, leave the file, I will call you if I need further assistance.'

The researcher did as Rosemary asked and left her deep in thought, and after maybe ten minutes she came back to life. Picking up each photograph, she held it up and inspected it in detail, looking behind the subject, searching for anything that might throw more light on what was going on. So, the Brits had provided another piece of the jigsaw, an important piece by the look of it, and she wondered what her next move should be. After a few seconds of deliberation, she picked up the telephone and keyed in several numbers.

Anita wondered how Rosemary was getting on with her request for information and was of a mind to send a further email. However, when she went to her computer a reply was already in her inbox. Surprised, she opened Rosemary's report and began absorbing the contents, first reading the notes and then studying the attached images. Like her American counterpart, Anita too wondered how the man in the pictures had remained hidden for so long. Apart from the two sightings in Istanbul, there appeared not to be any mention of him on the British databases though that was not necessarily true. There could be something hidden away and awaiting discovery, but for now all she had to go on were the reports from the embassy in Turkey. She sat back and then it dawned on her, of course the Russian, he was the connection and he was in London.

She picked up her telephone, called her section head and after a brief conversation made her way to his office.

'Come in, what can I do for you? You said it was to do with our previous conversation. The Russian billionaire I presume.'

'Yes sir, there has been a development. I received intelligence from the Istanbul bureau a few days ago and after some consideration, I put one of the researchers on to it and asked Langley for some help. Look here at the pictures I received and this one, generated by computer, showing a three-dimensional image of the suspect.'

'How did you do that?'

'I didn't sir, it's from Langley. I guess some whiz created it but that is not the point. Here, look at these taken about fifteen years ago in Iraq.'

The section head looked over the images while a silent, watchful Anita allowed him to draw his own conclusions.

'Same man?'

'I am ninety-nine per cent sure and what's more I believe he is mixed up with our billionaire. That is his yacht in the background.'

'And we already have the Russian under surveillance but as far as I know we have not acquired anything useful as yet.'

'I think we should try a bit harder sir and by the way I have given the Arab the code name 'Shadow' and the Russian 'Bullseye'. Sir, I read the intelligence gained from the Russian's house, not much so far but there is something of interest. He has a housekeeper, who seems to run things while he is away. The woman has a good command of the English language and it was difficult to place her but one of our people kept an eye on her for a few hours and heard her speaking in Russian to someone on her mobile telephone. So I'm sure she is Russian, and she was inviting someone to a dinner party.'

'You think we should infiltrate one of our people, see what we can turn up?'

'Yes sir, me.'

The executive officer lifted his gaze and looked at Anita with some incredulity.

'I checked the numbers she was calling and one was an outside caterer, no doubt to provide their services for his dinner party. I know a lot about wine sir.'

'Do you, I must admit that is a surprise. What has that got to do with the Russian's dinner party?'

'I want to join our party planners and serve the wine.'

'A wine waitress?'

'Yes sir, as a wine waitress, as you call it, I can get very close to the guests, listen out for any snippet of information and maybe the surveillance boys could fit me up with a camera to get pictures of the guests. See with whom Bullseye mixes, and widen our knowledge of him, and that might give us a clue as to what he may be trying to do.'

'Hmm . . . are you sure you can cope, I mean you could be infiltrating what might turn out to be a viper's nest? I think the idea is a good one but it is hardly unknown for an operative to go missing. Let us get hold of Special Ops and see what they can do to help.' He picked up his telephone and ten minutes later Brian from Special Operations arrived. Working with Anita on a number of occasions, he was well aware of her capabilities. He listened to the section head outline their basic plan, listened as Anita described her proposed involvement, and he considered the dangers.

'It seems to me we need to convince the caterers that they need a wine waitress first. I will send someone round to have a chat, to see how they hire and fire. My guess is they occasionally use agency workers if not on a regular basis. Most of the Europeans who did this type of work have gone back home and they may have a problem recruiting,' said Brian.

'What about protection if we can get her onto the payroll?.

'If this party is to take place fairly soon, then we need to move quickly, and as for your protection Agent er . . .'

'Sims, I will be Mrs Sims, my usual cover name.'

'Well Mrs Sims we can wire you with anything you like, sound recorder, camera, but I don't advise it until we see what kind of security they have. It does not take much these days for a sweep to find a device on a person. The devices that we introduce are normally passive but yours will be active, constantly transmitting and they are easier to detect with the right equipment. I think we need to find a safe place nearby and keep a watch. If you are in trouble a signal of some sort at a window and we will come running. It will be a difficult and dangerous job if you suspect Russian Embassy involvement, but not impossible. I will select a team to begin work immediately, send someone to talk to the caterers, and we'll deploy a listening van in the street.'

'I assumed I would not be able to carry a surveillance device, how will you know if I need help?'

'Can you scream?'

Anita gave Brian a blank look.

'We have sensitive enough listening devices to penetrate all but the thickest walls. If you scream we will be able to hear you and that will bring us running.'

The interior of the early Victorian house was spacious and decorated to a high standard. To anyone else it would be impressive but to Anita it was just another property, her mind was on a far more important issue as she meticulously wiped each glass with the microfiber cloth. She examined the glass she had just cleaned, holding it to the light before placing it on the enormous white tablecloth. One by one, she set down the gleaming wine glasses until twenty places were complete, ten on each side of the long table.

As in the way of Russian culture, the table had a central feature of fresh cut flowers, and arranged along its length were tall glasses each containing a coloured candle and apart from the ever-present worry of discovery, Anita was rather enjoying herself. It was more than six months since she had performed such a task. That was at her older sister's fortieth birthday party, catering for more than eighty guests. Marion had specifically asked for her help and she remembered her words when she phoned.

'You are so good at organising parties, you always were. I don't know anyone who can set a table like you and you are such an expert on wine.'

'The Old Lady has a lot to answer for doesn't she?' she had replied.

When she and her sister were teenagers, they would spend their summer holidays with their aunt and uncle on their small farm in northern Italy. It was there, in the Piedmont region that Anita had first learned about wines and wine growing from an old woman living alone in a nearby villa. The woman was Lady Pocklington, the last of an impoverished aristocratic line who spent her days painting and playing her piano in splendid isolation. She had befriended Anita and for three consecutive summers they were practically inseparable.

Each morning, during her holiday, Anita would visit 'Lady Moira' as she called her, watch her apply paint to canvas and listen to her amazing stories. Such was their friendship that it was not long before Anita obtained an easel and some paints herself. Together each morning the two of them would paint landscapes, and in the afternoons, the Old Lady would teach Anita to play the piano. When she reached sixteen, Lady Moira had taken it upon herself to school her in the advantages of the local Barolo wines.

'You are turning into a fine young woman,' she had said. 'You will, one day soon, meet young men who will try to sweep you off your feet. Take it from me you do not want to be a passive partner; you need to know more than they do if you are to meet the right one.'

Anita remembered her embarrassment, but it had soon passed and as the weeks wore on she enjoyed learning the intricacies of wines and table etiquette. When she returned home to England, she kept up her painting and her piano playing, and when she went up to Oxford, she joined the University Wine Circle. There she learned much more about fine wines, even taking part in the Varsity wine tasting match during her final year.

It was at a meeting of the Oxford University Wine Circle that she met Herman McGough, a man several years her senior. She had been extolling the virtues of her favourite wines to a few fellow students when Herman introduced himself, and offered what appeared expert advice. Then several more meetings later, he revealed he was with MI6 and suggested she should apply for a job with them. To begin with, she was sceptical, but he was persistent and after gaining her degree she applied and began life as a spy. A spy – she felt she was little more than a pen pusher and after a year in the job was finding it boring. Then Herman turned up once more.

'Hello again, how are you getting on in the service?'

'Herman, I could say fancy meeting you here but I know now what you do for a living. As far as getting on in the service I'm not sure.'

'What's wrong?' he had asked, frowning, and she had told him she found the work tedious. 'I have seen your file, how would you like something a little more demanding?'

She had said she would and within weeks she was on a training course with several other would-be field operatives and had never looked back. And now was one of those times to put some of what she had learned into practice.

The preliminary briefing at the offices of the Lakeland Catering Company had consisted mainly of a description of the client and his requirements, the running order of the evening. Unsurprisingly there would be a security check and to make things easy all the caterers were to leave their mobile phones behind when they arrived to start work. The Russian woman, Lyudmila, seemed to be in charge of the security check as well as almost everything else and when Anita first saw her she was running a metal detector over those entering the house. After that, all the agency staff were subjected to a quick and expert body search and Anita knew then for sure that she was Russian Secret Service.

After their security clearance, the chef, servers and Anita were ushered into a large room adjoining the spacious kitchen. The food was already on the premises, delivered during the afternoon, and without wasting time the principal of the catering firm, an overbearing woman named Sharon Binks, issued her orders, and preparations for the evening's event began. A girl and a young man worked under the supervision of the chef preparing the food, while Anita and one of the servers began setting the table, spreading the white tablecloth and carrying in cutlery and table decorations. Anita was halfway through setting out the wine glasses when the Russian housekeeper approached her.

'You are the wine waitress?'

'Yes.'

'You call me ma'am when I speak with you, understand.'

'Yes ma'am,' replied Anita without making eye contact.

'You are not setting the table the Russian way. You put the water glass here and here, only one inch from the wine glass, the white wine glass, and exactly the same distance for the red wine glass. Look, I show you. Your company tells me you know these things.'

'I'm sorry ma'am, I do know how to set a formal table but no one explained that it should be like this.'

'Well now you know. We have important Russian guests tonight and Mr Borisovich wants them to enjoy a Russian evening.'

Anita, still avoiding Lyudmila's gaze, nodded her acquiescence and carried on laying a place setting. The housekeeper watched, and seemingly satisfied turned her attention to a black woman arranging flowers. Relieved that another victim had taken her place, Anita proceeded to finish her task. This time she was extra careful to keep the distances between the glasses the same, finally standing back to admire her handiwork. She had known all along how the Russians liked their tables laid but to appear too knowledgeable was to invite scrutiny. Nevertheless, she had invited attention, and the officious head of the caterers was next to reproach her.

'Mrs Sims, Lyudmila seems to think you are not up to the job. These Russians are important clients of ours. If you are not capable of providing first-class service then we should part company now.'

'I'm sorry; I understand where I have gone wrong. The Russian lady showed me how they like the table set,' said Anita.

The woman Binks looked at the completed place settings, her face stern and unforgiving, until she could see that Anita had made an excellent job.

'Oh, I see you have done as Lyudmila asks. Make sure you keep to the same standard when serving wine. These Russians can be very particular and we do not want to lose their business because of sloppy presentation. All right, go and help prepare the wine and be careful. We have kept the bottles in a controlled environment and we do not want the wine spoiling. Here you,' she said, her attention drawn by another member of her staff. and Anita took the opportunity to leave the dining room. She made her way to the anteroom just as two men were carefully placing cases of wine on a table and beyond she could see that the kitchen was alive with activity. The white-hatted chef was snapping orders and cajoling his assistants as they prepared the food and Anita was glad she was not a part of it.

'Are you the wine waitress?' asked one of the men handling the wine.

'Yes.'

'Well we will begin opening the boxes; tell us where you want the bottles putting.'

Anita looked at the large table and the folded white cloth lying on it.

'On here,' she said, laying the tablecloth across the woodwork.

The men began passing her the bottles and one by one she examined the labels searching her memory, Hermitage red and Sauternes white, expensive, quality wines.

'That is the lot, we will get rid of the boxes and leave you to it luv,' said one of the men, casting his eye over her.

'Yes, thank you,' she said and turning away to avoid his stare walked back towards the dining room.

'Where are you going?' asked Lyudmila, appearing in the doorway.

'I was just going to make one final check of the place settings.'

'No need, they are just fine now, you have learned. The guests will arrive soon and will not sit down to dinner for a while. You should be serving aperitifs. Where is Sharon, she should have organised it?'

Just then, Ms Binks appeared and made for the two women.

'Ah, Mrs Sims, I have found you. I need you in the parlour to get the glasses ready to serve drinks to the guests as they arrive. Please see to it immediately.'

Anita did not wait, lowering her gaze and walking into the reception room. Apart from a side table and trays of glasses awaiting their charges of champagne, there was no one else in the room. She took a quick look round, wondering where Bullseye was as she arranged the glasses on silver trays. Then she heard the doorbell ring, Lyudmila rushed past her and ten minutes later the reception room was half full of people and Anita was busy serving them champagne. She began making mental notes as she served the guests, noting their accents and appearance and hoped that the spooks had photographed them arriving. The invitees were exclusively male and mostly in their forties and fifties, and seemed evenly split between Russians and British with one Asian-looking man. A hubbub of conversation engulfed the room as the guests made connections and reaffirmed old ones.

Anita tried to recognise faces but failed except for one individual, Mikhail Mikhailovich, the SVR bureau chief, and she hoped that he had never opened her file. She had been in the game long enough for the Russians to have at least something on her she was sure, how much she did not know, but it would be disastrous if she was recognised.

Watching Mikhailovich from the corner of her eye, she felt some relief that he showed no sign of knowing her. But would an expert in espionage keep his sentiments secret? Of course he would. She could feel her adrenaline beginning to flow, her heartbeat picking up, and breathing slowly in and out she fought it until calmness returned. It was a warning to be on her guard.

She had still not caught a first sight of Bullseye, since the first of the guests arrived, he had waited at the front door to welcome them and now, finally, he came into the reception room. Standing for a few moments, he cast his eyes over the assembly before he clapped his hands together to draw their attention.

'My very good friends I am so glad to invite you to my humble little dacha here in London.' Subdued laughs percolated through the room because with a price tag of twenty-eight million, the house was hardly a humble dacha. 'I have invited you here to celebrate my birthday.' Again, a few murmurs and one or two glasses raised in a mock toast. 'I have not been in London for quite a few months, more Mother Russia and southern Africa of late, and so I feel it is time to renew acquaintances, though the visa restrictions imposed upon me make it difficult at times.' He paused, looked at the Russians in the room, all suffering to various degrees in the new political climate. 'I have engaged the services of one of the finest catering companies in London and I am sure the fare on offer will not disappoint. Please, help yourselves to drinks and in a short time we will adjourn to the dining room.'

'We are never disappointed by you Leonid,' said a voice from the midst and Anita looked to see who it might be. He was British, she judged, full of self-importance, and speaking in a loud voice to his neighbour she heard him extolling the virtues of foxhunting.

Who were these people, what was the common denominator? Borisovich was a business tycoon, a possible Russian agent and, obviously, had contacts in high places. Perhaps there was no common denominator; perhaps it simply was his birthday party. She found that hard to believe, people like Bullseye always mixed business with pleasure, forever chasing the mighty dollar, or rouble. It was their lifeblood. She refilled her tray and returned to mix amongst the guests, offering full glasses in return for the empty ones and then she noticed Mikhailovich in conversation with a thickset man who looked to be of Slavic origin.

Then she looked past him, through the doorway, and in the corridor spotted Lyudmila speaking to a large, muscular man. The conversation was brief, the man disappeared, and Lyudmila peered into the room. Her eyes seemed to swivel in their sockets as she stood motionless looking around and Anita turned her head away before the gaze settled on her. There was a real sense of security about the place, something not normal with just business acquaintances. Now the guests were beginning to disperse, following Bullseye into the dining room where Anita's real job was about to begin. She had uncorked several bottles ready to serve and once the guests had pulled up their chairs she enquired as to their preferences. They hardly noticed her, chatting as they were, and gradually the conversation increased in volume. Anita began to take the wine orders in preparation for the first course, and moving round the table she eventually came to Mikhail Mikhailovich.

'Red or white?' she asked him.

'Not for me.'

He was proving to be the consummate professional spook, not drinking alcohol, and then it was the turn of Bullseye.

'And you sir?'

'Oh the Guigal for me,' he said, casting an eye over her.

'And you sir?' she asked the next man.

Twenty orders to memorise was a lot but Anita's trained mind could cope and as the conversation round the table continued she returned several times to pour each guest their chosen wine.

In the meantime, two servers hurried back and forth with plates of smoked salmon on buckwheat pancakes, and standing just inside the doorway Sharon Binks watched over them. Behind her, Lyudmila hovered like a bird of prey and Anita began to establish in her own mind that there did indeed seem to be a strong connection between Mr Borisovich and the Russian Secret Service. Then there was the added dimension of the host's superyacht and the mysterious Arab.

The room filled with conversation, the sound of cutlery on china, the occasional chink of glasses, and amongst it all Anita floated in and out with her fine wines. The guests were generally knowledgeable, some expert, appreciating the quality and more than once she was asked a searching question.

'You seem to know your wines, Miss er . . .' said Bullseye, the third time she filled his glass. 'I heard you talking to Sir Graham here. He is impressed by your knowledge.'

'I like to think I know my job sir.'

'Tell me, the Guigal, how you would describe it?'

'Well sir, I have to say it's not the best vintage but it is a very good one.'

'What do you mean not the best; my instructions were for us to have the best.'

'You could consider the Guigal La Turque Cote Rotie 2008 is better with the 1988 even better still, but the price is probably more than a dinner party would warrant. The 88 is a wine to savour, one to sit with a view, and dream.'

'That is a poetic description my dear, I might take you up on that.' Bullseye looked Anita up and down once more, his greedy eyes weighing her up. 'Perhaps you would leave your number with my assistant Lyudmila; I may want you to provide your services in the future.'

'That would be nice sir; I'm always looking for decent work.'

'You are unemployed?'

'Not exactly sir, I work as a freelance, filling in here and there.'

'Do you work abroad?'

'Occasionally, I have contacts in France and Italy who sometimes ask me to help out as a sommelier in their restaurants; I visit wineries for them, check out the vintages.'

'Sounds interesting and I notice you are single. No ties I presume.'

'No ties sir, I am as free as a bird and that is how I like to live my life.'

'You are an interesting lady.'

'Thank you sir, if you will excuse me I do believe one of your guests requires his glass recharging.'

Chapter 5

To meet with the ruling council always made Yusuf feel important and that day only a week before was no different. The four men, attired in traditional dress and smoking from the hookah, were waiting for him in the lobby of Cairo's Om Kolthoom Hotel. It was a hot, languid day and no one seemed in a hurry. Yusuf always marvelled at how open they were in a public place. Anyone could find them but he knew there would be bodyguards somewhere in the background.

'*Assalaam alaykum,*' said one of the men as he approached.

'Peace be with you,' Yusuf replied.

The speaker invited Yusuf to join them and he sat down.

'You have come a long way, how goes it in al-Sham?'

'We are making good progress in the northern enclave, the people trust us and our enemies are leaving us alone for now. It is because we are weak, we cannot take on the might of the Syrian state and the Russians, but that may change.'

Yusuf drew the tobacco smoke through the water pipe and gave his host an enquiring look.

'We have asked you here today to tell you of our plans for the future. You are an important part of our organisation, you have proved yourself over many years and for that, we thank you. However, the world is changing, old alliances are being broken and new ones formed. Syria is much subdued now that Assad is a puppet of the Russians; they are in charge and they have plans Yusuf.'

'Plans, for us?' he said intuitively, understanding the council member's message.

'Yes, you have carried American money provided by the Russians to our brothers in Syria and Yemen but now we are asking you to take their money to secret cells in Europe. There is a grand plan and we will be a part of it, our reward to instigate sharia law on the continent of Europe. The Americans are retreating and will not come to the aid of the Europeans.'

Yusuf was puzzled, his host carried on.

'The American President keeps saying America will be great again, yet he is abandoning his allies and creating fortress America. He is afraid of us and we will soon have the power to achieve that which he fears.'

These were big words indeed, as if the Prophet himself were foretelling the future, and Yusuf was impressed.

'What is it you want me to do?'

'The Russian ship is the conduit for the money we need to pay our soldiers and to buy arms. You, Yusuf, will carry on collecting that money but instead of bringing it here you will visit all the great cities of the infidels in Europe, distribute money to cells waiting to attack the Europeans in their own countries.'

Yusuf knew not to ask too many questions though there was much he wanted to understand and as if reading his mind the man introduced his companions into the conversation. For half an hour they spoke in low voices, of past successes, of their aspirations and of the al-Qaeda cells awaiting the order to attack. They gave him an address in Rome, the first of many he would learn of during the following months.

Yusuf, comfortable in his aircraft seat, was feeling pleased with himself, his work was bearing fruit. The policy of treating the local population less harshly than the overlords of Islamic State was working. They were also relaxing sharia law, encouraging businesses to grow, and were generally improving people's lives. Yusuf had wondered if this was the right strategy to begin with but in certain pockets the locals appeared loyal. He had seen their reaction when IS was defeated, seen how overjoyed they were. Although a coherent Islamic nation was still a dream, it did now appear to be a possibility.

The Sommelier

He looked out of the window at the blue sea
below and in the distance caught his first sighting of
Italy, a destination that was new to him. He worried
that his Arabic features might betray him because
this country he was visiting had suffered more than
most from the upheaval in the Middle East. He
hoped his Western clothes would render him
invisible and at least Syria had stabilised. The
Russians and the Iranians were helping to rebuild
the broken cities and a steady stream of refugees
was returning home, relieving the pressure on
southern Europe. Added to that, the Americans
were reducing their presence in the Middle East and
less pressure from the air attacks left al-Qaeda
unhindered and able to grow.

The administration in Washington had signalled
for some time it was considering an isolationist
stance and now it looked as if they were putting it
into practice. He had heard that the Sixth Fleet
would soon leave the Mediterranean and already the
Russians were filling the vacuum, building bases
and expanding their sphere of influence, leaving the
Italian, French and Spanish navies to take the place
of the Americans in the Mediterranean. The world
was changing; adversaries of the past were now
allies and the ruling council appreciated the
importance of Russian backing and recalled how,
during his last visit to Yemen, he had learned the
extent of al-Qaeda's involvement with the Russians.

Meeting the emir of the peninsula several times,
they had discussed the group's progress and he

remembered his words: 'We have come a long way since the overthrow of Saddam and Mubarak, recruits were plentiful then but many became martyrs and we have had to change. We have learned to convince the population that we are the true leaders of the Muslim world and it is we that will make the caliphate a reality. Jihad is a religious duty and we are carrying that out to the best of our ability but there are limits. We need recruits from all the lands of Islam, from the Mediterranean countries, Africa and from the East and we need money to pay our soldiers, provide them with the means to fight the war. You, Yusuf, are an important part of that. It is a dangerous business I know, you are a brave soldier of the Prophet and you must be careful not to let the servants of the West know what you do for I hear of great endeavours being planned.'

Yusuf had replied that he would be careful. 'Have I not survived so long? I know the dangers we face and I know the importance of my task,' he said with some indignation.

The emir had encouraged him. 'You speak as a true believer,' he said, 'go and fight the infidel in your own way with the followers of the Prophet and we will take the fight to the heart of the West's so-called civilisation.'

Yusuf smiled to himself as he remembered that conversation and reciting a silent prayer he steeled himself for the task ahead.

Under cover of darkness in the early morning, the box van pulled up at the dock gates and the driver produced his papers.

'You are early, can't you sleep?' queried the security guard.

The driver gave a forced smile before climbing back into his seat and slowly making his way along the dock towards the Lady Galina where the officer of the watch noted his approach. The long night of boredom had at last lifted and he stretched his arms across his chest, yawned and looked at his watch. Another hour to go before his shift finished but at least now there was something to occupy his mind. Rubbing his eyes, he stared out of the window noticing Alexie and Viktor appear from the shadows. He did not like them very much, the owner's bodyguards – the power on board – men who rarely mixed with the rest of the crew. Even Captain Rusedski deferred to them and Nikolay himself was not about to question their actions or motives. Better to keep his head down and just do his job rather than tangle with the GRU. He watched the men unload boxes from the van and although it would soon be time to write up the ship's log he knew that this activity could not appear in the ledger. Walking to the desk, he opened the logbook and picked up a pen, writing first the time and then he looked at the instruments, copying readings onto the page. Suddenly his heart jumped as without warning Alexie appeared, startling him.

'Uh . . . where did you come from?'

'I am checking our security. We have just had a special delivery, Russian food, the best, and the driver is in need of a rest and some breakfast before he leaves. Ask the chef to come on duty and make something for him and, while he is at it, Viktor and I would like breakfast. By the way the boss will be here in a few hours so I suggest you have the crew on their toes.'

It felt like a threat, it was, and he was not about to deny the request. He knew that the chef would complain when he dragged him from his bunk but he would make sure he attended to the thug's request. He was less afraid of a Michelin-starred chef than of the hulk standing beside him.

The car pulled into London City Airport's private car park. It was already bustling as business people left early for the continent or the Republic of Ireland and the departures queues were long. The tedious process of visa checking was causing some tempers to fray but for Leonid things became a little easier when a familiar face appeared.

'*Dobroe utro* my friend.'

'Good morning Mikhail.'

Mikhail Mikhailovich looked fresh and alert as he took a step towards Leonid.

'Come with me, I can fast-track you to your plane.'

It was a welcome gesture, Leonid had just taken in the orderly chaos that was the British queue and did not like what he saw.

'You are flying back to Italy in one hour?'

'Yes, that's the plan. The pilot telephoned earlier to tell me that the weather forecast is good and he does not expect any problems. You said you wanted to speak with me before I left.'

'Yes, we should go outside where we will have some privacy, follow me.'

Mikhail led the way, familiar with the airport layout. As the top man in this part of Europe, he was responsible for coordinating the Russian espionage effort and as such had taken many flights from London City to the capitals of Europe.

'Here,' he said, pushing a door open and walking out onto the edge of the runway.

Leonid followed, resisting the airflow and holding his free hand to his ear to shield it from the noise of a taxiing jet.

'Not much chance of a bug working here I think. Now down to business. I received confirmation that the packages are aboard your yacht and that the courier will arrive sometime tomorrow. You are to look after him, feed him if he so requests, make it appear as if he is a bona fide guest. We will provide him with small denomination bills, making it much easier for him and his contacts to dispose of the funds. You do not need to know the details but I can tell you the money is to oil the terrorist machinery in Europe, to give the Europeans and the Americans a headache. Mother Russia is in the ascendency, my friend, and you are helping. Please, not a word to anyone about this conversation. Now, you have two of our specialists on board your yacht. They have their orders and will carry them out as necessary but to make it appear you are simply a very rich man enjoying the fruits of his labours you are to cruise the waters of the Mediterranean until further instructions. We will let you know via Alexie as to which ports you should go and on what dates. We are counting on you Leonid; it would be a shame for you to let us down.'

Borisovich took the hint, he had mixed in Kremlin circles long enough to know the consequences of failure.

'It will be as you wish Mikhail; you know you can count on me.'

'Yes, Leonid my friend, I am sure we can.'

The SVR bureau chief held out his hand and Leonid reciprocated before the two men returned to the main building where Mikhail showed his diplomatic pass and ushered Leonid through.

The report was not an hour old when it landed on Anita's desk – a single sheet of paper with half a dozen lines of text but it was enough.

So, Bullseye was off on his travels again. An agent had followed him to the airport, seen him and a second man enter a restricted area and now the billionaire oligarch was already on his way in his private jet. The report did not name the other man but the agent suspected that he was Russian intelligence. The final sentence advised that photographs of the two individuals were on their way via email.

Anita turned to her screen, grasped the computer mouse and opened her inbox. There it was, an email with several hastily taken shots attached. Oh yes, SVR all right, Mikhail Mikhailovich. Twice now, she had come across Bullseye in his company and it seemed obvious that they were working together on something.

'What have we got?' she murmured under her breath as she reached for the file on her desk. Reading the notes and emails, she could see no evidence pointing to anything of substance, just a gut feeling simply because Mikhail Mikhailovich was involved.

Picking up her telephone, she rang the number for the MI5 liaison officer working with air traffic control, Swanick. After an exchange of passwords, she learned Bullseye's flight plan and was surprised to learn that its destination was Naples in southern Italy. Had Lady Galina moved? She had not thought about the yacht since Istanbul. Naples possessed a large port and could easily accommodate the vessel. Her next telephone call was to the British Embassy in Rome and the MI6 bureau chief. She needed to know if indeed the yacht was in Naples and if it was she required surveillance.

Getting up from her desk, Anita walked thoughtfully across to the coffee machine and pressed the button for black coffee, no sugar. She needed a dose of caffeine to sharpen her mind, to try to get her head around what was going on. There was a problem though, since Britain had closed its borders and pulled out of full co-operation with the Europeans she needed to be careful to avoid treading on the toes of the Italian Secret Service.

A car was waiting for Yusuf when his aircraft landed, a battered-looking Fiat with a young, fresh-faced driver and an older, swarthy looking man with a hooked nose – an Egyptian, though his features could be mistaken for those of an Italian and because of that he could move freely and unnoticed. His name was Abdullah El-Sherif, an ex-secret police officer of the SSI, the main security and intelligence apparatus of Egypt's Interior Ministry. At least that was until the upheaval of the Arab spring, a time when events had turned his allegiance away from his mother country and towards al-Qaeda.

His police work had focused on radical Islamists though eventually his attitude towards them had changed. The turning point came when his own colleagues murdered his sister and her family for nothing more than an accusation by a known criminal. The pain was acute, never-ending, and when he tried to have the murderers prosecuted, they turned their violence upon him, radicalising him from that day on.

Abdullah saw Yusuf first, a tall, good-looking man in his late forties and carrying a green rucksack over his shoulder, the sign he expected.

'*Ahlan wa sahlan,* welcome to Italy,' he said.

Yusuf swivelled his head, refraining from an Arabic greeting.

'You are from the Metropole Hotel?'

'I am and I come to take you there on this wonderful spring day,' he said.

Passwords exchanged, Abdullah opened the rear passenger door for his guest and Yusuf climbed in.

'This is Ahmed, my driver and bodyguard. Make no mistake his youthful looks conceal a warrior of the Prophet. He will take us to the safe house where you can rest and I will await your instructions. Allah be praised.'

'A word of warning my friend, it is dangerous to speak in our native tongue, believe me there are many ears straining to hear what we have to say, enemies who would readily kill us. English is safer.'

'I bow to your greater judgement,' said Abdullah, falling silent as the car sped from the airport towards a small industrial estate on the outskirts of the city.

'You will be staying here tonight, you can come here whenever you need a safe place,' said Abdullah, getting out of the car.

A minute later the tired, rusted roller shutter door began its squeaky ascent, and when it was high enough Ahmed drove the car through into an open space. Leaving his seat Yusuf stood and stretched his arms, looking up at the grubby roof lights illuminating the void and then at the rows of half-empty shelving. It was a drab-looking building, probably used as a storage facility, but it was isolated and it seemed secure.

'I run a magazine distribution business from here,' said Abdullah, 'it serves well as a cover. We have arms and explosives stored on the premises ready for the time we receive the word. I have contact with cells in Rome and the north of Italy as well as here in Calabria. You have brought us money to buy more?'

'Not quite yet. Where do I sleep?'

'Behind those boxes is a small office, we sleep in there.'

Yusuf felt disappointed, he had roughed it for months and had expected at least a safe house with a proper bed, if not a real hotel.

'We have cooking facilities and a toilet, all we need. I will make some fresh coffee for you after your journey and you can tell me what you want me to do. Ahmed, drop the door,' he said to the young man.

Abdullah signalled to Yusuf to follow him between the stacks of boxes towards the rear of the building where he opened the door to the small office. Yusuf entered and placed his rucksack on a chair while his host filled the coffee percolator.

'You will be in need of a coffee and a short rest before we go to your destination. Where is it you want to go?'

'To the docks, you can take me to the gate and leave me there to make the rest of the way on my own. I will call you when I need picking up but for now, as you say, I have time to collect my thoughts. You are sure this building is secure?'

'As secure as it can be, the authorities have never troubled us. Our problem is with the local mafia but, don't worry, I pay them regularly.'

Yusuf *was* worried, if the mafia discovered they were hiding munitions in this warehouse they would not hesitate to pay a visit. He could not allow that to happen and decided that perhaps it was not such a safe house after all. Maybe he could remain on the yacht for a day or so.

'Have we any handguns here?'

'Yes, I was told that I should make one available,' said Abdullah, pulling open a desk drawer and lifting out a metallic object wrapped in oiled paper. 'Here, and take these bullets. It is not much against the mafia, or even the carabinieri should they show an interest in us.'

'Then we must not draw attention to ourselves and move as quickly as we can to allow me to disperse the funds.'

Funds? It was the first time Abdullah had heard that word; he had believed they were to distribute arms and explosives to the al-Qaeda cell in Rome. What was the value of these funds, he wondered, perhaps enough for a man to disappear into a comfortable life?

Yusuf turned away, biting his tongue, for he realised that he had divulged sensitive information and that could prove dangerous. He decided there and then that he could not stay in this place more than one night for fear of betrayal; money was a strange bedfellow in such times.

On the Lady Galina, everyone was preparing for the owner's arrival: the sound of vacuum cleaners permeated throughout the living quarters, several crewmembers were busy cleaning the brass work in the spacious saloon bar, and on the bridge, the captain was checking his charts.

'What time is Mr Borisovich due aboard Captain?' asked the first officer, returning from his off-duty rest.

'Alexie says he will be here around eight o'clock this evening. He and Viktor are leaving to collect him later this afternoon.'

The first officer nodded his head slowly and began wondering if they had missed anything in their preparations. It was his responsibility to keep the yacht in a seaworthy condition and the engineer had assured him that they had a full complement of fuel and that the engines and ancillary equipment were all working correctly. He did not want another incident like the one when the ice-maker failed, and after speaking with the housekeeper was confident that the owner would not be disappointed.

'Have you checked the crew, are they all aboard? We cannot afford to be without any of them should Mr Borisovich invite his usual guests. They take some looking after as you know.'

'No, I haven't sir, not today. I will check right now.'

The captain nodded, the two officers parted company, the first officer to find the housekeeper. He guessed that she would be in the owner's suite and sure enough, he found her there with one of her staff making up the king-sized bed.

'Olga, there you are,' he said in their native language.

'Nikolay, hello, what do you want?'

'You sound defensive Olga, is something wrong?'

'That girl, the Romanian, she's a good worker when I can get her to work but today she will not come out of her cabin. She says she is ill and wants a doctor.'

'Damn, just the kind of problem I could do without. I had better talk to her.'

Amongst his other duties, he managed crew discipline and he had to make sure everything ran smoothly, he could not afford slackers. Annoyed that an unexpected problem had arisen he walked to the staircase leading below decks and the crew quarters. He came to cabin twelve and knocked on the door. There was no answer so he knocked again, louder. Still there was no answer and so he called out.

'Nicoletta are you in there?'

There was silence for a few moments until he heard something stir and a minute later the door opened a few centimetres.

'Nicoletta are you all right? We are expecting the owner later today and I need everyone at their posts.'

The door opened further and an ashen-looking face peered out.

'I not well, need doctor.'

Her appearance mildly shocked Nikolay and he instinctively realised that he really did have trouble on his hands.

'Stay here, I will talk with the captain and see about getting a doctor to have a look at you.'

After talking to the purser, Nikolay was relieved to see a local doctor arrive and after he gave the girl an examination, he diagnosed appendicitis.

'She cannot stay here doctor. I have a crew to consider and the owner is arriving soon. Can you get her into a hospital or somewhere until she is well enough to resume her duties?'

'Let me make a telephone call, there is a private sanatorium that will take her but it is expensive.'

'I need to speak with the captain but my guess is that is not a problem we just need to get her off the yacht.'

There was another problem with the Romanian girl. She was employed as a wine waitress, and though not quite up to sommelier standard as a good-looking girl she possessed additional skills. The captain was aware of those skills and they had kept her in her job so far. On a temporary basis, he would necessarily use one of the other girls to do her job but as Mr Borisovich prided himself on his wine cellar, he would need a competent replacement and fast. He pondered the question for a minute or two. He had a choice, a local whom he could not trust, or the agency in London, the one in Mayfair that had never disappointed him. He would contact them immediately and clear it with Mr Borisovich once they came back to him with an offer.

For Yusuf the night spent on the camp bed was not a pleasant one. He had roughed it in the desert many times, slept out in the open with nothing more than a blanket, but the poorly constructed, narrow excuse for a bed had just given him one of the worst night's sleeps of his life. His back was aching, his mouth was dry and even though it was early he felt he had no choice but to rise and dress.

Across the room, he could hear snoring and through the gloom made out the prostrate figure of the Egyptian. Rubbing his eyes he tried to wake up, puffing out his cheeks in frustration; he pushed himself up from the bed and standing for a few moments allowed his blood to flow unhindered. Arching his back, he took a deep breath and began to feel a little better just as Ahmed appeared, bright-eyed and fully dressed.

'Where did you come from?'

'I am a light sleeper and Abdullah said I am to keep an eye on you.'

Yusuf looked at him with hostile eyes.

'To keep you safe, master.'

Yusuf relaxed, the young man was good, alert and confident and he hoped that his newfound bodyguard was as good as he believed himself to be.

'Can you make coffee?'

'Of course, it's stuffy in here, why not open the door and let some air in and I will make the coffee. Hey Abdullah, wake up,' he called to the still sleeping Egyptian.

It was late in the afternoon when Leonid Borisovich finally came aboard his beloved Lady Galina and after a brief conversation with Captain Rusedski ordered the chef to send some food up to his cabin. One of the crew appeared to carry his bag to his cabin and after a shower, switched on his computer to catch up on his emails to see what was happening in the world. After satisfying his curiosity, Leonid gazed out of the window, happy to see a bit of sunshine after the dull, overcast English skies. However, he could not dwell, aware as he was of the courier's expected arrival and that he would need to talk with Alexie about the secret funds. Although he expected Alexie to report directly to his superiors, he was still the owner and the mission depended upon his co-operation. He had more than once during his stay in London met with Mikhail Mikhailovich and he remembered his words.

'Leonid, I cannot stress how important your mission is to Mother Russia. The people we are involved with are helping us in a great plan and it is vitally important that you are available where and when we need you. You already know that you are providing hard currency to help finance terrorists in the Middle East. Well we are expanding the operation and you should find suitable berths for the Lady Galina in Italy and France.'

'Europe?'

'I can tell you no more than that, but yes, Europe. On a more declassified note, you will be aware of the United States switching their focus eastwards towards the Chinese threat. Well we understand that they are about to abandon Europe and to reduce their commitment to NATO. It is an opportunity we must grasp. One day, in the not too distant future, we believe that the Sixth Fleet will leave Europe, probably for good, a situation we must take full advantage of.'

Leonid stared out across the waters of the harbour, for once unaware of the beautiful vista, his mind concentrating on other things. Finally, his eyes focused on the view and sighing inwardly he sat in silence until there was a tap on the cabin door. His food had arrived.

'I will sit out on the balcony, please put the tray on there,' he said pointing to the rosewood table.

The girl did as he asked and after pouring himself a gin from his personal bar he walked out onto the balcony and settled down to eat dinner and after he finished he rang for the housekeeper.

'Clear the dishes and ask the captain to meet me in the saloon in ten minutes. Where's Nicoletta, she usually serves me in my cabin?'

'She left the boat sir, before you arrived.'

'Why, do you know?'

'No sir only that she was taken ill.'

'Taken ill, why wasn't I informed?' he said, puzzled. He had been looking forward to seeing Nicoletta; she had a wonderful body and was discreet, one of the few women with whom he could still have a satisfying relationship.

With an image of the girl in his mind he walked into the spacious and expensively furnished saloon bar one deck below his master cabin, went to the period sideboard and took a Black Russian from the silver cigarette box. He allowed no one to smoke inside the yacht, himself included, and finding his lighter slid open the door leading onto the deck. Leaning on the rail, he shielded his lighter with cupped hands and drew deeply on the cigarette. Where had Nicoletta gone, what had happened?

'Excuse me sir you wanted to see me,' said a voice.

'Ah Captain, please join me out here, cigarette?'

'Er no, thank you sir, not if you don't mind.'

'Probably the right answer, I don't smoke a lot but they say one is too many.'

'Indeed sir.'

The officer stood, relaxed, silent, waiting for Mr Borisovich to speak.

'What is all this about Nicoletta?'

'She was taken ill yesterday, took to her cabin and would not come out. The first officer tried to get her back to work but discovered instead that she was quite ill and I decided to ask the purser to call a doctor. The doctor diagnosed appendicitis and advised hospitalisation.'

'How long will she be away, have you any idea?'

'The doctor mentioned two to four weeks, should there be no complications.'

'Good, good, at least she is in safe hands,' said a thoughtful Leonid, feeling some regret at losing such an accommodating member of his crew.'

'I am told there will be guests during the next week or so sir, we could really do with a replacement for the girl.'

Leonid, still distracted by the image of Nicoletta's figure, simply nodded.

'I have already contacted the agency in London for a replacement, at least short term, and they are getting back to me.'

Suddenly Leonid's mind filled with another image, the woman serving the wine at his last dinner party. She had impressed him. She was older than Nicoletta but equally attractive.

'There is someone in London who impressed me greatly, someone who knows her wine. Let me think, the name of the caterers – ah, I remember, Lakeland catering. Get back onto the agency and see if they can find the woman, offer her a decent salary and get her out here as quickly as you can. Now, more pressing business, I must speak with Alexie. Thank you Captain, do your best.'

'Yes sir, will there be anything else?'

'Not for now Captain, not for now. I will speak to you in the morning of my sailing plans.'

Captain Rusedski saluted and turned on his heels, his action betraying his connection to the

Russian Navy. Like his first officer, he was not a particular fan of their two permanent guests and loathed having to take a subordinate role. However, he knew who they were, where they were from and that it was dangerous to cross them.

Chapter 6

Rosemary held the newspaper in both hands, concern written all over her face as she read the headline: *SIXTH FLEET TO RETURN HOME*. The rumour mill had prophesied a retreat from Europe and this news report appeared to reinforce that view. Those in the know at Langley would have been aware of plans to repatriate the Sixth Fleet, probably even John. He had not mentioned anything but she did see that the United States needed to counter the growing threat from China, and India to a lesser extent. However, to desert Europe in the process seemed reckless.

She walked into the kitchen, still reading, and without looking poured herself a coffee from the pot. John was still in the shower and would soon join her but for a few minutes she was alone with the startling news. POTUS was certainly different to those who had gone before, a 'loose cannon' many called him. A loose cannon maybe, but a powerful one nevertheless, his only saving grace his executive order to reactivate the Second Fleet, but even there things were moving at a snail's pace.

'Morning dear, why the worried look?'

'Read this John, it seems the Sixth Fleet is leaving Europe.'

'Oh, I did wonder.'

'You know something?'

'Classified I'm afraid but I can tell you that there have been plans afoot for some time. The navy complained that resources they needed were going elsewhere, the new unmanned fighter program, and they are losing surface ships to the underwater program. The carriers are expensive pieces of kit to build and maintain and if a sixty thousand dollar missile, not even guided, gets through then a billion dollars is toast.'

'So you think it's money driven, not political?'

'I didn't say that.'

Rosemary peered at her husband, recognised the look in his eye and knew it was pointless pursuing the conversation in its present form.

'Are we keeping the base in Italy?'

Again, John was non-committal and again Rosemary withdrew, her mind considering the implications of the fleet leaving European waters. The Americans had been in Naples since 1953, almost seventy years a permanent fixture. Now however, the fleet seemed to be part of the Oval Office's realignment, a plan put in motion since the re-election of the president. Although the United States was still the pre-eminent power others, notably Russia and China, were trying to steal the crown and now it looked as if her job was about to become so much harder.

She filled a second cup and passed it to her husband, whose face betrayed his thoughts. The situation worried him too, he was involved with the strategic view, his office a party to any major shifts, and he must have known of the changes taking place for some time. The Sixth Fleet leaving Europe was momentous and would have far-reaching consequences.

'When will they close the base, can you tell me that?'

'No, I don't know and it hasn't happened yet, there's still time.'

'Time for what, I see reports almost every day about the Russians expanding their reach? The base they are building in Tripoli will be operational within a year, just as the naval base in Tartus is now. That will give them a stranglehold on the Mediterranean and the Black Sea not to mention their efforts to close off the Baltic to us. What next, the North Sea? Thank God we will not have this President for anymore than another year or so. Make America great again, piff.'

John looked at his wife and then at his coffee cup. He could no more tell her what he knew than the man in the moon, but she was a clever girl and she had access to resources. She would figure it out on her own.

In his cabin aboard the new Queen Elizabeth class aircraft carrier, Admiral Cunningham had not yet heard the news of America's retrenchment; his news was of an altogether different kind. At midday, a yeoman signaller had delivered a message from the Admiralty in plain English causing his left eyebrow to raise a little as he read it. The government were dispensing with the ship's original name. So, at least Nelson was still the spirit of the navy, he mused. After four hundred years of naval tradition, the authorities were sidelining the Royal family and renaming the warship after the national hero and by God did they need one. At least the two carriers were still the Queen Elizabeth class, or were they changing that to the King Charles class? He would not put even that beyond the politicians.

She was their first new aircraft carrier in forty years and another was to follow, but at two years late and with the project overspent by a billion pounds, there was not too much of which to be proud. His job was to keep this first carrier operational and so long as there were no other delays, he was on target to bring her back into service on time. The trials of the F-35s were going well though they had their own problems and their costs too had spiralled. Still, the admiral was confident that the Russians had no real answer to *Nelson* and her compliment of aircraft.

Geoffrey Aitkin was a little surprised as he read the email. He was used to problems with staff but this was an unusual request. Reading the message for a second time, he switched to searching the database he kept covering all personnel past and present. Mr Borisovich was a good client who had used the services of the agency on many occasions, now it seemed that he was in need of a temporary replacement.

Who was the woman Mr Borisovich wanted for his yacht? He did not even have a name, simply a brief description and the fact that she had worked for Lakeland Catering on a previous occasion.

'Oh well, here goes,' he muttered to himself, searching for their number.

'Ah, good morning madam, my name is . . .'

He discovered the woman was Lakeland's principal and she advised that she did remember the woman, a surly individual as she recalled. She would make enquiries and call him back.

'Martin, do you remember the wine waitress we engaged for the Russian's dinner party?'

'Which Russian?' asked the young man busy entering invoice details into his computer.

'Mr Borisovich, you remember, the Russian with the house not far from the Malaysian High Commission.'

'I remember the event; cost an awful lot didn't it?'

'Yes it did and it seems Mr Borisovich uses Jarred Imperial for his permanent staff and the wine waitress we used for his party is in demand.'

'I can't say I remember her. I can check the wages record if you like and maybe there is a staffing sheet with her name on it.'

'I think her name is Smyth, or Simson.'

Anita's desk phone rang and she picked it up.

'Thank you for that I will be right up.'

She put the phone down, her heart racing. It seemed Bullseye was looking for her. The caller was from the outsourcing department that handled enquiries to safeguard agents using false identities. The Jarred Imperial London Agency had been in touch, believing the number they had rung was the home of the sommelier Mrs Sims. 'We told them to ring back in half an hour,' said outsourcing. 'You will want to take the call?'

'Of course, usual place?'

'Yes, in there, the call will come in on the blue telephone.'

'Thanks,' said Anita, entering the small, sparsely furnished and soundproofed room.

She dropped her small notebook on the table, sat down to wait and when the telephone rang announced her name.

'Mrs Sims, I'm glad I have found you. My name is Geoffrey Aitkin and I run the Jarred Imperial London Agency. We place staff with exclusive clients and one has asked me to engage your services as a sommelier aboard a very exclusive yacht. Would you be interested? I can make it a very attractive proposition you know.'

Anita pursed her lips, Geoffrey Aitkin sounded almost desperate.

'How attractive, how long is the contract period or is it simply a one-time engagement?'

'It is up to you and the client to decide upon the final salary and the length of the contract but I am authorised to inform you that the job is aboard a superyacht, probably for a month. You will work as the sommelier, provide the client with the best wines available, and for that I can offer you five thousand pounds sterling as a signing-on fee and I would imagine your salary would be in the same region. Do I have your okay on that Mrs Sims?'

'When would I start?'

'Immediately, I have taken the liberty of purchasing airline tickets and am in the process of obtaining a work visa for the European Union. You will be joining the yacht in Italy and can fly out the day after tomorrow. Are we in agreement?'

Anita did not answer straight away even though there was no prospect of her turning the offer down.

'I do have commitments during the next few weeks.'

'Cancel them, my client is a very demanding man but he will pay well for what he wants. Look at the signing-on fee, I can stretch to six thousand, how does that sound?'

He *was* getting desperate, perhaps it was time to put him out of his misery, after all, she could not afford to let slip the opportunity to gain access to Bullseye's yacht.

'Give me your number and let me call a few people. I am happy to accept your offer Mr Aitkin but I will need to cancel several engagements. I will confirm within the hour.'

A somewhat relieved Geoffrey Aitkin gave Anita his telephone number and hung up, leaving her feeling pleased if somewhat apprehensive. Talk about entering the lion's den, she thought, as she scribbled a few notes on her pad and went to get herself a coffee. One of the first items on her agenda was to meet with the head of the department and once back at her desk she arranged a meeting with her boss.

'Why would he want you to travel out to Italy, why has he asked for you?'

'I don't know sir but the information I have is that it is a temporary engagement. It is an opportunity to have a look on his yacht, see what he is up to. Do I have your permission to proceed?'

Her boss slowly nodded his head. 'Yes, you have my permission but only on the proviso that you have proper backup. You have been out on a limb before and it caused me all sorts of problems.'

'Thank you sir,' said Anita returning to the room, soundproofed for privacy and picked up the blue telephone.

'Mr Aitkin?'

'Ah, I do believe it is Mrs Sims, I recognise your voice. Thank you for ringing back. Positive news I hope.'

'Yes, I have decided to take you up on your offer; I have cancelled all my commitments for the next week or so.'

'Just a week?'

'Well the work I have been offered after that is not confirmed as yet,' she said, realising she was cutting herself short. 'What exactly is it you want me to do, should I visit your office?'

'That would be a good idea. In the meantime, I can tell the client that his new sommelier will be arriving in two days' time. You have our address?'

The conversation ended and Anita sat back in her chair, her mind working overtime. She wrote more notes on her pad and then left the room to make her way back to her desk, stopping off at the section head's office on the way.

'Come,' called a voice. 'Anita, back already, what can I do for you?'

'The situation is developing sir and I would like to discuss some more details with you.'

The sun finally broke through the grey clouds hanging over the closed city of Severomorsk on Russia's northern Kola Peninsula. Admiral Sokolov left the headquarters building of the Northern Fleet to meet Captain 1st rank Krumlov, his guide for the day who was waiting for him at the base of the wide steps next to a car, its door already open.

'Good morning Captain, I'm looking forward to my visit to the General Directorate of Undersea

Research. I hope you have some interesting things to show me.'

'Yes sir, I think you will be impressed,' said the officer, opening the car door for his superior.

'We will not talk about progress in the submarine service until we reach the base Captain, understood?'

'Yes sir,' said the Captain 1st rank, climbing into the front passenger seat.

He was well aware of the recent scandals in the Russian Federation's military. Corruption was rife, always a problem, yet everybody had managed to live with the situation until the destroyer *Igor Panteleyev* caused a collision with a Swedish frigate, killing several Russian sailors. The incident caused uproar when the Kremlin discovered senior officers of the Baltic fleet had attempted a cover-up. That led to sackings all the way up to the Admiral of the Fleet and since then discipline and accountability had become a major issue. Dismissal from the service was the usual punishment for anyone seen to be slacking but, even so, the new rules had not completely eradicated the problem.

'I have a helicopter waiting for us Admiral; to go by road would take us many hours. Travelling by air we should be there by around nine o'clock.'

Admiral Sokolov said nothing; instead, he flicked through the messages on his mobile phone, stopping at the one from his wife. Svetlana was organising his fiftieth birthday party for early the following month and was not sure which of her husband's colleagues to invite. He smiled to himself; she knew some so-called friends could be informers or working for one of the secret services. The Soviet way of thinking had not left her and, indeed, he was himself well aware of the need to be careful. His next message was more sombre, it was a summons to Moscow as soon as he had conducted his business with the Northern Fleet.

After the short journey to the helicopter landing-pad, the car swept through the security gate, pulling up near the Kamov Ka-27, its rotor already spinning. The Captain jumped from his seat, opened the rear door for the admiral, and with their heads bowed the two men walked under the aircraft's rotor to climb aboard. The pilot gave them a wave and after a brief safety check, the helicopter took off for the journey across the waters of the Kola Peninsula to the submarine base at Gadzhiyevo.

Hidden deep inside a sheer cliff face the base was invisible to satellite surveillance and security was particularly rigorous, hardly surprising considering its importance to the Russian Navy. First, they had to pass through the outer perimeter gates, guarded by commandos, and then the guard post to the submarine dock. Both were used to tight security, both had served in submarines and both had spent time in the area. What was more surprising was the sight of two Severodvinsk-class attack submarines sitting silently side by side. They were the new stretched version able to carry the ST30M super cavitating torpedo, a weapon without equal in Western navies.

'Those babies will give the Americans and the Chinese something to think about Captain.'

'Yes sir, and what I am about to show you will too. Please follow me.'

The two men walked further into the underground cavern and then up a steel staircase to an area with yet another layer of security. This time they had their photographs taken, their fingerprints and irises scanned before entering the restricted area.

'Quite a security set-up down here Captain. I must say I am impressed.'

'Yes sir, the work we are doing here is concerned with top secret underwater technology and we really do not want anyone to know about it.'

'So, down to business, the Kremlin has sent me here to assess your latest development, we know it is an autonomous underwater system but the details are still not known. You will show me what I need to see so that I can report to the defence committee for their consideration.'

'Comrade Admiral we have organised a lecture and some video to explain the principle of the system to give you an idea of its capability, and after lunch we are to go to the testing area for a live demonstration.'

The admiral nodded his approval and following his subordinate into a spacious, windowless room he was surprised to see two men waiting for them. The first was in the naval uniform of a Captain 2nd rank and the other was wearing a white coat, a civilian he guessed.

'May I present Captain 2nd rank Sverdlovsk and Professor Muntoni,' said Captain Krumlov.

The officer saluted and the scientist bowed his head in a sign of respect.

'You are an Italian, Professor?'

'No sir, my great grandfather came here to fight for the revolution in 1917, met my grandmother and the rest, as they say, is history.'

'You are a true Russian if your ancestor fought for the revolution. Now Professor, I presume you are the one to tell me about the project.'

'In part, Captain Sverdlovsk will inform you of the deployment capabilities of the submarine. I am here to explain how it works. Please take a seat and we will begin.'

The admiral and his subordinate took their seats whilst Captain Sverdlovsk walked over to a computer sitting on a nearby table.

'We have prepared a presentation; Captain Sverdlovsk will run it as I speak. To begin, the military world has changed dramatically in the past few years. Gone are the vast armies of foot soldiers, gone the pilots of jet aircraft, instead we have battlefield robots with capabilities far in excess of their human counterparts. The navy is no different; yes, it is true we have our aircraft carrier and support ships, destroyers, submarines, and they are important as a show of force but the Chinese have shown the way. Because they could not match the Americans, and still do not, in fact even we cannot hope to match the United States Navy as equals, the Chinese have demonstrated that small, long-range and accurate weapons platforms bombarding a valuable target only need to penetrate the enemy's defences once.'

The professor cleared his throat before continuing: 'We are working along similar lines with our unmanned, autonomous submersible. We can in theory, and that theory is becoming more of a reality every day, launch an attack on an enemy from outside his territorial waters with a real prospect of success. Not only are the submarines autonomous but also completely silent, stealthy, almost undetectable. We have developed a strategy of stealth rather than brute force, caution instead of speed. The navy's new cavitating Shkval torpedo is all very well when we need to take out a capital ship on the high seas, but there is not much left when it has done its job.'

'Isn't that the object?'

'In most circumstances yes, but once we have used a Shkval the enemy will be in no doubt who launched the attack. This approach is to use very advanced artificial intelligence techniques to deploy an autonomous machine that can disable the target, leave the scene and make it difficult for the enemy to apportion blame. The new submarine is not a hare, more the tortoise. It will creep up on an enemy undetected, do its job and disappear before anyone realises that it has even been there.'

The admiral sat up in his chair, engrossed.

'But there is a problem Professor, we have not seen your submarine in action and only have your word for it. I understand there has not been a field trial and so you cannot be sure it will work.' He looked at Captain Krumlov as if to confirm his doubts.

'If you please sir,' said Captain Sverdlovsk, 'let me show you some video footage and the computer simulation of the system. We have been careful not to expose the sub to the outside world but we have tested the programming and the sensors and the results are impressive.'

The officer switched on a large screen attached to one wall of the room, dimmed the lights and for almost an hour showed video footage of the new submarine, charts demonstrating its capabilities and sensors. Then he alluded to the propulsion system.

'Comrade Admiral this is the vehicle's main strength.' He brought up a sectional drawing of the submarine and pointed to the rear section of the craft. 'The propulsion system we have developed is like nothing else, we have mastered laminar flow, eliminating eddies and cavitation so making it practically undetectable by any listening device that we know of. Here are the test results,' he added, bringing up a graph on the screen. 'As you can see we have little more than a straight line only just above the axis.'

'Meaning?'

'Meaning the sound profile is almost non-existent, and probably we can go anywhere undetected. As far as we know, the Americans and the British do not have a listening device sensitive enough to pick up the submarine's minimal vibration at any significant distance.'

'And how do you control it if it is unmanned?'

'Yes sir, it is unmanned and the sub is, to all intents and purposes, out of control.'

Admiral Sokolov's eyebrows lifted a fraction though his eyes remained unmoved. He was wise enough to realise that the Captain second rank was setting him up for something.

'When I say out of control I mean out of our control, temporarily that is. Thanks to our friends at Google and Amazon who have digitally mapped just about the whole planet, important geographic information is readily available if you are prepared to pay for it and we are. We created a company with the cover of exploring for minerals on the seabed and because it appears a bona fide exploration company, we have not encountered any problems in purchasing the ocean topography files. From those files, we can program the submarine to find the target on its own.'

'What is the range, how long can we leave it without interference?'

'Good question sir, firstly battery technology has come a long way in a very short time and due to the expertise of the spooks at the Foreign Intelligence

Service we have obtained the most advanced battery technology of both the Americans and the Chinese. For the past two years, our scientists and engineers have been perfecting a new design of battery for the submersible. We expect it will have a range of several hundred miles and the possibility of over seventy hours at sea without recharging. We believe that is enough to carry out even the most complex of operations. We have a demonstration for you in . . .' he looked at his watch, 'one hour and twenty minutes. First sir, if you are happy with the presentation, we will have lunch.'

Admiral Sokolov nodded his head, this time his eyes a little more animated.

'That was very interesting. I can see the advantage of an accurately mapped seabed and seventy hours submerged is a long time. How does the submarine navigate?'

'I think that is more for Professor Muntoni to explain sir.'

The professor walked in front of the screen and illuminated by the still active presentation began a brief description.

'We have an array of sensors covering the hull. These are not ordinary sensors; they have the ability to work together with the on-board computer to create their own three-dimensional map of the seabed and match it exactly with that purchased from Google. We also acquired some of the technology from another American company concerned with augmented reality and utilising that technology the submarine can precisely map the target area and superimpose the target on it. This makes it possible to target almost any craft in any unprotected waters.'

'What exactly do you mean by unprotected? Surely any navy worth its salt will have defences in place at their bases and what about Poseidon?'

'Yes comrade, the Poseidon Maritime Patrol Aircraft was our biggest obstacle when we began this project. The British have just taken delivery of the first two aircraft and are no doubt working up to operational readiness but as yet we believe the Royal Navy is relying on sophisticated towed array systems. We understand them and we believe our submarine can evade detection by such systems.'

'That still leaves Poseidon.'

'It does and we are confident that we can evade the aircraft's sensors provided we are careful.'

'Careful, that's an understatement. It is a submariner's duty to be careful.'

'Yes Comrade Admiral, what I mean is that there are evasive actions we can take that we are sure will allow the submarine to do its work undetected. For example, we have constructed the vessel almost entirely with composite materials and engineering plastics. The propulsion system is practically metal-free, the submarine will move into position to attack a target at very slow speed. With an almost undetectable signature, the sonar will think it is merely aquatic life on the move.'

'Fish?'

'Dolphins or seals, something they will have eliminated from their detection algorithms to avoid a false alarm.'

'You are sure you can do this?'

'Ninety-nine per cent.'

'Comrade Admiral, the plan is to program the submarine to leave the mother ship and cross the threshold into the target's territory. From the moment it leaves international waters, the submarine is on its own. It will find its way to a pre-arranged position close by the target, and once there it will use its sensors to more accurately map the target and, when ready, engage its weaponry. We believe we have a one hundred per cent chance of taking out the target once we are through bases' outer defences. Moreover, after the attack the submarine has a good chance of manoeuvring undetected away from the target area and back to the mother ship – leaving the enemy wondering what hit them.'

'And what if it can't, what if it is caught? The repercussions could be disastrous.'

'Indeed, and if that is the case the machine will self-destruct, scattering debris everywhere and hindering any forensic investigation.'

The admiral remained silent. He had become aware of the capabilities of autonomous submersibles ever since the discovery of MH370's wreckage in the waters off Western Australia the previous year. The skill and speed with which the last search effort had unfolded had left him captivated.

'If this works you have a lot to be proud of.'

'We did not do this alone sir; it was a team effort, a team effort by over a hundred dedicated scientists, technicians and intelligence experts who want nothing more than to serve the motherland.'

'As all good Russians should . . . I am impressed and I am hungry.'

Exactly one hour and twelve minutes later, the four men, the admiral, the scientist and the two serving officers, stood together on a pontoon reaching deep inside the cliff. They were dressed in survival suits in case of an accident and standing apart from them were two technicians in full scuba diving suits.

'You think I will fall in and these two here are to rescue me?' said the Admiral, looking a little puzzled.

'No sir, just a precaution, but we do expect that you will get wet,' said Captain Sverdlovsk.

'Hmm, well what have you brought me to see?'

'Our submarine sir, it has been on a mission for the past four hours and will surface in exactly thirty seconds.'

'Oh where?'

The admiral did not hear the answer, instead he was shocked to feel the pontoon sway as an upwelling of seawater spilled across it. But he was more shocked to see the dark grey shape of the submarine as it surfaced just metres away.

'Where did that come from,' he said, staring at the dolphin-like shape emerging from the depths.

'Sir, we set a mission for it to perform beginning four hours ago. The object was to cruise the waters of the sound, to search out one of the destroyers lying at anchor and to perform pre-ordained manoeuvres similar to those we envisage in a real attack. The destroyer has unique characteristics and these we programmed into the submarine's memory. The aim of the exercise is to show you that the submarine can locate a target, close in for the kill without any instruction from outside, and then return to surface at a pre-ordained time and place. As you can see sir, it did just that,' said Captain Sverdlovsk, turning to the two divers. 'You know what to do, secure the boat.'

'With your permission Admiral, we will return to the laboratory where I will establish a radio link and download the mission log,' said the scientist. 'In the laboratory we can consult the data and assess the accuracy of the submarine's movements during the exercise. From the log we will be able to demonstrate more fully the machine's capability, give you a more comprehensive understanding.'

'I am looking forward to that comrade; it is good to know we are one step ahead of the Americans.'

Colonel Vasyli Kazantsev had shown an acute interest in computer science as a young man, obtaining his doctorate in the discipline from St Petersburg State University. From the start, he

showed a natural ability and a year later, his
brilliance brought him to the attention of Russia's
Foreign Military Intelligence Service. After joining
the GRU, he had become involved with the
monitoring devices or black boxes known as SORM.
The boxes could intercept all data passing through
the Russian network, and the security services now
had access to that data, recording and analysing
every telephone conversation and every email
passing through the Russian service providers' lines.

Colonel Kazantsev realised that if the Russians
were doing covert spying within their own borders
there was a good chance that the Americans were
doing the same. He was aware since his student days
of nascent hacking groups such as the Legion of
Doom and the splinter group called the Masters of
Deception. It had intrigued him to learn that so-
called amateurs were regularly breaking into
computer systems and then came the Christmas
Tree EXEC worm and he realised where the future
lay.

Four years on from that time, in a Moscow
suburb, he found himself in command of a
nondescript Soviet-era concrete building of four
storeys, a cyber warfare hub. The top floor was a
large open-plan office full of young computer
specialists staring into computer screens, spending
their days hacking into the West's military systems.
The colonel enjoyed working there, enjoyed the
company of the young whiz kids of the computer

age, and during the first half hour of his working day he would spend time amongst them.

'Maksim, good morning, tell me what you are doing today.'

The man looked up from his work, eyes bright and receptive.

'We have penetrated the British Royal Navy's computer system and the code we planted is beginning to bear fruit. During the next week or two we should know a little more about their present capabilities and hopefully their plans for us.'

'Good, the British are weakened by their own political actions, and with some help from us they can say goodbye to their navy.'

'Yes sir.'

'Okay, keep up the good work.'

The colonel moved along the line, looking at each screen, talking to individuals and eventually he reached his office where a pile of envelopes and documents awaited him. Removing his jacket, he sat down at his desk and lit a cigarette. The smoke was reassuring but as a man of science, he knew that he was slowly killing himself. 'Ach . . . what the hell,' he thought. If things did not work out as planned they could all be dead within the year.

Putting those black thoughts to one side, he began to work through his mail. There were reports from the different work groups, routine correspondence; he began reading until the ringing of his telephone stopped him.

'Colonel Kazantsev?'

The earpiece hissed and as he listened the colonel's face became serious.

'I will inform security of your arrival comrade, yes I understand, thank you,' he said, putting the telephone down.

So, the head of military intelligence was paying him a visit. He had expected it. A visit from such a high-ranking officer happened only rarely, usually in times of stress, for example, when Russia had invaded Ukraine. His department had cleared the way, finding out the Ukrainians' order of battle, infecting their computers, sowing confusion, but more importantly, the department had ascertained the lack of political will within NATO to oppose an invading force.

In the end, it had been easy; a malfunctioning computer grounded the Ukrainian Air Force and their big guns had not worked for the same reason. It had taken less than five days for the Russian tanks to surround Kiev, almost as easily as the annexation of Crimea, and as help was not forthcoming from the West, the government had sued for peace.

Colonel Kazantsev knew that would not be the end of the expansion plans. So far NATO had proved ineffective, the Americans had refused to become directly involved and the president had ambitions to fulfil before the end of his final term in office. And that was less than a year away.

One week later Colonel Kazantsev walked into the room with the large oval table and took the chair next to Admiral Sokolov. During the next few minutes, more men in uniform arrived until there were just three vacant seats. Seconds later the double doors at the end of the room opened and the president made his entrance, flanked by the deputy prime minister and the head of the armed forces.

'Gentlemen we meet again, I hope you all have positive news for me,' he said, taking his seat.

The most powerful man in Russia looked around the room, reassuring himself of the strength of his position, and after a brief pause began to speak.

'The events of the past few years have been momentous for Mother Russia, the Americans are in retreat, NATO is now not a force we should particularly fear. We have concluded an agreement with the Chinese to let them have the Pacific right up to the western seaboard of the United States while we will concentrate upon Europe and the Middle East. The Indian Navy is a problem but even they are losing interest in the Americans who seem content to stay at home and wallow in their own self-pity. Gone are the days when they ruled the world. It is our world now, our world to shape as we please.'

He looked again at his audience, stony-faced, non-committal, what else could he expect, after all, they were Russians. A hundred years of Russian history gave them little reason to smile but a new age was dawning and before he left office, he would lead the country once more to greatness.

'Colonel Kazantsev would you like to enlighten us as to the extent to which you have compromised our enemies?'

The colonel nodded and opened the folder in front of him.

'As you all know we have been penetrating the West's computer systems for a number of years and we feel we can control many of their functions, for instance their power grids. Western countries are power dependent, from hospitals and schools to their transport systems. If we take out their means of generating power then the infrastructure will slowly stop. We can do that, we have code implanted in most of the power-generating plants in Europe and many in the United States and Canada. Once we receive the order, we can sabotage them and black out whichever country we choose. In addition, we can control government and military computer systems at will. They have countermeasures for sure but we can cause enough disruption to serve our purpose.'

'Thank you Colonel and now you, Admiral, please let us know the state of readiness of the Northern Fleet.'

Admiral Sokolov was ready, his own folder open and from it he took a single sheet of paper.

'We have been conducting manoeuvres for the past few months, in recent weeks stepping up the intensity, and the results show that we are at full readiness for any operation demanded of us. Each ship of the Northern Fleet is fully crewed and armed and in three days the nuclear capable ships can be mission-ready too. As you may be aware comrades, like the air force the navy is experimenting with unmanned craft. We have developed several autonomous submarines but one in particular stands out.'

The admiral went on to describe the exercise he had witnessed in the Murmansk Oblast, adding several operational scenarios the machine could undertake. When he finished speaking a few murmurs reached his ears, he had obviously impressed the military men by his presentation, and the president added his compliment.

'You have made great progress Admiral and you are to be congratulated. Now let us hear from the General of the Army, please tell us about your readiness and your strengths. The new tank how is that performing?'

The General of the Army cleared his throat and began to speak; he sounded convincing but one or two of the more experienced officers suspected a cover-up of some sort. It was not the first time the army had proved less efficient than expected, but in Russia it was not a good idea to lower expectations. If the president suspected anything, he did not show it and once the general had finished speaking the remainder of the committee delivered assessments of the readiness of their own departments.

After each of the heads of the various military and intelligence services had concluded their reports, the president declared a break for refreshments and an hour later the gathering reconvened. The mood was subdued yet an unmistakable air of confidence filled the room. The generals and admirals had listened to each other's addresses and realised that the power and reach of the Russian Federation's armed forces had never been greater. They were on the verge of Mother Russia's ascent to greatness, to a place in history where they would rule much of the Western hemisphere and a greater part of the East, leaving the rest of the world to the Chinese. America was almost finished as the pre-eminent world power and as if to confirm their private thoughts, the president began to utter his own.

'I have already said that a window of opportunity is presenting itself. Europe is in disarray, thanks in no small way to our long campaign of misinformation and factual distortions. The hard-right parties are winning elections and these people are our natural allies. The Americans are still a threat but if we handle the next stage of our plan well they will not bother us. If they do, they will pay heavily with the disruption to their infrastructure and, more than that, we have cells of militant extremists ready to break cover. Igor, what is the situation with the Muslims?'

Igor Ilyich Andresov was a small, bespectacled man who nobody would suspect as the head of the GRU. It was not his height that mattered but his intellect, one that towered above most men, his capabilities and Machiavellian intrigues second to none. Rising from humble beginnings, he had proved himself in counter-espionage, exposing and eliminating many of the West's agents. Distinct from the rest of the men around the table, he carried no notes. Wary of the written word Igor Ilyich Andresov was unlikely to leave evidence that in the future could become a death warrant and with a humourless smile, he began to speak.

'For almost ten years we have worked loosely with al-Qaeda, since the height of the conflict in Syria. To the outside world, they are the enemy of the Americans and of ourselves but that is not wholly true. We have found them useful in containing some extreme factions of militant Islam. Do not forget that we have a large Muslim population ourselves and it is prudent to keep them quiet. Performing this function for us are al-Qaeda, but at a cost. In part, we finance that organisation and have done for a while and they are intent upon causing damage to the Americans, which also suits us very well. An added bonus is that they will not attack Mother Russia and although I agree there have been instances, we choreographed many of them for popular consumption. For the coming large-scale operations we will employ them again, this time to hit the Europeans rather than the Americans. Cells exist in all the major European cities awaiting the order but first we have to equip them with the means to carry out their attacks. It is ongoing, a slow process by necessity, and the operation should be nearing completion within the year. These are not particularly disciplined groups nor do they seem capable of anything resembling a sophisticated attack but they are willing to die for their cause and we have convinced their leadership that their cause is our cause too. They will rise up across the continent under our control, create enough mayhem to wrong-foot western European governments and then we will make our move.'

There was silence for several seconds; an Islamic rebellion controlled by Russia was something no one had really considered. The military men had mixed reactions on hearing the news, a second front was welcome but many of those in the room were sceptical that an unruly group such as al-Qaeda could manage large-scale disruption.

Chapter 7

Sylvie lifted her glasses to her forehead, rubbed her eyes and then stretched her arms to relieve the stress of hours scrutinising satellite imagery. She had spent so much time looking at one particular picture she was beginning to feel that she lived in Moscow's Bakovka Oblast. The hours spent meticulously checking every detail had left her with a mild headache but she could put up with that, all part of the job she loved.

Sylvie Parker was a geospatial intelligence imagery analyst for the United States Army and right now she was keeping an eye on the Russian First Tank Army. The image on her screen was an overhead view of their base, a large open area containing several long buildings where the Russians supposedly housed or maintained their tanks. However, she had only seen two tanks at any one time and was beginning to wonder just how many there really were. Was it possible that there were no more tanks and that it was simply an intelligence feint to confuse?

Sylvie looked at the time on the monitor, six-thirty, still more than an hour until the end of her shift. Feeling a little more alert she replaced her glasses and returned to studying the image for a few moments longer and then she looked on the database for any later images from the satellite. Raw images were often available as soon as they came in from space but were not as good as the enhanced versions available a few hours later.

There was one, taken only half an hour previously, late evening in Moscow and the skies were clear, perfect for her job. She zoomed straight in on the coordinates of the base and immediately noticed a difference to the image taken a day earlier. Outside each of the long buildings, she finally saw some more tanks, twelve in total, and by their haphazard appearance they were on the move. She zoomed in further, to the best magnification without too much distortion, and searched every inch of the compound. Panning the screen, she came to the first of the hangars and poking out of the doorway she was sure she could see a tank beginning to emerge. It was a significant discovery; there had been little or no movement for months.

'Hi, could you come and have a look at this sir,' she called to her supervisor sitting across the room.

The major nodded and rose from his chair to walk to her workstation.

'What have you got Sylvie?'

'I have watched this base on and off for the best part of a year sir and never seen a great deal happening. They occasionally bring in tanks on transporters and then take them away again but only one or two at a time. This image here on the screen shows twelve tanks and it looks to me as if they are assembling for something.'

The major pulled up a spare chair, sat beside her, and viewed the image intently.

'Let me zoom in for you, look there, isn't that a tank beginning to emerge? And there, those are soldiers, tank soldiers by the look of their headgear, enough to crew more than just a couple of tanks.'

'I do believe you are right. One picture does not tell us a lot. Maybe you could check all the images of this place taken in the past month, compare them, perhaps you have missed something. Keep me informed if you turn up anything.'

'Yes sir.'

Her superior's remark did not offend Sylvie, she could well have missed something, to look at every image taken was time-consuming. Her initial job was to examine samples, search for anomalies and so she began to look at previous images of the base. Then she glanced at the time, her shift was ending and her mind began to move towards other matters, things she had to do at home, and taking one last look at the monitor she began writing up her log ready for Martha, her relief who was already walking towards her.

'Hi Sylvie, what you got today girl?'

'Hello Martha, this could be interesting. The tank base we have been keeping an eye on, the one on the outskirts of Moscow, something's going on I think.'

For ten minutes the women talked, Sylvie explained what she had seen and Martha nodded as she began to understand that she might have a busy shift looking through the many past images.

'Okay honey, leave it with me, I'll see you in the morning.'

At a quarter to eight the following morning a bleary-eyed Sylvie returned to work, got herself a coffee from the machine and walked across to the workstation.

'Morning Martha, how did you get on last night?'

'Good, real good. I worked through the images going back a month and I counted the tanks coming in and those leaving and I managed to compare most of them to make sure they were not the same and I reckon there were at least ten more tanks in those buildings by the end of that month.'

Sylvie took a sip of coffee and gave Martha a mildly admiring look.

'There's more, I logged on to the agency's account with Planet Incorporated in San Francisco and asked them to stream all the images coming in from their cluster over Moscow and this is one image we received.'

Sylvie looked at the screen and at first the overhead shot of the base looked no different to the one she had studied the previous evening. Then she noticed that those tanks she had seen manoeuvring had disappeared.

'The tanks have gone?'

'Sure have, look at this.' Martha brought up a series of images taken earlier during the fading daylight of late evening. The image detail was not as clear as those military satellites provided, but to Sylvie's trained eyes, they told a story.

'So they are on the move and there are a lot of them.'

'Yes, I've spoken to the team leader and he is putting in a request for someone from upstairs to come and have a look. My guess is they are deploying for some war game or other. Maybe they are heading for Ukraine. We will keep an eye on them and find out. All yours now Sylvie, I'll see you tonight.'

'Thanks Martha, sleep well.'

'Hu . . . sleep well, you know how hard it can be. I got shoppin' and washin' to do. Sleep well indeed!'

Sylvie smiled at the robust black woman as she gathered her things and began to make her way towards security. Sylvie's smile did not last long, she was getting that feeling, the excitement she felt when something big was unfolding. She took one last look at the image on the screen and then she opened her email folder to examine the latest information from the Surveillance and Reconnaissance Agency in Springfield.

The Sommelier

A few hours later at CIA Langley, Rosemary was surprised to see her husband enter the office.

'Hi John, I do not see you in here very often.'

She was making small talk, she knew her husband well enough and his face told her that something serious was bothering him. It had to be the Russians.

'Let's go to the quiet room, I have something to say.

'Oh oh, thought Rosemary, this did look serious.

John opened the door and waited for his wife to enter the soundproofed room, a few of the other analysts' heads tilting towards them as they went, and after closing the door John shrugged his shoulders and turned to face his wife.

'They are on the move – big time. We have received reports of troop and tank movements from our agents in Russia and the intelligence analysts working with the Moonpenny team at the West Virginia establishment have confirmed satellite imagery showing the army is indeed on the move. The Brits have done their part too; Carboy supplied some intercepts from the Russian Northern Fleet. It seems they are working up as well.'

'You want me involved?'

'I sure do Rosemary, there's no one at Langley with a nose for Russian misdemeanours as good as yours. There is a committee meeting first thing in the morning to discuss what we know but there is also a lot we don't know and I want you to make it a priority to investigate as much as you can of the intelligence we have and bring it along.'

'Am I working alone on this John, it sounds like quite a task if you are looking for fast results?'

'I will talk with your department head and get him to second one or two of his brightest. Anyone you have in mind?'

'Yeah, Sarah Lovell, she is the whizaroony who came up with the imaging analysis program. My guess is we will need some serious computing power to reduce time. There is another analyst in the department, Bryn Williams, he's good and he's been working on the Russian armed forces for some time, he could be useful.'

'Okay I'll arrange it and for now we'll keep the operation local. Once we have an idea what they are up to then we can decide whether to escalate. I will be late home tonight honey, so do not wait up for me. I'll be in touch about the things we've talked about and I'll get someone to brief you on what we already know and the sources so you can liaise with them.'

'Okay John, I'll get straight on to it. Send me the information as soon as you can and in the meantime I will talk with my team, oh and don't expect me home early either.'

John opened the door, kissed his wife on the cheek and walked off at pace leaving her to wonder what her best approach might be. She needed a drink first and going to the machine at the far end of the office she got herself a black coffee and returned to her desk. A coffee always helped when it came to thinking, and thinking was all she could do right now.

She glanced at her computer and noticed the number in the bottom right-hand corner; she had received three emails since she had left to speak with John. The first was routine traffic, the second a request from the Southeast Asia department for information and the third was from MI6 in London, a request for help in identifying two men. She looked at the image, the now familiar background of the Lady Galina and two men lounging on the dockside. That was not the only image, but the agent who took them must have rushed, afraid of discovery perhaps, for there was camera shake blurring the shots. After studying them for half a minute, she picked up the telephone.

'Sarah, can you swing by pretty soon, I have some pictures for you to have a look at, and I am putting together a small team and I need you to work with me on a more full-time basis.'

The conversation carried on for a minute longer before Rosemary replaced the receiver and sat back in her chair. The Russians and their agents were everywhere, were they playing out some grand plan or was it just normal intelligence traffic? It was her job to find out, to collate every scrap of information coming in via the satellites, and from agents on the ground. That was where Sarah came in and until she showed up Rosemary decided that a few emails were in order. She needed to let the relevant departments of the United States intelligence community know what she expected of them. She had been in the job long enough to have contacts in almost every branch, she needed favours, and almost as soon as she finished sending, Sarah arrived.

'Hi Rosemary.'

'Sarah, good afternoon,' said Rosemary, looking up from her computer. 'Take a seat and I will fill you in on a few details, what we think is going on and what I want you to do to help. We are seeing an increase in Russian military traffic and I had a report this morning that some of their army and naval units are on the move. The problem is we do not really have much idea about what they may be doing. We can speculate but that does not solve any problems. Your work with imaging impressed me, and that could be important right now because we are getting satellite images all the time and perhaps your techniques can turn up new insights. I am to pull a small team together to sift through the intelligence coming in and to try to make sense of it all. Experience tells me that we could be overwhelmed and miss the important stuff. Tell me, can you come up with something on your computers that can sift the information and maybe take a statistical look, tease out information that is relevant?'

'I guess so, radio signals, images, the lot, is that what you want?'

'Just about, I know enough about your discipline to appreciate the power you can bring to an investigation like this. There is no way I can do this on my own so I asked for you and one or two others to help. Let us start by setting an agenda, say a meeting every morning first thing to consider the ongoing situation and you will want access to the constant supply of intelligence to crunch the numbers. Let me know exactly how you would like that set up and I will ask those overseeing the project to sanction your request.'

'What do you think is going on?'

'I have very little idea at this stage; the Russians are masters of deception and intrigue. I am not a particular fan of football but I do know it is in the interests of winning that you confuse the opposition's line-backers, take them out and their defence is vulnerable to a swift and flowing attack. Maybe they are shaping up to do just that or maybe they are simply putting on a show of strength to keep us at bay. I really don't know, Sarah, but we're damn well going to find out.'

Sarah squeezed her lips tight together and looked thoughtful for a few seconds before relaxing and looking Rosemary in the eye.

'I have a friend at MIT who is heavily into data mining and he has written a new algorithm to collate information, to enable highlighting patterns that might otherwise escape scrutiny. That, I think, is what you require. I don't know if he has any security clearance though, he was always a bit of a rebel and I don't expect any government agency would risk him working for them.'

'People grow up. Bring him in and we will have a talk. In the meantime, I have had a request from across the pond to identify a couple of guys. Can you run the image through your system and see if we can turn anything up?'

'Sure, no problem, just email what you have and meanwhile I will sound out Jake.'

The head of Anita's department read the report from Langley with interest before finally looking up.

'These two are dangerous, Anita, GRU professionals. I'm not sure I like the idea of you being on that yacht without backup.'

'I can manage sir.'

'Your record says you can but your record is history. Each situation is different and this one certainly is. If you are out at sea and are in trouble how the hell can we help you?'

'It's part of the job, I'm sure I can cope sir.'

'I have to sanction this operation in the next few minutes – or not. I will not send you knowingly into harm's way.'

Anita held her boss's gaze, unflinchingly, knowing that it had to go ahead otherwise a big fish would get away and after all the upheaval of the past few years they were due some success.

'You are determined to go I see. It does look as if there could be some rich returns if we can infiltrate their operation. Look, I can see that I am going to have to sanction the mission, the defence committee has already intimated as much, but you do need backup. We have agents in Italy and the Italians are still our allies so I believe it prudent to involve them to some degree to keep an eye on you.'

'I am not too happy involving foreign security services. The Italians are not always the most efficient or trustworthy sir and the last thing I want is some incompetent agent compromising things.'

'Quite, though I do suggest you see Commander Pearson, your controller, as soon as you can. He will try to keep you safe but you will be on your own for most of the time. If the Russians behave as normal they will screen and search you I am sure. They are thorough and do not take chances. How long have we got?'

'I'm flying out at noon tomorrow, provided you sanction the mission.'

'You will talk to your controller?' the director queried, his pen hovering over the order.

At least the operation had official sanction, she mused as she walked along the corridor back to her desk. Her forays in the field of late had been low-key affairs with little in the way of real danger but sometimes it was the danger that drove her. She had always been adventurous, athletic and prone to taking risks that usually paid off. If they did not she had always managed to reach safety and a spell on the luxury yacht could be an experience as well as giving her the chance to get close to Bullseye. She needed to talk with Commander Pearson as soon as possible and if she were to be the sommelier on the superyacht then she needed to brush up on the current state of affairs in the world of wine. A quick look over her desk and a glance through her email inbox informed her that nothing was pressing. She had received the reply from Langley an hour before, confirming that the two men on board the Lady Galina were indeed GRU and now she needed to fill the gaps in her knowledge about wine. It was just after ten o'clock in the morning and she had an idea. Taking out her mobile phone, she skimmed through the directory and made the call.

Olivier Rousset was very happy to see her and, yes, he was free for the next few hours. She arranged to see him and then she rang her controller to make an appointment to discuss the operation. It took the best part of an hour, they talked about her cover, the kind of backup he could arrange, and they envisaged the sort of scenarios where things might go wrong.

'I can always swim sir,' she joked, eliciting a frown from the commander.

'I hardly think that is a serious option. Listen, I will contact M Squadron; let them know of a possible job. If things get too hairy you must try and let us know.'

Commander Pearson believed in his agent's ability but problems always arose and part of the art of espionage was to get your agent out safely. Anita listened to his advice and after leaving his office made her way back to her desk where she checked her briefcase, slipped on her jacket and signed out for the day.

The Sommelier

She was looking forward to seeing Olivier Rousset, Master Sommelier at the Royal Automobile Club. She was a member of the club and well aware of his reputation and now she wanted to tap into his extensive knowledge of fine wines.

Stepping out of the lift, she walked into the deserted underground car park and not twenty yards from her sat her black BMW i8. Although it was not new, it still looked good and if she enjoyed anything, it was putting the beast through its paces. She called out to it and immediately the door opened, beckoning her into the driving seat.

'Hello Anita,' said a man's husky voice from the surround speakers.

'Hello George, let's go,' she replied and the car responded by automatically starting its engine. 'Take me to the entrance,' she said.

The car, aware of its surroundings and without any further input from Anita, backed out of the parking space and made its way steadily towards the security barrier. The duty officer gave a cursory salute as the scanners verified her, and as the barrier began to rise she took control of the BMW and drove it onto the Albert Embankment.

It was no more than two miles to the RAC, and after crossing the river at Lambeth Anita dodged through the traffic past the Palace of Westminster, through Admiralty Arch, eventually arriving in Pall Mall and pulling up at the first available parking space. Using her mobile phone, she paid for the maximum four-hour stay and walked to the club. It took her less than five minutes and after announcing herself in reception she did not have to wait long before a good-looking, middle-aged man appeared.

'*Bonjour* Anita, how nice of you to take an interest in my work,' said the smartly dressed Frenchman and in the Gallic way he reached to kiss her on each cheek.

'It's good of you to see me at such short notice Olivier.'

'You said you wanted to discuss the current wine market.'

'Yes, I am in the middle of helping a friend open a restaurant in Blackheath. She is an excellent chef and knows I have an interest in wine so she asked me to help stock her wine cellar.'

'Have you any preferences, what sort of vintage and is there a price range?'

'Well, to be frank, my friend expects to have customers with expensive tastes. I have an idea of which wines I might choose but I am not a professional like you Olivier.'

'Well, I can give you some ideas of the best wines available at the moment. What is the food your friend will be serving?'

'Italian mainly, the usual fish and meat dishes together with pasta, oh and possibly Russian.'

The Frenchman's eyebrows rose slightly.

'Russian? Well I suppose we do still have some wealthy Russians living in London these days. I tell you what, we can have a light lunch, we are not busy today, and I think we should just have a general conversation about wines to begin with, that should help you to make your own decisions. If I give you my private number then you can call me if you are having a problem.' The Frenchman's eyes twinkled as he spoke and Anita could not help but smile.

The operation was on and she was learning a lot from Olivier, the wines that would impress those who were not quite so knowledgeable. The last thing she wanted was some so-called expert questioning her authenticity.

'I hope I have helped you *Madame*, do not forget to call me should you have a problem,' said Olivier as they parted company and again Anita noticed the twinkle in his eye.

Walking back to her car she wondered just how covert her operation would prove to be. Only a small group of people from MI6 had any knowledge of where she was going and what she would be doing – and maybe the whole of the Italian Secret Service. They did have a good reputation in parts but the mafia still infiltrated government agencies and what if there was a Russian mole, would someone reveal her real intentions on the superyacht? That was a worry.

The seat belt sign started flashing; Anita fastened hers and leaned back in her seat to gaze out of the aircraft window at the Italian landscape. Naples was just visible in the distance, sitting astride green-brown fields edged by a sparkling azure sea. In a perverse way it made her look forward to her task for she had not visited Italy since her early twenties. In a mood of black humour, she determined to relegate any worries about the mission to the back of her mind, at least in the short term, enjoy the sunshine and gaiety that was Italy.

She was aware of her vulnerability, aware that for long periods she would be on her own and that if she found herself in a tight situation she could not expect much help. The spooks at MI6 had warned her that there was zero possibility of her smuggling a firearm aboard the yacht, even her mobile phone had gone through a sanitisation process. The two GRU men would check everything, scan her for hidden devices and prevent any attempt to communicate with the outside world.. She would indeed be on her own.

At least she had prepared as well as she could spending some time with a communications specialist before leaving London. Her department head had sat with her discussing possibilities, things that might go wrong, what she could do in case of trouble. Their biggest fear was that the superyacht might put to sea for an extended period. Then she would be at her most vulnerable and they would find it almost impossible to help her. Before she could think too much about such a situation she felt the Airbus began its final approach. It wasn't the first time that she had entered the unknown and dangerous world of the spy, she felt the gentle rumble of landing gear extending, the ground was coming ever nearer and she wondered what kind of reception awaited her.

The sharp-eyed Alexie spotted her almost as soon as she emerged from the arrivals building. He still had the car's engine running, and letting out the clutch he drove past the line of waiting cars, pushing in at the front of the queue to the sound of irate taxi drivers' horns. 'They ought to try Moscow on a busy day,' he murmured under his breath just as he drew level with his passenger.

'Hey, Mrs Sims,' he called out from the open car window to the well-dressed woman towing her wheeled suitcase.

Alerted by braying car horns Anita had already turned towards the commotion. She instantly recognised the driver from the intelligence material, Warrant Officer Alexie Popovich of Naval Spetsnaz, the Russian equivalent to the British Special Boat Service, a capable and dangerous man.
The spooks at Langley had found him in their database from selfies taken during the Crimean incursion years previously. Young soldiers with little more to do than take pictures of themselves next to their war booty had made the mistake of sending them to their friends, a mistake Langley and Britain's GCHQ seized upon. The geotagged images had helped to build up a picture of the Russian Special Forces, their movements and the composition and strength of their units. Cross-referencing the geotags had enabled the secret

services to identify Alexie Popovich as one of the Little Green Men involved in the takeover of the Crimean Peninsula. Not so little, thought Anita as she began to cross the road.

'I have come to take you to the Lady Galina, here give me your case,' he said, climbing out of the car.

'It's nice to have a bit of sunshine at last,' she said, making conversation, but there was no reaction from Alexie and for the next half hour she sat in silence looking out of the car window as the car swept along the coastal road towards the port.

So this was her brief summer holiday, watching the outskirts of Naples flash past – if it was, then she might as well try to enjoy it. According to the signposts the car was heading for Pompeii; through one window the azure sea of the Amalfi coast filled her field of view and there through another the towering edifice of Mount Vesuvius. It left her feeling a tinge of regret that there would be no summer holiday, instead she had placed herself in danger and now she hoped that the volcano would not erupt to compound that danger.

The town of Pompeii itself became visible and within ten minutes the car reached the marina gate. Passing through Alexie drove along the quay and now Anita could see first-hand the impressive lines of the yacht They came to a halt and Anita stepped out to admire the wide expanse of the Lady Galina. For a minute she stood looking up; no one could fail to be impressed by the superyacht. A metre or two away, after retrieving her case, Alexie produced a shortwave radio and called to someone on board.

'Lady Galina, security two over.'

The radio fizzed into life.

'Lady Galina, permission to come aboard.'

The reply was short and in the affirmative.

The security *was* tight, realised Anita; she would need to be careful. Then, to her surprise, a panel on the boat's hull began to move, detaching itself, swinging sideways to reveal a deck hand in a crisp white uniform. From the confines of the interior she saw a mechanical device begin to unfold, a very modern gangplank that slowly snaked out towards the quayside. Skilfully manoeuvring the slowly extending floor the deck hand brought it to rest just on the dock.

'You follow me; I will take your case to your cabin,' said Alexie. 'You must first see the purser with your papers and then the housekeeper. She is in charge of all the domestic staff, but first we need to check you for anything we do not like and inform you of security obligations. This is a sensitive area, the whole of the vessel.'

'I am sorry, what do you mean?' asked a surprised-sounding Anita.

'Mr Borisovich is a rich man and he has important connections. We do not want journalists or somebody who might take unauthorised pictures and maybe try to blackmail him. Viktor here will check you out and explain the restrictions aboard that you must obey,' he said as a second man appeared from the yacht interior.

Viktor was even bigger than Alexie, and Anita inwardly shuddered at the thought of having to take both of them on but then of course the idea was not to find herself in such a position.

'Phone please,' said Viktor in a thick Slavic accent.

Avoiding his eyes, Anita produced her mobile telephone and handed it to him. Then the big man asked her open her small suitcase.

Anita obeyed, running the zip far enough around for him to peer inside and for thirty seconds he rummaged through her clothes and make-up bag. Then, as one last precaution, he produced a small device, scanned both her and the bag for electronic bugs and finding none grunted with what seemed like disappointment.

'You are clean,' said Alexie, watching closely. 'Your phone will be returned to you when you leave the boat. For security, no one carries a mobile here. Now take this paper, it tells what you must not do, and if you need to go ashore you ask Viktor or me first. Do you understand? Okay, follow me, I will take you to the purser then you meet the housekeeper.'

Anita hurriedly zipped up her case, picked it up and followed the Russian to a small office further along the corridor. He rapped on the door, pushed it open and invited Anita to step inside where a man in a white uniform looked up from his computer.

The Sommelier

'Mr Anderson, this is the new crew member, Mrs Sims, check her papers and sign her on then I want you to introduce her to the housekeeper.'

The man nodded, gesturing to Anita to take a seat.

'Good afternoon, I am the purser and my name is Colin. Have you your papers of engagement and passport?'

Anita reached inside her jacket and took out her passport and the letter of introduction from Jarred Imperial.

'Thank you, just need to check one or two things and then I can print out a contract of employment. You will need to sign two copies, one month initially I believe?'

'Yes, a month was what I agreed to.'

'Good, then all is in order. I see you have good references, just what we need to bring the ship's complement up to strength. There are twenty crew aboard the yacht divided into two watches but your job is unique. You will be required to work as and when needed and, on occasion, work long hours. When guests are aboard, they can be very demanding. I see you have the security notes, it is important to adhere to the procedures laid down. The two men you have already met oversee day-to-day running and I warn you now not to cross them. Okay, I will call for one of the female stewards to come and take you to meet the housekeeper.'

The Sommelier

He picked up the telephone on his desk and after a brief conversation told her someone was coming to collect her.

Having never been on a superyacht before Anita could not help but admire the sheer luxury. Dark and highly polished woodwork together with white leather upholstery seemed to be everywhere and the spaciousness of it all astounded her. However, she was not here to admire the vessel's architecture, instead, she was here to gather intelligence.

The housekeeper was a tall blonde-haired woman with china-blue eyes, probably in her mid-thirties, looked physically fit and to Anita she oozed Russian state security. It fitted of course; if Bullseye was working with the Russian Secret Service, it seemed only natural that he would have some of their people in place.

'So you come to work with us as sommelier, Mrs Sims, I think?'

'Yes, that's right, the agency sent me.'

'I know, agency from London. Mr Borisovich expects the highest standards from his staff. You must remember that. Come, I will show you to your cabin and then I give you one hour to rest and freshen up after your journey. My name is Olga by the way.'

'Pleased to meet you ma'am.'

'Well, you work hard and you make the owner happy and we are all happy but I warn you we not stand for sloppy work.'

The Sommelier

Anita was getting the picture, the people in charge were strict, running things in a semi-military manner, and she wondered how the civilian crew were taking it. They were probably happy enough to put up with it considering the size of their salaries.

'Come, I show you your cabin. In one hour you come to the dining room for me to show you your duties.'

Following Olga past private cabins and down a steep spiral staircase, the women finally reached a narrow corridor. Here the staff cabins were small with just a narrow bunk bed, integral shower unit and the minimum of furniture, very different from the spacious luxury of the owner and his guests.

'This is shower, use it carefully, one girl was sacked because she let it flood her cabin.' Swinging open a door, Olga revealed a tiny wardrobe. 'You can put your clothes in here and look, this is your uniform. Mr Borisovich expects the highest standards especially when he has important guests. You should wear just a little make-up and you will have a clean blouse every day delivered outside your cabin door. Try this uniform on and I will see you in the dining room.'

As Anita started to unpack she took in her surroundings, the porthole was no more than the size of a side plate and definitely no escape route. Removing her travel clothes, she turned on the shower and for the next fifteen minutes let the warm water splash over her. Feeling relaxed, the grubbiness of her journey removed, she wrapped a towel around her and after taking the uniform from the closet tried it on. The white blouse with its blue and gold epaulettes and the navy skirt fitted her well, figure-hugging but not too tight and for a minute or two she admired herself in the mirror, before brushing back her dark wavy hair, and following Olga's advice, applied just a hint of lipstick.

Chapter 8

Exactly an hour after Olga had left her Anita walked through double glass doors and into the dining room. There were two occupants, one a young woman carefully laying the large oval table with highly polished silver cutlery, and Olga arranging flowers.

'Ah, you are here and punctual I see,' she said looking up, 'and you are presentable. Mr Borisovich will be pleased I am sure. I understand that as well as serving drinks you are to source the wines if we need to restock the cellar. The girl you are replacing was not so good but she had the owner's eye and got away with it. I prefer someone who knows wines rather than a tart. You do not look a tart so tell me, what wine should we serve tonight with the smoked salmon and caviar starter and the main course of fillet steak and wild mushroom?'

Though taken a little by surprise, Anita quickly recovered and remembering Olivier Rousset's advice said: 'Off the top of my head I would recommend a Pinot Noir with the starter, and as we are in Italy I would recommend a Nebbiolo for the main course, a Barolo or a Barbaresco perhaps.'

Olga's eyes narrowed. 'An improvement on the last girl I think, maybe I should introduce you to the chef and he can show you the wine cellar. Come, we will go to the galley.'

Olga gave some instruction to the girl setting the table before walking briskly towards the far end of the room, closely followed by Anita. They descended a staircase and once they reached the lower deck walked towards a set of double doors and into the galley. The yacht's food preparation area was impressive and would not be out of place in a five star hotel. It took Anita by surprise yet it should not have, she had already experienced some of the yacht's high standard of design and workmanship. The first thing she became aware of was the noise level, a radical change from the calm throughout the rest of the boat, but she had to admit that the level of cleanliness was impressive.

From across the galley the chef looked up from his work, and Anita instantly recognized his Frenchness, a thin moustache and his *toque blanche* tilted at a slight angle.

Olga called to him. 'Pierre, I want you to meet your new sommelier.'

The man stopped work, wiped his hands and looked Anita over as he approached.

'Pierre this is Mrs Sims . . . you have a first name?'

'Er yes, Anne,' said Anita.

'Pierre this is Anne, she is taking over until the Romanian girl recovers. Perhaps she can add a bit of class to your establishment.'

Pierre's expression did not change; if Olga's comment was a reflection on him he did not show it but instead took Anita's hand, kissing it in the Gallic way.

'*Enchanté madame*, welcome to my kitchen.'

His eyes lingered and inwardly Anita felt flattered by the attention but flirting was not part of her remit.

'Pleased to meet you, *Monsieur*.'

She withdrew her hand and looked at Olga who glanced up at the ceiling as if mystified by the French chef's antics.

'Now the introductions are over I will leave Anne with you Pierre, make sure she wears the correct clothing in here will you?'

'Of course, madam, do I not run a hygienic kitchen?'

Olga did not answer as she walked away, content in the knowledge that she had ruffled his feathers.

'So you are a sommelier, you have qualifications for this work?'

'Yes, I trained with the Court of Master Sommeliers in London,' she lied, relieved to note that he appeared satisfied. She hoped Olivier Rousset's advice would stand her in good stead; the last thing she wanted was exposure as a fraud before she had even got started.

'Then you come with the best recommendation and if the boss thinks you are suitable then who am I to question your appointment. However, let me put one thing straight madam, this is my kitchen and I run it my way. I reserve the right to overrule your recommendations should I deem it necessary. The Romanian girl was competent but no sommelier and it was always my choice of wine served at table. I never have complaints.'

'Of course chef,' said Anita feeling somewhat relieved. If Pierre wanted to control things, then that was fine because it meant that there would be less chance of her making a fatal mistake.

'You will need a white coat and cap, come we will get you them and then I show you the wine cellar.'

From his office window in the Lubyanka building Igor Andresov looked out across the square towards the seven-lane highway filled with Muscovites' cars. Moscow was busy, the sanctions had worked to begin with but the country had got back on its feet, the oil price had returned to its peak and Russians were becoming more productive. Who needs America now? he thought. The consensus was that the new century would belong to China but the way things were going they would have to share that accolade with Russia.

At the far side of the square he could make out the towering cranes working on yet another high-rise building, a sign that the country was growing richer in spite of the American sanctions. The

Saudis had decided to reduce production, which had helped the oil price, and with the discovery of vast new gas deposits in Siberia and the Russian Far East the country's finances were returning to pre-crisis levels. On the political front the incursion into the Crimea had paid off and now the whole of Ukraine was back under Russian influence; food supplies were plentiful and the industry that once supported the Soviet Union was again churning out steel and machinery for the motherland.

He had played no little part in the country's success, obtaining classified American files through his network of spies. The files had provided a gold mine of secret information ranging from banking to aerospace and from that Russia had upped its game. The new stealth fighter was operational and could match anything NATO could throw at them except the F-35, a possible problem.

Igor sat back in his chair and folded his arms, a pose he often took when deep in thought. His rank was now as high as it could be before joining the inner circle of the Kremlin and he knew how important he was to one man on the Politburo. He had already made the most important decision of his life, aligning his loyalty with him, the man the president would support in taking over from him. The plan was never one of revolution, more evolution, a slow and methodical transfer of power, avoiding a vacuum when the president finally stepped down. If handled badly, the country could tear itself apart and the gains of the previous decade be washed away like the melting snow.

Most of the generals, admirals and heads of the security services were ready for that transition – a risk, for the president might change his mind. He had before and if that were to happen then there could be trouble and possibly bloodshed, but the event was still over a year away. Across the Atlantic, the Americans too were beginning their own political manoeuvrings to replace their president and from Igor's perspective, it did appear that interesting times were just over the horizon. He was a survivor and wanted to be on the winning side.

Taking a deep breath as his thoughts receded; he picked up the classified document lying on his desk. The Russian population were always in favour of a strong leader and if the plan the document referred to came to fruition then the man who could carry it out would have their support. Igor read it once more, contemplating possible ramifications before walking over to the document shredder.

At the same time, almost five thousand miles away in Rockville, a half-awake Rosemary filled two cups with fresh coffee. She had worked late every day for almost a month and fatigue was beginning to set in. She yawned, picked up the cups and carried them to the breakfast table where John was busy checking messages on his mobile phone.

'Anything I should know John?'

'Hmm . . . looks as if the last of the battle fleet has put to sea. They really are coming home.'

'It's a sad day for us *and* the Europeans.'

'It sure is, nearly eighty years of peace and security aided by the Sixth Fleet and now we are letting the Russians have free range. It's madness don't you think?' said her husband.

'Yes, madness, but then the skirmish with the Chinese in the South China Sea was madness too. That could have started world war three.'

'Thank God it did not happen, it simply served to focus minds and as a result, we are all but abandoning Europe and focusing the carrier fleets eastwards. The president believes that the Europeans should look to their own security instead of relying on us all the time. NATO exists in name only these days, he says, and the British and the French have competent navies so they should manage to take care of the Russians,' said John.

'Can they though? The French carrier, *Charles de Gaulle*, is just about obsolete and they have no more than half a dozen competent surface ships. As for the British, apart from their new carriers they have only a few guided missile destroyers and a dozen or so frigates, while the Russian fleets have around two hundred warships and seventy subs. I know they have maintenance problems and probably a large proportion of their ships are not fit for active service but still it is a worrying situation.'

'Very worrying Rosemary, the sooner the Brits can get their new carriers into service the better.'

by the way how's the European theatre doing? I have a meeting starting at ten to discuss the apparent build-up of Russian troops along the northern border. What can you tell me?'

'Not a lot at the moment John, let's get to Langley where we know it's secure and I will fill you in on what I know.'

Her husband nodded and sipped at his coffee, aware that even their home could be bugged. His wife's timely reminder that they could not consider anywhere one hundred per cent secure helped solidify the notion that the Russians were dangerous and clever. If some security issues were developing then they needed to get to the underlying cause, maybe convince POTUS to turn the fleet around and send it back to Naples.

'You about ready Rosemary?'

'Yes, we had better travel separately today because I do not know what time I will be coming home tonight.'

John was the first to leave and within minutes was driving onto the freeway, Rosemary followed a few minutes later, alert now and with her mind focused on the jobs in hand. An intelligence avalanche was beginning to overwhelm her and her colleagues, Russian troop movements, terrorist activity and aerial recognisance. Unravelling the various strands to try to form a clear picture was time consuming and at times tedious. The vast volume of signals traffic and wide-area motion imagery would take a normal person an age to decipher but she had Sarah to help her. After feeding in much of the information the powerful 'Pattern of life' analytical program she had helped develop would predict possible outcomes and that would be useful in seeing the bigger picture.

In times of crisis the staff at Langley and associated agencies would have to work long hours, using a wide range of techniques developed to assimilate intelligence. Rosemary knew that today there was a good chance incoming intelligence would inundate her but she had to get out a report for her husband's committee. They would discuss that and other sources of intelligence, develop an overview to advise the White House. Although the committee was just two steps away from the president, the volatile nature of his personality could not be underestimated. A false picture could create a situation with far-reaching and dangerous consequences.

Ahead of her, John Pennington had already parked his car and was just entering the European wing, first stopping off at the coffee machine. Taking the cup from the machine, he passed the desks of his staffers, stopping briefly to ask one of them a few questions and then, as he half expected, he found a yeoman signaller waiting for him near his office.

'Morning Ensign, what have you got for me?'

'Signals come in during the night sir, they are grouped by security classification,' said the young naval rating, laying several sealed envelopes on the desk. 'Would you sign for them sir?'

John took out a pen from the inside pocket of his jacket and after checking the envelopes signed the receipt. The rating left and he began to read his mail, mostly intelligence reports from military commands in Europe and signal interceptions from the British GCHQ. When he had finished he filed the low priority ones in his cabinet and the others he used to update his computer files.

Rosemary's morning procedure was little different, after clearing security she too was checking her mail, her half-empty cup on the edge of her desk, and she was wearing a frown. Security wonks at almost all the United States embassies in Europe were reporting increased activity by the Russians, military convoys, bases with increased security, though nothing obvious to the casual observer. She made a few notes, grouped embassies by the amount of traffic the spooks were generating, and before long, she could see that Germany and Poland were seeing some increase but for the Baltic States, it was a lot more.

It came as no surprise, previous reports had detailed an increase in Russian troop movements and of course there was the disappearance of the First Tank Army from Moscow. Running her finger across the computer monitor, she selected the file on the Baltic states and looked for updates for the past twenty-four hours. It seemed that someone had made the decision to assign one of the newly launched spy satellites to monitor northern Europe. The reason as stated in a note was that the cluster of civilian satellites were not returning clear enough images, even the decommissioned KH series had returned better images. The new spy in the sky could cover more than half the northern latitudes simultaneously and provide real-time intelligence.

Next, she turned her attention to the morning's emails and found a report from Sarah's department. An analysis of Russian troop movements along the border with the Baltic States and Poland had thrown up a few new nuggets. Then she saw a signal from the Nimitz Operational Intelligence Centre referring to the Russian Northern Fleet ship movements, something she deemed significant, convincing her that the Russians were on the verge of invading northern Europe.

Why would they do that? NATO still had a strong presence in the area; European troops had filled the vacuum created by some American forces returning to the States and the United States Air Force was still operational up to a point. Maybe they were going to try the same tricks they pulled off in Ukraine, a shadow invasion, plausible deniability. Was that it, were they using the American retreat from Europe as an excuse to spread their influence? It was not beyond the realm of possibility but to Rosemary it looked a risky strategy. POTUS had pulled quite a few stunts since his election and had gotten away with them so why would the Russian president not try one of his own. She sat back in her chair and interlocked her fingers, placing her thumbs under her chin as she tried to imagine the scenario, and then she remembered the Arab. Was he a part of a grand strategy, were he and his ilk somehow involved as well? She needed to talk to someone.

The First Tank Army had made good progress, travelling during the hours of darkness to avoid detection; but in the modern world that was not easy. The satellite cluster worked well during daylight hours and those with infrared detection could see the Earth during the hours of darkness, but they had neither the coverage nor the resolution to pick up the tanks' progress. The older KH satellites could but they were hovering over the Middle East and China and the recently launched MX2 was still undergoing calibration, but it *was* getting some results.

The imagery from the new satellite was truly amazing; the high-powered cameras could even discern the brand name on a soldier's cigarette packet from almost three hundred kilometres away in space.

Russian soldiers smoked a lot, too much according to the statistics; even the military command had tried to stop the daily ration. Young soldiers finding conscription boring and unable to afford much on their army pay welcomed the free cigarette ration and to withdraw it would create more problems than it solved and so it had persisted. The Russian Army had improved immeasurably in its capabilities during the preceding twenty years but it was still a mainly conscript-driven organisation and they were prone to ill-discipline, particularly when it came to disposing of empty cigarette packets.

Sylvie Parker was not particularly aware of the Russian Army's morale nor the behaviour of its soldiers. But for the past six hours she had pored over the imagery from the satellite. Six hours was a long stretch with only the odd cup of coffee to keep her going but at least she had just managed a proper break, a visit to the bathroom and then the canteen for something to eat.

Feeling refreshed she took her seat in front of the wide-angled monitor and again focused her attention on the image. She had looked it over before taking her break and not noticed anything out of the ordinary. She decided to spend just a few more minutes on it before moving on to the next image in the sequence. Zooming in on an area of road, she noticed a familiar object lying by the roadside, a red and white object. That was the beauty of the new system: colour, vibrant realistic colour, and that helped her immeasurably in the laborious task of searching every square metre of a foreign land.

She reached to the screen and gently drew her finger down the slider, increasing the magnification, and immediately the object of interest became large enough for her to recognise.

'Well, what d'you know, Marlborough cigarettes,' she mumbled to herself. 'They get everywhere.'

Amused by her discovery she zoomed back out again and by chance exposed another discarded packet; intrigued, she zoomed back in to find yet another. Sylvie had been in the job long enough to know that three identical items in a small area proved nothing but something was telling her that it was not so in this case. For several minutes longer she examined the image and was about to leave it when she noticed a wheel track, a deep track made only by a vehicle carrying a heavy load. Perhaps it was a construction crew moving heavy plant.

For several minutes, she sat looking at the screen, panning along the road looking for more tracks, but for once the Russians had made a proper job of resurfacing the highway. Sylvie was not wholly convinced that she had found anything of significance but still felt it was worth flagging and so she picked up her desk phone and called the section leader.

'Might just be a lorry stop, maybe it is a construction crew or several vehicles in convoy,' said the supervisor, scratching his head. 'You think the cigarette packets are significant Sylvie?'

'Well maybe. To find three identical packets points to an organisation rather than individuals. I may have got it wrong but that's why I called you.'

'I tend to agree with you, I'll get on to the science team and ask them to have a look. If you are right there will be a few more of these Marlborough packets around.'

Sylvie nodded and thanked the supervisor feeling pleased to know those at the top were taking her observation seriously.

Rosemary had not even left for her meeting with the department's director when the message arrived. It was obviously important for it was hand delivered and she had to sign for it. Slitting open the envelope, she retrieved the single sheet of paper and read the message.

'Bingo, they have found the missing tanks and it appears they are on their way to the Polish border.'

The boffins in imagery analysis had conjured up a search routine and turned it loose on the sequence of images. The focus of the search was Marlborough cigarette packets and one by one the program had found them, lots of them, discarded along many kilometres of road. The program had logged their positions, like the footprints of a prey animal, and like the hunter it had followed the trail.

It was clear from early on that it was probably a tank regiment on the move and a team of analysts was set to work gathering more evidence. They broke the route up into sections, began a minute search, and before long the first tank appeared. A sharp-eyed analyst managed to spot a gun barrel protruding from under a camouflage net narrowing the search area to reveal many more tanks.

Rosemary was relieved that the search for the First Tank Regiment was delivering results. The regiment was fully equipped with the new Armata T-

14 tank, believed by NATO planners to pose a particular threat. To move such a powerful regiment in secrecy was nothing new but the trail was leading to northern European borders, a worrying build-up of Russian capabilities. Stacking a few of the papers she needed and adding this new information, she called the head of the department.

He was waiting for her at his open office door and once he had closed it behind her, she told him that she believed that she had found something of significance. She felt that she had hard evidence that the Russians were massing on the borders of the Baltic States and Poland and that it was more than just war games.

'Interesting Rosemary, you appear to have made a thorough analysis of the situation as you see it and I commend you for that. But do we really believe that the Russians will invade Europe? Ever since the end of the Second World War we have half expected them to, but our system of deterrence prevented it.'

'Until now; our retreat from Europe has, in my view, emboldened them sir.'

'Hmm . . . it looks serious I will give you that. I think we should kick this one upstairs. I will contact the steering committee and ask for an immediate hearing. You ready to convince the Director of Russian and European Intelligence?'

'Certainly am sir.'

Rosemary had one heck of a reputation within CIA, her take on situations was insightful but where she really scored was in her thoroughness and the evidence she could produce. He picked up the green telephone and made the call. Replacing the receiver, and looking Rosemary in the eye, he said.

'Two o'clock, the director himself will chair the meeting. Anything else we need?'

'Not at this stage sir. Once they understand the situation more fully I am sure I will be called upon to furnish more information and I will work on that, but in the meantime let me put my case.'

Three hours later Rosemary and the head of the department were sitting at the large table in the meeting room on the fourth floor overlooking the vast car park. Sitting across from them were the Director of Russian and European Intelligence, his deputy, two specialists from the department and a secretary to take the minutes of the meeting.

'First let me welcome you all here this afternoon. As you already know I am Director Linley, on my right Deputy Director MacBain, Tom Hatcher from SIGINT, and Keith Andrews of DCGS, the drone surveillance arm of CIA. For your enlightenment gentlemen we have here department head Vince Criscioni, and Rosemary Pennington, one of our most capable analysts.'

'Would you like to start Vince?'

'Yes sir. Rosemary came to see me a couple of hours ago with rather disturbing news and I felt it was a matter for this committee.'

Criscioni went on to describe his meeting with Rosemary and the results of their discussion, stating that he believed her assessment credible. Then it was Rosemary's turn to present her case plus the analysis from imagery intelligence regarding the movements of the First Tank Army. Director Linley pursed his lips and after a pause invited Tom Hatcher from signals intelligence to speak.

'We have noticed a build-up of Russian military signals traffic over the past month, we have identified most of the units and where they are stationed. Here is a map of the area in question showing military emplacements at the beginning of the year and as of yesterday. You can see quite clearly where they have strengthened their line and see how it abuts the Baltic states and Poland. With the addition of a tank regiment, these troops will shortly achieve superiority over NATO. If I can add, I find that worrying particularly when viewed in the context of previous Russian adventures. The pattern looks familiar.'

'Keith, what can you tell us about our low-level surveillance?'

'No more than you have already heard. The drones do not cross any Russian border, it is too dangerous, and we do not want an incident. They get close enough and on a clear day from twenty-five thousand feet an Orion Unmanned Aircraft System can see around two hundred miles into Russian territory. What we are seeing bears out the analysis you have presented,' he said, looking at Rosemary and then Tom Hatcher. 'I have here copies of images taken a few days ago showing several tented areas, possibly temporary bases for their infantry. What does SIGINT tell us Tom?'

'We are fairly sure that is what they will be; agents on the ground report a lot of men in uniform and the signals traffic supports that.'

'So it would seem that your prognosis is correct Rosemary, what we need now is to know how, when and where the Russians will strike, if that is what they intend. I have to say I am not wholly convinced though. Is there anything else you can tell us Rosemary?'

'There is something bothering me but it's only a hunch.' She looked around the table for support to carry on and got it. 'I have been working with the Brits on something that may or may not be connected. It looks as if the Russians might be bankrolling al-Qaeda.'

Across the table, eyebrows were raised, and she noted the questioning looks.

'For several days I have been looking into the movements both past and present of a person of interest. Twenty years ago, we logged him leaving a training camp in northern Iraq, a camp destroyed in a bombing run. A British Special Forces patrol photographed him leaving before the jets arrived and after they destroyed the camp, the patrol searched the remains. They reported that after the F15 attack they noticed a large amount of cash in US dollars scattered about the camp. Ten years later, not long after Islamic State invaded Iraq, a drone spotted him again, this time in an IS controlled area and subsequently intelligence established that he had probably conducted some sort of financial negotiations with that terror group. We know that IS did enter into deals with al-Qaeda, selling oil to them for example, and now he has reappeared.'

Rosemary had gained the full attention of her audience and with hands spread on the table top to add weight to her supposition she continued.

'The man, code named Shadow, popped up several months ago in Istanbul and a spook from the British Embassy followed him. He boarded a superyacht belonging to a Russian with connections to the Kremlin, one Leonid Borisovich who the Brits have christened Bullseye. Bullseye owns the yacht the Lady Galina, an impressive eighty metre vessel. But it has a serious flaw: at such a length, it is difficult to easily find a berth for it and if they need to remain in port there are few marinas with the facilities to handle her. She could berth in an industrial port but in general that would be unacceptable to someone out to impress, and Bullseye seems to fit that category.'

'What about anchoring off some place?' asked Director Linley.

'It is possible sir; the point is that it's not easy to conceal such a vessel. The Brits picked her up because she had switched off her automatic identification transmissions somewhere in the Black Sea. Until then no one had noticed her but the Brits are keen on ship movements and from that moment on they went looking for her. We have a satellite surveillance capability that would soon find her if we so wished.'

'What's the connection with the Russians?'

'Well sir, I believe our friend Shadow is a paymaster for al-Qaeda, funnelling Russian money to terrorist groups.'

'To where, who?'

'We don't know but probably Syria, Iraq and now possibly Europe. MI6 and GCHQ are helping, doing what they can to find out.'

'What do you think the Russians are planning, you must have some idea otherwise you would not be talking like this?'

'It's only a hunch at this stage, but apart from the obvious places in the Middle East I believe that al-Qaeda is planning something in Europe, something spectacular.'

'Like what?'

'I don't know sir. MI6 are taking the threat seriously though and are on the case already.'

'You think we should too? You think we ought to throw some resources at the problem?'

'Well sir that is not for me to say. All I can do is offer advice; the evidence so far points to some connection between the Russians and the terrorists.'

'Is it credible that the Russians would work with terrorists who have operated on their own soil, killed their own citizens?'

Rosemary held Linley's gaze for a few seconds and his expression of mild disbelief turned to one of serious contemplation a realisation taking hold.

'The apartment bombings of '99,' he said, 'you think they are planning terrorist atrocities on Russian soil and to use them to legitimise an invasion of Europe, as they did with Chechnya?'

'Maybe sir, I don't know, I guess anything is possible. There have been bombings and terrorist attacks all across Europe since al-Qaeda and ISIS appeared. Al-Qaeda's mantra is one of attacking the West on home soil; to take the fight to the Americans in America.'

'And the Europeans in Europe, I see your logic Rosemary, this is serious but I will need more convincing if I am to take this to the White House intelligence committee. POTUS has his own ideas and I am afraid that he is a person who listens only when it suits him. I will need hard, indisputable evidence if I am to ask for resources. Do not forget we are pulling away from Europe, the president says they should look after their own security, not the American taxpayer. Get me concrete evidence, find out what's going on over there.'

Chapter 9

Bullseye liked the look of the woman, smartly turned out and with an athletic figure. He liked athletic figures and smiled as he considered the adage that opposites attract. Nowadays his figure was certainly not athletic, not that it ever really was, but in his experience athleticism in a man was not as important as the size of his bank balance, and on that score he could feel confident.

He could smell Anita as she leaned close to pour the wine, she smelled English, faintly perfumed, without the body odour of some eastern European women – probably because English women shaved their armpits, he thought – and as she stood back he cast his eye over her.

'What have we here?'

'A Pinot Noir, a perfect match for the smoked salmon and caviar.'

Bullseye swirled the wine for a second or two, then lifted the glass to his nose experiencing the bouquet, and then took an initial sip.

'That is very good, please fill the glass.'

Anita stepped forward and filling the Russian's glass asked, 'Will there be anything else sir?'

'Not for the moment, you may leave until I am ready for the main course. If the wine you have selected for the steak is as good as this then I will be very happy.'

He picked up the glass, lifted it in mock salute and Anita bowed her head slightly in appreciation before leaving him alone. She had cleared the first hurdle, Bullseye seemed pleased and if she could keep him happy then she might have a chance of getting closer, discovering what he was doing, and with a self-satisfied smile on her face she walked into the galley.

'You look pleased with yourself,' said the French chef. 'The boss must have approved your choice of wine.'

'*Our* choice, you were very helpful Pierre, thank you.'

'You,' he said to the server hovering by the double doors. 'Do not let him see you looking, just a glance now and then to see if the course is finished. Then and only then go out and see if you can clear the plates for the next course.'

The girl moved away from the porthole window, out of Mr Borisovich's sight. She was safe enough, he was facing the large picture window with a view over the sea and he was a slow eater. If she could have seen his face she would have noted that he was deep in thought. Eventually, Bullseye placed his empty glass on the table, half turned and raised his hand, waving the extended index finger to summon the server.

'He's finished chef.'

'Good, you Mrs Sims, you first, see if he wants his glass filling. Let her see to his needs first Mila, and don't forget to check the cutlery is straight.'

The girl gave him a blank stare before turning to look through the window again just as Anita pushed past her and from behind, she heard a steak begin to sizzle on the grill plate.

'Would you like some more of the Pinot Noir sir?' said Anita, standing to his side.

'No, not just now, tell chef I am ready for the next course. What delight do you have in store for me this time Mrs Sims? I can't keep calling you that, what is your name?'

'Anne, Anne Sims.'

'Very English.'

Anita smiled and picked up the ice bucket containing the half-empty bottle of Pinot Noir.

'Would you like the wine for the main course now sir?'

'Yes I would, I am intrigued to know what you have chosen to go with the steak. I hope your choice of red wine is as good as the white.'

Anita took the ice bucket and made her way back to the galley finding it hard to believe that it really was a ship's galley. The yacht was so impressive – spacious, well furnished, the height of luxury – but for all that Bullseye cut a lonely figure. Perhaps he had a girlfriend somewhere, he wasn't married she knew that. Anita pushed the galley door open, made her way past the kitchen staff and went to the climate-controlled wine cellar at the far end. She had already uncorked the bottle and picking it up returned to the galley just as Pierre was spooning his truffle sauce onto the succulent-looking fillet steak and mushroom puree.

'*Voilà*, the sauce is perfect, truffles from France with the best Angus steak. I hope your wine matches my perfection,' he said with a twinkle in his eye.

'A Monforte d'Alba and of course it will complement your food *Monsieur*.'

'I hope you are right, he knows his wines and he is very particular madam.'

Pierre was a very good chef and his sense of humour was not at all cutting, making Anita feel relaxed, but it was not to last. As she placed the bottle of wine onto a silver tray and returned to the dining salon, she saw through the large window the yacht's two security men talking and one gesticulating as if something was amiss. She felt herself tense up but they did not look at her, so maybe she was of no interest to them. That was a relief, but they were dangerous men and it was a warning to be vigilant.

'That is a good full-bodied wine,' said Bullseye, swirling the liquid around his mouth. 'Rather like you,' he added. 'Tell me, is there a Mr Sims?'

'No sir, we divorced several years ago.'

'I could say that I am sorry, but I would not be telling the truth now would I?'

Anita felt herself blush, not with embarrassment but with knowing that maybe she could get closer to this man – even if it did mean performing beyond the call of duty.

'I am glad you are happy with the wine sir and might I say your yacht is quite magnificent.'

'Why thank you,' he said, raising his glass. 'Yes she is rather special, I must admit. Ah . . . here comes my steak. Pierre makes the best steaks I have tasted and this smells delicious.'

The girl Mila arrived at the table with her silver tray to place Bullseye's food in front of him.

'Thank you Mila and you Anne, you may leave me now.'

As he began to eat, the two women left him in peace and walking back to the galley Anita glanced furtively through the large, dining room window. The bodyguards were gone.

The sommelier's work was just about over for the day and for a time Anita stood alone inside the wine cellar, admiring its impressive collection. She guessed that most would have cost one hundred pounds a bottle or more and reflected upon how the oligarch lived. A man with everything, a superyacht, houses in the most fashionable cities in the world, his own private jet . . .

As part of her initial investigation into his affairs, she had researched company records, crosschecking with his known associates, discovering his African mining interests and several companies involved in the construction business. Could they make him so rich, a billionaire? She doubted it, so where was his wealth coming from, was it borrowed money? If it was she could only find a few hundred million in loans, mainly from Russian banks. Did he have another income source or was it an empire built on sand?

Locking the cellar door, she returned to the galley and hung the key back on the rack in the small office.

'I have finished in the wine cellar Pierre. Is it possible for me to leave, I am tired from my journey?'

'Of course, the boss left a clean plate by the way and he finished off the whole bottle of red wine. That's a good sign so long as he doesn't suffer a hangover in the morning.'

'Where is he now?'

'With his two bodyguards, that is what they are; they accompany him everywhere when he goes ashore and when we have guests they pay close attention to them.'

'What about us, do they pay close attention to us?'

'Only if we stray. Let me give you some advice: do not go out on deck without their permission. You will have given up your mobile phone no?'

'Yes, when I came aboard. They scanned me as well, what do you think they were looking for?' she said innocently.

'I don't know, perhaps they worry someone might want to sabotage the ship. It happens, disgruntled employees getting their own back for some real or imagined slight. Keep out of their way; I have seen them in action. When one of the engine room staff became drunk and started shouting abuse they beat him up and threw him onto the dockside together with his belongings. I think they broke his arm but it didn't worry them.'

'Were the police not involved?'

'Of course not, they warned the young man that if he went to the police he would be fish food.'

Anita looked suitably shocked but did not say anything, it was no less than she expected. These were tough individuals without much in the way of scruples, and no doubt, the Russian Ambassador in the country feeling the effects of their endeavours would smooth things over.

She reached the door to her cabin, produced the credit card key and let herself in. She wondered if there were cameras or sound bugs in the room – probably, and to counter them she simply did everything expected of an innocent person. She took a shower, careful to have her robe on hand, and as she dried her hair looked round for signs of entry. There was nothing obvious though she expected they would keep a check on her, the spooks at MI6 had warned her so. As if she needed warning: she had lived the life of a spy long enough to know that nowhere was safe, nowhere was wholly secure. Her only defence was to appear clean, squeaky clean, that she really was a divorced woman making her own living. She looked at her watch; it was ten-thirty. She switched off the light and climbed into the bed and lying motionless allowed her mind to roam free. They could not stop her thinking, scheming and planning, yet if she put a foot wrong, she could be in mortal danger.

Alexie looked up from the screen as Viktor slid the door open to a room out of keeping with the opulence of the rest of the superyacht. It was small and sparsely furnished with no more than two business-style desks and swivel chairs. Large monitors sat on each of the desks and underneath powerful computers and communications equipment went quietly about their business. This was the communications and surveillance centre of the vessel and for all the spaciousness of the main living quarters, the room was a tight squeeze for the two GRU men.

'Anything Alexie?'

'No, she seems normal enough,' said the big man watching Anita. He had seen her enter and take her shower. He had found that entertaining to a point but he was a professional. 'She is sleeping; we can keep an eye on her tomorrow.'

'What about the rest of the crew, any problems there?'

'No, they are docile enough, the French chef can be a bit of a nuisance now and again but I give him a warning to stop going on deck for cigarette without our supervision. The boss does not like his staff smoking at the best of times but tolerates it; my worry is that the chef might see something he should not. It would be a shame to break his neck and then have to suffer second-rate food. It would be like living in barracks again.'

Viktor grunted at his fellow soldier's black humour. That was one of the benefits of taking care of Mr Borisovich's security; the food on board was first class.

'We have a visitor tomorrow, the Arab.'

'How much will he take this time?'

'State secret Alexie, if I tell you I have to kill you.'

'Don't joke about that,' said a slightly subdued Alexie who was well aware of his comrade's capabilities in that area.

'Sorry, I make bad joke, too many Western spy films. There is two hundred thousand dollars in fifty and one hundred dollar bills, easier to carry.'

'Does the captain know to keep his men away from the saloon?'

'Yes, I told him and the first officer that the pickup is tomorrow afternoon and we don't want prying eyes.'

'I don't trust navy men, they are not as security conscious as they should be.'

'Maybe they are too busy sailing their ships.'

Alexie shrugged his shoulders, having navy men aboard was unavoidable and it was preferable to have them sail the yacht than civilians.

The Sommelier

Yusuf passed through the airport security system
relieved the biometrics did not set off any alarms. At
least he could relax in the knowledge that he was
unknown to the authorities. He was still taking a
risk though but it was one he was prepared to take.
To avoid the overland route was a sensible option
for not only was it arduous but also a far more
dangerous proposition. Only months before, the
Turkish Government had cracked down on the
rebellious Kurds, a battle-hardened and well-armed
element ready to fight government troops, and that
made overland travel a risky business. For Yusuf any
disruption was unacceptable and so he decided to
take the risk of flying into Italy, a country he had not
set foot in for many years.

During the late nineties, he had studied civil
engineering in Britain in the hope of returning home
to build a better future. It was a noble enterprise but
politics and the Americans got in the way. After
gaining his degree, he started his career with a
multinational corporation building roads and for a
time worked in both France and Italy. During his
time in France, he met a group of young Arab
radicals, spending time in prayer and conversation
with them.

A strict upbringing had taught him the
importance of the Prophet to Muslim life and during
one of the Arab-Israeli conflicts, bombarded by
hourly news bulletins; these new friends had
convinced him to take the path he now trod.

The Sommelier

At times, this new life had been hard to bear, many friends had fallen by the wayside, but he had shown his worth and now the organisation had bestowed upon him the honour of paymaster. For some time he had moved surreptitiously around the Middle East, he was transferring his skills to Europe. It was the desire of the ruling council that the Muslim population should become strong enough to wrest control from the Christians and he was to help facilitate that goal.

Anita first noticed the tall, good-looking man walking towards the gangplank. To the untrained eye he could easily have passed as a southern European dressed as he was in Western clothes, but Anita had a trained eye and she had studied that same face on historic intelligence photographs. She caught no more than just a fleeting glimpse from the saloon window before Viktor escorted him aboard. She craned her neck for a better view but on the deck below, he was shepherded from sight to be frisked for hidden weapons.

'He is clean.'

'Good, let us take him to his cabin,' said the watching Alexie. 'I trust that you have had a good journey my friend?'

'Yes, though it was not without danger.'

'Indeed, would you like a drink, coffee perhaps?'

'That would be nice; I have not had a good strong coffee since I left Lebanon.'

'You flew this time we understand?'

'It is better than having to run the gauntlet through Syria and Turkey. Flying is quicker but dangerous. I took a chance but no one stopped me, no one questioned me, and I will not be flying again, I live in Europe now.'

'Come my friend, give your bag to Viktor and we will take you to the cabin you can use while you are here. You will not leave it unless one of us accompanies you, you understand. In the meantime I will call the galley and have them send some food and coffee.'

Yusuf stepped into the room and dropped his holdall onto the bed and the two GRU left him alone until he heard a tap on the door.

'Who is there,' he said in mild alarm, a condition born of years of living on his wits.

'Coffee sir, the chef has sent me to deliver coffee and some food.'

Yusuf relaxed a little at the sound of a female voice and opened the door just enough to see a smartly dressed woman holding a silver tray.

'Coffee, good, I hope it is strong.'

'Yes sir, that was the instruction. Shall I put the tray on the table?' said Anita, encouraging him to open the door wider.

She had heard the chef speaking on the internal telephone system and had taken her chance offering to deliver the refreshments.

'Yes, that will do there on the table.'

Anita put down the tray and from the corner of her eye managed a brief glance at Yusuf. He was a big man, not muscular like the two security men, and appeared more thoughtful, he was Shadow for sure.

Anita did not see Shadow again, she did not even see him leave the yacht, and as the sun began to set Bullseye summoned her to the saloon.

'Ah Anne, I want you to find me a nice bottle of red, perhaps a St Emilion. Bring it to the master suite in half an hour.'

'Yes sir,' said Anita, turning away, unaware of Bullseye's gaze.

Leonid found her attractive, not as attractive as the Romanian perhaps, the sommelier was older, but she had class. He watched her leave and walked out onto the open deck for one last look over the bay of Naples. A stunning panorama illuminated by the light of the setting sun, and in the distance Vesuvius provided a spectacular backdrop. The day had proved interesting; Alexie had informed him that their visitor had left the yacht.

He knew enough of what they were doing to find him implicated should the authorities discover what was going on. That worried him, but if it was the will of his masters in the Kremlin then he would have to live with it. They had promised him concessions in the Middle East and Africa and he was not about to lose the chance to expand his business empire. Oman's production of chromite had increased dramatically over the past five years, and with Russia's newfound political strength in the region he was in line to become a major supplier of the mineral. The stakes were high, Russia was emerging stronger and with more influence than it had for years and he stood to benefit.

Draining his glass he took one last look at the setting sun and left for his cabin, and two decks below Anita searched the cellar for the bottle of the 2010 St Emilion.

'I see you are still working,' said a French accented voice from behind her.

It was Pierre, a hesitation in his speech causing her to turn towards him.

'Yes chef, the boss wants a bottle of St Emilion for his cabin,' said Anita taken aback by Pierre. 'What's the matter chef, you look bothered about something?'

'Madam I feel that I must speak freely to you. It may be nothing and perhaps I am making a fool of myself but you are not the first to serve wine in the master suite. I know a little of what might happen when you are alone with him. And please do not mention to anyone what I am about to tell you.'

Ten minutes later, a thoughtful Anita tapped lightly on the stateroom door, chewing the inside of her lip as she waited for Bullseye. Pierre was a sweet man and she appreciated his concern but she was well aware of who she was dealing with and was prepared for his advances. The department had run a thorough check on Bullseye, discovering early on that he could be a sex pest. Stories had emerged of some of his dealings in both London and New York where several women had made complaints only to withdraw their accusations days later. To any sensible person it seemed abundantly clear that he was paying for their silence.

'Ah, come in my dear,' said Bullseye opening the door. 'Put the tray on the table over there.'

Anita stepped forward bemused by his appearance. He was dressed in only a white flannel dressing gown, his legs naked from the knees down, and his reptilian smile made it hard for her to feel anything but tense.

'You can pour me a drink; have one yourself, you deserve it for all the hard work you have put in since joining the Lady Galina. Here I will fetch another glass.'

He sidestepped Anita, his bare feet gliding silently across the luxurious carpet towards the small bar. Reaching up to a shelf, he grasped an upturned wine glass and waited for Anita to come to him. She understood perfectly the technique, he would slowly begin to dominate her, entice her into his web and then pounce. She felt the hairs on the back of her neck begin to rise, felt tightness in her abdomen and her adrenaline began to flow.

'You have a corkscrew?'

'Yes,' she said, retrieving it from her skirt pocket.

'Here, let me help you,' said Bullseye, placing his hand over hers.

She did not react; instead, she flicked open the corkscrew and began to remove the metal foil.

'Go ahead; I will help you hold the bottle steady.'

'Er, thank you sir. I can manage you know, really I can manage.'

'But it is so much easier if I help you.'

Anita was beginning to feel nauseous; close up and wearing nothing more than his short dressing gown, he was quite a repulsive man. She knew it was futile to resist; she must play along with his little game and taking hold of the bottle, she deftly scored the foil and peeled it away. Bullseye released his grip, his small dark eyes looking into hers.

'Teamwork my dear, teamwork, it is so much easier working together don't you think?'

'Yes sir,' she said, working the cork out but not before tilting the bottle as the cork made its noisy exit, splashing some of the red wine on Leonid's sleeve.

'*Der'mo*,' he retorted, pulling his arm away. 'What a mess you . . .' He stopped himself short, not wanting to alarm his prey. 'Oh never mind, it is just a stain, but I must soak it in some water before the garment is ruined. Wait here while I visit the bathroom for a minute.'

He gave her a dismissive glance and turned to cross the spacious living room to the bathroom. Anita watched him go and scanned the room for anything useful, her eyes alighting on a writing bureau where several sheets of paper lay. Convincing herself that Bullseye was not about to re-enter the room she sifted through the printed pages, finding a list of European cities and dates in

201

the past and the near future. Then she felt, rather than heard, Bullseye begin to open the bathroom door and with the agility of an Olympic gymnast returned to the bar before he had the chance to catch her spying on his private papers.

'Ah, my dear, pour me another drink will you?'

Anita took a deep breath and turned towards him, surprised to see that he was all smiles but more than that he was wearing nothing but a pair of skimpy pants.

'Certainly sir, I will bring it to you.'

'No need I can help you.' She knew the moment had come.

'I will use a fresh glass sir,' she said walking behind the bar.

She had only seconds and turning her back on him felt in her skirt pocket for the capsule. Grasping it, she reached with her free hand to the shelf to retrieve clean glasses. Behind her Bullseye savoured her figure, his eyes following her hand as it reached up, not noticing her put something in her mouth.

The capsule was a present from Pierre, a garlic concentrate for use in some of his dishes. She let it roll between her teeth, biting on it, forcing the plastic membrane to give way and allowing the contents to wash around her mouth. The taste was as repulsive as she had expected and she hoped that her admirer would feel the same. Taking the bottle, she filled a glass and Bullseye took several steps towards her.

'Please, pour yourself one, I do not wish to drink alone tonight.'

Hesitantly Anita poured just a thimbleful into the second glass, and as Leonid raised his glass, she did the same.

'We must drink as Russians, here put your arm through mine,' he said, guiding her glass over his, intertwining his arm with her own.

Those small dark eyes met hers once again leaving her feeling decidedly uncomfortable, but she had little choice but to go along with him. Leonid leaned towards her, attempted a clumsy kiss, pressing his lips against hers expecting her to yield but instead she exhaled and he recoiled in disgust. If he had expected the perfume of love, he was disappointed. The capsule achieved quite the opposite of a breath freshener, the decidedly repugnant odour of someone with a health problem.

In an instant, his ardour cooled and finding himself in a compromising state of undress his overriding reaction was to get rid of her as quickly as he could. Releasing her from his grip, his seduction thwarted, his face became angry and he gestured for her to leave. Without a word, Anita headed for the door, pausing at the last minute to say, 'I am sorry if I have caused any inconvenience sir but I have been feeling a little unwell of late.'

Bullseye waved her away and taking the opportunity to escape she left the master suite and hurried towards the staircase observed by Alexie and Viktor watching her movements on the security monitor.

'Mr Borisovich left instructions not to be disturbed this evening Viktor, and yet here is the sommelier leaving his suite after no more than fifteen minutes.'

'Fifteen minutes with her would be enough I think,' grunted the second GRU man, watching the security screens. 'Perhaps there is a problem. Look, she does not seem too well. What do you think?'

'Yes, she is walking a little awkwardly but I have not noticed anything odd about her until now.'

'Maybe she has women's problems, it hits them like that I think.'

'Perhaps the boss should have consulted her star chart. What a shame, she is an attractive woman and we know how generous he can be when he has had a good night. Maybe the Romanian girl Nicoletta will be back soon and he can have his fun.'

Chapter 10

Early the following morning Anita left her cabin, the lingering taste of garlic eclipsing the beauty of the view across the bay. Her experience of the previous evening weighed on her mind, would Bullseye react negatively towards her, perhaps dismiss her before she had even begun to penetrate the mystery of the Lady Galina?

'Good morning madam,' said Pierre as she walked into his galley. 'I hope last night was not too traumatic for you.'

His eyes, serious yet friendly, elicited a brief reply.

'The present you gave me worked well. Thank you.'

'You can only use that trick once. In future you will be on your own I think.'

Anita pursed her lips and nodded.

'He is in the dining room awaiting his breakfast. Do you want to serve him? It might be a good idea as he does not like to be snubbed.'

'Okay, I will take his orange juice and his coffee.'

She knew that she would have to face Bullseye eventually and perhaps it was best to get it over with, see where she stood.

'Ah . . . Anne, you are better this morning?' said Leonid in a friendly enough tone.

'Yes sir, I was ill during the night but I feel much better now thank you,' she said, wondering what he was really thinking.

'Good good. Has the purser spoken to you about several guests arriving on board in a few days' time? Not here though, the yacht will be sailing for Savona later this morning. I am leaving shortly on business and will re-join the yacht with my guests, Russian nationals who will require entertaining in the Russian way. You have some experience I recall.'

'Yes sir, should I have any special drinks available for them?'

'Just the usual, I think a bottle or two of the Barolo you served before would be nice. Do you have any in the cellar?'

Anita thought quickly about the wine, or lack of it, and wondered how she might turn the situation to advantage.

'If I may be so bold sir, if we are going to Savona then we are not far from the vineyards of the Barbaresco region. I could visit several of them in one day and perhaps find a special wine for your guests.'

Leonid fell silent for a few moments while Anita filled his glass with orange juice from the pitcher. He remained quiet, thoughtful, before saying, 'That

is an idea. I shall be leaving before midday, I will tell
Alexie to accompany you there in the BMW and
when I return with my guests, perhaps you can
impress them and we can have another drink
together. You would be foolish to spurn me. I am a
very rich man and I will make it worthwhile,' he said
lowering his tone.

'That is kind of you sir, I will consider your offer.
If there is nothing else I will leave you to enjoy your
breakfast.'

Leonid gave her a half-smile, and lifted his glass
of orange juice in a mock salute, confident that he
would be more successful next time, and Anita,
walking away realised that the game was not over
yet.

After motoring through the night and most of the
following day the Lady Galina finally picked up her
moorings in the busy port of Savona. It was a bright
cool evening when the yacht's crew finally finished
their work and were able to relax. Anita had made
brief acquaintance with one or two of the female
crew and now she joined them in the crew mess.

'Hi, I'm Lynn; I see you are replacing Nicoletta.
She has appendicitis I understand.'

Anita looked up from the magazine she was
reading.

'So I understand and yes I am her replacement,
temporarily might I add.'

'Do you want a coke; I am just going to get one
for myself? No alcohol I am afraid. They do not like

us drinking with guests on board. Can't see that it matters right now as there will not be any guests for another two days if my information is correct.'

Anita smiled, 'A drink would be very welcome, thank you.'

'Here you are me duck, you don't mind drinking out of the can do you?' said the girl, letting slip a Midland accent.

'No, I spend all my working hours with wine glasses so it's good to be a bit of a slag now and then.'

The girl laughed a coarse throaty laugh that Anita found amusing. The girl was chatty, liked to know what was going on and Anita thought that she might be a source of some useful information.

'Anne isn't it? Where are you from originally?'

'Yes, Anne, and I live in London but originally from Oxfordshire.'

'Pleased to meet you,' said the girl offering her hand as she sat down. 'I'm from Newark, near Nottingham. My mum says we are about as far away from the coast as anywhere in England so how is it that I wanted to go to sea?'

'A good question, now why did you want to work on a yacht?'

'Come on, it's not really a boat is it, it is a floating mansion. It's only like working in a posh hotel. Look at you, a sommelier; you don't get those on normal ships do you?'

'I suppose not,' said Anita, smiling inwardly. 'What do you do on board?'

'General dogsbody, I work mainly for the housekeeper making the beds and keeping the cabins up to scratch. It's a demanding job, some of the guests are very particular and they like to complain over even the smallest thing.'

'You work for Olga?'

'That's right.'

'East European isn't she?' queried Anita.

'East European my arse, she's Russian, just like those two who run things, and the captain.'

'He is Russian as well?'

'They all are this trip.'

'This trip?'

'Yes, the captain we had last time was French like Pierre in the kitchen. He was a good stick, would have a drink with the crew when he could but this lot!'

'Different?'

'I would say so. Talk about a slave ship, they do not even allow us ashore without permission. Before if we were off duty there was no problem, we even mixed with some of the passengers. They are rich, wow, I mean really rich. It costs half a million euros a week to hire this yacht. I have to say though that you couldn't tell with some of them.

'You like that don't you?'

'Yes, much nicer to have a friendly conversation now and then.'

'But it doesn't happen now?'

'No, not with the Russians.'

'I wouldn't have thought mister Borisovich would want to hire his yacht out.'

'Tax, I believe it's to do with tax but I don't know any more than that.'

Anita could believe it, the super-rich didn't get so rich without their accountants.

After a furtive glance around Lynn leaned over and lowered her voice.

'I think they are Russian mafia, those two who run the place, and Olga the housekeeper. They are often talking to each other in low voices. I don't know why, they speak Russian and hardly anyone else on board can understand them.' She took a drink, her chatter in need of lubrication. 'As for Mr Borisovich, we don't see much of him, he just comes and goes.'

'Where does he go, do you know?'

'We are not supposed to but we hear things. He goes to Africa and the Middle East a lot and they say he has friends in high places in Russia, even the president I believe.'

'The President of the Russian Federation?'

'Yes.'

'Wow, that is some connection don't you think?'

Lowering her voice further Lynn almost whispered, 'They watch us all the time, be careful. The engineer is good with electronics and he says they have a room near the bridge full of screens and communication equipment. He says they even monitor the staff with surveillance cameras in a room next to the purser's office.'

Lynn's eyes glazed over as she realised she had probably said too much. After all it was just a job, she didn't care what they did so long as she got paid and she had already decided that this would be her last trip.

Alexie seemed morose when the following morning Anita explained her plan to visit the wine growing region. That was not such an issue until she asked to have the use of her mobile phone.

'I need a map as well, I can manage using Google maps if we can print them off,' she had told him, 'but a paper one is easier to use and I do need to call ahead and speak to a number of *viticoltori*, to make sure I can taste their wines.'

'I do not like the staff using mobile telephones.'

'I can see that but you must realise we cannot just turn up and do I have Mr Borisovich's permission to visit the wineries.'

'Go to the purser's office and use his computer, your mobile phone is there. I will tell him to let you use it under his supervision'

Anita climbed the stairs to the deck and finding the purser's office, tapped lightly on his door.

'Come,' said a voice. 'Hello, you want to use a computer for some maps I understand?'

'Yes, for a few minutes. Can I print out some information?'

'Yes, there is a wireless connection to the printer over there,' he gestured.

'What about my mobile phone?'

'Yes, Alexie says you can use it for business calls. I will get it from the safe.'

Anita watched the purser punch numbers into the small keypad and opened the safe door. It was not large, simply a day safe containing a few papers and several mobile phones, belonging to the rest of the staff she presumed.

'If the battery has run down there is a charger you can use.'

'Thanks. Is there a toilet around here I can use?'

'There is one just along the corridor. I will put your phone on charge for you while you are gone.

Anita thanked him and stepped out of the office noting the doorway to the bridge area and next to it two more, one with a toilet sign above, the other she guessed it would be the control room. Taking a deep breath she boldly walked up to the door and tried the handle. She was in luck, it was open and the place was deserted, the screens were live and she could see people moving as the cameras switched every few seconds and to her relief she saw Viktor and Alexie together on the deck below.

They must have left for only a short while or she would have expected to find the door locked. She did not have much time and quickly she rifled through some sheets of paper on one of the desks. She noticed one had a list of European cities and dates, just like the one she had seen in Bullseye's cabin and then there was another containing actual addresses and the title "Operation Venenum".

Thoughtful for a moment she noticed the screen in front of her change, the figures of Alexie and Viktor coming into view and she could see them look up towards the bridge and then they parted company. At least one was returning to the control room she guessed and with time running out she scanned the paper in front of her memorising several of the addresses and one in particular stood out, Rue Lacroix in the eighteenth arrondissement.

'You found the toilet okay?' asked the purser as she entered his office.

'Yes thanks. How's the battery looking?'

'Not quite fully charged but plenty for you to make your calls,' he said handing it to Anita.

She switched on the phone and keyed in her PIN code, before slipping it into her pocket.

'You can't do that. I am under strict instructions to make sure it is visible at all times. They are sticklers for security our Russian friends. Make your calls and give it back to me.'

'I need to use the computer first, check out the vineyards and their numbers. Can you give me some time to do that?'

'Yes, I suppose so. The computer is connected to the internet so just start using it while I carry on with my work.'

Anita knew of several small vineyards in the Barolo region and set about obtaining directions, telephone numbers, before printing out the information. Then she began to make some calls.

'Hello is that . . .?'

For the following few minutes she worked through the list and in the end, she had secured appointments with two well-known wine growers.

'Finished?' asked the purser.

'Not quite, I need to ask a favour.'

'Oh.'

'It's my mother; I haven't spoken to her for a several days. She is eighty-five and still lives on her own. Can I give her just a quick ring just to make sure she is all right? She relies on me, my sister lives in Australia now and I am her only living relative. Please, it's important to me.'

'I don't know . . .'

'Only for a minute, I would really appreciate it. How would you feel if it was your mother?'

'My mother died three years ago.'

'Oh, I'm sorry.'

'Only a minute mind,' he said, his tone softening.

Anita wasted little time scrolling through the contacts list, finding the London number she used only in emergency.

'Hello, mother, it's me Anne. How are you? I am sorry I have not been in touch but I am out of the country. What is that . . .? Italy, Savona, near where we used to holiday remember. Yes I know you cannot get to the shops, perhaps social services can get it for you. Ask next time they visit you.'

Anita stopped speaking for a while as the trained operator took up the spirit of the charade, acting out the conversation, and then the office door opened and Alexie walked in.

214

'Thank you so much, I will speak with your manager tomorrow and I hope you enjoy the rest of your holiday, goodbye.'

Alexie glowered at Anita, suspicious, and reached for the telephone. I hope you have been ringing who it is you say. What is this number, it is England not Italy?'

'I was hoping to visit the Mascarello winery tomorrow. The founder's daughter runs it these days but it transpires that she is in London so I called her there.'

Alexie grunted and to Anita's relief simply turned off the phone.

'She has finished, put it back in the safe,' he said to the anxious-looking purser. We leave at six o'clock in the morning and we must be back here before eight o'clock in the evening. Mr Borisovich's guests are arriving a day early.'

Anita could do little else under the circumstances and gathering her printouts she gave the purser a naughty schoolchild look and his face filled with relief. In London, within minutes of the call ending, a recording of the conversation was in the hands of Anita's controller.

Alexie hardly spoke, his concentration was on the road ahead, and in the passenger seat Anita sifted through her paperwork, glancing up occasionally to note signposts drifting past. Her knowledge of Piedmont was not extensive though coupled with

215

the notes on her lap she hoped she could convince Alexie that she knew what she was doing.

'You need to turn off soon, for Mondovi. Take the 564 to San Lorenzo; it is about half an hour away.'

Alexie nodded, glanced in his rear mirror and then back at the road ahead and for some reason, perhaps it was the laid-back Italian way of life, perhaps the unfamiliar surroundings, whatever it was he did not notice the plain blue Fiat following them. It was, admittedly, of nondescript appearance and well behind, far enough not to present a driving hazard.

In the Fiat, the driver was having no such lack of awareness; Ernest Jones, a security expert seconded to the British Consulate in Milan, was concentrating hard on the BMW and sitting beside him Brian Thacker, a communications specialist, was equally alert. Anita's brief call had alerted MI6 and after a flurry of communications, the two operatives received orders to travel overnight to the port of Savona. Arriving in the early hours, they parked within viewing distance of the dock gates and waited.

An hour later, the BMW appeared and through his binoculars, Thacker watched two people get into the car. Within seconds it was heading for the gate and as it drove past them, the driver slipped the Fiat's engine into gear and began to follow.

At first the BMW could not move very fast in the built-up area of the town but soon it was accelerating onto the motorway and for many kilometres the driver of the Fiat easily kept it in sight. Dodging through traffic when necessary, dropping back when he felt they might see them, he eventually let slip an expletive.

'I think we might have a few problems Brian, the road he is turning onto is single lane. If we get too close he will probably see us and if we hang back you can bet your bottom dollar a truck or two will block our view and he could turn off anywhere.'

'We don't seem to have much choice, though someone had the forethought to send us a list of possible destinations. London said that it was more than probable they would go to a winery. The nearest is one called the Vineyard Bertolini and from the map they do seem to be heading in that direction.'

Jones grunted, acknowledging his colleague's comment just as the BMW disappeared round a bend in the twisting road. Increasing speed, he tore round the bend and, catching sight of his quarry, closed the distance. It was no more than fifty metres in front, the pursuit was proving difficult and then, after a fraught twenty minutes, the BMW turned off the road into a vineyard and came to a halt.

'I think we should stop here Brian, take stock. Can you walk over there and have a look, see if we might follow into the property. Some of these places have visitor centres. At least if there are a few tourists about we can park up and mingle.'

The communications man opened his door and jumped out, walking at a brisk pace towards the entrance to the vineyard. He paused for a few moments before waving the car forward.

'There is a farmhouse and a car park with at least a dozen cars.'

'Good, jump in and we'll risk it.'

The Fiat turned into the gravel-covered entrance, and into the car park facing a fine, four-storey stone farmhouse. Picturesque with its backdrop of vines spreading far up the hillside it was a pleasant sight for any tourist but Ernest and Brian were not tourists. Finding a parking place the two men left the car and wandered towards the farmhouse.

Inside the building, she began to feel very much at home, considering the place the epitome of the region. Aware of the vineyard's reputation she paused for a moment to savour the faint aroma of ripe strawberries, roses and tar permeating the air, flavours she was eager to sample.

'*Buongiorno*,' said a slim, dark-haired woman appearing from behind the counter.

'*Buongiorno*,' replied Anita. 'You must be Maria I think.'

'*Si*, I am, and you are the lady who called yesterday?'

'Yes, Anne Sims,' she said offering her hand. 'I am interested in purchasing some wine for my employer. As I explained I work for an important business man and he needs to restock his cellar.'

'Well you have come to the right place. Let us go into my cellar and have a look, taste a few of our vintages.'

The Sommelier

Anita looked at Alexie as if for permission and receiving it followed Maria towards a stout oak door.

'Watch your step,' she said, switching on the lights as she began to descend the worn stone staircase. Anita followed into the dimly lit cellar, lowering her head under the low curved ceiling as they walked between rows of large oak casks. Alexie followed several paces behind, silent, oppressive, keeping Anita within his sight. For once Anita hardly noticed him, finding the experience of the vineyard inspiring, and for a time she forgot her minder.

Ernest Jones noticed several tourists as he entered the farmhouse but of the two from the BMW there was no sign. Looking round he wondered where they might be when he noticed the door leading to the cellar. Making his way across the room he opened the door just enough to see a staircase leading downwards and hearing footsteps heading his way he decided to retreat.

He was just in time because the door opened only seconds after he had closed it. Squeezing behind a rack of cheeses and preserves he made himself scarce, letting the big man who emerged pass him by. His orders were to attempt to make contact with the agent, a Mrs Sims, and failing that to see that she was safe enough. Peering through a gap in the shelving, he watched the big man make his way towards the entrance. Perhaps now he would have the chance to communicate with the agent.

Outside Thacker was just a few metres from the farmhouse keeping watch, casting his eyes over the parked cars repeatedly manipulating a small plastic item with his fingers as he waited for his chance to attach it to the BMW. However, each time he had made a move someone intervened. First, it was a tourist leaving, and then a worker cleaning up litter, and now a man was walking towards it, tough looking and Thacker deduced he must be the driver. From the shelter of some trees he observed his progress, saw him reach into his pocket and pull out a packet of cigarettes. Time was running out; if he were going to plant the listening device, he would have to move soon but with such an obstacle in his way his options were fast evaporating.

In the cellar of the winery, Anita had just finished tasting a fourth wine, spitting the residue into a glass.

'Thank you, the wine is superb, a credit to you. After trying these vintages, I would like to buy some of the '96 and the 2001. What is today's price?'

For several minutes, the two women discussed prices and quantities, finally coming to an agreement.

'The driver has the means to pay; I do not handle the money,' said Anita.

'I will instruct one of my people to pack the wine for you. Come, let us go back upstairs.'

Jones, still loitering in the shop, noticed the cellar door open and to his relief saw Mrs Sims emerge with a second woman. They spoke for a moment, and then they parted, leaving the agent alone. Now was his chance.

'Hello, wine tasting are you? I must say this is a beautiful place.'

Startled, Anita's eyes swivelled towards the speaker, her head following.

'Erm . . . yes, it is a nice place.'

'And the weather is so good, much better than London Mrs Sims.'

That was a shock, he knew her code name and he talked of London. She had rehearsed a coded phrase before she had left London for the Lady Galina and now it was time to use it.

'I hear the Rolling Stones visit hear often.'

'I have heard that to. It must be the Italian way of life.'

So, he is MI6 but time is short, she thought. Alexie had said he was going for a smoke and she estimated he had been gone almost ten minutes and there was the chance that he would return.

'I can only tell you Operation Venenum. I don't know yet what it means but there is something happening on the Lady Galina.'

She said no more, walking away in case Alexie returned to find her speaking with some stranger. He would become suspicious and she knew that might blow her cover, but before he did, Maria appeared and called to her.

'I have a man packing the wine and so if you would like to we can complete the transaction.'

Anita smiled and turning her head noticed Alexie had walked back into the building.

'It is time to pay. I have ordered two dozen bottles and they are being boxed ready for us to take away.'

Alexie pursed his lips and produced a credit card. 'This will do, yes?'

'Of course, if you will put it in this machine then we can conclude our business.'

Maria left Alexie to enter his code into the machine and turned to Anita.

'Ah, here is your wine,' she said, instructing her employee to place the case on the desk. 'You know your wines and I am sure your principal will not be disappointed. I hope you have a safe journey. Where is it you are going to?'

'Savona, we are there for a few days more I think.'

'Ah yes you mentioned a yacht. It sounds an exciting life.'

Anita was about to answer when Alexie's impatience got in the way. Cutting short her conversation with the vintner, he picked up the cases of wine and motioned for Anita to follow him back to the car and amongst the trees, the agents noted their progress.

Jones said, 'You managed the plant okay Brian? No chance of it falling off is there?'

The communications man frowned disapprovingly.

'Okay, you're happy with it. Have you tested it?'

'Not yet, with no one in the car there's no signal.'

'There will be soon, look.'

Alexie had reached the BMW and was opening the boot and stowing the cases of win when Anita glanced round and noticed the blue Fiat. At least she had managed to pass on some useful information but if Alexie noticed them being followed then her work might all be in vain.

'Right, I'm getting something. I can hear them moving and he has just turned on the engine,' said Thacker, holding his smartphone to his ear.

'Yes, we got 'em loud and clear. Right, time to disappear, I will listen in for a minute or two but the battery only gives us about ten hours' transmission time. It's pointless listening to those two, we need to catch bigger fish.'

The BMW had visited two more of the vineyards on Anita's list and weighed down with several more cases of wine the car returned to the Lady Galina. It had been a long day, Anita was feeling tired and told Alexie that she would go to the cellar to receive the new consignment.

'You have had a successful day madam?' said the chef as she walked into the galley.

'Yes, successful and informative I think, expensive too.' She lowered her voice. 'We spent almost a hundred thousand euros.'

'Welcome to the world of the super-rich my dear. It is nothing to Mr Borisovich, money is no object.'

'The deck hands will bring the cases to the wine cellar in a few minutes. Can I have the key so I can make room before they arrive?'

Pierre walked the few paces to his office, retrieved the key and handed it to her.

'Thank you Pierre, I had better get a move on and then I need to update the records on the computer. We have enough stock for now but once the next guests have been attended to I might need to buy a few more bottles.'

'It is always the same, never-ending, but do you not find pleasure in looking after the cellar? I have to do the same with the food, only the best food, and to meet with the producers is always a gratifying experience.'

'I suppose that is professionalism Pierre.'

'Yes . . . I am professional I think.'

Anita smiled at his self-aggrandisement and left him preening.

The First Tank Army had travelled well over two thousand kilometres, south through Russia and then through occupied Ukraine before turning north. They had moved as fast as possible and taken a roundabout route to convey the impression that their destination was western Ukraine. Forty-eight hours later the convoy of tank transporters reached the base deep inside Belarus and the Russian high command issued a communique stating that there would be a joint exercise in western Belarus between remnants of the Ukrainian Army, the forces of

Belarus and Russian Federation forces. Rosemary picked it up on the morning news on her way to Langley, and though there was not much in the way of detail she was not convinced of the veracity of the report.

'John, this Russian statement about a joint exercise with the defeated Ukrainian Army, it does not stand up to close scrutiny.'

'In what way?' asked her husband as the car entered the parking lot.

'Traffic analysis suggests that there are no Ukrainian forces in any meaningful strength anywhere in the country. The Russians made sure that there could be no chance of a rebellion once they had taken over. Many of the army units are confined to barracks, I guess until they swear unswerving loyalty to the Russian Federation that will remain the position.'

'So what are you saying?'

'I am saying that something sinister is developing. We have experienced Russian misinformation and fake news for quite some time and when I look at the numbers I see a shift in emphasis.'

Rosemary closed the passenger door, joined her husband and together they walked towards the high security entrance of the CIA headquarters building. 'Okay, not much we can discuss here. Put together a brief and call me. I will have a word with the director and you can tell him what you suspect.

The Sommelier

Rosemary nodded her head thoughtfully; pleased to have the chance to explain her theory, and after passing through security, they parted company. John already had a meeting fixed for the first part of his day and headed towards the lift to the first floor whilst his wife walked down the corridor to her own workplace.

'Morning Rosemary, you're looking thoughtful this morning,' said a voice from near the coffee machine.

'Admiral Schmidt, Martin, I haven't seen you for what, four or five years? How are you, what are you doing here?'

'Classified, for now anyway, I have come to see you.'

'Me, if you want to see me should you have let me know? You have gotten clearance?'

'I have, I have clearance to talk to you, look,' he said, proffering her a plastic-covered pass.

'Hmm . . . let me get a coffee, I can't do anything without a cup of coffee.'

The German admiral smiled, getting coffees from the machine before turning back to face Rosemary.

'What's this all about, Martin, do we need to use the quiet room?'

'I would say so.'

'We will go there then and you can fill me in. How's Inga by the way, and the kids?'

'Inga died last year and the kids are kids no longer.'

'Aw heck, I didn't know, I'm sorry.'

'It's okay, you were not to know. Cancer I'm afraid, it was quite sudden.'

'You managing, where do you live now, still in Italy?'

'I manage, miss her like hell but I manage.'

Admiral Martin Schmidt of the German Navy looked a little sad and as his eyes looked down towards the floor he took a deep breath before transferring his gaze back to Rosemary.

'Italy, we had good times in Italy Rosemary, but since Inga passed away I asked for a transfer and now I work out of Kiel, the Centre of Excellence for Operations in Confined and Shallow Waters. They said they needed my expertise in submarine operations to help evaluate Russia's intentions in the Baltic.'

'I can see the logic in that; your department fed us a lot of useful intel down in Naples. I guess the Baltic is home ground for you and I know the Russians have been getting bolder.'

'They have, and cleverer, which is why I have come to see you.'

'Come on then, let's go to the quiet room where we can talk a little more freely.'

Rosemary led the way, her mind beginning to question why the German admiral would turn up at Langley and unannounced at that.

'Do I need to take notes Martin?'

'I advise against it at this stage. I really have nothing concrete to report.'

'Then why are you here and how come you turned up unannounced? There are protocols you know.'

'Rosemary you judge me too harshly. You and I are in the same business, at opposite ends I grant you, but you will agree we have common enemies?'

'Yes, I'm sorry if I offended you.'

'That does not matter. Let me explain as well as I can why I have come to see you. Firstly, I am not here unannounced, I had an appointment with Admiral Bradley of the strategic command yesterday afternoon and expected that meeting to be the only one but he insisted I came to see you. I think he made the decision too late to let you know but he feels that what I have to tell you could be important.'

Rosemary sat back in her chair and looked the German in the eye. She had known him for almost twenty years on and off and she trusted him. For his part he was aware of her reputation for deep analysis, had witnessed on more than one occasion how she had teased out the Russians' intentions from no more than a few intercepted messages and the odd aerial photograph. She somehow had an ability to think round corners, to see the invisible.

'Let me begin at the beginning. There was a report of a submarine sighting off the Swedish coast back in October 2020. You may remember it, an emergency telephone call in Russian, and then an increase in radio traffic between the archipelago and Kaliningrad. Shortly after that, there was a sighting of a research vessel towing an unidentified craft. The

Swedish Navy became involved and after a thorough investigation concluded that the Russians did indeed have one or more submarines in their sovereign waters.'

'I do remember and as I recall the Swedes never did find anything.'

'No, but the report stated that there were highly confidential matters not yet released, additional sightings, ELINT intercepts.'

'What are you saying; that the Russians have infiltrated Swedish naval defences?'

'In a word, yes, just think about it, with such a rugged coastline riddled with fjords and hidden inlets it's a perfect hiding place for Russian submarines and one in particular.'

Rosemary's attention was complete, her jaw set, her eyes focused on Martin.

'One in particular?'

'Yes, one that we know nothing about, have never seen nor do we have any intelligence on it except for one particular fact. I say fact; it is a report from a sometime-agent embedded in the Russian Northern Fleet.'

'That narrows it down, no sighting and no intelligence. What makes you so sure they have a sub in Swedish waters?'

'A hunch and a sighting of some disturbed water. Our spy in the Northern Fleet has reported a visit to the submarine base, by the commander of the Russian Navy. That is such a rare occurrence as to be significant and, more than that, Admiral Sokolov is no submariner.'

Rosemary's brain changed up through its gears, her curiosity increasing by the minute as Admiral Schmidt described the situation in Severomorsk. She had already subscribed to the theory that the fjords of Sweden would make a good hiding place for Russian submarines and at times of heightened tension, they could deploy fearsome new missile ships with the Baltic fleet in Kaliningrad right on the doorstep of Poland and the Baltic States.

'This submarine you have never seen and know nothing about . . . how does that fit in?'

'I mentioned the sighting of disturbed water. What I haven't told you is the fisherman who saw it is a lieutenant in the Swedish Navy, a submariner himself. More than that, he is an engineering expert working on secret developments for the Swedish Navy. Luckily, he was on leave and was spending the day fishing off the small town of Sanda, just south of the Karlskrona naval base.'

'The main Swedish naval base?'

'Yes, the same.'

'From what I know the area is full of inlets and islands.'

'Exactly, and our lieutenant, being a bright individual, kept a close eye on the disturbance as soon as he spotted it. Initially he believed it to be a very large fish, a bottlenose dolphin, for they are relatively common in those waters. He said it was moving at only two or three knots and because it was close to the surface he could make out a rough shape. He started his outboard engine, decided to follow it, and soon realised that it could not be a marine mammal. What surprised him most was its size and that was when he began to think it might be a submarine of some sort. However, it looked nothing like a submarine, more like a real dolphin only much larger, and in his report he stated that whatever its propulsion it had similar characteristics to dolphins, a slow side-to-side movement of the rear portion of its hull.'

'Might it have been a fish?'

'He said not, it was bigger than anything he had ever seen in those waters and its method of propulsion was not quite as smooth as a real fish, but it was effective. Now I have been put in charge of a project to try to determine exactly what he saw but from what I have learned, which isn't much I admit, I think the Russians are trying out a new form of submarine.'

'Manned?'

'That's the worrying part, we don't think so.'

'Are you trying to say that it is autonomous and if it can navigate those waters undetected it can go anywhere, threaten any surface ships?'

Admiral Martin Schmidt slowly nodded his head.

'And what do you think I can do to help?'

'Not a lot with regards the vessel but if the Russians are planning a build-up along the Baltic States' borders, they tell me you are the one to know.'

'Well thanks for the information Martin; I will certainly include it in future assessments of the Russian forces. Who else knows?'

'Only those who need to know, just my immediate superior and a small number of officers in the Swedish Navy. I informed your Admiral Bradley yesterday and now you know as well. The problem we have is that we only suspect it is a Russian submarine, we don't know. If there really is an autonomous submarine prowling the Baltic, we need to discover what it is and how to deal with it. I can tell you that our Type 212 submarines are actively looking for it.'

'I will speak with Admiral Bradley as soon as I can, see what he wants me to do. I have to say Martin your information does appear important and I think as few people as possible should know about it.'

'Don't worry Rosemary, as soon as I began to appreciate what might be going on I made sure any information is classified.'

'So where to now, are you heading back to Europe?'

'Yes, I am just making a whistle-stop visit this time. My boss felt it better to have a personal meeting with Admiral Bradley rather than go through the usual channels, keep what we suspect under the radar for the time being. This business may be significant, we have our own programs and we know the goals we are trying to achieve, but if the

Russians get there first and we are without countermeasures then we could be in trouble.'

Chapter 11

Alexander Luzhkov knew now for certain which way
the wind would blow when the president finally
stepped down. The Politburo had, for several
months, quietly prepared for change and the man
sitting beside him on the park bench was one of the
instigators of that change. More than that, the
Russian military machine was gearing up for an
historic endorsement of that change.

'Igor, your agents close to the British, are they
providing the kind of intelligence we need?'

'Yes, their civil service has had a requirement for
many more personnel over the past few years due to
the folly of the British and that has created openings
for us. They are still arguing over the depth of our
involvement in their internal affairs, if they only
knew eh?' he said, a wry smile showing on his face.
'We have infiltrated military computer systems and
for several years we have monitored their defence
plans, understanding the true breakdown of trust
between them and the Americans.'

'You believe the Americans will not move against us.'

'Personally no, but I believe that there are elements within the United States that would support the British. If they can motivate enough people then they might. They tried to support the Ukrainians a few years ago, supplying sophisticated armaments, but as usual, they did not follow through. We neutralised the Ukrainian army and the Americans did nothing. I can see that happening this time.'

'Do you really think that likely?'

'Only unless we give them good reason but that would need to happen well before the operation is under way. Statistically it is much more likely that once hostilities start the American public will have no stomach for another foreign war, especially to save the Europeans. POTUS has made them believe their European allies have not made proper contributions to NATO for years. The Germans for all their exporting success and surpluses are still not spending the required percentage of GDP, and that more than anything irks the Americans. Moreover, of course, our cyber warfare boys in Moscow and St Petersburg will be working overtime to feed the Western media with false reports aimed at controlling their public opinion. It worked in 2016 and 2020 in both America and the United Kingdom and it will work again.'

'How goes it with our Middle Eastern friends?'

'Our near Middle Eastern friends I presume you mean?'

'Of course, that is your project. The Middle East itself has no bearing on our plans other than to distract the Americans.'

'The Americans are losing interest in the Middle East. Ever since they returned to burning coal and discovered more natural gas deposits they have left it to us, and increasingly the Chinese, to take care of the Arab world.'

'Yes, the Chinese, which is tomorrow's problem but today we concentrate on Europe. I have a meeting with the Politburo this afternoon to discuss strategy in the Middle East. How it will affect relations with the Chinese is on the agenda so maybe tomorrow is not so far away.'

'It is a sensible approach *tovarishch*.'

'I also have a meeting with the head of the army and he will want to know just how far advanced are your plans with the al-Qaeda cells. What can I tell him?'

Igor pursed his lips, a thoughtful look spreading across his face, and he remained silent, gathering his thoughts before finally replying.

'I can tell you that we are moving towards our goal. The ruling council has issued orders to the various cells in European capitals, they are making preparations and the finance to purchase chemicals and explosives is almost in place.'

'That is good, the army is positioning itself along the border and I understand that the Northern and

Baltic Fleets are working up to a state of readiness as we speak. And you Alexander, your agents in America and Canada, what are they telling us.'

'Simply that the American military is not ready to return to Europe in force and we discovered recently a secret report on the publics expected response to our system of plausible denial. They swallow it hook line and sinker, they are unlikely to push for their military to intervene. We should not have a problem there.'

As he looked out of the train carriage window Yusuf could see the green-brown Italian countryside morph into the untidy outskirts of Genoa and soon he would meet the Russian. As the train came to a stop he quickly left the station precinct to find Alexie waiting for him in the BMW parked across the road from the station exit.

'Get in,' he said, driving the car slowly alongside the Arab.

Reaching for the handle, Yusuf opened the rear passenger door and threw his bag onto the seat before climbing in.

'You have good journey?' said Alexie in English.

'Good enough, the scenery was very beautiful but I did not really take much notice.'

'No, you have other things to think about. The yacht is not far, sit back and relax.'

Yusuf could not relax; the next stage of his mission would be a trying experience because he would need to travel to Munich and then Berlin alone. With the heightened state of security in Germany, he ran a real risk of discovery.

In a room on the third floor of the British Consulate in Milan, Brian Thacker was listening in to the conversation. The small device he had planted days earlier had pulsed to indicate that a conversation was taking place and he had activated the transmitter. Coming to life it was, surprisingly powerful and picked up every word but the battery was almost flat and he could not obtain very much more intelligence before the transmitter shut down for good. Today though, there appeared nothing much in the way of useful information, simply that the BMW was transporting someone to the yacht. He picked up a second mobile phone from the desk and called Ernest Jones who was at that moment sitting outside a small cafe in the warm afternoon sunshine and enjoying a cup of coffee.

'Ernie, I have something, it looks like they have picked someone up and are taking that person to the yacht.'

'How long?'

'I don't know exactly but I don't think the BMW will be long in arriving.'

'Okay I will take a look, see what I can find out.'

The line went dead, Jones felt in his pocket for some change and left the cafe for his car parked along the street. Reaching it, he unlocked the boot and retrieved the compact Leica camera, an ideal choice for surveillance with its full-frame sensor and a telephoto lens. In capable hands, it could record pin-sharp images from distance and the security agent's hands were particularly capable. Jones had no real idea when the BMW would show and looked round for a vantage point where he could keep a lookout unobserved. Due to the size of the superyacht, the commercial area of the port was the only place it could berth. If he tried to walk along the quayside, he would have to pass the security gate, and a myriad of industrial buildings obscured the view from the road. He needed a clear field of vision and then an idea struck him. The cruise ship moored in the next dock would offer the perfect platform, so long as he could get aboard her.

Making the decision to try he moved quickly, covering the distance in a little under five minutes. The white stern of the *Costa Diadema* rose up above him, but there was a security post placed well in advance of the gangplank that he would need to negotiate. From what Jones could see, it appeared to be a filtering point, probably the place where a crowd of returning passengers was slowly turned into an orderly line. If he were to go that way, he would have to pass the uniformed security guard.

Then a coach turned up and began to disgorge a group of noisy young women. It was now or never, thought Jones. Lifting the camera off his shoulder, he slung it round his neck to create the appearance of a returning tourist and began to mingle. The passengers were babbling excitedly as he joined them, the disorderly throng slowly funnelling towards the waiting security man, and he joined it behind the group of young women. They were wearing skimpy shorts and tight blouses, their midriffs tanned and firm, and this being Italy he gambled that the security guards attention would be elsewhere for a short period.

'*Regazze buon pomeriggio*,' said the guard, beaming a smile and tipping his head back slightly in a gesture he perceived attractive to the opposite sex.

Two of the girls began giggling which only served to encourage him.

'You are English, no?'

'*Si si*,' said one of the girls, wide-eyed and seemingly easy prey to the Italian's charm.

'You a like *Italia*?'

'*Si si*,' she said again, repeating the only word of Italian she seemed to know.

'And are you from London?' he asked, reaching out to touch the girl's cheek and causing more giggles.

Ernest Jones took out his warrant card and flashed it quickly in front of the guard, giving him little time to spot that it was nothing to do with the ship's security system, and it worked. The Italian paid little attention; Jones passed by and found there was no security at the foot of the gangplank, simply a few of the crewmembers half-heartedly welcoming the passengers back aboard the ship. Jones could not believe his luck and not wishing to push it too far stayed in the company of a group of passengers.

Once aboard the cruise ship he took the stairway leading to the upper levels, emerging eventually into the sunlight of the promenade deck. It was a perfect vantage point with an uninterrupted view of the *Lady Galina* lying parallel across the water. Lifting the camera, he brought her into sharp focus, using the lens as a magnifier to sweep the yacht and its immediate surroundings. He could see crew working on the upper deck, polishing the brass work by the look of it, and on the bridge's wing an officer was speaking into a shortwave radio. He lowered his view towards an opening in the hull where two women were in conversation and zooming in took several shots. Then he swung the camera towards the stern, just as the BMW appeared. As it pulled up he caught his first glimpse of the car's occupants, first a tall, dark-skinned man, then the driver appeared and together they walked towards the gangway. Agent Jones took several more shots before looking over the yacht for other points of interest, and finding none his mind turned to the problem of leaving the cruise ship. He had been aboard for no more than twenty minutes but instinct told him she might soon depart and he had no wish to leave with her. Then, at almost the same time, the ship's whistle blasted, forcing him to run towards the staircase leading to the lower deck. He had no idea how long he had to get off the ship nor if he were too late, but get off it he must. Reaching the deck below he took a few seconds to look over the rail and could see that there were still just a few passengers on the dock ready to board. Their numbers had dwindled dramatically and several crewmembers were beginning to dismantle the awning; time was running out. 'Damn it,' Jones swore as the ship's hooter sounded again. Taking the stairs two at a time, he rushed past sedately moving passengers, almost knocking a woman over who screamed after him, but he was not stopping for anyone not even the ship's officer stringing a white rope barrier across the open doorway.

'Hey you, what do you think you are doing? You can't go there, the ship is making ready for sea.'

'Press,' he called back. 'I work for a holiday firm; we're doing a spread for Costa Cruises.'

It was enough to impress the officer and soon after Jones landed both feet on dry land. He called out a thank-you to the officer who simply shook his head and waved him away.

Relieved to have escaped so easily, he walked back to his car, and could not help but admire the sleek lines of the Lady Galina. Just for luck he took a couple more shots of her then looked at his watch, five o'clock. That figured, the cruise liners often put to sea around now and as he looked across the water to the *Costa Diadema* he could see her bow thruster beginning to churn water and returning to the car, he quickly thumbed through the camera shots. Each one he transferred onto his mobile phone minutes later he had transmitted them to Milan and was ringing the consulate.

'Get me Thacker will you?' he said to the receptionist.

He did not have to wait long before a familiar voice came on the line.

'Ernie, how did you get on?'

'Okay, although I was a bit too close to going on a world cruise at one point.'

'Eh!'

'Never mind, look I have sent some images using the secure app and will hang about for an hour or two just in case anything of interest turns up. Have a look at the images and get them off to London.'

'Will do. For your information the bug has gone quiet, the battery is running down but if it fires up and acquires something useful I will let you know.'

Yusuf looked at the briefcase sitting on the table and then at Alexie busy printing out a map and a list of rail and road transport options for him. He knew the address where he was going, but getting there might prove difficult without some prior groundwork.

'There my friend, a map of sorts and a list of the trains that will get you to southern Germany. You will have to leave us first thing in the morning as the boss will be arriving with some guests and my instructions are to help get you on your way before they have a chance to see you. Also I have to inform you that we will be in Marseille next week for what will be your final pickup.'

'I understand, it is not good practice to wear a path that others can follow. I have used this boat too often already.'

The Russian nodded, he was a security specialist and well aware that to use the same methods or routes too many times was to invite trouble.

'You have your train ticket for the journey to Munich?'

'No not yet, from this printout the train leaves in the morning at around eight and as I have a multi-country rail pass I should have little trouble.'

'Good, then we are all set; bring the case and I will take you to one of the spare crew cabins. Stay there until I come in the morning to take you to the railway station, and in the meantime I will arrange for a stewardess to bring you food. We know all about Muslim eating habits.'

Yusuf bowed his head slightly in apparent gratitude, though in reality the Russian's mock condescension had made him angry.

Ever since catching sight of the returning BMW, Anita's curiosity had taken centre stage. She knew guests would be arriving shortly, and Olga began briefing her about arrangements. As they talked Anita saw the car pull up and from the corner of her eye spotted the Arab get out. So he was back.

'Are you listening?' said Olga.

'Oh sorry, yes of course, I was just wondering if Pierre has his menu ready for tomorrow.'

Olga frowned but let it pass, she had not seen Alexie return with the Arab and her suspicions were not aroused.

'Mr Borisovich has four guests for us to look after during the next few days and while they are here we are to provide the highest service because they are important guests. Do I make myself clear?'

'Perfectly ma'am.'

'Good, now let us run through the order of things. Breakfast will be easy going and relaxed, after all they are here to enjoy their surroundings and the sunshine. Mr Borisovich will be conducting some business and when he is, you are to serve the drinks but be discreet. Anything you overhear you are to forget instantly, do you Understand?'

'Perfectly ma'am.'

'There will be formal dinners each evening and I want the table dressed in the Russian style. Mr Borisovich was insistent that it should be so.'

From Olga's final statement it seemed obvious that the guests would be Russian, perhaps a mixture of business associates as at the dinner at the house in London. Olga had said that it was purely a male gathering; no females would accompany the men, so it did look more like business than pleasure.

Suddenly aware of Anita looking past her, Olga turned her head and her eyes narrowed. Anita froze. Fortunately, Alexie and the Arab were no longer on the dockside having come aboard but it was a worrying moment.

'Does chef have a menu for tomorrow evening? I really would like to know what he proposes so that I can take some time to select the wines.'

'I believe he is well advanced with that and he has already ordered the food. Go and see chef now.'

Anita turned to take the stairway down to the galley, her head full of the image of the man she had seen getting out of the BMW – it was Shadow she was sure. Why was he back aboard the yacht, why did he keep coming back? She did not know and was still speculating when she walked into the galley.

'Madame, good afternoon.'

'Good afternoon Pierre. I have come to see what menu you are creating for tomorrow evening.'

'Creating, a good word, I see you appreciate my skills as a chef.'

'Oh come now Pierre, everyone knows you are the best.'

The Frenchman beamed, wallowing in Anita's praise until he became more serious.

'Madam, if you will come into my tiny office I will show you what I propose for tomorrow,' he said, leading the way across the galley to the cubicle he called an office, and shutting the door he turned to Anita. 'They are all Russians I believe and important ones at that so we must make an extra effort for Mr Borisovich's sake at least. He told me before he left that some are important government figures, men who can help grow his empire, and that if they leave happy there is a bonus for me.'

'Lucky you, and no doubt you are now going to impress upon me the importance of the wine I will be serving.'

'*Exactement, ma chère amie,* we will both do well if they leave happy. Now down to business, here is a hand-written copy of the menu. To start will be a choice between asparagus spears with truffle, poached free-range duck egg and hollandaise sauce, or prawns with sorrel, cucumber and rye bread. For the main course, I will prepare roast guinea fowl with glazed carrots and spiced plums. Do you see any problems with that?'

Anita cast an eye over the list.

'No Pierre, your choices are perfect for me. I will spend a little time in the cellar to decide my final selection. I am sure our guests will be very happy when they see what you can do.'

'*Merci madame*, you are very kind.'

The chef smiled and Anita reciprocated, believing that perhaps she had at least one ally on board the Lady Galina and then her mind turned back to the Arab. Twice now, she had seen him aboard the yacht, and of course there were the images from Istanbul, then Alexie appeared at the doorway to interrupt her thoughts. When he was around, she was automatically on her guard and picking up Pierre's menu, she appeared to study it.

'Chef, we have an extra guest tonight who will need feeding. He is a Muslim and you know they only eat halal meat. Can you make him something?

And you,' he said to Anita, 'you can wait on him as you never seem to have a lot to do.'

Anita looked up from the page. 'I do what I am told.'

'Well there is a man in the guest cabin on the staff deck. He will be there for tonight only and you will attend to his needs. Take him his dinner and give him whatever he wants. I don't think you need to impress him with your knowledge of wine, an orange juice will maybe be enough.'

The Russian half-smiled, as he imagined how their guest might cope in a hard-drinking session with some of his GRU comrades. They had downed a whole bottle of vodka each on more than one occasion and still managed to appear on parade the following morning. This Arab looked as if just one glass would knock him over.

'He will want breakfast early; he will be leaving by seven in the morning.' Alexie snapped.

Anita acknowledged the order with a nod of her head and Pierre scratched his as he wondered where he had put the small amount of halal meat he usually kept for just such an eventuality.

'So we are feeding terrorists now are we?' said Pierre with some venom.

'Terrorist, how do you know that?' asked Anita.

'Because they all are, look what has happened in Paris and Lyon, in Brussels and Amsterdam, even you British have suffered at their hands.'

'You seem upset Pierre, have you been involved in something?'

248

'No, but my brother has, was. He lost the sight of one eye in the bombing on the *Champs-Élysées* two years ago, on Bastille Day. Before the parade began he was with some student friends and a bomber blew himself up. You remember?'

Anita did remember, she was working that day and saw the first reports as they came in. Although it was a nasty incident, it killed no one apart from the bomber, the device going off prematurely which had at least prevented him from mixing with the gathering crowd. If he had managed to get in amongst them the outcome would have been a lot worse. It was a near miss, some people were injured and it seemed that one of them was Pierre's brother.

'How is he Pierre, I am so sorry?'

'Most of his injuries have cleared up but he is blind in one eye, the real damage is more psychological.'

Pierre stood motionless for a moment, his eyes focusing on something far away and then he sighed and his assistant, who had moved away when Alexie had appeared, turned on a tap, began washing a large pan, and broke the spell.

'Ah . . . it is in the past, life goes on. I must not dwell and I am sure not all Muslims are the same.'

'No Pierre, I am sure they are not,' said Anita wondering how to tackle the one Muslim on board the boat who surely was a terrorist.

Yusuf's travels had left him feeling tired and he was grateful for the bunk in the small cabin. Lying back his mind drifted on the edge of sleep thinking of his days in the Iraqi desert, his wanderings through war-torn Syria and the brave fighters he had known, people he would never see again until he entered paradise. In his mind's eye, faces became clear, as if they were in the room with him, but many had faded, their memory slipping away and he became angry. They had fought the infidels for decades and had made only limited progress, it was time to achieve something more, something to send a message to the West, let them know al-Qaeda was still a potent force.

Opening his eyes, he reached for his mobile telephone, one of the few people on board allowed to and tapping in his security code, he scrolled to the app for Muslim prayer times and noted the time for *Maghrib*, the evening prayer. Then a soft knocking on the door disturbed him and frowning with displeasure he got up from the bed and pulled open the door just enough to see who was there.

'Yes.'

'I have been sent to ask what you would like for your evening meal sir,' said a female voice.

'What have you to offer, I prefer halal lamb, do you have that?'

'Yes sir, chef says he can make it with rice and mangoes if you would like that.'

'I would, and some strong Arabian coffee but not just yet. Come back in twenty minutes.'

'Certainly sir,' said Anita leaving him alone.

The Sommelier

She was disappointed yet not surprised that she had learned nothing, Shadow was living up to his name. Perhaps when she returned with his food she might discover something. She walked along the crew quarters' corridor and just as she was about to climb the stairs she caught sight of Alexie coming towards her carrying a small leather case, and standing to one side, let him pass. He had a hostile look in his eyes and Anita avoided them, glimpsing briefly at the object he was carrying.

'What you do down here?'

'You asked me to find out what he wants to eat.'

'Oh yes, do that,' he growled as he hurried past, in the direction of Shadow's cabin.

Yusuf had only just arranged his prayer mat and was about to kneel when he heard a knock on the door for a second time.

'Who is it?'

'Me, Alexie, open the door.'

Yusuf knew better than to argue against the muscular Russian security man, his evening prayers did not stand much of a chance and mumbling a prayer for forgiveness, he opened his door.

'This is for your next assignment, for Munich and Berlin.'

'Of course.'

Alexie smiled a thin mirthless smile as he lay the case on the bed and opened it.

'There, two hundred thousand euros, check it is correct before I leave you.'

Yusuf began, taking some time to count, finally looking up at Alexie with some disdain.

'It is all here as far as I can see.'

'The map and information about trains is there too. I will be waiting in the car for you at seven o'clock in the morning so do not be late because I hate tardiness,' he said.

'I will be ready, now please leave me in peace.'

Alexie said nothing more, leaving the room and closing the door none too gently behind him, and as he marched along the corridor he cursed every Arab he could think of.

'That Alexie seems upset about something Pierre, he snapped at me just a few minutes ago,' said Anita

'He gets like that now and then, usually when the boss is due back on board. This time Borisovich is bringing a few friends and business acquaintances and no doubt tomorrow, we will all be under pressure, particularly our Russian friends. It is always the same but we are experts are we not, we will conjure up a feast fit for a king? It is what we do,' said the Frenchman with a twinkle in his eyes.

'You must get a little bored at times Pierre, especially when there is no one aboard except the crew?'

'A little, but it is these little difficulties that make for an interesting job. And of course they pay me well.'

'Of course,' agreed Anita.

On the surface, yes, thought Anita, it was an easy number and they would be paying Pierre a six-figure sum but boredom counted for a lot when you expected daily adulation. Still it was not for her to judge, she thought as she looked at her watch, seven-thirty, another five minutes or so and she could return to the Arab's cabin.

'I have made our guest a *mansaf*; it's a traditional Arab dish. The meat is halal so there shouldn't be a problem if he asks, I will just finish off the sauce and you can serve him.'

Anita placed the bottled water she was holding next to the cloche-covered plate and waited until Pierre was ready to spoon on the sauce then she picked up the tray.

'Smells good chef.'

Pierre grinned, always amenable to flattery, and touched his *toque blanche* as he waved to one of his kitchen assistants to push the double doors ajar for Anita.

'He will believe he is back in the desert with his Bedouin friends when he tastes my food. I guarantee it.'

Anita did not hear him; she was already on her way, her mind focusing on the immediate future. She would have only a few seconds, a minute at best, in the company of Shadow and she did not really fancy her chances of discovering very much. Turning the corner, she descended the stairs and reaching the fire door put her hand out to push it open. Suddenly, through the wired safety glass, she caught sight of the bulk of Alexie emerging from Shadow's cabin and to see her hovering nearby might raise his suspicions. The last thing she needed was a confrontation with him, no matter how trivial, and retracing her steps, she walked back up to the galley.

'I forgot the serviette, sorry,' said Anita, picking one from a box nearby.

'I was sure you had one when you left,' said a surprised Pierre.

'I might have dropped it. I will have a look after I deliver the food.'

It was a narrow escape and she was lucky Pierre had not noticed the original serviette poking out from under the plate. No matter, she had managed to get away with it and, with luck, Alexie would have left the crew deck by the time she returned.

But he hadn't, Alexie had delivered the bank notes and now his mind was on the following morning's job, the BMW was running short of fuel, and petrol was something they did not keep on board the yacht. Taking out his mobile, he keyed in a memo to call in at a petrol station before he set off with the Arab and then he checked his personal messages. Reading the few messages, he slowly made his way along the corridor to the fire door where his nose twitched. He had not eaten since breakfast, almost eight hours earlier, and the faint aroma of spiced lamb hanging in the air reminded him of the fact. Suddenly he felt hungry, his gastric juices began to flow and he considered calling into the galley for something to eat, and then he saw the sommelier coming down the stairs towards him.

The Sommelier

Anita had miscalculated, Alexie had not left the crew quarters, and instead he was blocking her path. There was nothing to do except to carry on, to act normal, and it seemed to work as Alexie stood to one side.

'For our guest I expect?'

'Yes, Pierre sent me.'

Alexie nodded and let her pass, the food's aroma amplifying his hunger, and at the other side of the fire door Anita breathed a sigh of relief. She had managed to sidestep the Russian security man and now she had to tackle Arab.

'Your dinner sir,' she said, tapping lightly on the cabin door.

There was no answer immediately and she waited patiently until finally, the door opened halfway and an angry looking Yusuf glowered at her.

'Yes, what is it? Oh, you have brought food. I am praying and I do not want disturbing,' he said, reaching out for the tray, though to do so he had to open the door fully and Anita took advantage.

'Here let me sir, let me leave it on the table.'

She looked over his shoulder. 'The one by the bed, it is easier for you sir. Chef has asked me to tell you that he has prepared your meal in accordance with your customs. He is a very good chef sir, he understands the needs of the Muslim and has prepared halal lamb for you in the traditional way.'

She had Yusuf on the back foot for a few moments; he was just as hungry as Alexie and, involuntarily stepping backwards allowed Anita to enter the cabin.

'Here sir, let me leave your tray for you. When you require it removing you can use the telephone by the bed. Sixty-six will put you through to the galley. Chef sends his compliments and hopes you like his cooking.'

By now, Anita had her back to Shadow and her eyes were roaming everywhere, finally alighting on the partially open case unnoticed by Yusuf who at that moment was more concerned about his evening prayers. She had caught him off balance but he recovered and moved over to the briefcase, obscuring Anita's view, but not before she had seen the contents,

What she saw shocked her, banknotes, thousands of them and of high denomination, the sight of them leaving her heart thumping. She was beginning to realise that whatever Shadow was doing it involved a lot of money.

'There sir, enjoy your meal,' she said turning towards the door as Yusuf eyed her with suspicion.

Between the aromas rising from the plate and his need to conclude his prayers, Yusuf was happy just to get rid of her, to close the door and be alone while in the corridor, Anita's mind was full of unanswered questions. She turned over in her mind all that had happened to her on the yacht as she climbed the stairs. Reaching the deck she arrived at the swing doors only to see Alexie coming towards her. He was carrying a plate covered with an aluminium lid and this time it was her turn to smell the aroma.

'I told you they cannot resist my cuisine,' said Pierre. 'The Russian wanted some of the same food you took to the Arab. He is a lucky man because I made enough for an extra plateful.'

Anita had half-smiled at Alexie as she passed by, towards the sanctity of the cellar to think through what was going on. Alexie too was in pensive mood for although he could not put a finger on it, he could feel that something was not quite right about the sommelier woman.

'That smells good Alexie; it's a pity I have eaten already,' said Viktor as he entered the control room.

'This is the last of it Viktor my friend. You will need to be a little quicker if you want to beat me to one of Pierre's specialities.'

'Next time maybe I will,' said Viktor turning back to the security screen in front of him.

He watched for a minute as the images changed and seeing little of interest turned his eyes towards Alexie. Surveillance could be a tedious operation, nothing much had happened on board and the smell of the food was sapping his interest in surveillance.

'You are enjoying that I see.'

'Mmm . . . good,' said a preoccupied Alexie. 'I will say one thing; the food on board this ship beats anything the Black Sea Fleet can dish up.'

'Is that such a surprise?'

'Ha, no it is not a surprise. Military food is the same the world over, rubbish, but at least it fills your belly.'

'Do you remember when we first went into Ukraine, the naval base in Sevastopol? They had better food that we did.'

'It didn't last long though did it?'

'No, we ate the lot in two days,' laughed Viktor remembering the chaos the Special Forces caused as they ransacked the food store. 'What is it you are eating?'

'Lamb, in the Arab style.'

Alexie paused and using a fingernail to dislodge a piece of trapped meat, his mind suddenly switched to the moment he had first caught the dish's aroma. What was bothering him, what was not quite right? Casting his mind back to his visit to the Arab's cabin, the handover of the case, its contents, the woman on the stairs. Then his eyes involuntarily looked down at his plate. Of course, the aroma was already percolating the foot of the staircase even before she appeared. Had she had been there earlier and, if so, why? Why was she was not there when he first passed through the fire door, was there an ulterior motive, was she up to something?

'Viktor, we might have a problem. Can we view the recordings from the surveillance cameras?'

Chapter 12

Admiral Sokolov had become aware of the new submarine's operational potential the previous year and wanted to see it for himself. Initially he had despatched a subordinate officer to examine the submarine, to report to him. The results were promising; however, as an old hand with connections right back to the Soviet Navy, he had reservations. Exaggerated prognoses had abounded during the Soviet era, leading the high command to believe that the armed forces were in a high state of readiness when in fact they were not. Repeatedly it became clear that half of the equipment was not in a serviceable condition. He remembered the *Kuznetsova* and its deployment to the Mediterranean almost ten years previously.

It had started well, much fanfare and a slick video to impress the Americans, and reports made by the captain of the time seemed to support the view that the Russian Navy had lost none of its Cold War prowess. However, it did not last. To his knowledge, the Politburo never did learn the full truth about the breakdowns, the loss of aircraft due to mechanical failure. It was a reflection on the wider state of affairs that the captain was never court-martialled; the blame reached the very highest ranks of the navy with the potential to expose those ultimately responsible and so investigations were never followed through.

The Admiral began to read the latest report on the new submarine, wondering just how advanced it really was because every navy in the world was experimenting with underwater vehicles. Some had budgets he could never hope to match; the Americans, and now the Chinese, were throwing vast sums into their projects. The one redeeming feature was that the Russian scientists and engineers were more than capable of producing the goods on a limited budget. The Status-6 system was a case in point, a stealthy underwater platform with the potential for delivering a nuclear warhead right into an enemy's port. That had been a game changer, but to use it would herald in Armageddon.

A nuclear confrontation would not serve any purpose other than obliterating the world. But this new system promised a new paradigm, a way of attacking without accountability. To possess the ability to defeat the enemy without having to declare war was the future and who better than the Russian Federation to exploit this potential.

The telephone on the admiral's desk came to life, its shrill call shaking him from his thoughts.

'*Da.*'

The voice at the other end of the line spoke rapidly for less than a minute before he replaced the receiver. So the president was finally going to announce his preferred successor. It was a foregone conclusion that Feodor Grachyov would win the election, he would become President of the Russian Federation and for the next few months, there would be upheaval. Some like himself had already aligned themselves with Grachyov but others had not and there would be a scramble as powerful men repositioned their allegiances, disposed of their enemies, and once again, the Russian people would foot the bill.

For several minutes the admiral sat motionless, elbows on the desk, fingers clasped together as he considered the implications. There was already a plan to realign the country's borders, to consolidate the whole of Ukraine within Mother Russia and to push the Americans back even further. The Federation's cyber warfare community had already wrong-footed them and soon it would be time for a more overt assault on the West.

Returning to the report on the submarine, he read it with renewed interest. This one machine could potentially inflict so much damage that the Europeans would hardly put up a fight, so long as the Americans stayed out of any conflict. He had to admit that after all the years of jousting with the Americans they had never looked so weak or less committed.

Turning the page, he read the results of the submersibles trials at the base on the Kola Peninsula. With the new, improved batteries fitted, its range had almost doubled, and after initial teething troubles, the machine had worked flawlessly. He had taken the decision to move trials to the Baltic and conduct tests in hostile waters. The Swedes were the obvious target but it was a risk; they were alert, possessed a competent though small navy, but he'd argued that if they could fool them, then the way would be clear to tackle NATO and the Royal Navy.

He had held technical discussions with the designers and the admiral commanding the Northern Fleet learning that the submersible had performed perfectly, penetrating coastal defences and entering the Karlskrona naval base. The trials had been a resounding success, no mention of any sighting in news bulletins and, as far as the secret service could ascertain, no mention in classified communications. It appeared that the machine was indeed invisible to NATO surveillance.

Igor Andresov looked up from his work and then consulted his watch, two o'clock exactly as a knock on the door announced the arrival of his visitor. Punctuality was one of his strong points and he expected it in others. Getting up from his chair, he walked the few paces to the heavy oak door and swung it open.

'Igor, you have heard the news?'

'Yes Alexander, I have heard, but it was expected, we have known for months that the president would name Comrade Grachyov as his successor. My department has been working to facilitate a smooth transition and I have sworn allegiance to our new president already. I advised you to do the same some time ago if you remember, you should always try to be part of the winning team my friend.'

Igor's visitor sighed and nodded his head. His department was more in tune with events on the other side of the Atlantic than the motherland and managing a weak smile, produced a small package from his pocket.

'A small gift for you Igor, I never forget your birthday.'

'You brought that into this building without being challenged?'

'I was challenged all right but when I said it was for you, the guard insisted upon escorting me to your office, and I did not see a problem.'

Igor frowned, but accepted the gift and placed it on his desk.

'Take a seat. The plans for the invasion of Belarus and the Baltic States are complete, the ground forces are in position and the navy will put to sea shortly.'

Igor made the statement to shock his visitor and was mildly satisfied that Alexander's expression hardly changed.

'You are not surprised?'

'No Igor, believe it or not this is something I already do know something about. I have heard

263

nothing from our own people but there are noises coming from Langley that have led me to believe they suspect that we are planning something. That can only really mean we are to expand in Europe and the Near East, because we are not about to upset the Chinese or the Indians. It's a logical consequence of the Americans' decision to withdraw from Europe to face East. They know what we might do, realise that others will fill any vacuum, and because the Europeans are so weak it has to be us. But they do not know our order of battle?'

'No, they can only guess, and we are busy feeding them with all sorts of false information.'

'And they us perhaps? Of course, it is the nature of the game but my spies in Washington discern a distinct lack of conviction. Unusual for the Americans I admit, but their politics are in a mess and that is in no small way due to us.'

Alexander allowed himself a brief smile. He had watched the American political machine for many years as, from a great height, an eagle watched its prey.

'I have my orders from the high command no less, Alexander, and they have told me to meet with you and to begin a new strategy of disinformation both at home and abroad. Our plans are, in general, an open secret. Every secret service in the world has probably guessed that we will strike eventually but not when nor where. It is our job to keep them guessing until we are ready.'

Ten kilometres to the west of Trelleborg, a town on the southern tip of Sweden, stratus clouds were sweeping in, darkening a once blue sky. The wind was increasing and as rain began to fall the *Sergey Makarevich* altered course a few degrees. Launched in the early eighties, she had spent her early life catching and processing fish anywhere from the Baltic to the Barents Seas. Built to withstand the ice in the high northern latitudes she was an ideal candidate to act as mother ship to the submersible. No more than a rusting factory ship on the surface, but with underwater doors and a concealed dock, she was well suited to her new role. She had recovered the submersible after its penetration of the Swedish naval base and was now heading north through the Danish straits.

Captain Sverdlovsk lowered his binoculars and hoped that they would not draw the attention of NATO warships. Even the fishery protection vessels could be a nuisance; with powers to board, his ship at times they posed more of a threat than the Swedish Navy. And one of the navy's warships was out there, not ten kilometres away, amongst the black triangles littering the computer screen. Each triangle represented a ship and embedded within it the ship's name, course and position, and one in particular commanded his attention. The Swedish naval vessel the *Karlstad*, a modern stealth corvette and a ship he would need to avoid.

He watched the black triangle slowly move across the monitor on a parallel course, but as the channel narrowed she could not fail to close the distance. She had held her course and speed for the past hour and to Captain Sverdlovsk it appeared that she was indeed shadowing his ship and that was worrying.

'Steer five degrees to port, helmsman.'

Gradually the *Makarevich* altered course towards the Swedish side of the island of Ven several kilometres away. If the corvette was tracking them then she would very probably follow the same course and try to avoid the landmass in case it interfered with surveillance.

'Markov, keep an eye on our friend here,' Sverdlovsk said to the first officer standing beside the helmsman. 'I need to have a closer look at the chart.'

The officer took a step sideways, noting the small black triangle that was the *Karlstad*. 'Yes Captain.'

Captain Sverdlovsk turned to the chart table. He still preferred plotting his courses on paper, and his large-scale chart afforded a generous overview. The channel would be at its narrowest as they neared Helsingborg and his options were reducing. Taking his dividers, he measured off the distance to the port and the narrows, six nautical miles. Even if the warship was not looking for them they would soon close the gap sufficiently for several pairs of unwanted binoculars to scrutinise his deck.

Taking his own binoculars, he left the bridge and stood in the shadows of the overhanging roof to scan the sea. The *Karlstad* was no more than half a nautical mile behind them on the starboard quarter and following the same course. Then to his relief ten minutes later he saw that she was beginning to change course. She was making for Helsingborg, a huge relief. It appeared that his ship was of little interest to her after all and he lowered his binoculars.

'She has changed course?' he said to the first officer still watching the screen.

'Yes Skipper, she is heading for the port entrance. Do you think we have shaken her off?'

'Maybe, give it a little longer.'

The two men continued to watch the black triangle until it turned sharply towards Helsingborg at reduced speed.

'Good, she's off our tail. Helmsman, prepare for a course correction,' said the captain, glancing at his chart and then back at the screen. 'When I say, take her round to two eighty degrees true.'

'Yes Captain,' came the reply and five minutes later the ship began to turn to port and from the bridge window Sverdlovsk looked ahead. He had decided to intercept the ferry route, pass close to Frederikshavn on the Danish side and then make the turn toward the open sea.

He was grateful they were of little interest to NATO but he was taking no chances. The automatic transmitter's signal was not only alerting other ships to his position but there would be an historical record of their movements. That might compromise the mission should any marine tracking agency decide to investigate and so they would make first for the fishing grounds, appear to be carrying out her expected business as a fishing vessel then set a course north into the Norwegian Sea, and Murmansk. Somewhere just off Russia's northern coast, they would turn off the tracking and make a dash for the submarine base at Gadzhiyevo.

So far the mission had gone as well if not better than expected. They had evaded NATO ships and aircraft and apart from several minor hitches, the testing of the submarine had proceeded according to plan. On reaching the submarine base, the divers and technicians seconded to the *Sergey Makarevich* would be debriefed and their data examined before the ship was laid up for the winter months and the crew could enjoy some well-earned leave.

Rosemary took a first sip of coffee, a welcome start on such a cold morning. Her drive to work had taken longer than normal because of the first real snowfall of the winter that had tested the district's snow team to the limit.

'Hi Rosemary, how d'you get on with Snowzilla this morning?'

'Okay, I left home half an hour early after hearing the forecast yesterday. What about you Edward?'

The researcher smiled, pleased with his new four by four that seemed to be capable of wading through the deepest snow and he took pleasure in telling anyone who would listen.

'Waal,' he drawled, 'my new Chevy Tahoe got me here on time, it is one hell of a vehicle. Do you know the latest model has collision avoidance sensors and snow braking sensitivity? I would have finished up behind a tow truck this morning if it had not been for that combination. I was out on the Curtis Parkway behind a bobtailing Mack when he went into a spin. If the Chevy hadn't performed like it did I reckon I was in for one hell of a bump.'

Rosemary smiled, Edward was a nice kid and good at his job but she really did not want to hear about his four by four or his near miss.

'What have you got for me?

Edward laid the folder he was carrying on Rosemary's desk and opened it.

'I checked out recent Russian movements on the border region between Ukraine and Belarus as you asked and here is the report.'

'What about the Baltic states, what is happening on the Russian border Russia right now?'

'Nothing much at the moment, this is the report. Units are turning up all the time for some sort of exercise.'

'Exercise, hmm . . . I hope that is all it is. Thanks Edward, I will let you know if there is anything else, so do not go skidding off the road for a while.'

'No ma'am, I do not intend to,' said the young man, a smile filling his face.

Rosemary picked up the first sheet of paper Edward had provided, reading the text and casting her eye over the graphics. They depicted the assumed troop and hardware distribution with trails of dotted lines showing where they had come from, and dates. The dates were interesting; they seemed to indicate that it was a planned operation spread over ten days. That was, to Rosemary, significant because to move so many men and their equipment in only ten days showed how far the logistics of the Russian forces had improved. She picked up the second report, the one regarding the First Tank Army. They had dispersed throughout a forested region near the border between Belarus and Poland – well placed to invade not only Poland but also Lithuania and open up the Suwałki gap. Perhaps they were planning to cut the Baltic States off from NATO reinforcements stationed in Germany. It looked a risky strategy but then she never took Russian moves at face value. They would have weighed up those risks.

'Ma'am.'

Rosemary looked up to see an ensign signaller approaching her desk.

'Yes, what is it?'

'A signal ma'am. For your eyes only, can you sign for it please?'

Rosemary picked up a pen and signed for the envelope; it was from Admiral Schmidt. The message inside read: Following *our meeting back in September when I informed you of my suspicions regarding the sighting of a mysterious underwater object, I now enclosed all the information we have regarding the sighting. I hope with the resources of the United States and the importance this incident may have on NATO you might be able to discover more.*

Rosemary was intrigued and sitting back in her chair pondered the implications, the reliability of the information, its possible effect upon the security of the northern NATO countries and even that of the United States. Had the Russians really developed a new and dangerous underwater weapon? If they had, it might be one of those game changing moments. Then she picked up the desk telephone and called her husband.

'John, can we meet sometime today?'

John looked at his telephone receiver a little puzzled. Her request had come unexpectedly; they had no ongoing projects other than the Russian build-up in northern Europe and only the previous day he had convened a meeting about that issue to discuss progress.

'Sure honey, just a minute.' He consulted his diary: 'How about two o'clock in my office?'

'I'll be there.'

Replacing her receiver, she reread the signal from Martin and studied the diagrams then she searched her address book for a contact number for Commander Alan Jacks of the submarine service. She had known him on and off for several years, from the time he was a submariner with Submarine Group Eight in Naples. She had seen him only once since then, at the Naval War College in Newport, Rhode Island, where they had both attended the same lecture on undersea communications. She remembered them sitting together during the lunch break and recalled their conversation.

'You are looking well Rosemary,' he'd said, 'and how's John these days? I have not seen or heard of him since he retired from the navy.'

'He is very well and still working hard.'

'I heard he was poached by a certain agency.'

'I am not sure poached is the correct term.'

'It's not unusual for a senior naval officer to move across to the agency, I have known more than one officer being enticed away. It's a logical move, wouldn't you agree, for people with such a wealth of experience? I bet the extra money is useful too. I heard down the grapevine that you were probably going to join him. I guess you are still navy or you wouldn't be here.'

'No, I'm not, though in essence I do the same job but for a different employer. Enough about me though. What are you up to these days, are you still with the submarine service?'

'Sort of, though I can't tell you much except that I work in Idaho.'

Rosemary recollected that he'd fallen silent then and didn't seem to want to talk further about his job. But if he was still in Idaho, was he working at the high security installation at Bayview? With his experience of underwater warfare, he would be an asset to them and no wonder he had fallen silent. The work there was top secret, designing and testing futuristic submarines that would probably not see the light of day for years, maybe even decades. Alan could be just the person with whom she should be speaking.

She did not have a telephone number, or an email address for him and that necessarily must be the first step. She picked up the telephone again and punched in several numbers.

'Edward, can you take a walk over? I need you to find someone for me.'

Edward would have little trouble in locating Commander Jacks and once he did, she could obtain clearance to ask him some searching questions because from memory Alan Jacks was a special submariner. He had not only commanded a submarine with distinction but also innovated and spurred on several initiatives for weapons systems improvements. The navy must have recognised his achievements for it was not easy to join such a prestigious organisation as Bayview unless you had something exceptional to offer. She glanced at the time on her computer screen, she still had half an hour before her meeting and managed a search on Google.

It would be handy to brush up on her knowledge of the navy's Acoustic Research Detachment at Bayview. She was aware that they investigated new and visionary ideas in submarine design; the navy's Area 51. There were numerous articles and quickly she scanned several of the more interesting ones and realised she was on the right track. There was nothing classified but there was a wealth of general information and the phrases *exotic hull shaping* and *acoustic dampening* stood out. If anyone could shed some light on Admiral Schmidt's mysterious submersible then it would be Commander Jacks.

The door to the meeting room was open when she arrived and through it she could see John talking to one of the executive secretaries. Knocking lightly on the door, she drew their attention and John waved her inside.

'Rosemary, come in, take a seat. You know Joan?'

'Yes, hello Joan.'

The woman returned the greeting and after John had closed the door, she took a seat next to Rosemary and opened her notepad.

'Things are warming up a little Rosemary and the director is insisting that all meetings regarding the Russian build-up, no matter how informal, will from now on be documented. You have no objection.'

'No, no objection.'

'Well then, down to business. You called me this morning to request this meeting. What do you want to discuss, I presume it is to do with the events taking place on the Ukraine border?'

'Well I guess you are already aware of that. The Russian build-up on the borders of Poland and the Baltic states is a good place to start.'

Rosemary opened the loose-leaf folder she had brought with her and picked up a piece of paper.

'You are well aware that for some time now I have been working on the Russian troop movements and their possible intentions. I have to say that until today I believed that they were simply sabre rattling, running war games to keep us guessing.'

'What's changed?'

'Take a look at this signal from the NATO headquarters in Germany from Admiral Schmidt, he sent it this morning for release at my discretion.'

Rosemary passed over the communication and sat back in her seat as John read it.

'You think they have some new form of underwater weapon?'

'Possibly, we don't know but the German Admiralty obviously thinks that they do.'

'What about the Swedes? Have they said anything about it?'

'One of their warships has been keeping an eye on a Russian ship in the Baltic for the past few weeks.'

'But we are not even sure that there is a submersible, right?'

'Right, but the little evidence we do have points to the probability that there is, and that the Russians are using it for something we don't know yet. There is more, the First Tank Army is hiding in the forests of Belarus and other units are moving west. I am beginning to wonder if the time has come for them to attempt to seize the Suwałki Gap.'

'That is a dangerous move. They will have the whole weight of NATO down on them if they try to reconnect Kaliningrad to Russia. That is some undertaking, and will they annex Lithuania or part of Poland at the same time? Either way it will start a war, a war that would see us involved. You know how the POTUS feels about the Europeans – it would be a political nightmare, never mind the possibility of us taking on the Russians. We could sustain unacceptable losses and what would that do to public opinion. The president hasn't long to go before he leaves office and he will be thinking about his legacy, he will not want to be remembered for trashing America's armed forces.'

'That's the problem, the Russians will know that and if they run a campaign like the two they ran in Ukraine, POTUS will certainly not want to become involved with losers.'

'What about the treaties we have with the NATO countries?'

'You saw what the president did to Mexico and the trade agreements, same with the Europeans a few years ago. He doesn't care about treaties; right now he only cares about his legacy.'

'That's a serious allegation Rosemary.'

'Look, my job is to take the facts on the ground and interweave them with our enemy's probable aims. I have looked at this problem for some time and all the indications are that something spectacular is developing at a time when both the Russians and the United States will have a change of leadership. My guess is that the Russian power struggle has already taken place and the new leadership is about to flex its muscles in conjunction with the aims of the one who is stepping down.'

John fell silent for a few moments, taking in Rosemary's words, and then he looked at her.

'What's this got to do with a new type of underwater weapon?'

'So far just land forces, but what about the Russian Navy? I am starting to believe that there will soon be a maritime aspect. We have always considered that their navy would be no match for the combined fleets of the NATO countries. But they have been beefing up the Baltic fleet in Kaliningrad since two thousand eighteen and what if this machine can tip the balance? That would leave them in a strong position to push a corridor through to Kaliningrad.'

'As usual Rosemary your logic is impeccable but what you are telling me sounds like the prelude to world war three. You are very rarely wrong and that worries me. In that case, I will ask for a meeting of the Joint Chiefs. Can you put together a presentation to deliver to the meeting?'

Rosemary slowly nodded her head. She had never quite reached the same conclusion as John, never really believed that a full-blown war with Russia was likely . . . Was that going to be the case this time?

Chapter 13

Not long after the private jet landed at Genoa's
Cristoforo Colombo Airport, Alexie drove the BMW
and its passengers the fifty kilometres to Savona
where the staff had instructions to attend to their
every request. Even Anita had instructions to take
her place behind the saloon bar and not long after
the guests arrived a thickset, middle-aged man
dressed in a loud shirt and mismatched shorts
entered the saloon. Glancing round the room he
noticed Anita and made his way towards the bar and
at the same moment Bullseye walked into the
saloon.

'Sergey, welcome, you had a good journey from
Moscow?'

'Ah Leonid, yes, very satisfactory and the yacht,
it's impressive I must say. Where was she built?'

'Hamburg, the Blohm and Voss yard.'

'They made a good job of her.'

'They certainly did and I hope that you will enjoy
your stay on board. Would you like a drink?'

'That would be very nice.'

Leonid looked towards the bar and clicked his fingers at the waiting Anita.

'Yes sir?'

'My guest, pour him a drink.'

'What would you like to drink sir?'

'*Ya russkiy, my p'yem tol'ko vodku.*'

Anita looked at the Russian in some puzzlement with the appearance of not understanding him.

'You will have to speak English, she doesn't understand Russian. A fault, I admit, but with a figure like that who really cares?'

Sergey Ageyev found Anita's appearance attractive and, believing she would not understand, made a crude comment in Russian. He obviously did not know she was a fluent Russian speaker and she minded to keep it that way it was possible that she might more easily overhear useful information.

The Russian rubbed his palms together, and in competent English asked what she recommended.

'We have some very good wines on board, or maybe you would prefer a mixer . . . gin, vodka?' she said.

Reverting to Russian, he addressed his host. 'I am on holiday and they tell me you keep the very best vodka on this boat.'

'I do, you should try a cosmopolitan, which will get you off to a good start.'

Anita appeared indifferent, waiting, until Bullseye instructed her in English.

'Make him a cosmopolitan just as you do for me. He will like that I am sure.'

'Certainly sir,' Anita said, avoiding Leonid's direct gaze.

Filling a shaker with ice she added vodka, fresh lime and a dash of cranberry juice before mixing well, grateful to be working because Bullseye obviously still had eyes for her. Then the sliding door opened and Alexie appeared with two other men dressed a little more fashionably.

'Mischa, Ivanov, welcome. I hope you are settling in well. The woman here is preparing a vodka cosmopolitan for Sergey, would you care for one too?'

'Of course,' said the first.

'And make mine a big one, I haven't had a good vodka for weeks,' said the second.

Anita finished preparing Sergey's cocktail and poured it into a martini glass.

'You can make two more of those,' ordered Bullseye.

Acknowledging him, she added a twist of lemon and placed the glass on a silver tray before presenting it to Sergey. Returning to the bar she began refilling the mixer when Alexie reappeared, leaning against the open doorway and calling to her in Russian, asking if she needed anything from the cellar.

The hairs on the back of her neck stood up as she declined a response. He called again, this time telling her to turn round. He was obviously suspicious; it was a trap and the sudden realisation causing a flood of adrenaline within her.

The Sommelier

'You will need to tell her in English, Alexie.'

'I will leave that to you Leonid,' he said, striding out of the lounge.

Anita was now on full alert. Had she slipped up somehow, had she given him reason to suspect her? If she had, she could not think what it might be, and then the remaining member of the yacht's guests appeared and she quickly composed herself. He was discreetly dressed and when Leonid greeted him it was with particular reverence and Anita suspected he was a man of importance. She did not recognise him, nor any of the others for that matter, and she was able only to pick up snippets of their conversations. Then Bullseye came over to her.

'I need to be alone with my guests for a while. I suggest you make yourself busy until I need you again. Come back in half an hour to refill our glasses, knock before you come in. First though, please refill their glasses and pour one for Igor.'

Refilling the shaker, Anita topped up the Russians' drinks and then left the saloon, and as she did so Leonid put on his friendly face.

'Igor, the cocktail is to your liking?'

The head of the FSB's European section lifted his glass in mock salute.

'Very much to my liking, I have not drunk vodka like this since my sister's wedding twenty years ago. Your other guest Leonid, he has left? Borisovich's half-smile disappeared. Igor Andresov was head of the intelligence service, a powerful figure in the

Russian state apparatus, and he was straight down to business.

'Yes, he left yesterday.'

'Did he mention where he might be leaving for?'

'Germany I believe; the security team handle everything, I am sure Alexie said he had to drive him to the station to catch the early train for Munich.'

Igor pursed his lips.

'How goes the operation, has he completed all his collections from you?'

'Not all, there will be one more when we reach Marseille. That is the last one as far as I understand.'

'Ah yes, Marseille, that is right, and then you are free to take your yacht wherever you please – except across the Atlantic.' He spoke coldly, a smile struggling to spread across his face.

'I have no intention of crossing the Atlantic in the Lady Galina my friend; I have work to do in Africa and the Middle East.'

'So I hear, reward for your loyalty. Do we really need to buy your loyalty Leonid?'

'Of course not, I am a true Russian.'

'I am glad to hear it and I must say you are making a contribution to our plans. The Americans keep going on about making America great again but with their president's lacklustre performance it is Russia and not them that will be great again. Let them worry about the Chinese and the Indians, the Pacific Rim, we will look after the rest of the world.'

'I will drink to that. Would you like another?'

'Just one, I need to keep my wits about me, but for today at least I will indulge myself. You are aware I am sure that no one else knows about this meeting. I decided that a short break away where we could discuss private matters would serve as a welcome change for your guests and of course here on the high sea we have added security.'

Leonid's face took on a serious look and then he noticed the sommelier had returned and was waiting in the corridor. After a glance at Igor he waved her into the saloon.

'My friends would like more of your vodka mixers. They are Russian and never refuse vodka, eh Igor?'

Igor nodded but said nothing, instead he held out his empty glass for Anita to take, his eyes looking her over with the rapier-precision of someone well versed in duplicity. It was second nature to him.

'Your staff, who are they, where are they from?' he said, turning to his host.

'The captain and his team are all regular navy men and the rest are some of the best in the business. I only employ people who can provide the highest standard of service for my guests.'

'They are vetted, there is no chance you have been infiltrated?'

'No, Alexie and Viktor make sure of that. They are experienced, constantly checking everything on board. The housekeeper is GRU also; she keeps an eye on the girls working under her.'

Igor seemed satisfied, pursing his lips and sitting back in his seat.

'So, our friend will return when the boat reaches Marseille? We will be leaving well before then, so until we do, I will enjoy the sea air and your hospitality my friend.'

Leonid nodded to show that he understood – understood that for the time being the Lady Galina was not his yacht but Igor Andresov's floating office.

'Your drink sir,' said Anita, placing the glass in front of the intelligence chief.

Igor looked up at her somewhat taken by surprise. The woman had approached silently, slightly out of his line of sight, and he wondered how much of the conversation she had overheard. Leonid saw the look and to reassure him said, 'She speaks no Russian and Alexie has vetted her. He believes that she does not pose a security risk.'

Igor seemed to accept his host's explanation and lifting the drink to his lips took a first sip.

'That is very good my dear,' he said in English and Anita responded with a smile.

She had hoped to overhear some of the men's conversation but even though she understood Russian, she was unable to pick up very much, only a mention of a visitor, the Arab she assumed.

The Russians were settling in their consumption of vodka a good indicator and Anita had to find another bottle. She left the saloon and made her way towards the cellar.

'*Bonsoir* Anne,' said Pierre as she walked into the galley to collect the key. 'We will be ready to serve dinner in an hour. I have told Olga to inform Mr Borisovich and perhaps you should begin your own preparations straight away.'

'Of course chef, I understand that these are very important guests and Mr Borisovich wishes to impress them.'

'That's right; we need to be on our toes. Olga has already told my staff to be extra discreet, told them that these Russians are to be looked after as well as we can. *My* staff, would you believe it, I, a three-star Michelin chef, told to put on a good show, be extra discreet! Who does she think I am, have I not proved I am the best?'

'I am sure your abilities are not in question chef, it will be just a tightening of security, probably came from Alexie.'

Pierre's hurt look faded a little at Anita's words. However, she realised things were warming up, the new guests were important and even she could not afford to appear lacking.

She left Pierre to his preparations and returned to the saloon bar to service the Russians' glasses, then left to take a quick shower and put on a clean uniform before she returned to the wine cellar to collect the wine for dinner. Half a dozen bottles should get them started, she thought, the Russians had a reputation as hard drinkers and these men seemed to be proof. On her way to the dining room she passed the saloon, catching sight of Bullseye and his friends deep in conversation. Oh to be a fly on the wall, she thought.

Taking the stairs to the upper deck, she entered the dining room to see two of the domestic staff carefully placing the silver cutlery on the pristine white tablecloth, a third arranging the flowers at the centre of the table. She put the wine bottles down on the bar top before decanting them ready for the dinner and after that wiped the wine glasses with a microfiber polishing cloth until they sparkled.

Things were taking shape and looking at her watch Anita noted that it would soon be time to serve dinner. Then Olga appeared with a stern look and proceeded to cajole the girls. She was a bully, and although the girls looked up when she spoke, they were not prepared to challenge her and a strange silence pervaded. It seemed to herald a new phase; the carefree, happy banter that she had known was gone, replaced by a more morose, oppressive atmosphere.

Looking out across the Thames from his office in the secret intelligence building at Vauxhall Cross, Sir Nigel Bedlington had a fine view of a sea going barge making its way slowly up river. A peaceful enough sight in the late afternoon sun but his mind was elsewhere. He was aware of the ongoing infiltration on the super yacht and had read the report from the consulate in Milan, noting the agent's mention of Operation Venenum – easy enough to decipher the Latin but what did it mean, what was the significance of poison? He turned away from the window to face the case officer sitting in front of his desk and walked back to his own seat.

'Damn strange name for a secret operation don't you think? It almost tells you what they intend to do, poison someone, but who?'

'Could be a head of state sir, what about POTUS? He's Russia's biggest enemy now that he's wriggled out of the tight corner he found himself in during the early years of his presidency. Maybe it is payback time. The Russian president is stepping down and we know he was as mad as hell when the Americans produced evidence that the Russians were involved in the plot to undermine the presidential election.'

'You could be right Pearson, though during the president's second campaign he made sure that Russian interference was not a factor in his victory. Maybe they are trying something new, perhaps it is a play on words and they are not out to poison a person or persons but to poison the Western system of democracy. They have been trying for years to destabilise governments in the West. Look at us, what a mess we are in due in no small part to their meddling, their planting of disinformation. Our newspapers swallowed the Russian bait and they are still in denial about it. It's a pity our hands were tied, a pity we couldn't tell the public what was going on.'

'As you say sir, our hands were tied.'

'The agent on the yacht, is she safe?'

'As far as we can tell sir policy is to let agents get on with their job unhindered. If they call for help we try to give it.'

'How long has the agent been aboard the yacht?'

'About a week sir.'

'I understand security is tight on that vessel?'

'Very tight. I have a couple of operatives from the Milan consulate keeping an eye on the yacht and GCHQ is tracking it.'

'If the agent is in trouble what can you do?'

Commander Pearson remained quiet.

'I see, so she really is on her own.'

'We are keeping an eye out sir, I am sure that if anything develops we can cope. There is something else though.'

'What?'

'The guys from Milan have been forwarding images of the yacht, monitoring comings and goings so to speak, and yesterday they saw several people boarding.'

'Do we have an ID on them?'

'So far just one, a colonel general of the army called Sergey Ageyev, the Commander of the Border Guards.'

'What about the others, have you anything at all on them?'

'No not yet sir, but we have a team working on it and we should have results fairly soon.'

'What about your agent, presumably she will be rubbing shoulders with these individuals?'

'Yes sir, that was the plan, infiltrate the crew and try to discover what our Russian friends are up to. She is resilient; she has been in tight spots before and coped very well.'

'Do we have a team in place in case she is compromised and needs to get out quickly?'

'So far I just have the surveillance team from the Milan consulate.'

'They will be okay for keeping an eye on her but not much good if things get rough I shouldn't wonder.'

'Quite, I have briefed E Squadron sir. Would you like me to put them on standby?'

'Yes, I think so, see what they can do.'

'Could be a serious international incident if the fireworks go off sir, it is the Russians after all, not some Middle Eastern tin pot regime.'

'You think we should just leave her alone for the present?'

'Yes sir, we could add to the surveillance team already in place and cover more bases.'

'Such as?'

'Well as I understand it the team keeps the yacht in their sights for most of the day but not during the night. That means there are times when we have no idea what might be happening; more men means we can keep up surveillance for twenty-four hours.'

'What about us asking the Italians for some assistance?'

'We could but since the withdrawal from the European Union we don't have the old agreements in place and to ask for help would mean a high-level request and an awful lot of paperwork. That could take weeks and there is still no guarantee.'

The Acting Head of Special Operations bit his bottom lip and after a few thoughtful moments decided that an increase in surveillance might be a good idea, if he could find anyone. Even so, for the time being Agent Sims would have to manage on her own.

The Russians were beginning to relax, entering the dining room in good spirits and behind the bar Anita prepared aperitifs and picking up the silver tray, she made her way towards the men. Of course, their conversation was in Russian and Anita found it hard to take in the conversation, her mind more on serving drinks. The men hardly seemed to notice her and that gave her the opportunity to take a discreet look at each individual. She did not recognise any of them but judging by their bearing, she wondered if they could be military rather than business people? Before she could explore further Leonid ushered her away and began addressing his guests.

'My friends, may I formally welcome you aboard the Lady Galina and may I say what a privilege it is to entertain you all. You are the guardians of the Russian Federation and I salute you. To friendship,' he said, lifting his glass.

'*Za vashu druzhbu*,' said the men in unison and raising their glasses.

The Sommelier

So they are military, noted Anita, as she uncorked a second bottle, turning her head away to avoid unwanted attention.

'You will not be disappointed with the food I can assure you,' said Leonid, signalling with his index finger to Olga waiting by the doorway. 'Please comrades, take your seats.'

He then looked across at Anita and she responded by carrying wine to the table.

'I think you will like this wine my friends, it is a special Barolo, one of the best vintages from one of the best wineries. And this beautiful lady here helped me select it for your pleasure.'

'I think you selected her for your pleasure Leonid,' said one.

Luckily, the food was arriving, two servers appeared carrying the plates to the table and all eyes turned towards them. Feeling relieved Anita retreated to the bar and watched discreetly as they started to eat.

So far, their conversation had centred round trivia, families, an appreciation of their surroundings but none had given her the slightest clue as to who or what they were other than her guess that they were probably military or state security.

At Bullseye's London residence, she had encountered a mixture of guests, businessmen, financiers and of course the Russian Ambassador, but these men did not fit any of those categories. She did notice that the last guest to enter the saloon clearly commanded the respect of the others, Bullseye included and she learned that his name was Igor. From what she could observe, he appeared to set the agenda so who was he?

Bullseye caught her eye and signalled for her to refill their glasses, the one called Sergey had already drained his and Anita marked him down as a drinker and talkative individual. Then she caught Igor looking at her, his eyes penetrating and cold, but before she could react, the servers reappeared to clear away the dishes.

'Igor, the asparagus was to your liking?'

The spell was broken as Igor's host distracted him and he looked away from Anita.

'Yes, the best I have tasted in a long time,' he said savouring the wine. 'This wine *is* excellent, where did you get it from?'

'My sommelier here,' said Bullseye, gesturing towards Anita who did not acknowledge him. 'Alexie drove her into the countryside to find a special vineyard known for its fine wines. She is the one to thank.'

Igor looked again at Anita, this time with some respect.

'You must send me a few bottles. I will need a good wine to smooth the passage of the next few months. Great things are in the air; soon we will show the world our true worth. To Mother Russia,' he said lifting his glass in a toast and from around the table the others raised their glasses too.

The Sommelier

Did he say they would show the world Russia's worth? Anita was sure he had, but what did that mean? She had no time to dwell; Leonid called for the next bottle, a rare wine held back for the main course and insisted that Igor be the first to taste it. Anita moved to his side and poured a little wine into his glass for approval. Turning towards her he lifted it to his lips and took a mouthful whilst holding her gaze before declaring the wine eminently drinkable.

'I thought you were never going to give the woman permission to serve us Leonid. I must say this wine is very good, she is indeed an expert.'

Anita found it hard not to react, forcing herself to take a step back until Bullseye gave a wave of his hand instructing her to fill every other glass.

'Your good health gentlemen and now for the guinea fowl, one of my favourite dishes.'

'Guinea fowl, now that is something I have never tasted,' said Sergey. 'My boys in the regiments on the border would be envious of me if they knew.'

'But they will not know, eh Sergey?' said the man sitting opposite. 'We had guinea fowl once when we were stationed at the Borisovsky Khotilovo air base. I liked it but you don't get a lot, not enough to keep you warm in a Russian winter.'

'This isn't a Russian winter Mischa; this is the Mediterranean and tonight is a chance for us to try something a little better than military cooking.'

The men began to laugh, amused at the contrast between Russian military food and the food on the superyacht. Anita listened as she made her way round the table refilling glasses. Then she caught a snippet of conversation between Igor and Bullseye.

'The Arab has been busy I see.'

'Yes, we have suffered his company once or twice.'

'Suffered his company?'

'He is not particularly friendly. He comes and he goes, he keeps to himself and I see little of him.'

'Good, the less people know about him the better. We have used him to good advantage so far and after he leaves you in Marseille we will have no more use for him.'

'The operation is completed?'

'It will be once he returns to Paris.'

'More wine sir?' asked Anita, arriving at the left hand of Bullseye.

'Yes of course Igor, some more wine?'

Igor pushed his glass forward in response. Although not particularly suspicious of Anita, he knew there was always the possibility of a spy on board the yacht and changed the subject. So far, the distribution of money to the terrorist cells had worked well and his informants had heard nothing to the contrary. The European security services were silent on the subject and it would be only days before he closed the operation down. Then the critical stage would begin. Each individual cell was to acquire materials for an attack – chemicals to build bombs, a vehicle perhaps. The cells did not yet know their objectives and of concern was the fact that they were not military personnel. Some had received training in the camps of Syria and Yemen where they measured success not in body counts, more by the disruption they caused. He had used similar tactics in Chechnya many years before and knew that amateurs posed a risk, but with the right controls, they could prove very effective.

Anita tried hard to overhear the conversation but the man was competent and gave nothing away save for the one word Paris and several bottles later, their appetites satiated, the guests and their host retired to the outdoors, to sit on the loungers and soft seats to smoke and to talk. It was not a place for Anita, it was a place for men only and man-talk and so she retired to the galley to find Pierre wanting to know how his food was going down.

'Oh yes Pierre, they were impressed by your food. How could they not be?'

The chef's eyes lit up.

'That is good; I know Mr Borisovich wants to impress these people. Between you and me I think that back in Russia they are powerful people.'

'I'm sure you are right. I need some more serviettes.'

'Over there in the wall cupboard,' he said pointing.

'Ah yes, I remember.'

Anita had plenty of serviettes behind the bar but she needed an excuse to get away, to stand down and take time out to think. What had she learned? She was sure two were Russian military, the others she was not wholly sure of but the one called Igor, he was not military, he was different.

'You should be in the dining room,' said a voice with a strong Slavic accent, jolting Anita back to reality.

Olga must have noticed her leave the room and followed her. The sight of the woman was unnerving and reaching for a handful of serviettes, she turned to go back to the dining room.

Damnation, she thought, had she aroused suspicions, had she made some mistake? Had Alexie seen her talking to the agent at the winery? Perhaps they were keeping quiet, watching her until they had proof of her activities? She felt her mouth become dry, felt that time was running out and she should leave the Lady Galina, but not before Marseille, not until the Arab returned. She decided she would try to leave when Shadow did, try to follow him to Paris for she was convinced that was where he would go. First though she would have to get ashore unseen and then, without any means of contacting her controller or any money, somehow get to the French capital.

Commander Pearson looked up to see his office door open and the stern face from the previous day.

'What have you found out? Anything of use, do we know who the visitors to the superyacht are?'

'Er yes sir, we have turned something up. Here are the files for each of them.' He placed a beige folder on his superior's desk. 'Briefly sir, they are

Colonel General Sergey Ageyev of the Russian Federation Border Force, Colonel General Mischa Bonderov of the Air Force Special Purpose Command, and Admiral Ivanov Ushakov, Second in Command of the Northern Fleet.'

'There was a fourth man, have you anything on him?'

'Yes we do, and it makes fascinating reading. His name is Igor Andresov, he is FSB and not only that, we believe he is head of the European section.'

'A spook and three high-ranking military, quite a gathering, so what are they up to?'

'We are not sure, it does seem strange to see them on NATO soil having what looks like a jolly.'

'That is just a cover, obviously, but why would they risk being seen together in southern Europe?'

'We have no idea other than that they are well away from Moscow. There are rumours of a power shift in the Kremlin. It does make sense to plot well away from there, reduce the risk of discovery.'

'Hmm . . . Russian intrigue, we have seen enough of that in our time have we not?'

'Certainly have sir. My money would be on that scenario but where does this Arab fit in, the one our agent is interested in?'

The commander looked thoughtful for a few moments.

'We are not exactly sure all we know is that he has made several visits to the yacht and that they have pretty tight security, a couple of GRU men and maybe there are others. With these characters on board our agent could find herself in a tight corner if she is not careful.'

'There is more sir, the Lady Galina left Savona late yesterday evening. We are tracking her and she seems to be heading down the coast towards Monaco, perhaps Nice or even Marseille.'

'We need to know her destination as soon as possible. I want a team sent to the coast to keep her under surveillance, let us know wherever she docks. Those men on board are a puzzle, why would high-ranking Russian military instigate a clandestine meeting. They must be planning something and if there is a power struggle in the Kremlin, I'll wager it has something to do with that.'

'Perhaps it's a matter of privacy. It's not as if any listening device I know of could eavesdrop on a boat at sea.'

'If that's the case then could we plant a bug when she docks?'

'I doubt it sir, security is pretty tight.'

'Well at least if our agent has found anything out about their plans then we need to know what they are. What we do not want is to find her dead. I think it's time to call on E Squadron to see what they can do for us.'

'Can you sign here for the files sir; I will collect them once you have finished with them. Sir, what about the French, should we involve them?'

'No, these days it is far too complicated to deal with a foreign power, friendly or not. Until our politicians can sort things out, I will resort to calling in a favour from DGSI if I need to. Their internal intelligence service owes us a few favours, especially after our warnings of a couple of years ago.'

'I remember sir that could have turned out very badly.'

'But it didn't thank God; but we do know that there are still terrorist cells lying low in France. Okay, take care of what we have discussed and I will put it all in writing, apart that is from communicating with the French. For the time being that will remain off the record.'

The security officer and the Acting Head of Special Operations parted company, the security officer to complete his log entries for the day and the acting head to contemplate the wellbeing of the agent. She was isolated and could have vital information. It was paramount that she was able to deliver that information.

The dinner party went on until well past midnight. After smoking on deck, the Russians had returned to the dining room and consumed copious more quantities of very expensive red wine. Finally, they decided it was bedtime and Anita watched them trail out of the saloon bar a more than a little worse for wear. Giving them a few minutes to leave the vicinity she began to collect the empty glasses, tidy up the bar space, then Bullseye appeared.

'You have made my guests very happy tonight. They were impressed by your knowledge of wine and I must say they admired your figure.' He paused before saying, 'As I do.'

'Thank you sir,' she said, her guard up, aware that he too had consumed his fair share of alcohol.

'You have worked hard and I appreciate that, perhaps as a reward you can come to my cabin for a nightcap and relax a little.'

'I would like that sir,' she willed herself to say.

'Call me Leonid, no need for formalities; you are off duty.'

'If you say so . . . Leonid.'

His crocodile smile returned, even so she would attend to his demands for as long as she could stomach him.

'I just need to lock the cellar for the night Leonid, and then I will come to the master cabin for a nightcap. Should I bring the Glenmorangie from the bar?'

'That sounds like a good idea. I will see you in my cabin in ten minutes.'

'Ten minutes,' she said, forcing a smile.

She really did not want to sleep with the Russian but if it meant eliciting useful information then she did not have a great deal of choice. Piling the empty glasses on her tray she gave a reassuring glance in Leonid's direction and left to lock the cellar door for the night.

Minutes later, she entered the galley to find Pierre and his assistants busy cleaning up.

'You look tired Anne; you have had a busy evening looking after Mr Borisovich's guests no?'

'Yes, busy but interesting and now I am to take Mr Borisovich a nightcap, a special twenty-five-year-old Glenmorangie from the saloon bar.'

Pierre glanced towards her, aware of his boss's weakness for a good-looking woman and the sommelier certainly fitted that description. Avoiding her eyes, he turned away and went towards his small office. Anita noticed then a sharp kitchen knife on the work surface. Pierre's assistant was nearby cleaning the oven, but her back was turned, and Anita took her chance. Grabbing hold of the knife handle she slipped the implement into her shirt and turned towards Pierre's office door.

'Pierre, I will need to lock the cellar, can I have the key please?'

Pierre reached above his desk and lifted the key from its hook, handing it to Anita and catching her eye.

'Don't worry about me Pierre,' she said, reading his mind, 'I have handled difficult situations like this before. Remember the garlic; I don't think I should try that again just yet though do you?'

Pierre gave her a concerned look before a smile crossed his face and he returned to his bookwork. Anita left him to it and made her way to the wine cellar, where she looked for a hiding place for the knife. She hoped that she might not need it but at least she had a weapon. Moving several bottles on the shelf nearest to her, she placed the knife out of sight but within easy reach and leaning back against the wall, she closed her eyes for a few moments. She wondered how she might handle Bullseye for she did not relish sleeping with him but she would have to go through the motions. Her only hope was one of the buttons from her blue blouse issued by the dirty tricks department.

The saloon, one deck below the dining room, was in semi-darkness when she arrived to collect the whisky bottle, the only illumination provided by the half-moon and some deck lights, enough for her to make out the bar. She approached through the gloom and as she reached for the whiskey bottle, she noticed two shadows pass the window . Taken aback to begin with she recovered and silently made her way towards the big picture window and the doorway covered by lace curtains. Very slowly, she pulled one half of the curtain aside and peered out across the deck. There was a flicker of orange light as someone lit a match and two pinpricks of red appeared, She carefully slid the door open a few centimetres and strained her ears. Two men were smoking and speaking on low voices but they were unclear, muffled by the glass, and so she dared to slide the door open further, enough to distinguish their words.

'Ivanov, this business with the American war plane the F-35, surely we can counter it once operations begin.'

'Sergey, you know as well as I do that the Americans are more advanced in electronic warfare than we are. Our best hope is to try and neutralise them before we move. I believe there are plans to achieve this but I do not know any of the details. If they can be prevented from operating near our forces then the operation has a good chance of success.'

Anita strained her ears but the two men began to stroll away along the deck and then she remembered Leonid. She had said ten minutes but she guessed she had been away for almost twice that length of time already. Quickly she sprinted back to the bar, grabbed the whisky bottle in one hand, two shot glasses in the other, and ran up the stairs past the dining room and up to the master cabin on the deck above.

'Ah there you are, you are late, I expected you here sooner.'

'Sorry . . . Leonid, I had to lock up the cellar but I had a small accident, er, I knocked over an empty bottle and smashed it in my rush to get back here. I couldn't just leave it.'

'No matter, you are here now and I see you have our nightcap and you have changed out of your uniform. I must say that you do look very attractive.'

'Yes, thank you, how do you like your whisky, with water?'

'Yes, just a little, come into the cabin, I have water in my fridge. I suppose I should keep some whisky there too but since the Romanian girl went into hospital I have had no need.'

The Romanian girl, of course, she must have experienced this self-same situation but in her case, the girl was probably a willing participant.

'How much?' asked Anita, unscrewing the cap.

'Make it half whisky and half water. I will get the water,' he said walking across the room to the bar.

Immediately Anita felt for the top button of her blouse and pulled, breaking it in two and dropping the pieces into the shot glass before adding the whisky. The two small pieces did not fully dissolve and she worried that he might notice them as he took a drink. It was time to cast caution aside and in a provocative manner, she undid the next button of her blouse, exposing just a hint of her breasts. It had the effect she hoped for, Bullseye could not help but stare, his eyes widening as he imagined her, or better still himself, undoing the rest of the buttons.

Holding his gaze, she took the bottle of water from him and topped up the glasses, swilling them round provocatively and licking her lips before handing him his.

'I remember you showing me the Russian way to drink,' she said, lifting up her glass.

'Ah yes,' he said, reaching his hand out to entwine it with hers. 'To an enjoyable evening my dear.'

'I will drink to that,' said Anita placing the shot glass to her lips and drinking just a minute amount. Bullseye was less cautious, consuming half of his drink in one gulp.

'You like the whisky?'

'I do and this one is certainly special.'

'Another?'

He nodded, finished the rest of his drink and handed her his glass. As she turned to retrieve the whisky bottle, she felt his hand on her buttocks.

'You don't waste much time Leonid, do you?'

'With such a beautiful woman as you I cannot afford to waste time.'

She handed him his drink, watched his greedy eyes roam across her breasts, down over her stomach. Then with a flourish, he downed the contents of the shot glass and put his arm around her waist.

'That was quick, would you like another one?'

She filled his glass for a third time and instead of drinking quickly, he rolled the liquid around in his mouth, savouring the taste, and without releasing his grip, looked Anita in the eye.

'Tonight I want you; I can make it profitable for you. Name your price?'

'I have never been propositioned like this before,' Anita managed to respond, shocked by the sudden direct approach. 'I don't know what to say.'

'Come now, you are a woman of the world and you would not be here in my cabin if you were not prepared to, shall we say taste forbidden fruit. How about it if I give you a thousand dollars? I can transfer it to your account right now with my smartphone.'

Anita looked at him and could not help but smile, he was offering a large sum of money for something she hoped he would never experience. Why not?

'Let's make it five thousand dollars, now, money transfer. I pay for all my women with Moneytrans, a Maltese company in which I am a stockholder. It's easy; give me your email address,' he said yawning.

Under normal circumstances, Anita would have rebuffed him but she had to concede that he was persuasive and these were not normal circumstances.

'ladyfromlondon at gmail dot com, lady from london all one word, lower case.'

She held his gaze, felt a power she had not known before as she watched him fumble with his phone. This was one of the richest men in the world and he was prepared to pay a lot of money to have sex with her. Although she viewed it as work, she really did not want to enter into any sleazy contract with Bullseye if she could help it and to her relief she could see the combination of alcohol and her presence was beginning to have an effect upon him. 'There it's done, now tonight you are mine,' he said beginning to slur his words. 'There, you are five thousand dollars richer. Now come, sit with me on the bed, let me taste you,' he said in a commanding voice, grasping her hand leading her into the master bedroom. 'You like my bedroom?'

She did not reply, recoiling slightly as he turned to face her, his hands first touching her neck then across her shoulders. Standing firm she allowed him to kiss her on her lips, felt his fingers fumble as he unfastened the rest of her blouse buttons. It was not an altogether unpleasant experience, his hands were soft from a lack of manual work and his kiss gentle enough, but once he started to undress her further and press his body against hers she became alarmed.

'It is for King and country,' she said to herself as she tried to respond and then, quite suddenly, he pulled her onto the bed and his hands began to explore more thoroughly. In the dim light, she could make out his closed eyes and could feel his breath on her as his passion rose. Then, without warning, his body became limp. The drug had worked and for a few minutes she lay still and not daring to move until she was quite sure that he was unconscious. Carefully she slipped out from under him and wondered what to do. To leave the master suite and return to her own cabin would undoubtedly raise doubts in Bullseye's mind. She could pursue that course of action, see what the morning would bring, or she could do her job. Making up her mind, she slid off the bed, picked her blouse up from the floor and placed it on a chair and then she kicked off her shoes

Chapter 14

Well before seven o clock the following morning the Lady Galina was standing off Antibes awaiting permission to enter port and in the master cabin, Anita was just waking up. Next to her she felt Bullseye stir, groaning quietly before he opened his eyes and turned his head towards her.

'Oh my head, what on earth happened last night?'

'You had your money's worth Leonid; don't tell me you do not remember anything of our passion.'

He lay on his back and stared up at the ceiling, his mind a blank. The drug had done its job. Closing his eyes again, he tried to recall the previous evening but, apart from the dinner, nothing came to mind. However, a man of his standing had a reputation to maintain and until his memory restored itself, he would go along with the sommelier.

'Was it good for you?' he asked.

'Oh yes, you are a very sexy man Leonid.'

'Good, that makes me happy,' he said, a frown creasing his brow. 'I must get up, my guests are departing today and I must leave for the Emirates for a business meeting. I will be gone for two days at least. You must leave now my dear and perhaps we can get back together when I return.'

Still looking somewhat puzzled Bullseye got up from the bed and went to the bathroom and Anita, without hesitation took her chance. Dressing quickly she left the master suite, closed the door silently behind her. For the time being at least, she had escaped Bullseye's clutches and walking quickly along the corridor, she descended the staircase unaware that Viktor was watching her on the monitor.

'The boss has all the luck,' he grunted, watching until Anita left the camera's field of vision.

She hurried down the staircase, through the decks to the crew accommodation, she was already late for duty and she needed to change back into her uniform. The last thing she wanted was the overbearing Olga breathing down her neck.

She took a quick shower dressed in her uniform and applied the minimum make-up and just ten minutes late she hurried into the dining room and through the panoramic window, she could see that they were already entering port. Below crewmen were busy preparing the moorings and the Russian guests were leaning on the ship's rail watching the yacht's progress.

This morning the drinks were strictly orange juice and sparkling water and as Anita busied herself filling jugs, she hoped she might at least learn something useful. Minutes later, in ones and twos, the men wandered into breakfast their

The Sommelier

conversation just small talk and Anita felt some disappointment. If she had been able to overhear them just a little earlier as they leaned over the rail, she would have heard something of far more interest. The quiet revolution within the Kremlin walls was the topic of conversation, the power struggle that was nearing its climax. As the servers removed the plates and the coffee arrived Igor Andresov instructed the staff to leave the room.

'Comrades, I thank you for coming here,' he said, commanding the men's attention. 'We will soon part company but before we do I can announce that I have received a message from the Kremlin. There has been a development; Comrade Grachyov has consolidated his position with the backing of the president and most of the Politburo. When the president steps down, Grachyov will ease into the presidential shoes and the Russian Federation will carry on as normal. Those who are loyal can expect promotion and those that oppose him . . . well we know what will happen to them. After our discussion last evening, you are aware that there are plans to expand our borders. Your commands are important for that expansion drive and when you return home you will receive your orders. Events are taking place that will shape our country for years to come and during the next few weeks, we will begin executing the plan. The president has spent his terms in office pushing back both the United States and NATO, recreating the Russian sphere of influence that is out birthright. Very soon, we will be

310

back in our rightful place, a world power, commanding a large part of the northern hemisphere. To regain that influence has taken a generation. Comrade Grachyov intends to carry on that work, and on top of that, our president wishes to leave a legacy the Russian people will remember for a thousand years. The ultimate goal is to return Russia to the great days of the past when all Europe envied us.'

Igor paused for a moment to take a drink of water and as he did so looked at each of the men in turn.

'You were contacted many months ago and have proved your loyalty. We have consolidated our grip on Ukraine, brought the country back into the fold. Belarus will do as we ask, as will the former Soviet satellites. The next step is to take over the Baltic States and consolidate Comrade Grachyov's hold on power. In the coming weeks you will be privy to more detailed plans and will be required to mobilise for a possible war with the West. Are there any questions so far?'

Colonel General Bonderov, his face somewhat troubled, was the first to reply.

'Comrade Andresov, we will not be able to keep troop movements secret from the Americans for long and although we would expect to overrun their positions within hours of any invasion we do not have complete air superiority.'

'We have a greater number of combat aircraft and manpower I believe. Should we be concerned? Of course, they have the F-35, a dangerous adversary.

It is invisible to our radar installations and its battlefield capability is superior to our fighters.'

'I understand our Su-57 stealth fighter is more than a match for the American fighter?' a puzzled General Sergey Ageyev interceded.

'In one-to-one combat it is, but the total battlefield control of the F-35 and its stealth capabilities make it superior in many situations and NATO have quite a few of them in service,' said air force General Bonderov.

'Gentlemen,' continued Igor, 'please do not talk down our weapons systems, we have plans to neutralise a large part of the NATO force and to do that we will make sure a significant portion of their F-35 assets never come within range of our air force. Our cyber warfare capability will slow down any response their military may take and more than that, public opinion in the West will be against hostilities. We have proved before that we can manipulate news and opinions and that is what we are planning for, a short war with substantive gains before a stalemate.'

Igor, his expression cold and humourless, added, 'Any Russian grandmaster will be proud of us.'

Then Admiral Ushakov spoke: 'I can assure you Comrade General, plans to neutralise NATO are at an advanced stage.'

'Not here Ivanov, our plans are secret. Once it is officially announced that Comrade Grachyov is to assume power, a meeting of the General Staff will be convened and more details of the plan revealed.'

The Sommelier

Igor paused for a few moments, noting the expressions of those sitting round the table, all high-ranking military men, all showing little in the way of emotion.

'We leave the yacht after lunch; Comrade Borisovich's private jet will take you to several sites in southern Russia under cover of darkness. It would not do for you to be seen together, suspicions would be raised and we do not want that. I will not be coming with you; I have a meeting planned with our ambassador to France. And finally, I do not expect that I need to impress upon you the need for utmost secrecy.'

'Of course not Comrade Andresov, we all understand that,' said Colonel General Ageyev.

'You would like a drink Sergey?' said Igor, lightening the mood.

'Yes, and I am hungry too, the food on this boat is very good. What time is lunch because by mid-day my stomach will think my throat has been cut?'

Alexie stroked his chin thoughtfully. 'You saw the woman leave the master cabin this morning?'

'That is what I said Alexie. You can see on the video recording.'

Leonid was becoming careless, drinking too much and now he had apparently spent the night with the English woman. Something at the back of Alexie's mind was beginning to tell him she was not what she seemed, and the fact that she had spent the night with Mr Borisovich only heightened those suspicions.

The guests were to leave for the private jet after dinner and the following morning Mr Borisovich would be flying out to the Emirates for a business meeting. From then until his return Alexie would be in overall charge of the vessel and then he could examine the video footage in detail.

'Viktor, look through the tapes again, find out when the woman was working unattended, whenever she was alone. I want to see what she did; I want know if she is doing something she should not.'

'You think she is foreign intelligence?'

'I am not sure. She is making Borisovich happy and I do not want the blame for spoiling his fun but we have our job to do Viktor. We don't work for him, we work for GRU.'

Several decks below, the galley staff were busy preparing lunch for the soon to be departing Russians, and Pierre was his usual single-minded self. Holding a spoon to his lips he was in the process of tasting his sauce when Anita walked through the door.

'*Bonjour madame.*'

'Morning Pierre. What have we on the menu for today?'

'Just a light lunch of roasted langoustines with asparagus puree and truffle sauce with a crab salad and a sweet potato mash.'

'Hmm, I will need to think about that. A dry white, perhaps I should serve the 2006 Chablis Grand Cru.'

'Very good madam, I am sure it will complement my dish and then our guests can leave satisfied. To prepare yourself for tomorrow I can tell you that I do believe the Arab, who only eats lamb, will be returning, for Alexie has asked me to make extra portions for him and Viktor.'

'Returning, when?'

'Tomorrow, after we reach Marseille.'

'Is he stopping overnight?'

'I do not think so; I have instructions to prepare a lamb dish for a late lunch tomorrow and in the evening to cook only for the crew. With Mr Borisovich away and without any guests on board we can relax a little.'

'I will have a look at the wine for lunch today. No need to worry about tomorrow's guest, he doesn't drink alcohol, and if the boss is away the crew can finish off the wine.'

Pierre gave her a smile and returned to his tasting, leaving her to retrieve the cellar key from the rack, her mind already working on the problem of the Arab. As she walked along the short corridor she wondered how she might get close to him.

Alexie and Viktor were not privy to the wider plans of the Politburo; their job was simply to look after security on board the yacht and to guard the safe and its contents.

'This will be the last time our friend visits us and after that we can expect fresh orders.'

'I will be sorry to leave,' said Viktor, 'this has been one of my better assignments. I don't think navy food will ever be the same again.'

Alexie managed a grunt, the chef's creations had seduced him too, but he had other more urgent matters to attend to. He looked at his watch, almost two o clock, the flight was due to leave at five that afternoon so it was time he checked the car for fuel.

'I expect Mr Borisovich will be saying goodbye to his friends soon. I will be away for a few hours so keep an eye on the sommelier during that time. You know how Borisovich likes women and I worry that particular one could be a spy.'

Viktor nodded, he hadn't considered that the sommelier was a particular security risk but Alexie had made him think and after Alexie left he began a search through the security camera footage. Alexie left to instruct the deck crew to put the BMW on the quayside and then he decided to look for Olga.

'You wanted to talk Alexie, have we a problem?'

'I am not sure yet but maybe I soon will be. The English woman, the sommelier, I am beginning to believe she is not all she seems, I think that perhaps she is a foreign agent, British secret service probably.'

Olga's eyebrows lifted in surprise.

'The sommelier, she is an agent of the British Secret Service, really?'

'Not so loud, someone might be listening. I do not know for sure but while I am travelling to the airport, I want you and Viktor to keep a close eye on her. She spent the night with Borisovich and there are one or two small incidents that don't quite add up.'

'I could take her somewhere and interrogate her, find out what she is doing.'

'I don't think we can use those tactics here Olga, maybe if we have some proof, also we are in France don't forget. The rules we are used to don't necessarily apply here.'

'What do you want me to do exactly?'

'Just keep close to her and if she does anything beyond her normal duties then I need to know. I will talk to you when I get back from the airport later this evening. If you want to talk before I go then call me on the radio, now though I am going to speak with Viktor.'

After a lazy afternoon and a late lunch, the Russians took their seats in the saloon. Soon they would be leaving to return to Russia but before they left they chatted while the sommelier charged their glasses.

'You have enjoyed your stay aboard the Lady Galina?' asked Leonid, taking his seat opposite Igor.

'Indeed we have Leonid and we are appreciative of the privacy afforded by this magnificent vessel.'

'You must bring your wife later in the season; have a few days together, cruising the Mediterranean perhaps.'

'That would be very nice though I would prefer the Black Sea.'

'Of course, just inform the ship's purser and he will arrange everything. My private jet can take you wherever you wish.'

Igor inclined his head slightly in response.

'Perhaps next year, I am afraid I will be busy for a while. We are all going to be busy are we not comrades? To Mother Russia,' he said, raising his glass.

The response was immediate and, as one, the men touched glasses before drinking the toast. Igor became thoughtful, taking just a small sip from his glass, conscious of the dangerous times in which they were living. Ever since the president had declared that he would step down at the end of his term in office a power struggle had ensued. For over a year secret messages had circulated, clandestine meetings had taken place and behind the scenes the new order had begun to emerge. In a matter of days, the president would reveal the name of his successor to the public and Igor felt pleased he had backed the right horse.

Russian politics were divisive, secretive and to be on the wrong side could be disastrous. He had learned early in the struggle for power that those who held the most cards and commanded powerful backing were the likely winners. After several discreet conversations with those near to the Politburo, he had worked towards the elevation of Feodor Grachyov and once he received the nomination, he was as sure as he could be that his position would remain secure.

'Sergey, Mischa, Ivanov, we have had a productive few days together, a useful prelude to what is to come. We will meet again in the near future.'

'Yes Igor, to the future,' said Admiral Ushakov, raising his glass.

'Leonid, no one should know of our visit here, certainly for the next week or so. I can tell you in strict confidence that the succession is resolved.'

Bullseye's ears pricked up, he was a very rich man, useful to the state apparatus, and he enjoyed privileges not afforded to the mass of the Russian population. Nevertheless, he relied upon the patronage of powerful politicians to survive and he worried that a change at the top might affect his business interests.

'There will be an election?' he asked.

'Of course Leonid, otherwise we could not present to the world how free and open we really are, though we will know the winner in advance.'

Leonid shrugged his shoulders; nothing had changed since the revolution, those in power still ran the country without recourse to the people and he had to admit, in his situation, he preferred it that way.

'I will watch out for the announcement. You still have some time before you need to leave for the airport. Why not look round the rest of the yacht, explore parts you have not yet seen and then maybe have a coffee before you depart? I have a gym on board and there is a Jacuzzi.'

'How the other half live, eh Leonid? I would imagine losing all this would be a disaster.'

Leonid felt his stomach lurch and he shivered as Igor's words struck home.

'Have no fear, I am a true Russian and you know how useful I have been in the past.'

'I did not mean to worry you my friend. We know how useful you are,' said Igor, his expression not of much encouragement to Leonid. 'The lunch was superb by the way, compliments to the chef and now I think that I would like a cigarette.'

The other men were of like mind, finishing the last of their drinks and ready for some fresh air out on deck. Most of them smoked and as they ambled out of the dining room, Igor followed lighting his cigarette and blowing the smoke skywards.

'The courier will make his last visit tomorrow Leonid?'

'I believe so, Alexie and Viktor handle the details, it is their operation and I have nothing to do with the courier.'

Igor pursed his lips, well aware that the GRU men were handling the operation, they were under his control and reported to his department. It was his brainchild and he did not want an amateur interfering.

Just over an hour later, Anita was polishing glasses and using the activity as cover. The visitors were leaving the Lady Galina and she leaned forward just enough to observe them. The Deck crew carried their bags, the BMW was already on the quayside waiting with Alexie standing nearby, a pair of sunglasses enhancing his thuggish appearance. Below she could see Bullseye and one of the party walking off the gangplank, having a few final words. She still did not recognise yet was sure that they were Russian military. the one with Bullseye though was different, a man with an authority beyond his travelling companions. They treated him with respect, deferred to him in conversation and it appeared that he was not leaving with them.

Why, she wondered, watching them and then suddenly Alexie turned his head towards the yacht and she pulled away. After a few minutes she dared to take another look to find that the BMW already moving towards the dock gate. She turned her attention to Bullseye and his remaining guest walking slowly back towards the gangplank deep in conversation

'Leonid,' said Igor, consulting his watch, 'the ambassador's car will be here in an hour, perhaps a coffee is in order.'

'Would you like something stronger Igor, vodka perhaps?'

'In my line of work consuming alcohol at the wrong time, impairing one's judgement, can have disastrous consequences. No, although you have a well-stocked cellar and I have enjoyed savouring some of your exquisite wine, coffee is my preferred beverage. Let us sit a while in the sunshine and while away the hour, you can tell me about your mining interests, advise me perhaps on investments I should buy with my meagre salary from the defence department.'

Leonid took a sideways glance at his guest: was it an opening gambit in a bribe request? It would not be the first time he had been approached by a powerful salaryman looking to supplement his income. It worked both ways; a payment inevitably bought a favour, the size depending upon the power the man wielded and, of course, the magnitude of the bribe.

'Just a moment,' Leonid said, waving his hand and beckoning Anita who had just reached the foot of the stairs. 'Anne, arrange coffee for myself and my guest and serve it on the aft deck by the swimming pool. Would you like a swim before you leave us Igor? I see you have been too busy for any real relaxation.'

'Thank you no; I have to confess that I am not too happy in the water. A coffee and a little time in the sun will be just fine.'

'Please, come this way then and let us find comfortable seats. Perhaps a choice of cakes would be nice.'

For once Igor smiled.

'That would be nice as I rarely have the chance to satisfy my sweet tooth. Yes, a taste from your sweet trolley to go with the coffee will round off my stay here very nicely.'

The Sommelier

'And bring a selection of cakes . . .'

Anita nodded and walked in the direction of the galley, returning ten minutes later with a tray of cakes and a coffee pot. As she reached the door to the outer deck, she met her acquaintance from the Midlands carrying a mop and bucket.

'They look inviting,' said Lynn, I wouldn't mind one of those with a coffee myself.'

'Hello Lynn, sorry, not this time, they are for Mr Borisovich and his guest by the swimming pool,' said Anita pushing past, eager to get rid of the girl.

'Ah, here we are,' said Leonid as Anita reached him.

'I must say we rarely get anything as tempting as these in the Aquarium,' said Igor.

Addressing him in English Anita said, 'Would you like to choose your own sir or should I serve you.'

'Oh I think it would be best if you serve. What do you think Leonid?'

A pang of jealousy at Igor's attentiveness shot through Bullseye. 'Yes, if that is what you want Igor,' he said, his eyes meeting those of Anita.

Good, Bullseye still had a yearning for her, that was useful, and more importantly his guest had let slip that he worked in the Aquarium and that could mean only one thing. Lowering her gaze, she placed the tray on the low table in front of the men and began to pour the coffee. Topping each with whipped cream, she moved the cups nearer to them and picked up the silver tongs, inviting them to choose a cake.

'Thank you, that will be all for now,' said Bullseye, eager to break Igor's attachment to her.

As she walked away, a mildly coarse comment about her in Russian reached her ears. She hardly noticed, her mind concentrated more on Igor's comment about the Aquarium, the nickname given to GRU headquarters by those who worked there. From the respect shown by his now departed colleagues, Igor must be of some importance in Russian intelligence and Anita began to ponder why they had congregated on board a superyacht. What were they doing, what was the reason for them being here? Apart from a few hours relaxation, they had spent most of their time locked in discussion. Then there was the Arab, how did he fit in to all this?

Half an hour later, she was in the galley when the telephone rang and one of the assistants answered it.

'It's Olga, she says you have to go and clear the table by the swimming pool.'

Anita left the galley and for a few minutes visited the washroom nearby, tidied her hair and used the little finger of her right hand to remove a smudge of lipstick, and looking presentable, she made her way back to the pool area. As she arrived, she saw that both Leonid and the other Russian had left, but out of the corner of her eye she noticed a car pull up at the quayside. It was a black limousine, the registration 315 CMD, definitely a diplomatic plate and one from the Russian Federation Embassy in France.

The Sommelier

Her attention now fully focused on the car as a heavily built man climbed out and walked towards the yacht. Viktor was there, standing guard she presumed, and the two men seemed to know each other.

Anita watched them for several minutes until Bullseye and his departing guest appeared with a deck hand carrying his bag. Both men turned to look at the Lady Galina and Anita felt a wave of anxiety. Was it a sixth sense telling her that she was the subject of their conversation? Had the man realised his slip of the tongue? If he were Russian intelligence then he was no fool and if he had made a mistake, he would look to rectify it. But they did not dwell, shaking hands before Igor climbed into the back seat of the limousine and Bullseye made his way towards the gangplank.

When Alexie returned from the airport, he went straight to the control room to find Viktor seated with his feet on the desk. He had a cup of coffee in his hand and a still shot of the staircase outside the saloon filling one of the monitor screens.

'Found anything?'

'Some bits and pieces, I have been at it since you left. I looked through a couple of the recordings and I cannot say that I have found anything obvious. She does disappear on occasion and we know that she spent last night in the master cabin.'

'All night, but did she leave at all during the night?'

'Not the master cabin I am sure but she could have gone missing for a short time before she went in there. I saw her enter the saloon for maybe ten minutes but what she was doing there I don't know. There is something on this recording that shows only her silhouette for brief periods.'

'What is in there that would be of interest?'

'She came out holding a bottle of some sort but it shouldn't have taken her that long.'

'Who else was about at that time?'

'I don't know. Everyone had gone to his or her cabins except this woman. Even Mr Borisovich was alone in the master suite.'

'While I check with the captain about leaving for Marseille just have a scan through the recordings from all the other cameras. Let's see if anyone else was about at that time,' said Alexie, taking a glance over Viktor's shoulder before leaving to walk the few metres to the bridge.

When he entered through the sliding door, he found the captain and the first officer huddled over a chart.

'Captain, at what time will we be leaving for Marseille? How long will it take?'

'We will get underway at around ten tonight. We are planning our course at the moment and estimate that we will be safely inside the Marseille Old Port area in the early morning.'

'The motor boat, is it serviceable?'

'Yes, why do you ask?'

'I might take someone for a ride. Make sure that it is easily accessible when we arrive in Marseille will you?'

'Of course, Nikolay here will take care of that.'

The first officer nodded his head and Alexie, seemed satisfied. He had the beginnings of a plan for dealing with the sommelier if he could prove that she was a spy. Leaving the bridge, he made his way down several flights of stairs to the galley deck and the strong room, his private domain, a place he had prohibited the staff from entering. It was not far from the wine cellar and as he passed its door, he made a mental note to pay a visit in the near future. Perhaps the room contained something he should know about.

Reaching the strong room door, he unlocked it and swung it open, felt for the light switch and stepped inside. The shiny stainless steel combination lock was as precise as a Swiss watch and turning the dial both clockwise and anticlockwise several times, he felt the telling click of a successful attempt and opened the heavy door to reveal several shelves still holding wads of banknotes and the dark shape of a sub machine gun.

Chapter 15

Ernest Jones had spent the past hour on his own, bored and now he was hungry. He lifted his compact binoculars and zoomed in on a man with a sack barrow moving an oil drum, and then he switched to the far side of the dock and focused on a car that had just pulled up. It was no good his concentration had gone. After a day of not doing very much his mind was becoming a little addled.

Sighing and sitting back in his seat he felt a yawn coming on. However, before he could manage it, there was a tap on his window.

'The car Ernie, the one near the yacht, isn't it a diplomatic one?'

Damn, he thought, he had switched off. Brian had gone off to do a little snooping around the dock area and to find a shop to buy some food and now he had returned.

'Oh, bloody hell, I do believe you are right, Russian Federation by look of the number plate. Things must be warming up,' said Ernest, coming back to life. 'Get the camera; let's get some shots of those men near the gangplank.'

The Sommelier

Brian Thacker did not need telling; already he was twisting the telephoto lens onto the body of the Leica, lifting the camera to his eye and for half a second the near-silent buzz of the autofocus was the only sound. Firing the shutter, he captured a succession of images and within seconds was uploading the file to his computer in Milan.

'That's done Ernie; I'll get some images of the car and a few of the yacht while I can. There are two people on the bridge in uniform; it might be useful to know who they are.'

'Don't hang about, the car is heading this way.'

The agent captured a few more images and then he and his partner slid down in their seats, out of sight of the driver of the passing diplomatic vehicle.

'I wonder what's going on,' said Jones, regaining his driving posture and looking intently into the rear-view mirror.

'I got a good look at them through the viewfinder, one of them looks like security, I don't know about the other two, they were older I could see that. Look, this is one of them,' he said, enlarging the image on the camera screen. Jones turned in his seat. The face was unfamiliar to him but he could see even from so small a likeness that the man was more used to giving orders than taking them.

'What are we going to do Ernie, I am knackered and do not fancy following that car? It could go anywhere, Russia even, and we don't have a lot of juice left do we?'

Jones glanced at the instruments to confirm his partner's observation. The tank was almost a quarter full, enough for not much more than a hundred and fifty kilometres and the embassy in Paris was a thousand kilometres away and Milan the best part of four hundred. He looked in the rear-view mirror again, noting the embassy car and that their window of opportunity to trail it was fast closing.

'No good following it. I will make a call to the consulate; see what they want us to do. It will be dark in a few hours, let's have something to eat and grab a few hours' kip.'

Commander Pearson chewed at his bottom lip as he digested the information. The operatives from Turin had made their report and it left him feeling uneasy. He glanced at the text once again, picking out key words to help make a judgement. Earlier reports had indicated that high-level Russian military men had spent time on the yacht and now there was this sighting of a Russian diplomatic car. To compound the situation the two agents on the ground had made it clear that although they were still in position at the port of Antibes they were fatigued and could not guarantee to carry out their work efficiently for much longer.

Where did that leave his agent? He needed to consider her safety, good field operatives were a valuable commodity, highly motivated individuals who took years to train, and he was not about to lose this one. Picking up the telephone receiver, he punched in the number for his superior.

'Yes sir, it is late but I do need to speak with you urgently.' Bloody bosses, he thought to himself, why did they have to go to the theatre just when you needed them the most?

Replacing the receiver, he gathered several sheets of paper on his desk when a girl from the operations department knocked on his door.

'Sir, the urgent despatch you are waiting for,' she said, handing him a brown official envelope.

'Thank you, nothing to go back.'

The girl turned away and Commander Pearson tore open the envelope, taking out several A5 photographs together with a sheet of paper. There were six images, good quality, showing several men's features and a shot of a car's number plate, instantly recognisable as a Russian diplomatic vehicle. He scanned the faces, identifying them from previous intelligence. It seemed that they had left the yacht, so where did that leave his agent?

Picking up his papers, he stood for a moment, his mind piecing together the jigsaw and he wondered what was missing. He let out a long shallow sigh, perhaps the operation had run its course and it was time to extricate his agent. Biting his lip again, he looked at his watch and realising he was late for his meeting, hurried along the corridor to the director's office.

'Ah Pearson, come in will you and close the door. You wanted to see me, said it was urgent.'

'Yes sir, I do believe it is an urgent matter and I will come straight to the point. I have been running an operation in the Med on a superyacht called the Lady Galina.'

'Yes, I know all about that. Found anything out?'

'That's the problem, I don't know.'

The director's right eyebrow lifted a little.

'We have an asset in place aboard the yacht which is pretty well locked down. She went in there alone, without weapons or a means of communication. We suspected there were GRU aboard taking care of security. Those boys know what they are doing and today we received information suggesting that FSB are involved in some way.'

'In what way, have you any idea?'

'I haven't a complete picture by any means sir, but I am hoping our agent can fill in a few details. She has been on that yacht for a week or so and must have learned something, but worryingly those GRU boys could be on to her.'

The director clasped his hands across his chest and sat back in his chair, thoughtful, and after a few seconds said, 'You want to extricate your asset?'

'Yes sir, as soon as possible security on board the vessel is tight and we are not able to communicate with our agent. She is in a dangerous position and if we want to learn more I believe we need to get her out of there pretty soon.'

The director unclasped his hands and leaned forward. 'I take your point, how do you want to do it?'

'M Squadron, just in case there is a problem. They are the logical choice for a water-borne target and I have already briefed them about the possibility of becoming involved.'

'Hmm . . . I will need permission from above, we don't want a diplomatic incident should things go wrong.'

'Quite.'

'Give me ten minutes and then come back.'

'Sir,' said the commander, beginning to worry.

As the yacht cast off for the overnight passage to Marseille Pierre was in his galley preparing Leonid's dinner and in the dining room Anita was standing by the picture window uncorking a bottle of wine. She watched as the French coast slowly passed by and for a brief moment understood the impressionist painters' motivation. The sun was almost touching the distant hills, its low penetrating light illuminating the landscape's colours in a way that excited the senses.

The beauty of the Mediterranean coast was lost on Leonid Borisovich though as he made his way down the wide staircase to the dining room. His mind had other concerns, worries that the regime change might remove all the advantages he had secured for himself over the past twenty years. The man destined to become the President of the

Russian Federation was not one of his associates – a man with military leanings rather than business.

What the future might bring he did not know but the fate of several oligarchs riding high in the past was a stark reminder of how far he could fall. There would be a fair and free election, of course, and the people would elect Comrade Grachyov on a landslide. It was always the way in Russia and at least Igor had told him that it would be Grachyov.

'Would you care for some wine sir?' asked Anita as he seated himself, the lone diner in the expansive opulence of the Lady Galina's dining room.

'Yes, that would be nice. What have we this evening?'

'Chef is preparing a bouillabaisse, bok choi and saffron aioli to start and I would suggest an oaked Chardonnay to complement the dish.'

'Sounds very good, I don't believe I have had that before, and what is this evening's main?'

'Roasted duck breast with Romanesco broccoli, wild mushroom and a lemon garlic sauce. Might I suggest the Chardonnay with this dish as well sir, I believe that to mix the wines with this menu could be a mistake.'

Bullseye looked up at her, gave her a knowing half-smile and left her to wonder where the evening might lead. She had been lucky to ward off his advances twice but she did not believe that she could be so lucky a third time.

Under the cover of darkness, the Airbus H160 skimmed low over the French landscape and inside four men of the Special Boat Service sat hunched in their seats. It had been a mad rush as usual. When the order came to move they had grabbed equipment, loaded the vehicle and headed for the airfield at Boscombe Down and now they had time to sit back and catch up on some rest.

Earlier in the evening, after receiving ministerial approval, the Director of Operations had telephoned Poole requesting the assistance of M Squadron. Then he called his opposite number at the French General Directorate for Internal Security. There was a real risk of an international incident if things went wrong and at the very least, he should obtain permission to overfly France.

In his office, Commander Pearson realised that once the cat was out of the bag there would be repercussions. Conducting a covert operation on French soil was bad enough but since the country had disengaged from Europe, several important treaties had lapsed and his job had become much harder. He would be responsible for the successful conclusion of the operation but if the French complained then his defence was that it was in both countries' interest. GCHQ was providing a lot of intelligence to the French it was only right for them to help the British on occasion.

Darkness had descended over London and as he looked out at the city lights, his thoughts were with those in the field and at that very moment, flying low over the French countryside, its soundproofed rotors making no more than a muffled hiss the helicopter sped towards the Istres-Le Tubé Air Base. Just northwest of Marseille the base was in an ideal position and on the ground, two men and a four by four waited..

'Welcome to France,' said a man dressed in dark civilian clothing as the first of the Special Forces personnel stepped onto the tarmac. 'If you will follow me we need to take a few photographs and your fingerprints, after that you can proceed. I am to tell you that we will not tolerate needless violence though we understand some may be necessary. We have agreed with London to provide a second level of security and so some French personnel will be in the background. Once the mission is complete you must leave France.'

Alexie looked at his watch, almost midnight, in a few hours he would hand over the last of the safe's contents to the courier and then the mission would be over. He had not particularly enjoyed his time on the yacht, the twenty-four hour responsibility for security was a strain and he was ready to relinquish that responsibility for a while. The visiting military men had created problems, the discretion their visit demanded had stretched both him and Viktor, and adding to his problems was the disturbing notion that the sommelier might be a foreign agent.

He had personally checked her references, matched them against the Russian intelligence database and received only negative results. In his opinion, it was a risk employing foreign nationals but necessary cover for the operation. The woman was interesting, he had to admit, but the Romanian girl was much easier to control, particularly when it came to the owner's infidelity. He wondered about Viktor, had he turned anything up from the security camera? He decided to have a word with him but first he would cast an eye over the saloon, check out the sun deck for any unusual activity.

Hunching his shoulders and with a scowl on his face he climbed the broad staircase to the saloon expecting it too to be deserted but in the shadows he caught sight of a figure. Wondering who it might be he approached, treading silently over the lush carpeting. The person was facing away, watching the distant lights of the French coast slowly passing by. Then, as the head turned, he recognised the profile.

'Olga,' he called out in a low voice.

'Alexie, stop creeping up on me like that,' she said, whipping round to face him.

'I did not creep up, you were miles away. What is on your mind?'

'Nothing in particular, I was just catching a few moments of peace before I turn in. You are checking everything is in order?'

'Yes, before I too turn in. I have to be up early to take mister Borisovich to the airport.'

Alexie paused for a few moments before looking Olga in the eye.

'The woman Sims, what do you make of her?'

'How do you mean, her work or something a little more serious?'

'Something a little more serious I think. You were aware of the importance of our last guests?'

'To a degree, I do not know everything that goes on but I did suspect that they were important state functionaries.'

'Yes, a fair description. One of them is part of our state security apparatus and he is suspicious of our sommelier, he thinks that she might be a foreign agent. Have you seen anything to substantiate that view?'

'Not really, she keeps herself much to herself, doesn't mix a lot but then she is only here until the Romanian girl returns and that should be quite soon.'

'She has recovered?'

'Just about, the sanatorium has been in touch to inform the purser that she is about to be discharged. He is arranging her travel.'

'You know the Sims woman spent last night with Mr Borisovich?'

'Interesting, in my younger days I worked the honey trap. It is an effective weapon in the espionage arena, as I'm sure you are aware Alexie.'

'So you think that there is a good chance she might be a foreign agent.'

'I believe that there is a very good chance. Without wishing to compromise my position, would you willingly sleep with the boss?'

'Thanks for that Olga, not a word to anyone about our conversation please.'

'Alexie, I have been in this game long enough, I'm surprised you need to ask.'

'Good night.'

Olga reciprocated and turned back to watch the lights as Alexie left the saloon to look for Viktor.'

'Found anything?'

'Maybe, the purser says you let her use her mobile telephone.'

'She only used it to arrange the visit to the vineyard.'

'I checked the number she rang and could not find anything, no address, no record on Google, nothing. Does that look suspicious? Then there are the missing minutes when she was going to the accommodation deck. There is no explanation for that either. I think she is not what she seems.'

'I will tackle her after the Arab leaves with his final consignment.'

By the time dawn was beginning to break, the Lady Galina was within a kilometre of the Old Port of Marseille illuminated by the early morning light of the new day.. The sea's dark, night-laden colour was changing back to Mediterranean blue and aboard the yacht the staff were starting their day's work. In his kitchen, Pierre was giving orders as his assistants prepared the crew's breakfast, and high above on the bridge the captain was conning the vessel through the breakwater.

'Order the deck hands to prepare the mooring lines,' said Captain Rusedski. 'This is going to be a tricky manoeuvre and I want everybody in place before we reach the marina.'

The first officer acknowledged the captain's request and walked out onto open area of aft of the bridge where he had a panoramic view of the lower deck. Assessing the situation, he lifted his radio to his mouth and made contact with the two men of the deck crew waiting below. Manoeuvring the eighty-metre monster past pontoons full of yachts and motor cruisers would take time and care and it was his job to make sure that there were no mishaps. Back on the bridge, the captain ordered a reduction in speed, and finally, the bow thrusters cut in, churning the water, gradually nudging the Lady Galina onto her new berth.

Yusuf watched the superyacht easing her way through the narrow marina channel from the perimeter railing. He had walked there an hour earlier from the tiny flat situated in the Saint Louis district, a run-down area of high-rise buildings housing a large North African and Middle Eastern immigrant population. He had made contact with the al-Qaeda cell, a group of young men with a perceived notion of discrimination had radicalised them.

The men were courteous yet somewhat distrustful of the tall Arab in their midst, and apart from a few words with their leader he had hardly spoken to them. He would have liked to engage with them, talk about the need for change, the introduction of sharia law into France, but time was short, he had a mission to fulfil.

The Lady Galina's bulk seemed to fill the Port and as she came to a standstill, Yusuf marvelled at the skill of the sailors. Shrugging his shoulders, he considered that the wealth needed to own such a vessel belonged to the very class he was determined to overthrow. He had received the usual text message in the early hours instructing him to come aboard the yacht by mid-afternoon. He looked at his watch; it was still only eight o'clock in the morning and he had little else to do. He looked across the water towards the floating white mass and decided to wander the streets until it was time to board her.

Leonid had just taken his morning shower before leaving for the airport when his mobile phone rang. It was Igor, what did he want?

'Igor, good morning, what can I do for you?'

'More what I can do for you my friend?'

'You are still in France?'

'No, I am just about to cross into Holland, then I fly back to Moscow later today. Before I leave Holland though, I wanted to let you know that the Kremlin will be announcing the succession this afternoon. Of course, this is confidential information but for a man like you necessary I think, to beat the markets.'

Alert to the possibility of adding to his fortune, Leonid concentrated his thoughts. A few companies and individuals would win from a change at the top, however there were many who could lose influence and, more importantly, value. He needed to study his portfolio, decide what to sell and then there would be buying opportunities.

'Thank you for that Igor, how can I repay you for the favour?'

'You have the Swiss bank account details, eight million roubles will suffice. Have a nice day Leonid.'

'You too Igor.'

The line went dead and Leonid could do no more than stare at the silent phone in his hand. 'So, the long-expected transfer of power was in motion and he had just a few hours to gain from the news, eight million to start with.

In the control room on the deck above, Alexie was also aware of the changing situation back home. The word was out and those whom a change at the top would affect were re-examining their allegiances. To back the wrong side in Russia usually meant ruin or worse. That was a path for those seeking power and those with ambition, not for a lowly GRU Special Forces trooper. Of more immediate interest to Alexie were the video recordings that Viktor had turned up.

While he waited for the order to take mister Borisovich to the airport he watched Viktor run the tapes. The first showed the sommelier leaving the galley carrying a tray of food and the next showed

342

her walking along the corridor on the crew deck. The times of the recordings showed on the top right-hand corner of the screen and it was that information Alexie was primarily interested in. He ran a third video, one of him leaving the crew deck, it too time recorded. She is missing for six minutes, he said to himself. Why and where did she go?

The fourth recording was of the corridor and staircase leading to the saloon and again the subject was the sommelier.

'What was she doing in the saloon?'

'I don't know Alexie, probably collecting the bottle but it shouldn't have taken her so long.

Then Viktor fast-forwarded the recording.

'Look there, shadows outside on the deck.'

Viktor jumped back a few seconds and ran it again to show two shadows pass by on the outside deck.

'Who was it out there?'

Viktor looked up the file for the camera most likely to have recorded the shadowy figures and found one spanning a similar time.

'Let's try this one, it might show who it was.'

Fast-forwarding he stared intently at the screen until there was movement and then ran it at normal speed, rewinding several times until it showed two figures emerging onto the deck, Ageyev and Colonel General Mischa Bondarev. They seemed deep in conversation and Alexie wondered if that was the reason why the sommelier had spent so long in the saloon. Was she listening to their conversation?

Pierre was just pulling his *toque blanche* over his hair when Anita appeared in the galley.

'Good morning chef, you are looking smart today,' she said, trying to make conversation. She had not made much in the way of friends on board the yacht apart from Pierre and the girl from the Midlands and wondered if her night with Bullseye was common knowledge. Secrets like that rarely remained secret for long in a close-knit community, sooner or later someone somewhere would get scent of the liaison.

'*Bonjour madam*, how do you like Marseille?'

'I haven't seen much of it yet, just a glance out of the porthole as we came in earlier. Are you making the lamb dish again?' she asked, noticing Pierre's assistant unwrapping cling film from some meat.

'Yes, we have the Arab on board and Alexie has instructed me to cook the lamb dish again. It needs to cook slowly for four hours to be at its best.'

'There will not be much requirement for alcohol then?'

'No, and Mr Borisovich will not want wine either, Alexie is driving him to the airport soon and he is expected to be gone for two days at least.'

'Are any more guests expected?'

'Not for now. Some of Mr Borisovich's friends are bringing their families on board next week. That could be interesting.'

'In what way?'

'They are business acquaintances and from previous experience their children can be quite a handful, particularly if they are Russian.'

Yusuf looked at his watch for what must have been the tenth time. Having to wait was getting him down but his instructions were not to approach the superyacht until the afternoon. For a time he sat in a small cafe not far from the yacht's berth watching female crew cleaning the vessel's exterior brass work. There was a sailor in a smart white uniform leaning on the rail smoking, and there were men carrying out some duties on the aft deck and then he noticed the crane begin to extend and the men on the deck lifted a small car onto the dockside. He found it fascinating and for maybe fifteen minutes, he watched until two men appeared from the boat's interior and got into the vehicle.

He finished his coffee and sat back to watch the car's progress towards the marina gate and as it passed no more than ten metres from where he was sitting he recognised the driver as the one he dealt with during his visits to the yacht. If he was to deal with this same man today then he wondered just how long he would have to wait.

And then as if to answer his question his mobile phone beeped. The text message he was expecting had arrived, giving him further instructions for boarding the yacht. The message advised him that there was a delay but that he should come to the marina gate at three o clock and one of the security men would come to escort him to the vessel. At last, things were moving; he could collect his final delivery from the yacht and by tonight he would be in Paris, and could celebrate the culmination of his mission.

Olga had finished supervising her staff and allowed them to take their lunch break when Viktor came walking down the main staircase.

'Mister Borisovich has left for his business trip Viktor?'

'Yes Alexie drove him to the airport earlier this morning. He should be back soon. He mentioned the sommelier?' he queried.

'Yes he told me of his suspicions and I will keep an eye on her. If I can be sure that she is spying on us I will let you know.'

Viktor did not reply, simply nodded his head thoughtfully and carried on towards the sliding door leading out onto the open deck. The boss was away, he was in charge and he needed a cigarette.

For Yusuf the rest of the day was uneventful and boring as he wandered the streets near the old port looking in widows, watching the boats come and go. Twice he found secluded seating in waterfront cafes to while away the time, and then he saw the car return and pass through the gate on its way to the yacht.

So his contact had returned and looking at his watch noted that it was still only two thirty. He still had half an hour to kill and he was finding the waiting excruciating. He called for the bill and leaving the smallest of tips made his way to the quayside with a good view of the yacht. He stood in the shadow of a single story building and waited, looked at his watch again. It was ten to the hour and then he noticed a man leave the confines of the yacht and begin walking to the security gate. That would be his contact he thought, and he began to make his own way towards the gate.

It was the one who he had seen driving the car, the one with whom he always dealt and after the big man had swung the security gate open he spoke to Yusuf.

'Come with me.'

Yusuf did not hesitate and passing through into the marina followed Alexie along the pontoon, past a row of lesser vessels, and towards the Lady Galina.

'You will not be here long. My instructions are to provide you with the holdall and, while I fetch it, the chef will provide you with some food. You can wait in one of the crew cabins, come I show you.'

Minutes later, they reached the base of the spiral staircase leading to the now familiar crew deck..

'Someone will bring you food and I will return with the bag. You have your travel arrangements?'

'Yes, the early evening TGV to Paris.'

Alexie nodded and left Yusuf to his own devices as he went to arrange for the transfer. For Yusuf it afforded him the chance to spend time alone and to pray, he had managed the mid day prayer in a quiet corner and was grateful for the chance to recite the afternoon Asr prayer in a proper manner.

A short time later Alexie walked into the galley and spoke to Pierre to tell him that the Arab was in cabin sixteen. Pierre did not answer, simply nodded his head in reply. He was no fan of the Russian thugs or the housekeeper; his contract ended in two months and until then he would simply obey their orders and avoid a confrontation.

'Margarita when I finish plating up I want you take the dish to the Arab in cabin sixteen on the crew deck.'

The girl reached up for one of the silver trays on a shelf and Pierre slipped a plate into his oven to warm it.

'It smells good chef, do not forget me,' Alexie said, a rare smile crossing his face.

'Of course, will you eat here or take it elsewhere?'

'Oh, here will do, I do not stand on ceremony when it comes to food. We sat on the tanks in Ukraine, no tablecloths there.'

'Help yourself to cutlery,' said Pierre, picking up another plate. It will be ready in ten minutes, I just have to heat the sauce.'

Alexie hardly noticed the chef's reticence in his eagerness to savour the dish and for a few minutes stood back to watch. Pierre was an expert at his profession and was soon dishing some lamb and rice onto the warm plates.

Alexie took his and went to sit at a small table in the corner of the galley, devouring the food like a starving dog. Pierre watched him from the corner of his eye, wincing inwardly. He would not know real gourmet food if it hit him in the mouth he thought, chuckling at his own joke.

'That was very tasty chef; you can make me that again. Have you fed out guest?'

'Margarita has just taken a tray,' said Pierre, ignoring the compliment.

'Good, we need to keep him happy, for now at least,' he said preparing to leave the galley only to see Anita enter.

She was clutching an ice bucket and taken by surprise at seeing the security man, caught her breath and trying to ignore him, reached inside the office for the cellar key. She could almost feel the Russian's eyes burning into the back of her head and felt decidedly uncomfortable. She just had to get away from him, to the sanctity of the wine cellar at least and without a word, she walked from the galley. It was only a short walk to the cellar and after fumbling with the key for a few seconds, she finally managed to swing open the door.

Alexie's attitude towards her had changed, he had become decidedly hostile and she worried that her cover might be blown. Switching on the light, she reached behind some bottles to check the position of the knife. She was feeling vulnerable and for a minute, she stood quite still and took control of her fears. Taking a deep breath to steady her nerves she examined the situation. Shadow was of great interest and he would be leaving soon. She had to try to follow him, find out who he was meeting and at the same time avoid the two Russian thugs. But she was too late.

'So I find you here, in your cave.'

'Cave, I hardly think so,' she said, her heart pounding in her chest as she half turned to see Alexie enter the room and stand not a metre from her, a menacing look in his eyes.

'Yes, your cave, your secret hideaway, a place where you can scheme and cause trouble for me.'

'Trouble?' she said, feeling afraid to be alone with Alexie in such a confined space.

'You are not what you seem are you, British intelligence, MI6 perhaps?' Come now, you cannot deny it, you are a spy for the British Secret Service.'

'I don't know what you are talking about. Now let me past I need to talk to Pierre about the wine for this evening.'

Alexie did not stand aside; instead, he blocked her path, staring at her with those hostile eyes.

'Who are you working for?' he snarled.

Anita did not answer and Alexie, angered by her silence, reached out to grip her by the throat.

'I ask you again, who are you working for?'

Anita could do no more than gurgle as she felt the pressure of Alexie's large hands and she knew she must act.

'I . . . I . . .' she began to say, and as Alexie relaxed his grip to allow her to speak, she seemed to stumble, falling back half a metre and steadying herself against a shelf. 'I . . . I . . .' she managed as if to speak and for a second he dropped his guard.

It was now or never. With a deft flick of her wrist she threw the ice bucket, aiming for his head and as he ducked she brought her knee sharply up into his groin. He gasped in surprise, no more than a brief respite but it gave Anita the opportunity to reach out and grasp the knife. She wrapped her fingers around it and stabbed at him with all her strength, driving the blade hard into his ribs.

The swiftness and force of the blow caught Alexie by surprise and he could do no more than stare at her in disbelief. Nevertheless, he was tough and recovered enough composure to lurch at her, but she was ready for him. Her training and an instinct for survival triggering a series of well-rehearsed moves and twisting away from his outstretched hands she lashed out with her fists, prompting a tirade of expletives.

'I kill you, you bastard,' he growled, pulling the knife from his chest and staggering towards her.

He was still a potent force, Anita needed a weapon, something, anything, and the nearest to hand was a bottle of champagne. Grasping it by the neck, she dragged it from the shelf and retreated out of range of the lunging Alexie. Reading his intention, she sidestepped his onslaught and at the same time swung the bottle at his head. To her dismay, it simply bounced off his thick skull doing no more damage than slowing him. Then he came at her and she hit him a second time, smashing the bottle across his temple. It was enough, the blow rendered him unconscious and he slumped to the floor.

Gasping for breath and feeling decidedly shaken, Anita stood over the prostrate form, her eyes focusing on his blood-covered shirt and specks of red spattered all over her own white blouse. It was something she would find hard to conceal and leaning back against the shelving, she forced herself to calm down and to consider her predicament. Alexie was unconscious but would probably recover and when he did he would raise the alarm.

The big Russian began to moan, he was already coming round, time was pressing and she had somehow to disable him. His belt would do for a start and with some effort, she managed to roll him over and pull the belt from the loops round his waist. Securing his hands behind his back, she then took the roll of tape she used to label the half-empty bottles for staff use and gagged him. It was no more than a temporary measure she knew, but it would at least give her time to get off the yacht.

Earlier that same day, dressed unobtrusively in jeans and tee shirts, three of the men of E squadron made their way towards the Old Port. It was still early morning and the area was just waking up. Cafe owners were setting out chairs and tables in preparation for another day and suppliers' vehicles were offloading. The three men kept themselves far enough apart, appearing unconnected, and through nearby streets the fourth member of the team circled in a their vehicle.

Their initial objective was to find positions with a good view of the Lady Galina, integrate themselves into harbour life and to keep an eye on the yacht. If the embedded agent should need assistance, then they would be ready.

For a few minutes, Sergeant Charlie Downey watched as female crew lifted some soft furnishings from a locker and fit them to the deck furniture. A few metres away, reading a newspaper, Warrant Officer Graham Forrest sat amongst several tradesmen who were drinking coffee before the start of their working day and he too glanced at the women from time to time.

It was a tedious exercise but a necessary one and after two hours of nothing happening Warrant Officer Forrest finally spotted him, a tall man of Middle Eastern appearance. He was leaning on the railings approximately fifty metres away, an insignificant sight to most people but not to the trooper. Anyone showing an interest in the vessel was a suspect and Forrest guessed that this man had more than just a passing interest. For a time he kept the man under observation until a waiter appeared and distracted him. He felt obliged to order a bottle of water and when the waiter left, he turned his attention back towards the tall man only to discover that he had gone. He searched the vicinity to try to find him again but it was no use; perhaps he was wrong, maybe the man was just admiring the superyacht's graceful lines.

As the day wore on the number of people around the marina increased, creating a chance for Sergeant Downey and his men to move closer to the yacht. The sergeant sized up their surroundings, strolled past Forrest and corporal Mills giving his orders and gradually the team readjusted. The sergeant found a seat not far from the marina gate and after positioning himself he watched as Mills and Forrest both found new perspectives.

Then the tall Middle Eastern man appeared again, walking steadily towards the marina gate, and Forrest immediately recognised him and took out his mobile phone.

'Charlie, the target is approaching the gate. A tall man, Arab-looking, was here earlier and very interested in the yacht.'

Downey spotted him, saw a man appear on the gangplank and then stride along the pontoon towards the gate. If he was in any doubt that there was a connection between them then his curiosity was soon satisfied. The two figures reached the marina gate within seconds of each other, the gate opened and the target passed through.

'Subject of interest,' said the sergeant into his radio, enough to alert the rest of the team, even the fourth member of the patrol who steered the car down a side street and onto the quayside not far from the Lady Galina.

The Sommelier

The waterfront was crowded with vehicles presenting a problem but seeing space in front of a cafe he pulled up, lowered the window for a better view, and for several minutes observed the yacht until a voice interrupted him.

'*Vous ne pouvez pas vous garer là monsieur.*'

'What?'

'*Vous ne pouvez pas vous garer là monsieur.*'

'Sorry mate, I don't understand a word of French.' Corporal Mick Beadnall did not have time to argue and without a word closed the window. The waiter tried to attract his attention but the tough marine was having none of it, his action enough to discourage the Frenchman for the time being. Then his radio came to life. It was Sergeant Downey.

'You need to park up somewhere Mick, somewhere nearby where you can leave the transport. And bring the camera.'

'I'll have a look,' he retorted and slipped the still running engine into gear just as the waiter returned accompanied by another irritated-looking man.

'Fuck you two,' he said under his breath and pulled away from the kerb in search of a more permanent parking space.

'Who is that guy who went through the gate?' asked Forrest catching up with the sergeant.

'I have no idea but the other one has security written all over him. Look at the size of him.'

'The bigger they come the harder they fall.'

Sergeant Downey said nothing, just shrugged his shoulders and watched the subjects disappear onto the yacht. Then he looked round to see Corporal Beadnall appear from a side street carrying the camera.

Anita's main concern was her bloodstained shirt, Alexie would present no immediate problem but the shirt would. No one seeing her could fail to notice the blood and that would bring questions she was in no hurry to answer. It was imperative that she got rid of it. Then an idea crossed her mind, some of the Barolos were similar in colour to blood and there was a bottle of Monforte d'Alba on the shelf in front of her. Pulling its cork, she spilled a quantity of wine over her shirt, rubbing it into the still wet blood. The ruse worked, the colours blended together well enough to give her the confidence to return to the galley and as she walked in a startled Pierre said, 'What happened to you madam?'

'Nothing, just a little spillage, I must change, excuse me.'

'That looks a little like blood on your cuff. Are you all right?'

'Oh, I nicked myself on the broken bottle, it's nothing.'

Pierre frowned and stood back to let her pass. He might be a hard taskmaster when the galley was in full flow but he did take pride in the well-being of his staff and here was something rather odd. The sommelier seemed agitated, her cheeks were very red and he was sure that there was more to the blood on her cuff than she was prepared to admit. If there was a broken bottle then perhaps one of the other girls should look in the cellar and clean up. No, he would do that himself but when he looked at the row of hooks in the office, he noticed that the key to the cellar was missing.

Chapter 16

Igor Andresov had enjoyed his few days on Borisovich's yacht. It was not often he could indulge himself in food to the standard of a cordon bleu chef and with fine wines to boot, but he had, and it felt good. But that was in the past, today he had more pressing matters to attend to. He had worked on the succession for quite some time and the plan was finally coming to fruition. He had the ear of the president in waiting, had helped gather support to the point where his position looked unassailable. However, there was still work to do, the officer corps of both the army and the navy might be onside but there were still a few malcontents. He needed to weed them out, have them demoted or send them on special assignment to Siberia.

He reached into the ornate silver box on his desk and took out a cigarette, lit it and sat back to savour its fragrant aroma. Exhaling he watched the smoke rise to the high ceiling, saw it slowly dissolve into invisibility. A metaphor for the dissidents' lives perhaps.

The Sommelier

So, the world had not changed, neither had Russia's enemies and as an instrument of the state Igor would do his best to defeat them. The expansion of the borders was progressing steadily; Ukraine had come under full control due to NATO's weak response. It had been a worry for a time, but now the whole country was under the Russian Federation's umbrella they could consolidate their gains. To the east, the former Soviet satellites' economies were too dependent upon Mother Russia to cause problems and Belarus had signed a cooperation agreement that guaranteed subservience. That just left the Baltic states and with luck, Poland.

Drawing more smoke into his lungs Igor turned to look at the map on the wall behind him. Poland, the Baltic states, they would be next. First though, the campaign of fake news and disinformation before disruption of the West's basic infrastructure and then it would be the turn of al-Qaeda. They would receive their orders to begin a campaign of bombing and murders from him and after that, the Russian Army would cross borders to bring back peace and order where there was only terrorism and disruption.

Anita hurried up the staircase towards the passerelle deck in the hope that she could just walk off the yacht. It seemed easy enough if she could avoid Viktor. After leaving the puzzled-looking Pierre, she had returned to her cabin and in a flurry of activity had changed her bloodstained blouse and the tight uniform skirt for more practical clothing. Next, she had pushed her soiled blouse under the bed, grabbed the few banknotes, her credit card and a change of underwear from the bedside drawer and stuffed them in her travelling bag before leaving the cabin without so much as a backward glance.

She was on the run and, making her way to the deck above, she recalled the last words of the controller before she had set out on the mission. He had said that he could not guarantee oversight of her on board the yacht; however, he would have people monitor the yacht's progress and have agents on the ground where possible. If her position became untenable and if she signalled that she needed assistance, then he would take what steps he could to protect her. For her part, she had remained confident that she would not need outside help but during the past hour things had changed. She had shown her hand and could feel the walls closing in on her.

She reached the recreation deck a little out of breath and saw the walkway leading ashore. Then her stomach began to churn as she caught sight of Viktor. He was no more than three or four metres away, standing with his back to her. He would not let her simply walk by, she needed another way off the yacht.

Unseen by the Russian, she retraced her steps and made her way to the saloon deck hoping that some means of escape would present itself but just as she reached the landing, Olga appeared.

'What do you think you are doing!' she exclaimed.

'I am, er, just taking a few things to the bar, serviettes.'

'There are plenty of serviettes there already, and your uniform, why are you not wearing your uniform? I think you are up to no good. Come with me.'

She reached out and grabbed hold of Anita's arm and taken aback at the woman's strength, Anita allowed herself to be led towards the doorway.

'I think we will talk to security, find out what it is you are up to.'

Olga, still holding onto Anita's arm, produced a shortwave radio with her free hand.

'Alexie, Viktor, come in.'

Almost immediately, there was a response.

'Olga, this is Viktor, what do you want?'

'I have . . .'

She got no further. Anita had to act quickly because once Viktor arrived she knew she would struggle to deal with the two of them. Twisting away from Olga's grip, she slammed the elbow of her free arm into the housekeeper's ribs and knocked the radio to the floor. The woman reacted, taking on the classic defensive stance, but Anita kicked her hard on the shin and she staggered backwards with a howl of rage and pain. Clenching her fists, she held her forearms vertically to protect her face and tried to recover from the shock of the assault and for a second or two there was a stalemate. Olga's eyes flashed menacingly until Anita deftly sidestepped and, with a single knuckle punch, dislocated the Russian's jaw and then, with an expert karate chop, hit her again on the back of the neck. It did the trick, the heavy woman sprawled unconscious to the floor, leaving Anita gasping for breath and believing that her chest would burst.

The exertion and the adrenaline rush had taken its toll, but there was no going back now, she thought, as she fought to control her emotions. Putting her foot in the middle of Olga's back, she rolled her prostrate body into the saloon.

At least she was out of sight of any casual observer but then the radio, still lying on the floor, crackled into life again. It was Viktor trying to make contact. Feeling shaken, she stared at the black plastic element and there was no doubt in her mind that Viktor would soon come looking for Olga. After a sharp intake of breath she composed herself enough to pass through the saloon door, side footing the radio under a seat as she went. Although she had little idea what to do, not even an inkling of a plan, her training and previous experiences told her that opportunities always presented themselves. The secret was to keep moving and to take those opportunities when they arose, to turn them to advantage. With that thought in mind and with renewed confidence she took the stairs two at a time to the dining deck and emerged onto a deserted outdoor bar area to overlook the quayside. She decided that she had come far enough but now any retreat to the lower decks would be more difficult. She needed help.

Finding an open space at the rail she faced the town and outstretched her arms, slowly raising and lowering them, a way to signal an SOS. She hoped that her controller had done his job and that somewhere out there someone would see her. Initially no one did but then an observant Warrant Officer Forrest noticed some movement.

'Shit, game on,' he muttered before pressing the transmit button on his radio. 'Subject is on the aft section of the second deck down.'

Three more pairs of eyes scanned the deck, catching Anita's last frantic signal before she disappeared into the interior on her way back down the staircase and in her haste she almost ran into Viktor. She had no time to hide.

'Have you seen Olga?' was all he said.

'She went up to the bridge I think, about ten minutes ago.'

Viktor looked thoughtful for a second before pushing past. This was her big chance, her opportunity get off the yacht. Running headlong down the stairs, she reached the saloon deck, it was deserted and through the glass doors she could see the outdoor furniture arranged neatly alongside the swimming pool but it was all of little concern to her as she took the final flight of stairs down to the telescopic gangway. However, when she reached the foot of the stairs she saw that the walkway had retracted into the vessel's hull and the outer door shut and she could hear voices at the top of the staircase. Now she really did feel trapped and in blind panic, she dived into the shadows under the staircase.

Yusuf and Viktor were making their way down and from her hiding place, she watched as Viktor operated the mechanism to open the door and extend the gangway. It looked too easy for her to run out onto the pontoon and escape but the sight of Viktor was enough to deter anyone and she did not want to spook the Arab.

With hardly a word spoken the Arab left the yacht and Viktor retracted the gangway leaving Anita to worry about her next move and outside the four concealed troopers of E Squadron watched the Arab pass them by. Sergeant Downey slipped a piece of gum into his mouth and considered the retraction of the gangway a piece of bad luck. Perhaps it was just a routine security measure, but it was effective because there was now no easy way to get aboard the yacht. Chewing on the gum, he reflected on the fact that it would have to be a case of using the grappling hooks. Keeping his distance, he loitered amongst several deserted yachts watching for movement on the Lady Galina. He knew the agent was in need of help but in broad daylight and in a foreign country, he dare not risk an assault. They would wait for nightfall and then attempt a rescue.

The Sommelier

With her means of escape cut off Anita found herself presented with a dilemma. She had little chance getting ashore from the lower deck and to retrace her steps would take her back into danger. If she were to get off the yacht, she would have to find some other means of escape. She paused for thought, her mind running through possibilities and she considered shinning down one of the mooring lines from the saloon deck. It would be risky but there seemed no alternative and in her favour was the fact that there were no guests left on board and most of the domestic crew were off duty. With luck, she would be unobserved and she bounded up the staircase to the open deck above, confident in the knowledge that no one had seen her.

Making her way forward she peered over the side and there no more than fifteen metres away lay relative safety. Without a pause, she took hold of the rail and swung her legs over the side, stretching out for the mooring warp and gaining a toehold, she gingerly reached down to take hold with both hands. Then she swung her body over the warp and hooked her feet round the thick rope. Hanging upside down she slowly began to shuffle along towards the dockside, her heart beating fast, her hands feeling the pain of the hard fibres. And then she heard a voice raise the alarm. It was Olga, she had recovered from Anita's blows, it seemed that her injuries were not so bad after all.

'Viktor,' she screamed, 'Victor, shpion *shpion.*'

Dammit, thought Anita, she had blown her cover and in a blind panic, she tried to scramble faster across the void.

But it was hard going for her and even before she had reached halfway she heard another thick Slavic accent.

'My dear Mrs Sims I suggest you stay where you are. There is no escape for you.'

It was Viktor, and now he was glowering down at her from the deck rail. She realised what was coming but kept shinning along the warp. It was hard work in her agitated state and then Viktor grabbed at the line in an attempt to shake her into the water. The thick warp hardly moved, causing the big Russian to growl in frustration and seeing Anita spurred on to greater effort he began to follow her. He was muscular, very fit and had performed the exercise of rope crawling many times during training and Anita felt the rope jerk as he climbed onto it.

Unlike her, his approach was to lie face down with his legs crossed at the ankles, a much more stable position from which he could pull himself forward with ease and from the corner of her eye Anita could see that he was gaining on her. The rope began to sway, causing her to redouble her effort and pulling hard, she began sliding her feet back and forth to give extra push. It seemed to be working until, with an outstretched hand, Viktor grabbed one of her ankles. His vice-like grip was irresistible, halting any further progress, and the more she kicked the stronger his hold became. Tiring now from her exertions, she realised she could not keep hold of the rope much longer and rather than risk falling into the water she would take her chances back aboard the yacht.

Watching the event unfold, sergeant Downey felt helpless and unable to intervene for he had rules of engagement to consider. If he, a serving member of the British armed forces, openly challenged a Russian national on French soil the political implications could be disastrous. Without exposing the existence of the patrol, there was very little they could do but they would act when darkness descended.

On the Lady Galina Viktor manhandled Anita back aboard, then manhandling her to the nearest guest cabin he flung open the door and pushed her inside.

'You stay here for a while until we decide what to do with you. I think Olga would like to be the one to interrogate you, she is expert.'

That comment sent a shudder down Anita's spine, she had heard about female GRU and she began to believe that she had little time before they would hurt her. If they disabled her, then the possibility of escape would become ever more remote and she braced herself. Then there was Alexie, if they found him, or he escaped, as he eventually would, then she would probably disappear, either to Moscow or to the bottom of the sea.

There was a tap on the door and Viktor opened it, Olga had arrived and she was carrying a gun. She pointed it at a chair, indicating that Anita should sit down

'What are we going to do with her Viktor?'

'For now you will keep an eye on her. I need to ask Alexie for it will be his decision. I haven't seen him for some time and he did not acknowledge when I called him on the radio, have you seen him?'

'Not since he returned from the airport.'

'Hmm . . . I wonder where he is. I will ask the crew. It is unusual not to be able to contact him at short notice.'

The pure whiteness of the Lady Galina's hull shone a dull orange in the glow of the fading sun and as darkness began to fall, four shadowy figures crept towards the yacht. The sergeant was leading and as soon as he reached the vessel, he gave the order and his men closed in, hurling the rubber-coated devices skywards to tumble over the yacht's rail. Then, after a tug on the trailing lines, they were ready and almost as one, the four men climbed cat-like up the yacht's side, landing silently on the deck and spreading out. The sergeant and Petty Officer Mills moved towards the wide glass doors leading to the saloon, while Forrest and Beadnall remained hidden in the shadows guarding the open deck. Carefully the Sergeant Downey reached out to the glass door and slid it open just enough to squeeze inside the darkened room. The task of finding the agent appeared daunting and he was just about to explore the corridor leading off from the main room when Beadnall appeared unexpectedly at his side.

'She's in a cabin for'ard Skipper,' he whispered, 'saw her through a porthole, I'm sure it's her, recognised her from the briefing photograph.'

'Where, can we get to it easily?'

'Only from inside I think.'

'Okay, we'll give it a go. You two keep a lookout on deck. Mills, over here,' he whispered.

Petty Officer Mills followed close behind the sergeant and cautiously they made their way across the saloon's rich carpet. They entered the short corridor leading to the cabins, noting the layout as they went. Four cabins, two on each side, and their target was in the forward cabin on the starboard side. Downey reached it first and pressed his ear to the door, listened and heard the voice of a woman speaking in a strong Slavic accent. He knew then that they had found the MI6 agent.

'You are lucky you are still alive but just to give you a taste of what Viktor and Alexie will do to you,' said Olga, clenching her fist.

There was silence for a second or two before a howl of pain as the GRU woman struck Anita across the side of her head.

'It leaves no obvious mark; maybe you would like me to try the other side, eh?'

Anita looked at Olga and braced herself for a second blow, but instead the cabin door flew open and a man holding a handgun burst in and then a second man appeared.

'Drop your weapon,' he said, his blackened face adding to the drama.

Olga was well-trained, tough, but she was not ready to die just yet. The gun she was holding slipped from her grasp and she raised both hands level with her head.

'Higher. You okay ma'am?'

A much-relieved Anita nodded as a strong arm lifted her to her feet and Sergeant Downey ordered Olga to turn round and without warning dug his knee into the back of hers, forcing her to the floor. Keeping his gun trained on her he produced an electrical wire tie and skilfully secured her hands behind her back. Next, he pulled a roll of tape from his pocket, sealed her mouth and hauled her helpless into an armchair.

'It will keep her off our backs for a while ma'am, but we need to get going. Can you manage?' said the sergeant.

He had no need to ask twice, Anita had mostly recovered and as they evacuated the cabin she took a backwards glance at the forlorn figure of Olga.

'Yes, we need to get off this vessel, Russian security are prowling around somewhere.'

'I have seen one of them,' said the sergeant, pulling gently on Anita's arm, guiding her through the doorway. 'I saw him bring you back on board after your abortive escape attempt.'

Anita shrugged her shoulders, the memory of the incident all too vivid.

At almost the same time, unknown to the escapee and her rescuers, Viktor had finally found Alexie. Pierre was not a brave man and when confronted by Viktor had revealed that Alexie had visited the galley to eat dinner and then had left in the direction of the wine cellar and it did not take a great deal of brainpower for Viktor to deduce that the sommelier had a hand in Alexie's disappearance.

'Where is the key?' he snarled.

'It's not here, it's gone,' said Pierre, 'I don't know where.'

Viktor had no time for recriminations; picking a meat cleaver from the rack, he made for the wine cellar, and as he expected found it locked. Swinging the heavy cleaver, he hacked through the door bit by bit until finally, he was tearing it open and there, lying on the cellar floor, he found Alexie.

'She is spy, British intelligence I think,' said Alexie, as Viktor sat him up and removed the tape. 'Where is she now?'

'Cabin four on the saloon deck. Olga is watching over her.'

'Good,' replied Alexie, rubbing his wrists, feeling both the circulation and his anger returning. 'She has a lot to answer for this Sims woman.'

The sommelier had not only outwitted him but also beaten him in a fight, leaving him with a burning desire for revenge. He had never liked the idea of foreign nationals working on the yacht during such a sensitive operation but his superiors felt it added authenticity. Authenticity, more a liability, Alexie thought as he raced up the spiral staircase to the saloon deck and as he neared the top, full of anticipation, he felt a hand grip his leg.

'Something is wrong,' whispered Viktor.

Alexie froze, his senses suddenly alert.

'The lights are out. I did not switch them off and Olga is in the cabin. It might be a crew member but I don't think so.'

'And we are unarmed.'

'*Da.*'

As they retreated, Marines Beadnall and Forrest guarding the deck area failed to notice the two Spetsnaz who were now busily retracing their steps. They almost jumped down each flight of stairs and ran back through the galley to the strong room. Alexie produced the key, burst in and within less than a minute, they had retrieved two Grach semi-automatic pistols and a PP-19 Bison sub-machine gun from the safe. Handing one of the pistols to Viktor, Alexie took the sub-machine gun and at the run led the way back towards the saloon deck.

The staircase was in darkness, affording decent cover. Alexie slowly crept up the last few steps to the floor level and peered carefully across the room. At once he became aware of figures moving towards him and ducking back down, prepared himself. Several steps below Viktor sensed danger and felt for his weapon's safety catch. The figures passed by seeming not to notice the two Russians and made their way towards the sliding glass doors. Alexie raised his head and challenged them.

'We have you covered, drop your weapons and raise your arms,' he snapped.

Sergeant Downey froze, dropped his weapon and raised his arms, Mills followed suit and Anita lifted her arms, a feeling of dismay flooding over her.

'So we have intruders and our sommelier wants to leave us. I do not think that is possible. Viktor check them for weapons while I keep them covered. I warn you I will be happy to kill you all should you resist,' he said climbing the last of the stairs

Viktor followed, moved forward and expertly ran his hands over the prisoners, removing several knives with a disdainful grunt, and then he picked up the two pistols lying on the floor, stuffing them into his belt.

'Done, they are clean.'

'Good, now are you alone or do we need to shoot somebody?'

'Quite alone,' said Downey.

'Viktor go and have a look for Olga.'

Anita began to feel drained, helpless; the game was up. Unable to escape with the intelligence she had gathered, she and her rescuers were now prisoners of the Russians, the mission an abject failure. She had been through a lot, she was fatigued, her brain less active than it might have been; it hadn't yet occurred to her that there could be more than just two men in the snatch squad and so the sound of splintering glass surprised her. It was the first indication that the mission was not yet over. Observing events from the shadows, the remaining members of the patrol were alert to the situation. Without thinking, they had shot the two Russians through the glass door, shattering it to smithereens.

'Sorry Skipper, we must have missed them,' said a blackened-faced trooper rolling one of the bodies over with his foot as he looked for signs of life.

'Well you didn't miss them this time. Come on, out of here before the alarm is raised.'

Chapter 17

Rosemary took off her reading glasses and rubbed her eyes. The reports from sources in northern Europe had occupied her for most of the day and taken together confirmed her strong belief that the Russians were preparing for a significant operation. More tank units were moving west and, from satellite imagery, several strategic airfields in western Russia were showing signs of increased activity.

She had suspected for several months that the build-up of troops and armour on the border were more than simply a preparation for war games. Normally she would write a report and submit it to the strategic planners who would discuss it in conjunction with information from other sources. This time though she had one of those feelings and could not wait.

'What do you make of it?' asked the deputy director after Rosemary had briefed him.

'Well sir, I cannot remember so many tank units moving our way since the Cold War. There is certainly a build-up going on and the Russians are not denying it. They say that it is merely an exercise and that they have fully informed us of their intentions through the usual channels. Somehow sir, the numbers don't add up.'

The deputy director bit his bottom lip in thought before looking Rosemary in the eye.

'They are playing the plausible deniability game. It worked for them in the Crimea and again in Ukraine and to some extent in Syria. They are going to chance it are they not? They are calling our bluff and they are going to invade Poland.'

'That is my guess, certainly the Baltic States.'

'The Suwałki Gap?'

'Yes, it will be a pushover for them to take control of the land bridge connecting Kaliningrad with Belarus, something they have wanted to do since the breakup of the Soviet Union and I believe we do not have the assets in place to stop them. POTUS has been ordering our troops home for almost five years now and the Europeans alone will not be able to hold them back.'

'Not unless it becomes all-out war,' said the deputy director. If it does come to that, the F-35s would enter the theatre and we are sure that the Russians' aircraft, even their radar defence system, cannot match their capabilities. We would give them a bloody nose and I do not believe they are stupid enough to escalate to that level. An all-out war in Europe? God it doesn't bear thinking about, what else can you tell me?'

'Well sir, we have been monitoring several strands to this problem and we have also noticed some movement of the Northern Fleet around the Kola Peninsula. The Germans are reporting that they suspect the Russians have developed a new type of autonomous submarine.'

'You think they could take out some NATO ships?'

'It's possible sir, Kiel or Portsmouth maybe.'

'Their defences are pretty sound I believe, but it would do no harm to inform NATO command of our suspicions even though we have nothing concrete as yet.'

'There is one thing more; I'm not sure how relevant it is to the present situation but the Russians already have form on this one.'

'Explain.'

'I have been liaising with an MI6 operative for several months. She is working on the hypothesis that there is a terrorist involvement. She has been investigating a mysterious Arab who has made several visits to a Russian oligarch's superyacht. We have helped her identify the man; he has affiliations to al-Qaeda.'

'What have you found out about him?'

'We think, now we have more to go on, that he is the paymaster for terrorist groups affiliated to al-Qaeda. We came across him originally during the first Gulf war, or at least historically we did, and after that he has turned up periodically. It was my contact at MI6 who really got on to him and with our help put some flesh on the bones so to speak.'

'Where is he now and what is he doing?'

'The latest information I have is that he has recently visited the yacht of Russian oligarch Leonid Borisovich.'

The deputy director looked thoughtful for a few seconds.

'Borisovich, I know that name. Was he involved in mining, some scandal in Africa a few years back?'

'The same and now he is cruising the Med. We have seen our Arab friend board the yacht in Istanbul and again in Italy.'

'If he is a person of interest didn't we put a tail on him?'

'Until now he was not really on our radar, he was the Brits problem.'

'What are they doing about it, anything? They don't seem to have the resources these days to do a great deal. We are always riding to their rescue and I can feel the need for yet another posse coming on.'

'That's not quite fair sir, they may not have the resources they once did but the quality of their work has never diminished.'

'Okay, maybe I am being unfair but from what you have already told me we have provided the intelligence.'

'Yes, we have, but they made the discovery, they put us on this outlaw's trail to use your analogy.'

'Let's hope he doesn't head for the hills then. So what do you think he is up to and what can we do about it?'

After a hectic ride through the darkened streets of Marseille, the Special Forces and their rescued agent finally reached Istres-Le Tubé and the waiting helicopter. Its rotor blades were slowly turning as the car screeched to a halt several metres away and in a flurry of activity, the men of M Squadron transferred their equipment and their extra passenger to the aircraft.

Anita was strapped into her seat, finally able to relax, and sitting back, she closed her eyes. The situation had a touch of the surreal about it, one minute serving drinks on a superyacht and the next sitting in a military helicopter after a mission in which men died. It was not the first time she had found herself in such a situation but the rapid transfer from tranquillity to a life-threatening situation had certainly pumped up her adrenaline and now she was feeling the after-effects.

'You all right?' asked the sergeant.

'A bit woozy.'

'Here, take this; it will bring you round for a few hours.'

'What is it?'

'Modafinil, let's just say it's a staff to lean on. You will feel more alert for the next few hours than you might have been. We use it now and then, I can recommend it.'

Anita took the capsule and popped it into her mouth

'Thanks.'

Closing her eyes again, she tried to clear her mind and as the drug took effect, she began to feel calmer. After a few minutes, she felt the helicopter lift off and she opened her eyes to look past the trooper sitting next to her towards the receding air base lights. She could still not fully relax. The cat was out of the bag, she told herself, the Russians would deduce a sequence of events; recognise her involvement and that would compromise the whole operation. She hoped not, certainly not until she found out what Shadow was really doing. Then her mind seemed to go blank and she slipped into a deep sleep for the next two hours.

It was just after one o'clock in the morning when she took her seat inside the small room deep inside the Northolt terminal building.

'Good morning Sims,' said a calm voice. 'I presume a coffee will be in order?'

'Yes sir, it would.'

'Have someone send in some coffee for us will you Flight Sergeant?'

As the airman left the room Commander Pearson sat back in his chair and cast a neutral eye over Anita.

'Good to have you back safe and sound. How are you feeling?'

'Well enough sir, just a little tired that's all.'

'Good, then perhaps you can fill me in on a few details before we leave for London. I have convened a meeting with the European counter-intelligence section for ten o'clock tomorrow morning. We can debrief you more thoroughly then but in the meantime would you like to tell me what you have learned?'

There was a knock at the door and seconds later the flight sergeant appeared with two cups of coffee and a plate of biscuits.

'Will there be anything else sir as I am due to go off duty? My opposite number will be available, shall I tell him to wait outside the room?'

'Yes, for now, we will need him to escort us off the base when we are ready to go.'

Anita waited until the door closed again before speaking rapidly in a low voice.

'Sir, I think maybe the debriefing should wait.'

'Oh, why, shouldn't we know what you have learned?' said the commander, picking up his coffee cup.

'This isn't over, not by a long way. I need to go to Paris and soon.'

The commander paused, his eyes narrowing, and he put his cup down.

'How soon and why?'

'Tonight, now, there is unfinished business to attend to and I think we need the help of the French authorities. The lid is coming off and we need it holding down for a while longer.'

Commander Pearson's jaw dropped only slightly as Anita recounted the past few days, telling him everything that had happened, even her intimate moments with Bullseye. The intelligence was valuable, extremely valuable, and he understood exactly his agent's anxiety.

'You are right, I need to make one or two telephone calls first, but yes, I think you will serve us better in Paris.'

The flight to Orly airport was a tense affair for Anita; there was so much to think about, so much to consider. She had spent no more than half an hour talking to the commander who had listened with interest and then had telephoned his chief who in turn had contacted the Foreign Office and now she was back in France. This time she was not on her own, she would be working under the supervision of the British Ambassador. He in turn would keep the French informed of developments, call upon them should events spin out of control. Then there was the Lady Galina and the mayhem visited upon her. To prevent any of that getting out the French had already begun locking the vessel down and had removed the crew.

'This address in the eighteenth arrondissement is significant I am sure,' she had told Pearson, 'and I believe that is where we will find Shadow, but there is little time From what I have seen, he keeps on the move but like everyone else he needs to eat and he needs to sleep. He rested on the Lady Galina once or twice and my guess is that he will spend the night at this address. I want to be there when he leaves, find out where he goes, arrest him maybe.'

'That will not be easy; we do not have the resources to mount a full-scale surveillance operation. That is what it will take, a full-scale operation, believe me.'

'I know sir, but I think this thing is big and getting bigger, another possible Operation Crevice in my view.'

'The fertiliser plot fermented by al-Qaeda what, twenty years ago, and you think they are going to try again?'

'I don't know sir but my feelings are that al-Qaeda is building up to something and our friend Shadow is the key. And of course there is the Russian connection.'

'It's not my decision I know but if you are right I think we have to tell the French everything, enlist the help of their internal security services.'

'If we do inform them of what we suspect they will want to take full control, after all it is on their soil, for now anyway, but I think it will spread,' said Anita with a grim expression.

'Okay, I am promising nothing except to ask permission for you to fly back to France immediately. While you are in the air, I will talk with the director again and he no doubt will liaise with the Joint Intelligence Committee if he sees fit. From what you have told me and from what you suspect I believe involving the French security services is exactly what he will do. Now let me have a word with the fly boys.'

The conversation had taken place less than three hours earlier but to Anita it seemed like days. Things were beginning to move fast and she could well be back on Shadow's tail very soon. Shaking off the last vestiges of what was no more than a nap, she watched the landing circle lights grow large and then she was stepping back onto French tarmac for the second time in eight hours.

'Mrs Sims, good morning, name's McGregor, Hamish McGregor,' said a man stepping forward to greet her. He was dressed in a dark suit, a man of medium build and with the air of someone who could take care of himself. 'I am here to escort you to the embassy. Have you any luggage?'

'Afraid not, I am not on holiday,' she snapped, her experiences and lack of sleep beginning to tell. 'Sorry, just woken up and I feel a bit grotty.'

It would not do to alienate the Paris Bureau so soon; she was entirely in their hands. Luckily, McGregor showed no emotion, he simply opened the rear door of a black Citroën parked a few metres from the helicopter and motioned for her to get in and as dawn began to break the car pulled out of the airport entrance. Traffic was light at such an early hour and the Citroen was soon speeding along the E5 towards Paris. Half an hour later it crossed the river, entered the fourth arrondissement and threaded its way between seventeenth century baroque buildings, finally turning into a street almost devoid of traffic to stop outside the British Embassy.

McGregor pulled out a key fob, and after activating it, a pair of stout wooden doors automatically opened to reveal a small covered courtyard. The Citroen lurched forward inside and after the doors closed behind it McGregor climbed from his seat.

'If you would follow me ma'am.'

The building was one of splendour, built in an earlier age when form and detail mattered but Anita had little time for the finer points of French architecture. From simply surveillance, her assignment had moved on to an altogether loftier plane.

'Would you like some breakfast Mrs Sims?'

'I would, I haven't eaten since lunchtime yesterday – I have been rather busy of late. I didn't know Paris could be so cold,' she added, shivering.

'Can be, the heaters will be on soon and in another hour you will be as warm as toast. We need to go up to the second floor, follow me please.'

The two of them began climbing the stairs in silence to a landing where McGregor opened a door to a high-ceilinged room.

'I will telephone the night desk and ask someone to rustle up some eggs and bacon, I presume that will do?'

'Oh yes, and a black coffee, made the French way if possible.'

'We can. There is a fan heater here somewhere, I will have a look and get you warmed up. What about your clothes, it's no wonder you are cold in just a shirt and slacks?'

'I had to leave in a hurry. I left warmer weather and I had no time to pack.'

'I will get the night desk to send out for something a little more in keeping. What size should I tell them?'

Anita reeled off several critical measurements leaving McGregor to relay them to the night desk and then he turned to her.

'Take a seat and you can fill me in on a few details. We have not met before. I am the head of the security here at the embassy and it is my job to assist you wherever I can but also I am to liaise with the French. I am afraid they are in on it now and I must say they were none too pleased to learn that they had not been in the loop before. By the way, they know about your little trouble in Marseille and are keeping that quiet for as long as they can.'

'Do you have the address I passed on, the one in the eighteenth arrondissement, is it under surveillance?'

'Er, no, not exactly. The French are very touchy about any possible terrorist activity on their patch. Since our madness, they say we are not really part of the team anymore and are insisting on complete control. If you ask me, they are acting like de Gaulle did. Maybe it will all be sorted out in future and we will be close again.'

'Hmm . . . politicians.'

'As you say, politicians, but that is not our problem right now. I believe they are in fact about to mount a surveillance operation in due course but in the meantime Commander Pearson has instructed me to accompany you on a more clandestine foray. We are to have a look for our friend Shadow and to stay out of sight of the French for the time being. I have two of my colleagues coming to join us.'

'You know of him?'

'Oh yes, for several months now we have had instructions to keep an eye open for him.'

'But you have never seen him?'

'No, that is where you come in, you will easily recognise him I am told.'

By the time the rescue squad had spirited Anita away from the yacht, Yusuf was already well on his way to the French capital. Catching the late afternoon train, he arrived at Paris-Gare-de-Lyon just after eight in the evening and from there he took a taxi to the address in the eighteenth arrondissement. The security guard on the superyacht – Yusuf never did learn his name – had passed him the address and a telephone number to allow an exchange of secure messages.

'I hear the weather in Paris is very nice at this time of year,' said Yusuf as the door opened to his knock.

'So long as it rains only on the ungodly.'

'The ungodly deserve no better, Allah be praised.'

The man, satisfied with the exchange, ushered Yusuf into the building.

'We have to be careful, since the bombings. The police are everywhere and think nothing of breaking down doors.'

Yusuf passed over the threshold into a dimly lit passageway that had seen better days, faded wallpaper was starting to peel off in places and there was no sign of any carpet. As his eyes adjusted he noted his host, a man wiry rather than muscular and several centimetres shorter than himself. Yusuf guessed that he was in his late twenties or early thirties. His most prominent feature was a pair of dark penetrating eyes that examined Yusuf, hate-filled, revengeful and belonging to the kind of person al-Qaeda needed in its ranks.

'You are ready to fight for the cause my friend?'

'Ready and willing to serve Allah, be of no doubt.'

'You are a true believer and I am here to help you in the struggle. I have brought you money to buy the necessary ingredients to wage war on the infidels.'

'Allah be praised, come with me to meet the soldiers and to break bread with us.'

The rest of the terrorist cell was waiting in a room at the rear of the property, sitting at a bare wooden table.

'*Assalaam alaykum*,' said the man in greeting as he and Yusuf entered.

'Pour our guest a coffee Abdul. Take a seat my friend, tell us how goes the fighting in Syria and

Yemen. We hear that it is difficult for our brothers in certain parts.'

'It is but they are brave fighters and they are making it difficult for our enemies. Now we are to spread the struggle, attack the soft underbelly of the West. We have used bombs, vehicles and singular acts of violence for many years and caused great anxiety, and now the ruling council want you to carry out more of these attacks but this time on a particular day.'

'That may not be so easy.'

'You must try to attack as near to the prescribed time as possible, the plan depends upon it.'

'What plan?'

'Across many countries we will rise up together and cause as much damage to the infidels as possible, al-Qaeda is still a force the West should fear. Pick your targets carefully and kill as many infidels as you can.'

The men sitting round the table looked at each other, their eyes a mixture of apprehension and delight. They found the prospect of hitting back invigorating and looked pleased that the time for action was fast approaching. They were North Africans, from Tunisia and Morocco, from poor, deprived backgrounds who had had come to France in search of work and a better life. Instead, they had found themselves shunned and treated as outcasts, their lives no better than before and all felt a desire to hit back.

'We are ready,' said one, 'I have the skills to manufacture explosive devices but it is always difficult to obtain the parts without money.'

'It is a problem we know and I have brought with me money to help you buy the chemicals and control circuitry needed for the explosives, and to buy vehicles if you plan to use that method. You must tell no one of my visit, destroy your mobile telephones as soon as I leave and replace them with new.'

'We will do as you ask. You will rest here a while my friend after your journey?'

'I will stay for the night.'

McGregor switched off the ignition, sat back in his seat and surveyed the street.

'You said the French police were taking over the surveillance of the house. I cannot see anyone and there are no other cars parked nearby. Where are they?' asked Anita, sitting beside him.

'I do not know, maybe they are well concealed, in a nearby building perhaps.'

Anita began to search the windows of the properties in the street but could see nothing and was beginning to believe the French had not yet put their assets in place. If Shadow managed to elude them at this stage, they might never find him again.

'I cannot afford to lose him Mr McGregor; too much depends on finding out the purpose of what he is doing.'

McGregor lifted his mobile phone to his ear and spoke. 'Temple, you and Clarke seal off the end of the street, make sure our friend cannot leave without us knowing.'

Anita did not hear the reply but felt at least a little reassured.

'Are you sure he as at this address?' asked McGregor. 'And if he is, then what do you intend to do if he appears?'

'I am not absolutely certain he is here yet but my best guess is that he is.'

'If he is and he leaves the building we can follow him of course but if he suspects he is being followed he will have ample opportunity to give us the slip.'

Anita weighed McGregor's words. It was not the first time MI6 were too thin on the ground to have much effect but there was a good chance that Shadow *was* still in their sights and she could see no other logical path than the one she was taking.

'I want to take him out.'

McGregor remained silent, thoughtful for a few seconds before he took a deep breath and turned to look at her.

'I know this man must be important to us but to snatch him off the street of a foreign capital? We will be no better than the Russians, we should consult upstairs.'

'Call the ambassador and tell him to speak to Commander Pearson, tell him I intend bringing Shadow in, we cannot afford to lose him at this late stage.'

The Sommelier

Yusuf slept for no more than four hours, rising in the pre-dawn to conduct his first prayers of the day. He had reached the end of his mission and for the next few days he could relax and make his way home to take a well-earned rest. First, he would pray and then he would talk with Salan, the leader of the cell, discuss the means of causing havoc and then they would pray together.

'I am glad to see you are all worthy followers of the Prophet,' he said, entering the lounge area to see that the men had their prayer mats and a copy of the Koran.

'It is important to pray, to know the true path.'

'Of course, and as we are all together I have things to tell you before I leave.'

'We will break bread together first, with your permission.'

Yusuf nodded his head in agreement pleased that the men were following the faith and would be ready to make the ultimate sacrifice when the time came.

'*Allahu Akbar,*' he said with some pleasure. 'Tell me a little of what you plan to do when the day of action arrives, tell me how you intend to kill the enemies of the Prophet and I will educate you on the ways of al-Qaeda.'

No more than fifty metres away McGregor's telephone came to life and after speaking with the caller for less than thirty seconds he turned to Anita.

'It's a green light, we have permission to try to take out Shadow and move him to a safe house. Now it is up to us. By the way, Commander Pearson will shortly be arriving in Paris. You have certainly stirred things up.'

Anita pursed her lips well aware of the enormity of the situation, but as she perceived it there would not be another chance and it seemed that McGregor agreed with her.

'The ambassador has told me to make an attempt to apprehend out friend Shadow, but he knows we have limited resources. If this thing gets out of hand, there will be repercussions at the highest level. The ambassador has given us one hour – after that he is informing the French Government and requesting their help. I would have thought they would already be here; maybe those that matter have yet to receive instructions. It happens. One hour isn't long, particularly if Shadow doesn't show. Are we still sure he is in the house?'

'Not entirely, but we have to presume that he is and act accordingly.'

McGregor spoke a name into his mobile phone and almost immediately, the speed dialling brought a result. 'Temple, you and Clark park your car and proceed on foot. We have a package to collect.'

Five minutes later McGregor glanced in his rear-view mirror and then signalled for Anita to get out of the car.

'This is the difficult bit. I need you to join our agents and tell them what it is we are expecting to happen. They are quite capable of taking our man down once you have identified him and they should be somewhere towards the end of the street. I will be watching and as soon as they have him I will bring the car and we can take him away.'

'He might have a gun; the Russians will probably have armed him. We do not want him dead. You had better tell your men that he is far more valuable alive than dead.'

'Do not worry; they are not in the business of killing, well, unless I tell them different.'

Anita got out of the car and began walking. She could see the two agents; they had appeared on the opposite side of the street, fifty or so metres away and they were walking slowly in her direction. For the time being the street was deserted but Paris was waking up, people would soon begin appearing on the street. That was a worry because once the operation to abduct Shadow was underway it would draw the attention of passers-by. And if the Arab put up a fight and should anyone feel more than a little heroic then things might prove very difficult.

The agents drew level and she crossed the street, catching them up as they stopped to look in a shop window.

'I will take the lead,' she said in a low voice, 'keep as far away as you can without losing contact.'

She looked away from them, towards the opposite of the street and noticed the door to the building of interest begin to open. A man emerged onto the street, a tall, swarthy and confident-looking man. It was Shadow alright and, luckily for Anita, his attention was pointed in the opposite direction. She could not risk him seeing her before she got close, he would surely recognise her, and stepping into a doorway, she waited to see which way he would go.

Yusuf was wary, he had not managed to survive for so long in such a dangerous occupation without taking extreme care and today was no different. He scanned the street looking for anything unusual, any person or vehicle that might offer a threat, but seeing nothing obvious began walking in Anita's direction.

She saw him turn, felt her adrenaline begin to flow and she waited. This man was the key she felt sure, the one whose trail had led her here, the link to the Russians. She was still not sure what his end game was and this was probably her last chance to apprehend him. She took a backward glance, noted that the embassy men had separated, one peering into a shop window, the other stooping down behind a parked car ostensibly to tie his shoelace. She looked back at Shadow and could not believe her luck as she saw him cross the street towards her.

Yusuf was feeling safe enough, the street was deserted save for a man looking in a shop window and he decided to cross over to the opposite side. He was exposed he knew but once he reached the junction with the next street he would be close to the metro station and the safety of the crowds. His plan was to take the underground to Montmartre, mix with the tourists, and from there he would disappear for good. His task was complete, he was weary from the years of evading death, and with the money he had saved, he would return to the Middle East and find a quiet place to live in comfort.

That was his mistake, thinking ahead. In all the years that he had done the bidding of his masters, he had always stayed in the present, alert to the possibility of death or capture in every passing car, around every corner, and it was that awareness that had protected him for so long. Today was different, with only himself to worry about, he had relaxed and slipped into a fantasy world and that was his undoing.

She surprised him, the slim woman in dark clothes who emerged from the doorway. She was attractive in a business-like way and she seemed familiar. For just a few seconds he was completely off guard until recognition dawned and as shock registered on his face he found the words to address her.

'You, you were on the yacht, you served me food. Who are you?'

'Never mind who I am,' she said, sticking her arm out as a signal to the two agents. 'You are to come with me.'

Yusuf was going nowhere and struck out at her, but Anita was ready for him and administered her own kind of violence. A bare-knuckled punch into his solar plexus and a second to his left ear incapacitated him long enough for the strong hands of the two agents to restrain him.

It happened so quickly that any witness would have had no time to intervene and McGregor was soon on the scene. With a squeal of tyres, he brought the car to a halt alongside the commotion. Anita pulled the door open wide and with some difficulty Shadow was bundled into the rear seat and pinned down. He was distraught, devastated that they had taken him so easily.

Chapter 18

The blue, cloudless Moscow sky had turned grey and overcast the warm sunshine of the past week no more than a distant memory. In his office on the fourth floor of the Lubyanka building, Igor Andresov hardly noticed, occupied as he was with reports from his agents embedded on the border. Every day the Politburo wanted to know how the operation was developing and every day he would correlate the reports to present to his superiors.

Picking up a sheet of paper, he read several paragraphs, stopping for a moment to utter an oath. Why had the ambassador to France only now informed him that the authorities had impounded the Lady Galina and arrested the crew on the pretext that they were drug smuggling? He knew very well that this was not the case. Why would they make such a move, what had they discovered?

Igor sat back in his chair, considered what might be happening, how the consequences might affect the operation, and scribbled a few notes on the sheet. Suppose the French were interrogating the two FSB men on board, what might they discover?

The Sommelier

Not much, he was sure, because apart from Alexie no one knew the money's destinations or the object of the operation. The navy men were there purely to sail the yacht and were not involved. Then there was Borisovich, the owner of the Lady Galina, but he had too much to lose to involve himself with the enemies of the state and too tied to the Kremlin to risk its wrath if deemed a traitor. Leonid Borisovich had only one interest and that was making money.

So what was going on? Igor closed his eyes for a few moments and cast his mind back to his few days on board the superyacht. Had there been a spy in their midst, was one of the military men with him working for the Americans? It had happened before, enticing people to turn for money – that was more a driver than ideology and the Americans had plenty of money. Then he remembered the woman, the sommelier, and recalled his suspicions. Was she a spy, was she working for a Western intelligence agency?

Considering all facts, he concluded that the French authorities were treating it as a police matter rather than one of national security. Perhaps it was a genuine case of drug smuggling. To be sure he would instruct the embassy security team to check thoroughly their sources and he would find out what the GRU men on board were reporting. It was an irritant, no more he was sure. The courier had done his job, and the individual cells were isolated from one another. However, the Arab did know a lot, the addresses where cells were located. He was a danger and he needed to eliminate him.

Writing several notes on his pad, Igor put his immediate thoughts to one side and turned his attention to the matter of the invasion. The president had set a date for a time when he would see most of the glory bestowed upon him and that date was fast approaching. It was a shrewd move for should things go wrong then his successor would have to pick up the pieces.

The main operation would start within days of al-Qaeda operations in the various European capital cities. Attacks designed to propagate maximum panic amongst the centres of population and to tie up the security forces for as long as possible. In the meantime, Colonel Kazantsev and his team of whiz kids would activate their denial-of-service strategy. This combination of terrorist incidents, computer system failures and a lack of electrical power would cripple large swathes of western Europe. Then the false news stories would begin to percolate; news-hungry media would grasp at any information that had a ring of authenticity and individuals would help to spread the panic through their mobile telephones so long as their batteries held up. Then the army would move on the pretext of protecting the Baltic States, a *coup de main* to open up the Suwałki Gap.

Taking back control of the land bridge between Kaliningrad and Belarus might prove a dangerous move, one that could lead to all-out war with NATO.

However, the military planners had factored in the West's weaknesses. Already the same techniques that proved so valuable in the Crimea and Ukraine were underway; Special Forces in nondescript uniforms were roaming across the borders and convoys were massing on the pretext of delivering humanitarian aid to the Baltic States. The armed forces of the Republic of Belarus would offer no resistance, in fact, the planners would have preferred them to join the Russian Federation in its endeavour.

The task of the invading army would be to cut NATO's lines of communication, sow confusion and panic and to establish an unassailable bridgehead. Nevertheless, there was a problem. The Russian Air Force would find itself more than evenly matched against the combined weight of the NATO air forces even though the Americans had largely withdrawn from Europe.

On paper, the Russian Air Force could and would win the air war but NATO had an ace up its sleeve. The F-35, with stealth technology, advanced sensors and weapons capacity, was the most lethal, survivable and connected fighter aircraft ever built. That posed a serious problem except for the fact that, in the grand scheme, it had a limited range, even with drop tanks, and they would create a visible radar signature.

A second drawback for NATO was that they simply did not have very many of the aircraft in service. Only the British possessed them in numbers that would tell in a conflict. It was common knowledge in military circles that almost fifty of the F-35B variant were on order or had entered service with British forces and at the very moment, the brand-new British carrier *Nelson* was taking on board the last of its war load of twenty four aircraft.

Igor had discovered that the British Admiralty had decided to increase the deployment from nine aircraft and that was worrying. Although the Royal Air Force had not yet received any of the fighter jets and was not a particular threat, the carrier and its compliment of F-35s was. It had the ability to steam within range of the unfolding conflict and that would most likely tip the balance of the air war in favour of the NATO alliance.

Lighting a cigarette, he blew the smoke into the air as he digested his thoughts. If the carrier managed to come within range and launch the F-35s then the whole enterprise could be in jeopardy. Without air cover the land forces, particularly the tanks, would be vulnerable to even the less sophisticated NATO warplanes and without the tanks spearheading the push towards Kaliningrad the advantage would be lost.

The carrier was the key to success. He would bring that to the attention of the chiefs of staff during the meeting scheduled for the following afternoon and picking up his desk telephone, he called his deputy.

'Valery, come to my office immediately, alert your staff because we have work to do.'

Igor replaced the receiver and lit another cigarette. He would need evidence to prove his assumptions and that meant looking through all the relevant information they had on the deposition of the NATO air forces and the capabilities of H.M.S. Nelson. He knew that the head of the air force would be at the meeting and decided to ask him to bring an up-to-date assessment of his forces and he must not forget to tell Valery to speak with the Paris embassy security team.

The double doors and the high-ceilinged room were becoming a familiar sight to Igor, as was the echo of his footsteps as he walked in. Nodding a subdued greeting to those already there, he headed straight towards Colonel General Mischa Bonderov.

'Mischa, *dobriy den.*'

'*Spasibo* Igor, good to see you again. What can I do for you? I received your message from my staff officer and as I already had a folder prepared for this meeting, I presume I have in it the information you would like to discuss. If I might be so bold Igor, I believe you are concerned about the F-35 fighter jets of the British?'

'I am.'

'Here comes the president, take your seat and we will discuss that problem when the time comes.'

Two smartly dressed guards had appeared at the entrance doors and as they stood to attention the president and his nominated successor, Feodor Grachyov, walked into the room. All eyes were upon them, the most powerful men in Russia, and as the guards pulled the doors shut behind them the assembled luminaries, high-ranking military men and agents of the security services, rose to their feet in a sign of respect. Acknowledging the gathered assembly the president responded with a brief nod of his head and taking his seat declared the meeting in progress.

He began by reading a prepared statement to welcome Comrade Grachyov who would officially take up the reins of power within the next six months and by then it was hoped that the Baltic states, and quite possibly a large slice of Poland would be back under the control of the Russian Federation.

'Comrades, we are here to take a momentous decision, to regain what rightfully belongs to Mother Russia. Our forces have been gathering, training for the next phase of our expansion to regain our place in the world as a pre-eminent power. As you all know I will be stepping down and Comrade Grachyov will carry the momentum forward. It will not be long until we are once again equal to, or better than, the Americans. They are withdrawing into their own backyard and that has created a once-in-a-lifetime chance for us to take.'

The room erupted with the enthusiastic sound of fists banging on the surface of the polished table and the president regally lifted his head in response. It had been a long and difficult path but he was finally reaching his goal.

'And now down to business. Each of you in turn will address the meeting; detail the strengths and weaknesses of the forces under your control. We still do not know how NATO will react but if it remains as passive as it did during our takeover of the whole of Ukraine they will do no more than make a lot of noise. The Americans are still a threat but a diminishing one and I have it on good authority that the President of the United States will not oppose us.'

Around the table, the men remained silent, some looked thoughtful, pursed their lips. Ever since the American voters had elevated POTUS to the presidency rumours had abounded. One or two in the room knew the truth and Igor was one of them. Not only had his agents spied on the Americans but also on certain members of the Politburo and the President's statement that the Americans would stand aside did not surprise him.

The French were understandably furious when they discovered that the British Secret Service had snatched Shadow from under their noses. It was not the first time the department's machinations had ruffled feathers and after intense diplomatic exchanges at the highest level, the British Prime Minister ordered MI6 to work with the French Secret Service whilst on French soil.

For their part, the French had not taken long to realise what had happened. The British had acted unilaterally, the furore that followed had gone right to the top, and now the ambassador was annoyed at having to deal with the problem. In an effort to determine what had gone on he had summoned both McGregor and Agent Sims to his office and shortly afterwards Commander Pearson had joined them from London.

'Pearson, this is your operation I understand. Can you tell me what the hell is going on?'

'What happened?' he asked, turning to McGregor. 'I thought it was to be no more than a surveillance operation and the French were to take the lead, after all, it is their country.'

'Yes sir it is, but Agent Sims here imparted some sensitive information and convinced me to act. It was a successful operation sir; we would not have acted as we did if the Frogs had turned up when they should have.'

'I have told you before not to use that term McGregor, our French colleagues are a little sensitive about that. Reminds them of Waterloo I think,' said the ambassador.

'Sorry sir.'

'So you had better include me, tell me about this sensitive information.'

'Sir, it is my responsibility, Mr McGregor was acting with the best of intentions,' said Anita.

'Quite, he usually does and I usually have to pick up the pieces. Please explain.'

'With your permission sir?' she said, turning to Commander Pearson.

'Everyone in this room has clearance, go ahead.'

'I have been working on a project for several months and it concerns a certain subject code named Shadow, the object of this morning's action. There is also another person of interest code named Bullseye, a Russian oligarch whose superyacht, the Lady Galina, is berthed in Marseilles.'

'I know about that, my opposite number called me an hour ago to discuss the situation and said the yacht was impounded, something about drug smuggling, but they seem to think that there is more to it than that.'

'There is sir; I have been working on the yacht as relief sommelier. We picked up some noise in London; I started working for Bullseye at his house in Belgravia, a dinner party for some interesting people. Then a few weeks later we had a lucky break. We knew something was going on, found out that Shadow had visited the yacht and that he was at one time with al-Qaeda. That posed the question as to whether he was still active or not and why he would visit a Russian's yacht. I might add that the yacht was cruising with its AIS transponder switched off until it appeared quite suddenly in the middle of the Black Sea. GCHQ spotted it and that was when we began to take an interest. I have kept an eye on both Shadow and Bullseye and I believe that Shadow is in possession of useful information that we might never have known if we had not apprehended him. He could have disappeared without trace, leaving us unable to discover his connections with the Russians.'

407

'Are we any the wiser?' asked the ambassador.

'Not at the moment sir. Can I ask, is the French Secret Service keeping an eye on the house in the eighteenth arrondissement?'

'More than that they have raided the place and arrested the occupants. You tell an interesting story Mrs Sims and I can advise you that they recovered a large quantity of United States dollars and euros.'

'He's a paymaster, that's it!' exclaimed Anita, 'we suspected that was his role for some time and now we know. There was a locked room on the yacht and only the two security men ever entered it. That must be where they stored the money. They also had a small control room near the yacht's bridge from where they must have kept in contact with Moscow. We checked out both individuals before I started working on the boat: GRU, Spetsnaz specialists. They were in the Crimea a few years ago, part of Russia's shadow army. What about the Arab sir, do the we have anything from him yet? He has the hallmark of one who will not talk, a zealot, committed to the cause so I do not expect we will get a great deal out of him.'

'He may well be tight-lipped, might very well withstand interrogation, but he made one miscalculation. He did not get rid of his mobile telephone,' said McGregor with a wry smile.

'What have you learned from that McGregor, anything?'

'Nothing yet sir, he used encryption apps, the telegram app for one.'

'Hmm . . . it is impossible to read those messages as I understand it.'

'For most people I guess,' said Commander Pearson, 'but it is amazing the things the boffins at GCHQ can do. I am flying to Cheltenham within the hour with the telephone. and Mrs Sims here is coming with me.'

'What are we going to do with this Shadow character?'

'Where is he now?'

'In a safe house,' said McGregor.

The ambassador let his glasses slip to the end of his nose and peered over them at the three people sitting opposite.

'You have put me in a difficult position; the French Minister of the Interior has rung me already today and wants answers. What am I going to tell him?'

'Ambassador, I think we should come clean, tell them everything we know. This thing will affect a lot of other countries and I believe the last thing we need is our friends turning against us,' said Commander Pearson.

'You have a solution?'

'Sir, give them Shadow. I will tell them all we know but we will keep the mobile phone and let GCHQ have a look at it first. I think we will get more from that than throwing our Arab friend in the Bastille.'

The ambassador frowned; his job was difficult enough without Anglo-Saxon humour upsetting people.

'Okay, sounds a good short-term solution but if you turn anything interesting up we will have to share it eventually. Leave it with me for now. I shall be contacting your superiors, Pearson, we can't let things escalate, and dealing with the Europeans is hard enough as it is these days.'

The flight back to the United Kingdom was uneventful apart from the rainstorm they had to endure on landing. Anita reflected on the British weather, cold wet and windy, very different from the warm sunny days she had so recently spent in the Mediterranean.

'Welcome home,' said Commander Pearson with a humourless smile.

'Yes, it's good to be back even though I must endure this weather. It's strange, but now I am back the weather does seem almost welcoming.'

'Quite, a car will meet us at the terminal building to take us to GCHQ and then we can see what the phone has to tell us. I have no idea how long it will take nor if there is anything of use on the SIM card. He may have swapped SIM cards on a regular basis, it's the easiest way, so I wouldn't expect too much intelligence.'

Later that day Commander Pearson's face creased in a rare smile as the specialist handed him his initial report.

'You seem to have extracted quite a bit already. I must say I am both surprised and impressed by these results.'

'It seems your friend was confident that his messages could not be read, used an encrypted messenger app but we have access to telephone company servers and our software can make short work deciphering the messages. They are not as secure as people might think.'

'What do you say Sims?'

Anita read the page from over Pearson's shoulder, noting that even some parts of the decoded messages were cryptic.

'I think *the Russian maid* could be the Lady Galina. He mentions that he will arrive shortly after a visit to *the Russian maid*. Do you know where he sent this message from?'

'Not yet, I have someone working on that at the moment. Once we can establish from where he sent and received each message then I will furnish you with a list.'

'What will that prove, where he has been yes but it would be nice to know his future plans.'

'I'm sorry I can't do that,' said the specialist, 'but we can extrapolate from the information we have to give an overall picture of where the subject has been and when. Not only can we determine the places where he used his SIM card but we can run a network program to include the numbers he contacted, who contacted him and when, and then we trace their calls and eventually we can represent them on a Venn diagram. That, coupled with some statistical analysis, creates an accurate picture of the subject's movements, who he communicated with, then we use the subject's acquaintances' phone numbers and before long we can have a fairly accurate idea of his movements even though there is nothing on his SIM card connecting him to these other contacts.'

'So you can show not only where he has definitely been, but where he has probably been in the recent past?'

'Yes ma'am.'

Anita and Commander Pearson both looked thoughtful for a few moments.

'We need to be heading back to London soon, will you forward what information you can extract as soon as possible to the Embankment?'

'Of course, give me the name or department to whom I should send it.'

Commander Pearson was a military man and when it came to organising troops or confounding the enemy, he was the best, but when it came to pure technicalities he left that to others.

'I think Mrs Sims here would be best for that.'

The expression on Anita's face was non-committal yet inside she was bursting with excitement. This could be the culmination of all her hard work, reward for the risks she had taken, and

without hesitation, she provided a secure email
address.

Across the channel, the French were not having
much luck with Shadow. Yusuf had prepared
himself for the day when his world might end,
learned to suffer the pain of torture and learned to
give nothing away. He would rather die than
capitulate to the infidels but to his surprise, they
had been courteous, and he was not in a prison cell
but a nondescript villa on the outskirts of Paris.

'*Monsieur*, we know exactly who you are and
what you have been doing on French soil. However,
there are some things we are not wholly sure of, for
instance, what was the object of your visit to the
house on the Rue Jean Robert, what was all that
money for?'

Yusuf looked straight ahead saying nothing.

'*Monsieur*, you would be wise to answer our
questions. You are a terrorist sympathiser and after
all the terrorist attacks France has suffered, we are
in no mood to be lenient. Our laws have changed; no
longer can people of your ilk dance around behind a
lawyer prolonging the case, hoping that in the future
some judge or other will allow you to go free on
some human rights defence. We can hold you
indefinitely until you decide to help us and when I
say indefinitely I mean indefinitely. It could easily
be a life sentence; you will finish your days rotting in
some obscure jail the world has never heard of.
Come Mr Muhammed, cooperate with us, who

knows, in only a few years you could be walking free into a new life.'

Yusuf was unmoved, still staring at the floor as if the interrogator's words had passed right through his head.

'You are well known to both the British and the Americans. They have been tracking you ever since Al-Kasrah. Do you remember Al-Kasrah, the training camp, the jet bombers that came to destroy it? We saw you there and we have seen you in many places since. You may think you have kept a low profile my friend, but the truth is you have been useful to us all these years. You have led us to terrorist groups all over the Middle East lied the interrogator, and now you come to Europe with your mayhem.'

Yusuf hardly flinched, but it was enough to cause his interrogator to allow himself an inward smile. It was true that there was a file on this man but it was historic and of no real use. The secret services of Britain and the United States had not realised Shadow's importance until only recently but it was useful to have him believe that they knew practically everything about him and the ploy worked in part.

It came as a shock to Yusuf to think that the Americans had known of his clandestine activities and more so that he may have caused the deaths of brother fighters due to his own carelessness. He would not let it happen this time: he would say nothing, even if it meant his death.

'If you knew about me you would have arrested me earlier. You lie, infidel.'

The interrogator said nothing, remaining silent, allowing Shadow to vent his anger. Most of those from the Middle East that passed through his hands were headstrong, arrogant and perhaps this one was the same; but eventually he might divulge a useful nugget of information that would be of future use.

'You cannot stop us, you cannot kill us all. We will win in the end. Allah be praised.'

'Win what, it is not defined. You have not declared war. You simply bomb innocent civilians. That is not war and is certainly not a conflict you can ever win.'

'Just watch us; the tide will soon be turning.'

'What tide is that my friend?'

Yusuf suddenly realised he had said too much, closed his mouth and returned to staring at the floor. The interrogator asked more questions, goaded him gently enough not to make him clam up completely, but after a further half an hour he realised he wasn't going to discover anything else today.

'I trust your quarters are comfortable enough. Is the food to your liking? We do not want to alienate you; we prefer to be your friend. I will leave you for a while; the guards will take you back to your room. Good afternoon Mr Muhammed.'

The two guards came into the room and between them escorted Shadow to his confinement whilst the interrogator, Captain Le Grande of the General

Directorate for Internal Security lit a cigarette,
inhaled slowly and began scribbling notes on his
pad.

Chapter 19

A thoughtful Commander Pearson was sitting with his chin resting in his cupped hand deep in thought when Anita entered the room.

'Ah, yes, come in Anita, take a seat,' he said, lowering his hands and sitting back in his chair. 'I have asked you hear to help me fully understand what might be going on. What is your reading of the situation?'

'I'm not sure sir, but some ideas are starting to crystallise. Shadow is a paymaster for al-Qaeda I am sure, and he is distributing what must be Russian-supplied funds. That is a strange affair to say the least.'

'My sentiments exactly and there are other forces at play of which you may not already be aware. The build-up of Russian forces in the Baltic continues though we cannot determine the exact reason. As usual, they are playing their cards close to their chest and pumping out false news to wrong-foot NATO. Rosemary Pennington at Foggy Bottom, you know her I believe.'

417

'Yes sir, we have worked together before. I asked for her help in identifying Shadow.'

'Yes I know. Well I want you to speak with her again as soon as possible, immediately in fact.'

'You want me to go to Washington?'

'I'm sure we do not have time for that. No, I have arranged a conference call via the secure line. I want us to have a brainstorming session, see if we can second-guess the Russians. I will be with you and Director Linley will be sitting in with Mrs Pennington. We're in luck; they have already started work over there so we can get right on it.'

Half an hour later in a secure communications cubicle Anita almost felt she was in the same room as the Americans what with the combination of the big screen and the ultra-HD transmission.

'Director Linley, Mrs Pennington, good morning.'

'Good morning,' said the director. 'It's good to hear from you Neil. You know Rosemary.'

'I am very much aware of her reputation but we have not actually met.'

'Hello Anita, I hear you have been in the thick of it again?'

'Hi Rosemary, you could say that but I am just doing my job.'

'Of course. I saw your report on Bullseye and his yacht and it made interesting reading. Now that you have Shadow in custody, we should be able to gather more intelligence. What have you learned so far?'

'I think Commander Pearson has more on that.'

Commander Pearson cleared his throat and paused for a moment before speaking.

'The French are still interrogating him and our people at GCHQ have done wonders with his mobile phone. They checked out the numbers, the calls he made and of course incoming calls too. They seem to be providing the best intelligence. From that, GCHQ were able to draw up a picture of his movements and his contacts.'

'What exactly did it tell you?'

'That during the past month he made a visit to Munich and Berlin and that his trail led back to the Lady Galina from where we believe he was collecting funds for distribution to the terrorist cells. Now that the French are fully involved we have been working closely with them and the German security service. They have provided what intelligence they could, and we are now are busy liaising with the rest of the European agencies. Since the boffins worked on the statistics we actually have a much fuller picture of his movements for the past year and at the moment each security service is actively trying to lock down the terrorists in their own countries.'

'Good, so you are keeping the lid on for the time being?'

'Not exactly, many of the groups we have identified are on the move. Some flew the coop when the police arrived and we are busy looking for them. In time, most will be found but the worry is that they will have already caused havoc by then.'

'Oh dear, that is a problem.'

'It is but we are working on it.'

'What else can you tell me commander?'

'I think perhaps Anita should fill you in on her findings, it make for an interesting scenario.'

Anita looked at the big screen, at the two Americans and began to relate some of the intelligence she had garnered from her time on the Lady Galina.

'While I was on board some high-ranking Russian military arrived for what appeared to be a short holiday but it was far from that. You have their names I think. I could not get close to overhear much of their conversations, the two goons running security kept me away as much as they could, but I did pick up something. They talked about the new fighter, the F-35, and it seems to be a problem for the Russian military.'

'I would say so; the Russians cannot match it no matter what propaganda they put out to the contrary. The jets are invisible to their radar and can hit targets from over a hundred miles away, never mind their total battlefield capabilities.'

'You think it significant Mrs Pennington?' asked Commander Pearson.

'Call me Rosemary, please Commander.'

'Then you should call me Neil. Again Rosemary, do you find the F-35s a significant part of the equation?'

'Let's paint the whole picture. So far, Anita has been working towards identifying Shadow and his connection with the Russians. That in itself is significant for it seems to demonstrate that the Russians are working directly with al-Qaeda. Now why would the Russians want to work with them when they have had terrorist incidents on home soil perpetrated by the self-same organisation?'

'They do have a bit of history working with terrorist groups.'

'It is true, they have, but in Syria mainly and never as far as I know on home soil.'

'But they are now,' interjected Anita, 'and since I got back to London I have discovered that one of the men on the yacht is Igor Andresov, head of the FSB's European section. Shadow was not, to my knowledge, on board at the same time. As a director of the FSB wouldn't he have an interest in using al-Qaeda? 'I am beginning to believe that is the case,' she said, her mind reliving some of her time on the Lady Galina.

'So what you have for us is one, al-Qaeda and the Russians are working together and two, the Russians are in the throes of an advanced build up along the borders of the Baltic states and three, they are concerned about the F-35s. How do we connect them?' queried Director Linley. 'What can you add Rosemary?'

Rosemary Pennington gripped her glasses between thumb and second finger, repositioned them at the end of her nose and looking over the lenses, pausing for a few moments.

'My work has recently focused on the movement of Russian forces along the borders of Belarus and

Ukraine. In my considered view it is obvious that if the Russians are intent on invading Europe, particularly the Baltic States, then they are in the right place and in the right numbers to do it.'

'You think they really would invade, Rosemary?'

'No Anita I do not, but I do believe they will carry on pursuing their program of creeping annexation of former Soviet satellites. If they are in fact progressing with that program then it looks to me that they are upping the scale somewhat and that should motivate NATO to oppose such a move.'

'That could mean war,' said Commander Pearson.

'It could, though on what scale and for how long I really could not say because we haven't had a peer-to-peer conflict in Europe for over eighty years. To unleash modern weapons on a large scale would be a disaster for both the antagonists and the defenders. No one will win and the Russians know that.'

'Is that where the F-35s come in, Rosemary?' queried Anita.

'Yes, I believe they are the key. The Russians have superiority on the ground. Well to a point, they have greater numbers though I do believe their fabled Armata tanks are not quite as advanced as they would have us believe. They work the numbers game, will suffer an attrition rate for longer than we can and in that way stand a good chance of winning, except that the F-35 in all its variants is a game changer. They know this and they know that their air superiority would not last long once the F-35s arrive in theatre. An appearance on the immediate battlefield is not necessarily the real threat because those aircraft can operate successfully from over a hundred miles away, are invisible to Russian radar and are equipped with the latest missile tracking, and defence system. They are to all intents and purposes they are indestructible so long as they do not get drawn into a dog fight.'

'Where are NATO's F-35s right now Commander?'

'I do not know exactly the whereabouts of the them all Director, but I can say that the majority of the British F-35s are on the *Nelson*.'

'What about your other carrier, how far has she progressed with her fighter complement?'

'Not very far I'm afraid, financial constraints and all that.'

'I do know the Italian Air Force has a number of them in service but whether the Italians would commit them to northern Europe is another matter,' said Director Linley. 'What do you think Rosemary?'

'The range of an F-35 is not so good for the B variant, maybe nine hundred kilometres in stealth mode. That is why they are carrier-based, so they can always be within range of a conflict. Land-based versions have a greater range but there are none, as far as I know, anywhere near the Baltic.'

'What about inflight refuelling?'

'It's a possibility but until the first strike takes out radar installations the tankers are vulnerable. I don't think it's worth the risk.'

'So we are totally reliant on the *Nelson* sailing within range to counter the Russian threat,' said the director.

'Yes,' said Rosemary, replacing her glasses and sitting back deep in thought.

'Have you anything to add Commander?' asked Director Linley.

'Rosemary has described the Russian threat and the response we can make but where does al-Qaeda fit into all this? Anita, what do you think?'

Anita watched Rosemary, noticing her eyes were looking inward, as if some revelation were unfolding and it was catching.

'I am of the opinion that al-Qaeda is a diversion,' said Anita

Both Director Linley and Commander Pearson looked at her in anticipation and Rosemary's lips parted in a thin smile.

'In what way, why?' asked Commander Pearson.

Anita did not answer; she did not have the chance because Rosemary sprang back into life.

'A diversion to wrong-foot us, use them to light many small fires, tie up the security forces of the Europeans and while we are busy chasing our tails they will have the chance to invade the Baltic states on the pretext of defending Russian nationals and assisting the local police to contain the threat. After that, they will open a corridor through the Suwałki Gap saying that Kaliningrad is under threat.'

'Its certainly possible, we have war gamed such a scenario for years but always believed the presence of NATO forces provided a sufficient deterrent,' added director Linley. 'Do you not think that deterrent will work anymore Rosemary?'

Rosemary turned her head to look at the director as if his statement was false.

'Times change, weapons change and although we appear to have the F-35s in sufficient numbers there is the possibility that the carrier cannot get within range to launce meaningful operations. That, as I see it is our weak link.'

'She has protection; the new Type 26 frigates and the Type 45 destroyer can handle any surface or air threat from distance and the Astute class submarines will be protecting her from underwater threats,' said commander Pearson. 'Those ships and submarines are equipped with the latest and best hi-tech sonar. With the F35s up in the air nothing can get close enough to initiate an attack and the carrier has her own sophisticated defences. I think it possible though highly unlikely that the Russians will attempt to sink her.'

'Sounds convincing commander but is something else. The small matter of an autonomous submersible we believe the Russians have developed. We have little idea of what it is capable and limited intelligence as yet. What we do know is that the submersible has an advanced stealth capability and that the Russian navy probably penetrated the main Swedish naval base sometime late last year. We know it has been undergoing testing on the Kola Peninsula with the Northern

Fleet. I recently held a discussion with some people at the Directorate of Undersea Research I can tell you that we are building and testing similar machines. My belief is that an autonomous submarine with a serious stealth capability is the greatest threat to your new carrier commander.'

Captain Sverdlovsk was grateful for the mug of hot coffee his steward had just handed him. He had been up all night studying his charts, plotting their course and keeping an eye on the helmsman. The waters of the North Sea could be treacherous, its shallows and currents ready to grasp an unwary ship in its icy fingers and drag it to a watery grave. He looked at his watch, three-thirty. In another two and a half hours he would open up the safe and take out his sealed orders.

Before leaving Murmansk, the Commander of the Northern Fleet had summoned him to a meeting. There was a civilian present, a thin, bespectacled man to whom the Admiral deferred. He was probably FSB and very high ranking at that. Anyway the civilian had sworn him to secrecy, made him aware of the consequences if he ever divulged the substance of the meeting and then he had learned a little of his impending task. The admiral had indicated the general area to which he should sail but that the operation would remain secret and his orders locked away until six in the morning on this particular day.

Returning to the *Sergey Makarevich*, Captain Sverdlovsk had then overseen the arrival of extra crew – four men, specialist technicians who would be responsible for the detailed execution of the mission. They brought with them sophisticated computer and communications equipment and as soon as the ship put to sea they began work on the 'Fish' as the submarine was now fondly known. Leaning back in his seat he took a long, deep breath and stared ahead through the bridge's windows just as the first glimmer of the new day began to spread across the eastern horizon. He had waited for this day after a long career in the navy, the day when he would begin to bring all his knowledge and experience to bear.

Finishing his coffee, captain Sverdlovsk slid off the seat and walked the few steps to the chart table to examine chart of the northern North Sea. Their cover as a factory ship was nothing new and he was well aware that the enemy might be keeping an eye on his activities. A visit from a NATO warship was the last thing he wanted though they had seen none since leaving Russian waters. He cast his eye over the chart again, noted the ship's course and issued an order to the helmsman.

'Steer one eight five helmsman.'

'Aye aye sir.'

The vessel hardly seemed to move, changing course a mere ten degrees, but it was enough to take them past the Shetland isles and out into the Atlantic. Then, at five minutes to six, he left the bridge in the capable hands of the first officer and went to his cabin.

Portsmouth was just coming to life as the tugs pulled the bulk of the aircraft carrier towards the dock, her flight deck and twin islands towering high over the historic buildings of the naval base. In contrast to a bygone age, the warship was far more powerful and capable than the whole of Lord Nelson's navy.

She had recently returned from the Western Approaches where her complement of F-35Bs had practised take-off and landing manoeuvres. Two hundred miles further out in the Atlantic a Royal Navy frigate had shadowed her and presented a potential threat. It gave the radar personnel a chance to familiarise themselves with their new equipment only recently installed and in general, the ship's systems were working well. Her sixteen hundred sailors, marines and aviators were battle-ready after months of training and the Captain was pleased with their progress.

'Steady as she goes Captain,' said the officer of the bridge as the three powerful tugs skilfully manoeuvred sixty-five thousand tons of steel alongside, and below he could see the sailors winching in the dock lines.

'Thank you number one. Carry on, I shall be in my day cabin should you need me.'

'Aye aye sir.'

The Sommelier

From the Spinnaker Tower the aircraft carrier presented a wonderful sight. The tower, a structure one hundred and seventy metres high overlooked not only Portsmouth but its naval base. As the tugs guided her into the harbour, townspeople lined the quays and one group of schoolchildren who had managed to evade the afternoon's lessons were with their teacher at the top of the tower.

'What do we know about the ship's name?' asked the teacher and several hands reached for the sky. 'Bell, what do you know?'

'Sir, Nelson was the best sailor we ever had.'

'Was he?'

'Yes sir.'

'Can you tell us why?'

'He stuffed the French sir.'

Laughter broke out amongst the boy's fellow pupils and, as they berated him, a middle-aged man holding a pair of binoculars and wearing a faded red baseball cap could not help a wry smile. The French were not the Russian Navy of today, he thought. The Russian navy was capable of presenting a more formidable opposition than the combined French and Spanish fleets of Trafalgar and having seen enough he lowered his binoculars. Casually he left his vantage point and walked away to a secluded corner where he took out a mobile telephone. The message was simple: 'Nelson moored alongside Princess Royal jetty.

The conference call had been a sobering experience for Anita because if she believed Rosemary, and there was no reason not to, then the world appeared close to conflict. Would Russia risk open warfare with NATO? She could not really believe it but there was certainly serious trouble brewing.

She had left the conference cubicle less than an hour before, it was almost ten in the evening local time and she was hungry. She put that down to nervous energy rather than the fact that she had not eaten since the early afternoon. After the discussion with Langley, she had spent some time in conversation with Commander Pearson when they had considered the implications of a Russian invasion of the Baltic States and, worse, Poland. Their main worry was not that NATO might be unable to defeat an invasion force but that the political will would be missing. For eighty years, the watchwords had been all for one and one for all but since the Americans' quicksilver president had changed tack they had run down or abandoned most of their European bases. Would countries such as Turkey join the alliance against the Russians now that they were such good friends? Appeasement was the new mantra. Anita was tired, she was hungry and it was late. She should really go home and have a good night's sleep and perhaps in the morning the situation would appear less bleak. She yawned, her eyes watered and she really did feel that she had had enough but one small voice broke through her fatigue and she realised that her day was not over, not by a long way and picked up her desk telephone and made two calls.

'Can someone send me up a sandwich please,' she asked the canteen on her second call.

She had a hunch; she had no idea where it came from, probably her tired brain working on its own initiative. Something in Rosemary's appraisal had struck a chord, her final comments, the fear of world war three and the worry that the Russians had a new advanced underwater capability. She remembered when Rosemary was speaking how the image of the aircraft carrier had entered her mind. Now why was that?

She leaned her elbows on her desk and supporting her chin in cupped hand she concentrated on the reasons why she would be thinking the way she was. It was obvious from Rosemary's presentation that the F-35s were important players in any modern conflict. Hadn't the Russians on board the Lady Galina expressed their own reservations about the fighter jet? Then there was this new information about a Russian underwater capability, which added a completely new dimension as she saw it. Still trying to work out the significance of it all, she sat back in her chair and drummed her fingers lightly on her desk. Her mind was beginning to focus and then the door opened and the security guard ushered in one of the canteen staff.

'Thank you for that, I do appreciate it,' she said to the woman as she deposited the paper plate with the cling-film-wrapped food onto her desk. As she left Anita walked to the coffee machine, pressed the button for black, double shot, and took her drink back to the desk. For the next ten minutes, she ate the food and tried to relax. Then she looked at her watch, almost midnight, six in the afternoon in Washington. She hoped Rosemary would be still at work and reached for her telephone to make the call.

'Anita, hi, so soon getting back to me?'

'Yes, something is bothering me.'

'Oh?'

'You mentioned the possibility that the Russians might have a new underwater capability, a drone I suppose?'

'Yes, but we do not have a great deal on it, only that we believe it penetrated the main Swedish naval base undetected and by inference maybe others.'

'Can this submersible be detected?'

'If it can we haven't managed it yet. That is if it has penetrated any of our naval bases.'

'That's the worry, if it has, and we don't know about it, then it can do it again.'

'And again, I take your point. You are worried about your aircraft carrier aren't you?'

'Yes I am. Question: if the sub can penetrate NATO naval defences and enter a base where did it come from in the first place?'

'Well done Anita, I like your thinking and the answer is we do not know that either, but one would suspect a mother ship of some sort. I do not believe the submarine would have the battery power for more than maybe a hundred miles.'

'So I need to look for the mother ship?'

'You do, where are you going to start, we do not have much for you to go on.'

'My last mission began because a superyacht turned on its Automatic Identification System in the middle of the Black Sea.'

'AIS, yes, good idea, now what do you need from me?'

'The date and rough coordinates of the Swedish sighting will be a good start.'

'Give me half an hour and I will dig out the report, email you its contents.'

'Thanks Rosemary.' Anita replaced the receiver and for the next half hour studied what she could find on the new generation of submersibles.

Their stealth capabilities were impressive but, more importantly, their artificial intelligence capabilities seemed to know no bounds and the more she read the more concerned she became. Then a noise caused her to look up, it was James Hill.

'Good boy, that's what I like to see, enthusiasm.'

'I wouldn't call it that ma'am, more a worry about losing my job. I came as soon as I got your call.'

'I don't think you need to worry about that.' Anita smiled at the young secret service officer. 'Now, down to business,' she said, checking her inbox; the email from Rosemary had arrived and Anita was able to brief James on what she wanted him to do.

She told him of the Russian threat in the Baltic, explained that it was problematic whether the Americans would ride to the rescue or not.

'If they do not we could have a big problem and you know what POTUS has said about Europe standing on its own two feet.'

James nodded, his weariness melting away.

'I have been thinking, there is a maritime element to all this and if you remember that is where all this started for us, when the superyacht went missing.'

'You think it's involved?' said James, a puzzled look on his face.

'Not anymore, the French have impounded it and threatened the crew with serious repercussions if they so much as breathe a word. No, we have bigger fish to catch this time I think. There is the suspicion that the Russians have developed an advanced autonomous submarine. A Swedish naval officer fishing near his base briefly caught a glimpse of it and from his description, the Americans have an idea of its capabilities. I have spoken to Langley who first alerted me to its existence and I requested as much information as is available. The result came in just before you arrived.'

She turned to her monitor and after hitting a few keys brought up Rosemary's report.

'This is a section of chart near the Karlskrona naval base where the submersible was sighted and the time. We strongly suspect that the sub needs a mother ship to get it within striking distance of any target and you my dear boy are going to find that mother ship.'

James's eyebrows rose a little in surprise.

'Can you do a printout of this?'

'Yes of course,' said Anita sending the file to the printer. 'What do you think?'

'First I need to find an historical record of AIS transmissions in that area, see what vessels were around at the time, and then have a close look at each one in turn.'

'What if the signal was turned off?'

'I will look at several days either side, see if something appears.'

'And what if it doesn't?'

'Whoa ma'am, let us not depress ourselves so early,' he said with a frown.

Anita watched him go and picked up her lukewarm coffee. It was not particularly palatable but she needed the caffeine and finishing it off she turned her attention back to her computer and as a matter of interest, she logged on to the Ministry of Defence website. First, she looked at the current assessments of the Russian military capability and it made disturbing reading. A note made it clear that since the war in Chechnya back in ninety-four the Russians had realised just how far they had fallen behind the West in their military capabilities.

Gosh, she thought was that really thirty years ago, thirty years since the conflict that had served as a wakeup call to the Russian military. Since then they had modernised, reorganised and now the number of ships, tanks and aircraft they could field were far in excess of the combined European force. Only the might of America, or the Russians' poor serviceability record, had any chance of holding them back.

Widening her search, she found specifications for the various configurations of the F-35 and its comparison to the best Russian fighters. It soon became clear that the F-35s really were superior in most combat scenarios. Their only drawbacks were their lack of comparable agility in a dogfight and the effective combat range of the B variant. The Russians were probably right to fear the aircraft if NATO could launch sufficient numbers and *Nelson* probably carried enough of them.

Anita's research came to a halt by as James returned.

'Hi, I have found your ship; she was loitering in the Baltic on the day in question. I checked out several vessels that were in the area on the date you gave me and all but one performed as you would expect.'

'Which one did not?'

'She is a Russian-flagged factory ship called the *Sergey Makarevich* and right now she is at the western end of the English Channel, making around ten knots. Once I had her on my radar so to speak, I checked out her historic AIS transmissions from several weeks before the incident near the Swedish naval base and I followed through right up to the present.'

'How did you manage that?'

'There are civilian sites with lots of information run by enthusiasts and professionals alike. They provide a treasure trove of information on just about every ship sailing the seven seas. After the date of the sighting, the *Sergey Makarevich* sailed out of the Baltic and then north along the Norwegian coast but as soon as she passed the North Cape and entered Russian waters where she switched off her transmitter. That was a puzzle but an indicator, at least, that she did not want to be found.'

'Where do you think she went?' asked Anita.

'My best guess is the Kola Peninsula to one of the Russian naval bases up there. The Northern Fleet have a research facility at the Gadzhiyevo submarine base and if they are working on a new type of underwater vehicle then my money is on that base.'

'I presume you picked up the signal again when she returned to the North Sea?'

'Indeed. That was over a year ago and interestingly enough the *Sergey Makarevich* has returned to the North Cape twice and each time her AIS stopped transmitting at roughly the same coordinates.'

'A pre-planned manoeuvre?'

'Of course.'

'That seems a little irresponsible of them, James, wouldn't they expect they were being tracked?'

'Not necessarily; if there had not been any incidents or diplomatic traffic referring to the ship then maybe they presumed their operation remained secret.'

'Mmm, seems a risky strategy given our sophisticated tracking and listening capabilities.'

'Sometimes it is easier to hide in plain sight. The fishing quotas are a contentious issue and I would imagine most eyes would be on her fishing ability not on some possible clandestine activities. I did a quick search of our database and found nothing to suggest she was of interest. Her recent movements show that two weeks ago she appeared yet again in Russian waters off the North Cape.'

'And where has she been in those two weeks?'

'Here look, I have mocked up a rough chart of the British Isles and superimposed her course on it. As you can see she was fifty nautical miles to the west of the Shetland Islands on the twenty-first and two days later, after skirting the west coast of Ireland, she was heading for the Western Approaches where she stayed until yesterday.'

'If the *Sergey Makarevich* is on the move, where is she now?'

'Here, look, about one hundred and twenty miles west of the Isle of Wight.'

'And heading towards Portsmouth?'

'Exactly ma'am.'

'You have done well James. I want you to write up what you have just told me and include your chart to show the ship's track. I am going to need to take it with me to convince the Director of the veracity of my argument.'

James sat at a nearby desk, typing rapidly into his laptop, finally taking his leave at seven in the morning he left Anita whose adrenalin was keeping her going.

'Ah, Anita, you wanted to see me accompany you to see the Director. God you look awful, what were you doing last night?' said a fresh-looking Commander Pearson appearing at her workstation.

'I was here sir, working. I have been here all night and my researcher has been here too. I believe that the *Nelson* is in imminent danger of a covert operation by the Russian Navy.'

'Rosemary mentioned that. You obviously took her at her word.'

'You could say that sir. James Hill and I have been looking at the movements of a Russian factory ship named the *Sergey Makarevich* and she is, I strongly believe, the mother ship for this new submersible of the Russians. The ship is somewhere in the English Channel not far from Portsmouth and I believe priming for an attack.'

'That is a serious allegation, we need proof, you can't go accusing the Russians like that.'

'I'm sorry you feel like that sir, we are dealing with a potentially very serious situation and I believe the time for pussyfooting around is over. If the Russians take the *Nelson* out then northern Europe will be at their mercy. Not to mention the cost this country will have to bear. There is around ten billion pounds worth of carrier, jets and equipment riding on this and I for one am not prepared to stand idly by while the politicians speak nicely to the Russians.'

'Putting it like that makes me tend to agree with you. What do you have? I will need something to take upstairs and when I say upstairs I think this will have to go all the way to the Prime Minister.'

'I have this,' said Anita, handing him several sheets of paper detailing the movements of the *Sergey Makarevich* going back over a year. 'Here is a brief description of what we think she has been doing in that time and a statement of the repercussions if the *Nelson* cannot be on station if and when the Russians decide to move.'

'Okay, give them to me and I will get moving on it. I must say Anita you have done sterling work and just for that your reading of the situation deserves an airing. Listen, you look all in; why not use one of the overnight rooms to get some rest. I will start pulling some levers and when I feel you should become more closely involved I will send for you. It could be only two or three hours, I don't know but you do need a break.'

'Thank you sir, I will do that.'

Fifty kilometres west of Vilnius lay the Elektrėnai Power Plant, supplying almost two-thirds of Lithuania's electricity. Recently modernised, it was a showcase of carbon reduction with one of the most up-to-date switching systems capable of monitoring the supply of electrical power. It had saved millions of euros in wastage, cut emissions by a quarter and reduced household bills. Today though there were outages almost every hour, the capital's hospitals had already switched to emergency generators and now industry was beginning to shut down.

Ivan Moskvichev, an ethnic Russian whose family had settled in the country after the Second World War was not a great fan of the Bear lurking nearby and had no wish to become a Russian surf. He had worked hard, gained an engineering degree at the Vilnius Gediminas Technical University and done well for himself. As the Director of the Elektrėnai Power Plant, he had a responsible job and a good salary but today was proving traumatic. The telephone never stopped ringing, his team were at a loss to understand what was happening, and he was worried. That went for all the management except for one man, Doctor Wolfgang Fathi, the plant's chief scientist who appeared to have a good idea of what was the root cause of their problems.

'It's started Ivan; the Russians are interfering with our remote controls, it is what we have feared for some time. I tell you my friend this is the start of a takeover just like Ukraine experienced. Since the Americans left I have not slept for worrying about the possibility.'

'What can we do? The power to vital industries and to the military establishments must be kept going.'

'We have little choice. We have to switch over to manual. As you know, since the takeover of Ukraine we have been working on a plan to defend our power supplies should it happen to us. If we are to beat them at their own game, we have to bypass the automatic control system. You need to put our best people in place as soon as possible if we are to keep the grid in operation.'

Similarly, in the control tower of the Siauliai Air Base air base two hundred kilometres away, radar and computer screens were experiencing their own problems. It was not much of a glitch, nothing was missing when the screens died and then returned to full operation, but it was worrying.

'We need the wing commander up here straight away,' said the operations manager, 'something weird is going on.'

At approximately the same time in the capitals of the three Baltic states timed explosions shook several buildings and anyone looking out could see the black clouds beginning to rise across the rooftops. These were not isolated incidents, the news wires were already singing with reports of terrorist activity in both Berlin and Amsterdam. From those initial reports, it appeared to be the work of co-ordinated terrorist groups, a new and worrying development.

In the Baltic States, however the terrorists were home-grown. Russian Special Forces dressed as civilians who had infiltrated the country planting bombs and when they exploded, they had already crossed the borders back into Russia.

Chapter 20

Alexie looked angry, very angry, and the knife in his hand mesmerised Anita. She knew that he wanted to kill her and he would use it because he blamed her for everything that had happened to him.

'English bastard I kill you for what you have done. You spy on us, you try to kill us, but you didn't and now I will kill you.'

Anita could not take her eyes of the bright shining blade as it swung from side to side, coming ever closer. Then he struck, lunging at her ready for the kill but he did not make it, the sound of a double bang stopping him as the bullets came crashing through the glass door. He stumbled forward, blood gushing from each bullet hole but still he came at her seemingly unstoppable . . . 'It's okay ma'am, you're okay. Please, calm down.'

Anita felt her body shake, sweat roll down her forehead and she opened her eyes, to see the duty sergeant peering down at her.

'It's okay ma'am, just a bad dream, you're in safe hands.'

'Ooo . . . that was scary, yes, a bad dream. Any water, my mouth feels like a vulture's crutch?'

The sergeant could not help laughing, such an unladylike expression seemed so out of character, but he knew that some people in this building courted danger. He had heard tales of spies caught up in difficult situations who were lucky to be still alive. Some were not so lucky and he told himself he would not have their job for all the tea in China.

'Commander Pearson telephoned to ask you to come to his office. Shall I give you a few minutes ma'am?'

'Oh, yes please. Wait outside while I freshen up. Thanks.'

Still feeling shaken by her nightmare Anita hurried through her ablutions, tidied her hair and applied a little lipstick before joining the duty sergeant and together they made their way to Commander Pearson's office.

'Come in, take a seat. I must say you are looking better, how do you feel?'

'I'm okay sir, still a bit groggy but that will pass.'

'Good, good. I can tell you that I have had a meeting with the Cabinet Office and the Chiefs of Staff but there have been developments.'

Anita noticed how grave his face looked.

'There have been multiple incidents in several European capitals. A bomb was detonated in a Berlin department store, at least twenty dead, in Amsterdam another bomb, this time in the central station, at least fifty dead, and a lorry has ploughed through a crowd in the Czech Republic where luckily only one person has died as far as we know.'

'Nowhere else?'

'Yes, all the capitals of the Baltic states. In Vilnius, a bomb went off in the central station, between ten and twenty dead, and driving here I heard reports that bombs have detonated in both Riga and Tallinn Those incidents have stirred up the hornet's nest. The Russians are livid, saying that ethnic Russians are in danger in Latvia, Lithuania and Estonia and if the authorities cannot contain these terrorists then they will. They have issued an ultimatum; if calm is not restored within the next forty-eight hours then they will have no alternative but to go to the aid of fellow Russians.'

'Bloody hell sir.'

'Bloody hell indeed. But you saw it coming didn't you?'

'Not just me sir.'

'That's as maybe.'

The commander paused as his mobile phone beeped and he looked at the screen.

'We have a problem now, just got a report that the power supply has gone down in all three Baltic states.'

'And we have a rogue submarine hunting our new carrier. I think that is our immediate problem sir, if I may say so.'

'You may and you are right. What a mess.'

'You said you have met with people that matter.'

'Yes, the Prime Minister has convened a meeting of COBRA and that should be under way as we speak. I also had a brief meeting with Sir Hugh Chalmers, the Chief of the Army Staff, and Admiral Sir Peter Marks, the First Sea Lord. They are all too aware of the disaster that will unfold should we lose the *Nelson* and its air arm. We have assets but they are too few and too thin on the ground to have much effect upon the Russians, and they have asked me to come up with a plan to keep the *Nelson* out of trouble as we are the only ones who seem to know what's going on.'

'Surely that's not true sir?'

'What they meant was that we have a handle, or we believe we have, on the submersible and its mother ship.'

'That's true, but what can we do?'

'You could try some creative thinking perhaps.'

'Yes sir, I have been giving the matter some thought. The *Sergey Makarevich* is a factory ship, a fishing boat, right.'

'Go on.'

'If she is in British waters then she is subject to British law regarding her catch and to enforce the law we have our much-depleted fishery protection vessels and the fishery protection officers. What if we could board her on the pretext of examining her catch – see what we can find. If there is any proof she is attempting to attack the *Nelson* then we can impound the vessel.'

'Sounds a bit far-fetched, how would we do that?'

'Get me some naval-looking overalls and an official-looking cap and get me aboard her. They will either put up some resistance, in which case it is probable that we have guessed right, or she will simply allow us on board and we have it wrong. Either way we can play the Russians at their own game of plausible denial.'

'And in the meantime their tanks are rolling across the borders of the Baltic States.'

'Not if they know the *Nelson* is on its way. They have set a forty-eight hour deadline you say. How far can *Nelson* get in that time, seven, eight hundred nautical miles? If she can then the fighter jets will be near enough in range to operate extended sorties in stealth mode and it might just deter them. They will soon have a new president and we do not yet know what he will do. The outgoing president will still have a lot of influence over the military and will be pulling the strings. I say this is a high stakes poker game and we need to out-bluff them at the very least.'

The down draught of the helicopter blades caused Anita to hold her hair with one hand and a briefcase in the other. Ahead of her Commander Person was already on the flight deck with a naval officer.

'Welcome aboard *His Majesty's Ship Nelson*, the captain sends his compliments. I am Lieutenant Commander Nicholson and I am to take you to the operations room. Please follow me.'

The Sommelier

The lieutenant commander was not alone, two marines accompanied him and after taking up positions on either side of the visitors the group made their way to the forward island and the lift to the fourth floor, where they emerged to see, a further two marines guarding a door.

'This way please,' said Lieutenant Commander Nicholson showing his authorisation pass to the marines. 'The captain wants to see you together with the Rear Admiral.'

He led them towards a room overlooking the operations deck.

'Your visitors' sir,' he said, as the door opened to reveal two fit-looking middle-aged men dressed in short-sleeved white shirts with epaulettes stating their high rank.

'Commander Pearson, welcome, I am Captain Sykes and this is Rear Admiral Buxton. We understand that you have something of importance to tell us.'

Commander Pearson saluted and reached out to shake the extended hand of the *Nelson*'s captain.

'Yes sir, we have. This is Agent Sims; she has been involved with this affair for some time. Her work revealed the Russians' suspected intentions, particularly those relating to this ship. If you would be so kind, we are ready to make a short presentation to bring you up to speed. As you know this comes right from the top, do we need to clear the room?'

'Not the lieutenant commander, he is in charge of the security on board and I think he should know what we are up against. The marines can wait outside.'

'As you wish sir. As you are already aware the Russians are continuing their build-up along the northern borders of Europe and this morning they issued an ultimatum . . .'

It did not take long for the commander to convince his audience of the seriousness of the situation and as he finished speaking, the captain of the *Nelson* was already ordering action stations.

'You say they will probably try to attack using a remote submarine. What do you know about it and what can we do to protect the carrier?'

'It's probably a very slow-moving machine, certainly in these waters as it will be important to protect its stealth capabilities. I suggest you deploy picket boats with powerful lights to search the immediate depths during the hours of darkness. That should give you around eight hours.'

'The Mark One Eyeball went out with the Second World War, Commander; we have far more sophisticated listening equipment these days.'

'Sir, with respect I do not think you have grasped the fact that we believe that even our most up-to-date sensing arrays are not capable of picking anything up from this sub. We believe the Mark One Eyeball is as good as anything in a situation such as this is. Again with respect sir, please use everything at your disposal but you should consider picket boats and powerful searchlights.'

'Very well Commander, we will and thank you for your help. Is there anything else?'

'Yes sir, a pair of your female crewmembers' overalls and a petty officer's cap.'

'What!'

'There should be a helicopter arriving shortly with a squadron of SAS and SBS troopers. We plan to land them on the fishery protection vessel that has recently left Dover harbour. The Admiralty ordered her to sea several hours ago and Agent Sims here is going to attempt to use the vessel to get on board the Russian factory ship under the cover of a routine catch inspection. She believes the ship is controlling an attack on your ship sir and if she finds that it is, then she will call in the special forces.'

'Good luck Commander, give these people all the help they need Lieutenant and make it quick.'

Captain Sverdlovsk looked at the sheet of paper and felt his heart race, their target was the British aircraft carrier confirmed alongside Princess Royal jetty in Portsmouth harbour. The signal was one he had expected, the order to begin the operation, and that he probably had a minimum of forty-eight hours in which to conduct the attack.

'Markov, tell the lead technician to come to the bridge.'

The Sommelier

The first officer nodded and walked to the steel ladder attached to the superstructure and descended to the main deck where two men stood talking.

'Popenko the captain wants to speak with you on the bridge.'

The first officer turned and the chief technician followed him to the bridge.

'You want to see me Captain?'

'Yes Kerzhakov, come into the day cabin. Take over Markov.'

The ship's captain led the man into his cabin and closed the door.

'I have just opened our orders for our mission and am authorised to tell you what is expected of you and your men. We are to disable the British aircraft carrier *Nelson* just enough to stop her sailing. I believe you have trained for such an event.'

'Yes sir, for the past year we have run simulations and tried the Fish in real-life situations. It has managed to enter our own and other bases to conduct trials and they went without incident. When do you want us to deploy the submarine?'

'We have an expected window of forty-eight hours from now. That will be enough I presume?'

'Yes, how far off Portsmouth are we right now?'

'One hundred kilometres approximately I believe.'

The technician nodded.

'The submarine has a range of about that so I do not see a problem if we can sail to within say a twenty kilometre range she will have enough power in her batteries to get back to us,' he said 'Our biggest obstacle will be time. We must move slowly during the latter stages of the attack so that we appear as no more than a small fish to the British sonar. We have detailed charts of the sonar buoys protecting the port but some may have moved or they may have added others. I will plot a course for the machine to give us the best chance of remaining undetected and then we will blow holes in its propellers so that their balance is disturbed enough to keep the carrier in port for repairs for at least a week. With luck we might even damage the shafts and that could mean several weeks in port.'

Four hours later the *Sergey Makarevich* was within sixty kilometres of the Isle of Wight and Captain Sverdlovsk was pacing the wheelhouse deck. What they intended to do was an act of war and if he and his crew were captured and the Kremlin could not face down the British then they could expect many years in a Western prison. On top of that, his orders explicitly instructed him, that in the event of capture, he was to scuttle the ship and destroy all evidence of the submersible.

Lighting a cigarette, he walked over to the large, colourful radar screen, far more sophisticated than would be expected on even the most advanced fishing vessel. It was leading-edge technology and capable of highlighting ships up to fifty miles away, a useful addition to his ship's capability. Right now, it showed two warships in the vicinity, a French frigate moving along an almost parallel course some ten miles away, and a corvette of the Dutch Navy steaming up the channel towards them. They seemed innocuous enough but more satisfying was the lack of a British warship of any description on the screen. He felt confident of his ship's invisibility and decided to leave the bridge to visit the cavernous hold to inspect the submarine and talk with the technicians making their final preparations.

'You are ready for launch Comrade Popenko?' he asked the lead technician.

'Yes, the three-dimensional model of the *Nelson* is in the submarine's memory and already it is working with the topography file. Once the machine is in the water and released from our direct control it will fix its position and then follow the course we have set. Once it is close to the target its sensors will match exactly the *Nelson* and its relative orientation. We have programmed the Fish to manoeuvre close to the target and when it locks on it will take full control. Then it will position itself so that the robot arm can deploy and attach the explosive charges to the propeller blades. We have developed an adhesive that will stick to the propeller material and once the submersible has attached the charges, the machine will leave the area at an increased rate of knots. With luck, it will be well away by the time the charges go off, and as they are not powerful, the British may not even realise anything has happened until they try to move the ship. The object is to unbalance the props, making it impossible for the vessel to move at anything more than a snail's pace.'

'Good, then we are ready to go,' said the captain, his hands behind his back and looking intently at the submersible.

'We just need your order to launch Captain.'

'How long do you expect before the submarine reaches the target?'

'We need at least twenty-four hours; we work on stealth. This baby is no *Khishchnik*; the last thing we want is cavitation noise. It's all very well hitting the target at speed and destroying it but our job is to quietly disable the carrier, not to eliminate it, and then to disappear.'

'Then you have my permission to launch when ready. I will enter the instruction into the log and you can countersign.'

Clearing the mainland, the twin-rotor Chinook flew at a height of no more than fifteen metres above the waves on a course that took it towards the fishery protection vessel *Arran*, five miles out in the English Channel. Heading towards her was the container ship *Sumo Maru*. One of the largest vessels in the area, the Monrovia-registered leviathan had been making her way to Rotterdam when she received a request from His Majesty's Government for assistance.

Her captain was obliging, he had experienced the pirates of the Malacca Straits and was more than willing to co-operate. His task was to be a shield, to position the *Sumo Maru* between *Arran* and the *Sergey* Makarevich long enough for the low-flying helicopter to discharge its cargo of men, boats and Agent Sims onto the fishery protection vessel out of sight of the Russian ship.

'Five minutes to evacuation,' crackled a voice over the loud speaker and inside the helicopter the eight Special Forces troopers checked their weapons and as the minutes counted down they began manhandling two semi-rigid inflatable boats towards the rear door. As the pilot took the aircraft to within five or six metres of the sea they opened the door and at the end of a ten second count down the men slid the boats out into space and followed them in quick succession into the water.

For Anita there was no such dramatic exit; the Chinook simply hovered above *Arran* and the winchman hooked her onto the cable. Lowered onto the deck, she found willing hands ready to help her find her feet and with hardly a pause she stood free of the winch cable while the helicopter turned and headed back to *Nelson*.

'Welcome aboard ma'am, I am First Officer Donnelly, please follow me.'

The officer led Anita across the deck and through a door in the superstructure where two men dressed in the navy's working blue awaited her.

'Good afternoon ma'am, my name is Lieutenant Chittenden and this is Lieutenant Dale, we are your armourers and communications conduit. We have a two-way radio that is constantly active. You are to take this with you if you manage to get aboard the target. If you have a problem, you can signal us with a simple voice command and we will send in backup. We need a code word in case of emergency. You tell us, that way we will be sure you remember it, even in the most difficult circumstances.'

'That's easy, red wine.'

'Okay, red wine it is,' said Chittenden. 'And here is your gun, a Glock semi-automatic, easy enough to conceal in this document case you can use during the inspection. Are you ready for us to begin? The Special Boat boys are already hooked up alongside and can be across the water in seconds should you need them.'

'Ma'am, I will be coming with you,' said First Officer Donnelly. 'You will need someone with you who knows about fish if you are to conduct a bona fide inspection.'

'Thanks, how long until we can try to get aboard?'

'We are still a couple of miles from the target so I think around fifteen minutes. The skipper will call them up and inform them that as they are in British territorial waters and that they are obliged to allow us on board to inspect their nets and their catch. They usually shit themselves when they see us and if they have been catching undersized fish they will be busy jettisoning as much of their catch as they can before we arrive.'

'Okay, let's get to it then. How do we get on board?'

'Tender, it will be lowered just before we need it and then it's a case of motoring across and climbing on board. Put this life jacket on and here is one of our caps to give you an air of authenticity,' said the officer, handing over a black life jacket and a fishery protection badged cap.

Anita fastened the life jacket straps and swopping caps, looked out of the porthole to see the *Sergey Makarevich* for the first time, still several hundred metres away and hardly moving.

'Looks like the skipper has made contact,' said the first officer and to confirm his suspicions his radio came alive.

'Boarding party stand by.'

'Good luck,' said Lieutenant Chittenden, standing back to let Anita pass.

'Thanks,' she said, and with determination written across her face. Anita followed the fishery officer to the ship's rail and down the steps to the waiting boat. 'Skipper says they are lowering a rope ladder for us and adds that they do not sound too pleased.'

Anita hardly heard the first officer, the sea was never her favourite element, not since the operation in Amsterdam when she had suffered seasickness, and now the tender's rise and fall had her attention.

'I'll go first, you follow and I can help you into the boat.'

Anita was not about to argue and taking a deep breath followed the seaman down the sloping steel ladder. As soon as they boarded the command to cast off was given and the tender began to pull away towards the dark shape of the Sergey Makarevich.

'Take her alongside boatswain and hold station while we get aboard, then I want you to hang about and come back for us when you get the signal.'

Gradually the gap between the tender and the Russian ship narrowed and then the first officer was reaching for the rope ladder.

'Quick, grab this and get aboard.'

Anita reached out for the rung at shoulder height, grabbed it with both hands and swung her feet onto the ladder and then she was scrambling up the ship's side where a pair of strong hands grabbed her boiler suit and dragged her over the rail. Stumbling, she fell to her knees, and looking up was dismayed to see a man in the same mould as Alexie and Viktor observing her.

'Your case ma'am,' said the first officer climbing over the rail and to Anita's relief he stole the man's attention. 'Good afternoon, I am First Officer Donnelly of the fishery protection vessel *Arran* and this is Lieutenant Sims. She is our scientist and she will be helping me conduct the inspection.'

'Come, we must see the captain first,' the big man said as he gestured towards the superstructure.

'So you are come to inspect my ship,' said a gruff sounding Captain Sverdlovsk meeting them at the doorway.

'Yes, regulations demand that we carry out a thorough inspection of your nets and your fish hold to determine what you have caught and to make sure you are fishing within the law.'

'We are Russian ship; we do not need to fish in your waters. We have plenty of fish in the northern seas and the Atlantic.'

'That's as maybe Captain but we still need to examine your nets and your catch as you are in British waters.'

'No need to see catch as we have no fish, we transferred our catch to another of our fleet two days ago and now we go north out of your waters to start fishing again.'

'I still need to see your nets,' Anita said with conviction, 'and I would like to inspect your fish hold Captain.'

'Very well, Vladimir here will escort you.' He then turned to the member of the crew and spoke to him in Russian. 'Vladimir, take this woman to see our nets and then take her below to the fish hold. She cannot be allowed to see anything down there so arrange a little accident and we will get rid of these pests.'

'*Da*,' said Vladimir, a hint of emotion beginning to show.

Anita was also feeling some emotion – fear. She had understood the gist of the captain's words even though his dialect was unfamiliar and she knew she had a problem. Her next concern was for the officer accompanying her, he had no idea he was in danger though his commanding officer had briefed him on the possibility, and then her radio burst into life.

'Arran One this is *Arran*, routine radio check please, over.'

'*Arran* this is Arran One, receiving over.'

'*Arran* standing by.'

Anita put the radio back in her pocket and Captain Sverdlovsk glowered at her.

'What do you need that for, you are just looking at our nets?'

'Regulations sir, I will need to contact the tender before we leave.'

'Vladimir, take them to look at the nets and I will talk to Boris.'

Vladimir grunted and indicated to Anita and First Officer Donnelly to follow him. They walked out onto the open aft deck, and spread out between two large winches was a huge net.

'If you will allow me ma'am, 'said Donnelly, removing a plastic gauge from his pocket.

Anita and Vladimir watched him and as the big Russian's attention focused on the first officer busy measuring the mesh of the fishing net Anita slid the zip open on the document case and felt for the gun. It was too risky to attempt retrieving it just yet and instead she took out the clipboard with several sheets of paper attached.

'What sizes are you getting?'

'So far the net is undersized but as I move along I can see the mesh is getting larger.'

'Can you give me the sizes?'

'Yes, sixty millimetres increasing to ninety millimetres just here,' said the first officer looking up at Anita and that was when he first realised all was not well, nothing obvious, just the look in her eye.

'Try the end and let's see if it is legal.'

Officer Donnelly slipped the gauge into the net and noticed some undersized and illegal diamond-shaped holes in the mesh but under the circumstances, he decided to let it pass.

'Borderline ma'am, not quite enough to cause us a problem.'

'Good,' said Anita scribbling anything she could think of on the clipboard sheet. 'It just leaves the fish hold then. Can you show us the fish hold please?' she said to Vladimir.

'This way,' he said, leading them to a staircase set into the deck.

As the door at the base of the steps swung open, Anita caught sight of a man in the shadows and she was suddenly alarmed. It was a trap; they did not intend to let either her or the first officer anywhere near what might once have been a fish hold. She was convinced they had indeed found the mother ship.

'Do you eat much fish Mr Donnelly? I mean you must get a bit fed up of the stuff.'

'What, er, I like a bit now and again.'

'I have found a new recipe; I must give it to you one day. It involves red wine. Do you like red wine Mr Donnelly?'

'Yes I do as a matter of fact.'

'What you talking about?' said an angry Vladimir standing just behind him.

First Officer Donnelly half-turned to answer when he felt a blow to the back of his head and losing consciousness slid down the last few steps knocking Anita sideways as he fell. Then the door opened fully and a man with the looks of a second-rate boxer appeared carrying an iron bar. Anita knew that she was next and reached into her leather case for the gun, closing her finger round the trigger just as the fighter raised his arm to strike.

The crack of the gun in the confined, metallic space was deafening but the unfortunate boxer heard nothing as he slumped to the floor with a bullet lodged firmly in his brain. Behind her, Vladimir tried to climb over the prostrate body of the first officer but his actions were clumsy. Stumbling forward and unable to manage a firm footing he allowed Anita time to take aim and fire the gun a second time, hitting him squarely on the forehead and he was dead before he hit the floor. She looked down at the unconscious Donnelly and realised there was little she could do for him. He was still breathing and the best she could hope for was that he would survive long enough to receive medical treatment once they got him off the ship. She didn't dwell, her priority was to find out what it was they didn't want her to see. The boxer had fallen across the doorway and she had to use her foot to force the door open wide enough to squeeze through. It was some sort of machinery compartment, a compressor was running and that must have masked the sound of the gunshots. She

looked round and could see no one, but several
metres away there was another door, one with an
external locking lever, the same as on a warship.
Why would a feature like that be on a civilian vessel
she wondered and reaching the door she pulled it
open just enough to peer inside the surprisingly
cavernous interior.

What she saw was like something out of a low
budget James Bond film set: a miniature dock, an
overhead crane and several men hunched over a
laptop computer. They were so engrossed that they
did not notice her swing the door open wide enough
to dodge inside the hold. There was very little cover
only a mechanical lift on a track that ran the full
length of the miniature dock and a stack of boxes
just about big enough to conceal her. Moving
carefully she crouched behind them and tried to
overhear the men's conversation. It was difficult, the
voices had an echo to them in the steel walled void
but she was sure she heard the words 'target' and
'British'. Not much but it was enough. Then she felt
rather than heard the twin explosions.

On board *Arran* not more than seven or eight
minutes earlier the communications expert had
picked up the agent's alarm – red wine – and he had
immediately alerted the waiting soldiers. Their
engines were running and it took no more than
fifteen seconds for the two boats to emerge, one
round the stern of the fishing vessel and the other
round the prow. It took the elite force not much
longer to cross the few metres to the *Sergey*

Makarevich and to be clambering up grappling lines. As the first of them reached the ship's rail, he lobbed a stun grenade into the bridge area and from the second team came another.

Captain Sverdlovsk became aware almost immediately that they were under attack when he saw a man's head appear over the rail. Even before the soldier was halfway over, he had grabbed his machine pistol from the chart table and was running towards the internal stairs leading to the hold. There had always been the worry of such an assault and he had ordered charges laid for such an emergency but he had never foreseen the speed at which it was now taking place. He had to get to the detonators, he had to close the watertight doors, lock the technicians into their watery graves. Failing that, he would shoot them, but he had to act before the attacking force had a chance to stop him.

From above he heard gunfire, his crew were putting up resistance as he expected. Each man was handpicked and all were primed to fight. His worry was that now the British had discovered them, even if his men repelled the attack, other more powerful forces would eventually overcome them.

A career officer, Captain Sverdlovsk had joined the navy as a sixteen-year-old and worked his way through the ranks. He had seen service as first officer on the *Yantar*, one of Russia's most modern spy ships tasked with searching for, and plotting on charts, the West's subsea cable network. That experience had inspired him and on his promotion

to Captain first class he had volunteered for the
secret operations branch of the service and for the
next few years had run clandestine operations along
the Mediterranean coast. He was proud of the
Russian Navy, proud of its traditions and had
jumped at the chance to command the *Sergey
Makarevich* and now it was up to him to save the
mission.

Running down the steep steel staircase, he
reached the door leading into the hold and
wrenching it open stepped inside. In front of him, at
the opposite side of the secret dock, the technicians
were standing and looking aimlessly at the high
ceiling, vaguely aware of the commotion above
them.

'We are under attack and must scuttle the ship,'
he shouted across to them. 'Open the sea cocks
while I prime the charges.'

The men became animated, began to perform a
drill practised numerous times as Anita watched
from her hiding place. Valve wheels turned,
sensitive equipment destroyed and it soon became
clear to her that they were scuttling the ship. She
had to make a decision, to run for it, to try to get out
of the steel coffin unnoticed, or she could fight her
way out. The chances of that working looked slim,
she was cornered and in a desperate situation. Her
one slice of luck so far was that the man who had
just appeared was still unaware of her presence.

He was pre occupied with the scuttling process
and Anita guessed that he was one of the senior

officers on board if not the captain himself. She watched as he opened a small electrical cabinet fastened to a bulkhead and reach inside. Straining her neck, she was horrified to see that he was setting some sort of mechanical timer and she knew then that he was setting explosives.

Captain Sverdlovsk checked the dial one last time and confident that the countdown timer was in operation, he turned his attention to his men. They must have opened the valves, he could hear the seawater rushing in and already the level in the dock had risen several centimetres. Soon it would be overflowing and once the charges went off the ship would begin to sink, but first he had another task to perform.

Anita peered out of her hiding place and saw the officer gesture to the men, waving them towards him, his voice useless over the din of the rushing water. As they drew near, eyes anxious for leadership, she was horrified to see him lift his machine pistol and before the men had time to react, he shot each where they stood. The act of cold-blooded murder caused her stomach to churn and remind her of her own need of survival.

The officer had turned away from his grizzly deed and was hurrying towards the door, leaving destruction and Anita in his wake. Then she heard the door slam and the sound of the locking wheel turning and she was alone. However, she remembered that she had entered by a second door at the far end of the dock and realised that she must get out and quickly. It was obvious that once he had locked the main door he would run to the second door and lock that too. He could not afford for any of the men he had just shot to survive and escape that way.

Feeling her adrenaline pumping and her senses sharpen, Anita made her way back along the dock impeded by the rising water by now reaching halfway to her knees and making the going difficult. Then she heard footsteps on the steel ladder. The captain must have known a shortcut for it sounded as if he was already at the door. It was still half-open as she had left it but, to her consternation, it began to close. She had no choice, she lifted her gun and took aim at the gap hoping that she could distract her jailor long enough to get out.

The adrenaline flowing through the body of the *Sergey Makarevich's* captain was no less powerful than Anita's, his vital organs no less stressed and over the din coming from within the dock he did not hear the sound of the gun firing but what he did experience was the sting of the ricocheting bullet as it whizzed past his ear. His reaction was to release his hold on the steel door and to feel for his ear. Half of it was missing and his hand, now covered in blood shocked him into pausing just long enough for Anita to force open the door and squeeze through.

They came face to face, the Captain first class and the spy but it was the younger Anita whose reactions were the quicker. She fired twice more, hitting him in the chest and the arm, and with a gasp he slid to the floor. His eyes were already clouding as he looked up at his killer and then a smile crossed his lips.

'You are too late; you are coming to the bottom of the sea with me and my ship.'

They were his last words, his head drooped to his chest and Anita felt panic overtake her. Of course, he had been setting the charges to blow up the ship, destroy the evidence and the act of murder was part of that exit strategy. What should she do, should she go back and attempt to disarm the explosive device? If she did, she had no idea how to do it and time was running out. Then, as if to help make a decision, a voice ordered her to drop her gun and doing so she turned round to see a man in a black scuba diving suit pointing his weapon at her.

'Come on ma'am, let's get you out of here.'

'What about Donnelly, is he all right?' she said remembering the officer who had accompanied her onto the factory ship.

'We found him, he is being evacuated now.'

'They have set charges, the ship will blow anytime.'

'We expected that, come on, hurry up.'

Anita found her legs would not work in conjunction with her brain and she fell against the wall. The trooper grabbed her before she fell and dragged her bodily out onto the deck and into a scene of carnage. The Russians had put up a valiant fight, but they had not stood a chance against the

The Sommelier

Special Forces and the bodies of their dead and wounded lay strewn across the deck.

Then the charges blew, just a short series of dull thuds and within minutes the deck began to list. The ship did not have long and beside her the troopers began evacuating the wounded, Anita being one of them and Second Officer Donnelly another.

The *Arran* had stood off once the shooting had started and was now edging closer to the sinking *Sergey Makarevich*, however, time was short and it was a dangerous manoeuvre. Closing the gap, the *Arran* came within a metre of the *Sergey Makarevich* and for the brief periods when the two ships touched the wounded were transferred.

The whole episode had taken less than an hour and after another hour the *Sergey Makarevich* finally settled and disappeared beneath the waves. By that time, Anita and half of the elite troopers were back aboard the *Nelson,* and the *Arran* was steaming at full speed to the nearest port

'A harrowing experience for you I would imagine,' said Admiral Cunningham. 'But more to the point, my information is that the advanced submarine was in fact not aboard the mother ship.'

'That's right sir, the dock was empty and I saw some technicians. They appeared to be discussing the sub and monitoring its progress on a laptop.'

'What do you make of that Professor?'

Professor Cowper was the head scientist at the British secret underwater establishment charged with developing submersible weapons.

'I say we still have a problem. If they were in control of the machine at that time and the link was broken, it could have gone off anywhere. I think that is unlikely, more they were simply monitoring its progress. As I understand it, the submarine will have carried instructions to make its way to within striking distance of its target and then the artificial intelligence algorithms will take over. That is the most dangerous time from our perspective for then it will be in kill mode and there is probably very little we can do to stop it other than blow it out of the water.'

'How long would you say we have got?'

'A few hours at most. It is more logical for the final phase of an attack to take place during the hours of darkness. The submarine will probably be in fairly shallow waters by then and in daylight could possibly be seen with the naked eye,' said the scientist.

'Yes we know about that.'

'Apart from the sophisticated sonar at our disposal that is probably the best we can do Admiral.'

'What about the sonar, Captain Sykes? What are we doing about finding this damn sub?' asked the Admiral.

'Everything we have is operational and I requested the assistance of the two Type 23 frigates already in Portsmouth to do a sweep of the approaches. Their sonar arrays are the best we have and if anyone can find this thing, they can. They are at this moment deployed covering the approaches to Portsmouth harbour.'

'Don't be too sure Captain. I can tell you that we have classified information that this Russian autonomous submarine is the most advanced anywhere and is almost invisible to even the best sonar detectors,' said Professor Cowper. 'What about putting to sea, would that be a better option?'

'Under normal circumstances it probably would but to get the tugs in place and to manoeuvre in the dark would take too long. The best option is to find this thing, said Admiral Cunningham. 'Have we any news from the pickets Captain?

His Majesty's Ship Bristol had entered service with the Royal Navy only six months previously and had spent most of that time working up. She was the newest of the Type 26 frigates, almost eight thousand tons, with an array of weaponry from missiles to the phalanx rapid firing gun. Designed as the eyes and ears of the fleet, she was equipped with the latest Artisan radar and Thales Sonar and in her low-ceilinged, low-light operations room the men and women who worked with these highly technical systems sat hunched over their screens.

Petty Officer Jim Stockdale was an expert with the new sonar, able to tune the sensors with precision to extract sensitive information from the sea. On his screen a series of numbers and coloured icons gave, in real time, an accurate representation of the situation beneath the ship and for many square kilometres around. The petty officer scanned his screen continually, searching for any sign of movement, for anything that was not a natural element.

The concentration required in such an environment was intense and after a further hour in front of the screen he was feeling a mild migraine coming on and it was with some relief that he vacated his seat to his opposite number.

'See anything Jim?'

'No, we've been at it for hours and there is nothing to report other than a few fish and a couple of seals.'

'They told us at the briefing that this sub could look like a dolphin or some other sea creature. Are you sure, you did not catch a glimpse of anything that could be this submarine? Keep looking, see what you can find.'

Leaving his relief to carry on the search the petty officer left the operations room and made his way to the mess to take a break, have something to eat and to clear his head before his next period on duty.

Half a kilometre away and similarly engaged, the crew of *HMS Sunderland* monitored their sonar sensors. The ships were in constant contact with *Nelson*, with each other and on board the carrier, the tension was very real.

The Sommelier

'Have you anything to report yet lieutenant?' Captain Sykes asked his communications officer.

'Nothing of any real substance sir.'

'Keep me informed, I want to know the moment we get a contact.'

He turned away and walked over to a row of monitors connected to the ship's own sensor arrays and looked at them one by one. Although he appeared calm, he was in fact very worried, the threat to his ship was real and untested. All during his naval career he had been aware of potential enemies' capabilities and the countermeasures at his disposal – but this was different. Having no detailed information on an enemy's weapons system left him feeling at a disadvantage. They were playing cat and mouse with a slow moving adversary that was invisible to British defences and the tension was rising.

Returning from his off watch time, Petty Officer Stockdale spent the next twenty minutes checking over his previous results looking for any anomaly and found it hard to believe that a submarine, no matter how small, could remain hidden. Perhaps there was no submarine, perhaps this was just an exercise and that the admiral would eventually call it off. He did not really believe that, the scale of the search was too large. Looking at the clock on the wall he noted that he would have to return to the monitor in just over five minutes.

'Seen anything yet Dave?'

'No, quiet as a mouse, not even a dolphin to break the monotony. Here, your turn and good luck.'

'Thanks,' said Jim, filling the vacant seat.

Her break had done him good, he felt fresh, felt his concentration was there and he settled in to watch the screen. Under normal circumstances, the computer would monitor the on screen action, look for movement, compare the signal with the database for a positive identification but the admiral in charge had decided that this was no ordinary search.

Carefully adjusting the sensitivity of the electronics he watched for change, for movement, and finding none decreased it to the standard setting. Then he tried the pixel fine-tuner, a method of separating out fuzzy signals, sharpen the picture to leave behind any positive contact. His eyes scanned the screen as the icons and colours began to fade, and then, in the top corner, he noticed a shape that was not changing and it appeared to be moving. He zoomed in on the object and instructed the computer to track it, extrapolate its course and overlay that course on the screen. It took no more than a nanosecond for the dotted red line to appear and just a little longer for Petty Officer Stockdale to realise that the course pointed straight at the *Nelson*.

'Got it,' he said excitedly and immediately drew the attention of the supervising officer.

'What is it Stockdale?'

'I think I might have the sub we are looking for.'

The Sommelier

Artificer first class Harold Davis was nineteen years old and loved his life in the Royal Navy. His father had been in the navy for twenty years serving on the old *Ark Royal* and was as pleased as punch that his youngest son had followed the tradition.

'Not much chance of a decent job in these parts son,' he had said when Harold left school with what were considered decent technical qualifications. He was good at maths and technical drawing but he was also exceptional with his hands. 'Engineering has all but disappeared from Middlesbrough lad, why don't you think about joining the navy? You could learn a trade and see the world at the same time. I did and now I have a decent pension to supplement the job at the distribution centre.'

Harold was a tad young to consider a pension but the fear of having to work in the distribution centre for the rest of his life was a real incentive so after leaving school and kicking his heels for six months he realised the sense in his father's words and signed on.

'See anything Davis?'

'No sir,' he said, sweeping the searchlight from side to side and peering intently into the waters of Portsmouth harbour, 'not a thing.'

'You two?' said the Sub-Lieutenant to the ratings peering over the gunwales.

'No sir, nothing.'

'Keep looking, the officer of the watch told me that we might all be out of a job soon if this submarine gets through.'

'I thought subs were huge, sir.'

'Not this one, it's supposed to be a drone and only about twenty or thirty feet long.'

'Like a big fish, a dolphin?'

'Aye, enough talk, get back to looking for it,' he said just as his radio came on.

He listened to the broadcast, noted the coordinates and checked them against the boat's chart plotter.

'Blimey, we are supposed to be right over it, keep looking you lot.'

The boat was one of more than fifty strung out across Portsmouth harbour searching the black depths, their searchlights turning night into day. Each boat had an area no bigger than a football pitch to search, a tedious but necessary exercise. By three o'clock in the morning, the searchers' concentration was wilting then the news of a possible sighting came in and tired eyes found new strength.

Harold swung his searchlight through yet another arc but this time his endeavour bore fruit when a dark shape just beneath the surface suddenly became visible.

'Sir! I have something I'm sure. Over there, look, on the port side,' said an excited Harold.

'Where?'

'Take the boat a few feet in that direction,' said Harold.'

The Sommelier

'Right, hang on,' said the Sub-Lieutenant putting the engine into gear and nudging the cutter forward at a snail's pace.

'There Billy, can you see that shadow moving?'

'Bloody 'ell Harold, I can,' said the bemused sailor. 'It looks just like a dolphin.'

'Picket control, picket control, this is bravo one six, bravo one six, we have a sighting.'

Within minutes of his call, a Lynx helicopter appeared out of the darkness, its searchlight suddenly illuminating the waters of the sound. The sailors below waved their arms, pointing towards the mysterious slow-moving object and within seconds the hovering helicopter's powerful light picked it out. There was little doubt that they had found the object of the night's exercise and it did not take long for a pair of black, neoprene-clad shapes to appear out of the darkness and drop into the sea.

Once the divers had made a positive identification, a specialist team arrived, amongst them two bomb disposal experts. Their job was to assess the level of danger posed by the sub and if necessary arrange to tow it out to sea and sink or destroy it. However, the Admiralty preferred to recover the advanced weapon and take it to a dry dock to unlock its secrets.

The bomb disposal experts entered the water and for more than ten minutes carried out a thorough inspection. When they finally surfaced, it was to give the thumbs up signal and, on board the cutter,

Harold Buxton and the rest of the crew heaved a sigh of relief.

'Your eagle eyes have just saved us from disaster young Davis. Let me be the first to buy you a beer,' said the Sub-Lieutenant.

Harold's smile was just about broad enough to reach his ears. His dad would be proud of him.

On the bridge of the aircraft carrier, Captain Sykes took the hot drink from his steward while keeping his eyes firmly the flight deck. The sun had just risen and below him, he could see the crew bringing the small boats back aboard the carrier.

'It's been a long night number one.'

'Certainly has sir.'

'A long night but a profitable one I think. How are the salvage team progressing?'

'They are still towing the submarine into number two dry dock.'

'Quite a catch I think. What were the Russians intending do you think?'

'Well sir, as far as I can tell the bomb disposal guys do not believe it is full of high explosives, not a torpedo, so its intended use was probably to disable rather than sink us.'

'Hmm . . . I must say I am of that opinion and the latest news is that the Russians are already threatening to cross over into the Baltic States. It will be up to us to stop them. Make ready for sea number one, signal the escorts and let's be on our way.'

Epilogue

The attack on the *Nelson* never did reach the ears of the public; the costs of breaking the Official Secrets Act was impressed upon the crew and newspaper editors found themselves summoned the Cabinet Office. Equally, the Russians did not become aware of the significance of the activities taking place at the entrance to Portsmouth harbour until almost twenty-four hours after they happened. The man in the faded red baseball cap, attracted by the searchlights, had watched the concentration of small boats out in the sound, trained his powerful binoculars on them and witnessed what appeared crucial details, but he was not alone, reacting with dismay on hearing a voice from the shadows.

'Mister Morris, or should I simply call you comrade Ivan?' queried the voice.

The man said nothing, carried on observing the movements in the harbour but his heart was racing, the moment he had feared for most of the years doing this job had arrived. Lowering his glasses, he still looked out across the sound until he felt a hand on his arm.

The Sommelier

'Mister Morris you are under arrest, I must caution you that anything you say can be held against you in a court of law. We do not need to dwell on the niceties though do we. You have been under surveillance for some time now so it is no good denying that you are an agent of Russian intelligence.'

The man finally turned to look at his protagonist and saw he was not alone. It was useless to resist. Commander Pearson, in discussion with Captain Sykes and Admiral Cunningham had decided to activate MI5 who were keeping an eye on the suspected spy and to order all shipping either to remain in Portsmouth harbour or not to enter at all until further notice. The pretext for such a move was the alleged discovery was the largest Second World War German bomb ever dropped on the British Isles. Therefore, as the story of a bomb gained traction it was logical that the Nelson would slip her moorings and head out to sea.

The news was not good for Igor: eventually an agent did report that the carrier had left Portsmouth and from a Russian military satellite, intelligence showed her half way towards the Baltic. Had the crew of the British carrier found what they were looking for, was it a bomb. He doubted it. It was not Igor's operation but he knew an attempt to keep the *Nelson* in port for as long as possible was a vital strategy and it appeared to have failed.

The Sommelier

For the rest of the day he watched the news wires, waiting for the terrorist mayhem to erupt throughout European capitals, but apart from several isolated incidents, there was nothing. What had happened, why had his plans not produced the expected result? He lit cigarette, contemplated the situation and hoped that he was premature in his disappointment, but something was telling him the strategy had failed. It would be only a matter of time before the power in the Kremlin summoned him, and the prospect of not having another birthday became very real. Then reports of the explosions in Riga and Tallinn came in and Igor began to feel a little more confident. It was time for the next phase, to unleash the barrage of claims and counter claims on the West's media. He picked up his telephone, rang the Moscow number and on the other end of the line he heard the voice of Colonel Kazantsev.

'*Da.*'

'Good afternoon, it seems that someone has lit some fires in the west.'

'Thank you for that information, we will look into it.'

The line went dead and Igor sat back feeling a little more confident that not all was lost. During the next few hours, stories would appear on social media and in the press confirming the Baltic States were under terrorist attack and that their own governments were incapable of protecting their ethnic Russian citizens and were on the verge of asking the Russian Federation for help.

In the capitals Europe, worried men were scrambling to understand what was happening and at the headquarters of MI6 in London Anita read the news on her screen.

'So, it had started, her worries were coming to fruition and she hoped that the measures her government were taking would dissuade the Russians from all an out invasion of the Baltic States. The stakes were high, the Russians had shown their hand, to go back now would lose them face and embolden NATO. After the shame of such tepid resistance when the Bear swallowed up Ukraine, there was a new mood amongst the European politicians. Finally, they were waking up to the threat and their military was mobilising.

'Morning Anita,' said a voice behind her.

Turning in her chair, she looked up to see a grim faced Commander Pearson.

'Morning sir looks as if we judged the situation correctly.'

'I should say so. You did sterling work and your contribution might just have saved a lot of lives.'

'How so?'

'Nelson is on station and already flying sorties over the Baltic. Since the more positive response from NATO initial intelligence suggests that no Russian fighter has entered the airspace of Latvia, Estonia or Lithuania.'

'What about ground forces?'

The Sommelier

'They started moving towards the border at first light but the spearhead, the first tank army, has halted its advance.'

'That is good news. Do you think the Russian's are having second thoughts?'

'Not really, they have opened the diplomatic front; their Foreign Minister is flying to Geneva to meet representatives of the European Union and who knows where that might lead.'

'What about the Americans, have they said anything, the news wires don't seem to have much, only that POTUS has called a meeting of The Joint Chiefs of Staff. That sounds promising but his tweets do not help. Do you think they will keep out of it?'

'He will try, after two terms the rumours of Russian collusion have not gone away. He only has six months left and will want to leave office without that stain on his legacy.'

'What about the election, are the candidates saying anything. There was a statement from the Republican Presidential candidate about not giving in to Russian aggression.'

'It's early days; both the Republican and the Democratic candidates will have to face up to this development during the coming weeks. The 2023 presidential election is fast approaching and this will be an important platform for them. America first was all very well eight years ago but the world has changed.'

'I see Prime Minister Corbin is to make a statement in the house today. He must have given the order for Nelson to set sail, perhaps his pacifist illusion has met with reality.'

'We will see, the Chiefs of staff will have spoken with him and the Defence Minister and my guess is that they will have told him that a policy of containment is better than standing back and letting the Russians walk all over their neighbours.

Anita remembered vividly her conversation with the Commander and as the days passed so did the crisis. The United States Presidential election had taken place and yet another hawk would be President and the Russian Federation had begun to realise that NATO would fight and this time round NATO's armoury was rather more muscular, and a flurry of diplomatic effort on behalf of the European Union had borne fruit. Both sides had made concessions but at least they had managed to avert war and the Baltic States were still free.

For her it was a personal triumph. Between herself and Rosemary Pennington, they had figured the situation out and their contribution was a major factor in averting that war. Only yesterday morning she had received a letter from the Cabinet Office asking whether she would accept membership of the Order of the British Empire in the King's birthday honours list. Of course, she would and feeling excited at the prospect decided to treat herself with a shopping trip to Bond Street. her purchases were normally restricted to a scarf or a middle of the range pair of shoes but today she would look for a full outfit and realising that it would be expensive she thought it best to check her finances.

Since getting back to the United Kingdom, she had been too busy to check her account, all the activity at the Embankment had relegated any money worries until today. Internet banking was all very well but in her business, she knew that nothing was ever completely secure and so she went to the branch and stood in line, preferring a real person to a machine.

'Can you give me a statement for this account please,' she had said to the cashier and within a minute she was standing alone scrutinising her print out.

Something was wrong, although her monthly salary was showing as paid into the account the total was wide of the mark. Why there was so much? There must be an error somewhere she reasoned and was about to return to the cashier when she noticed an unfamiliar payment. An amount of almost four thousand pounds and that puzzled her until it occurred to her that four thousand pounds was near as damn it five thousand dollars.

'Bullseye,' she exclaimed and several faces turned towards her.

Feeling somewhat embarrassed she quickly made her way towards the exit, re-living as she went that awful night in the master cabin. 'So it was Bullseye, his payment for the sex he only thought he had,' she chuckled as she put some distance between herself and the bank.

Four thousand pounds was enough to buy a descent suit and a pair of shoes but was it hers to spend? Not really and if she were in line for an MBE she should remain honest and report her windfall to SIS. Then she began to wonder what had become of the Russian oligarch, her benefactor. She had heard nothing of him since her traumatic escape from his yacht; perhaps she could check with border control, to see if he was back in London. Then again, perhaps she would not.

Other novels by this author:

iGoli city of gold. - Set in South Africa between 1912 and 1922, the story of a fraudulent mining venture and the violence of the miners' revolt.

Pickpockets and Zulus. In 1879, war erupts between the British Empire and the Zulu nation. Two young men from very different cultures find themselves on opposing sides and have to cope with events in their own way.

The last Zulu Warrior. – The aftermath of the war with the British Empire, the destruction of a way of life and how one man comes to terms with the upheaval.

Amsterdam Traffik. – Corruption and violence mar everyday life in Ukraine and because of that, a young woman finds herself sold into sex slavery.

The Vaporetto Driver. – Venice of the nineteen nineties, two lovers, their relationship and how the mafia's violent activities almost destroy them.

The Sommelier

The Sommelier

The Sommelier